14

AND THE WORKS OF PETER CLINES

"*14* is a wholly original story that weaves together mystery and the apocalypse like a finely tuned band."

—Evan Roy, Bricks of the Dead

"*14* is a riveting apocalyptic mystery in the style of *Lost.*"

—Craig DiLouie, author of *The Infection* and *The Killing Floor*

"[*Ex-Heroes*] is fun… the story telling is great and I was entertained."

—Jason Weisberger, Boing Boing

"I geek jizzed on your book."

—Nathan Fillion, star of *Castle* and *Firefly*

"[*Ex-Patriots* is] fast paced, full of action, humor and heroism…"

—Heather Faville, Double Shot Reviews

"*Ex-Patriots* is a crackerjack of a sequel… which readers can get lost in."

—Mihir Wanchoo, Fantasy Book Critic

"[In *Ex-Patriots*] Mr. Clines has created a compelling world filled with fascinating characters."

—Patrick D'Orazio, author of *Comes the Dark*

Other Books by Peter Clines

Ex-Heroes

Ex-Patriots

The Junkie Quatrain

The Eerie Adventures of Robinson Crusoe

14

PETER CLINES

A PERMUTED PRESS book
published by arrangement with the author
ISBN-13: 978-1-61868-052-5
ISBN-10: 1-61868-052-8

Cover art by Conzpiracy Digital Arts.

FOUNDATION

ZERO

He ran.

He ran as fast as he could. As if Hell itself were chasing him. As if his life depended on it.

He was quite certain it did.

The truth was, he was dead already. He'd seen enough men bleed out in medical theaters to recognize the wet pulse jetting between his ribs. The knife had done its job with almost surgical precision.

He mustn't think about himself, though. Not now. There was too much at stake. He had to keep running.

If the Family caught him, everyone would die.

ONE

Nate Tucker found out about the apartment as people often learn about the things which change their lives forever—by sheer luck.

It was a Thursday night party he didn't want to be at. 'Party' was too big a word for it, but calling it 'a few rounds after work' seemed too minor. There were half a dozen people he knew and another dozen he was supposed to know. He hadn't really paid attention when they'd been introduced, and none of them seemed interesting enough to go back and learn their names after the fact. They sat around tables that had been pushed together, shared communal appetizers some people would argue they'd never touched, and sipped overpriced drinks they made a point of claiming they'd first had at more exclusive restaurants.

Nate had realized a while back that nobody talked with each other at such gatherings. People just took turns talking *at* each other. He never got the sense anyone was listening. He wished his coworkers would stop inviting him.

Nate was being talked at by a man he remembered as the Journalist with the Hot Redhead Girlfriend. He'd been introduced to the man at one of these things a month or two back. Like everyone else at the table, the Journalist considered himself part of the film industry, even though, as far as Nate could tell, the man's job had nothing whatsoever to do with making movies. At the moment, the Journalist was lamenting a cancelled interview. His subject, a screenwriter, had to dive into last minute rewrites demanded by some producer. Nate wondered if the man got to put that sort of thing in his articles—*idiotic revisions made to climactic scene to pacify self-centered executive.*

There was a break in the Journalist's monologue and Nate realized the man was waiting for a response. He covered the pause with a cough and took a hit off his beer. "That sucks," Nate said. "Do you lose out altogether or can he reschedule?"

The Journalist shrugged. "Maybe. My week's packed, and he's going to be busy pulling his hair out." He took a sip of his own drink. "Anyway, enough about me. What's up with you? I haven't seen you at one of these things in ages."

Nate, who remembered waving to the Journalist at last week's almost-party and getting a raised chin back, shrugged too. "Nothing much," he said.

"Weren't you working on a script or something?"

Nate shook his head. "No, not me. Not my thing."

"So what have you been up to?"

He took another hit off his beer. "Work. Trying to find a new place to live."

The Journalist's brow rose. "What happened?"

"The guys I've been living with, they decided to do their own thing," said Nate. "One's moving back to San Francisco, the other's getting married." He shrugged. "We had a house, but I can't afford it on my own."

"Where are you now?"

"Silverlake."

"You looking for anything in particular?"

Nate considered it for a moment. It was the most anyone outside of his roommates had asked about the search. "I'd like to stay near Hollywood," he said. "I don't need much space. I'm hoping to find a studio for around eight hundred a month."

The Journalist nodded and took another sip of his drink. "I know a place."

"You do?"

The other man nodded. "A friend of mine suggested it when I first moved here from San Diego. Older place in that Koreatown-Los Feliz gray area around the 101."

Nate nodded. "Yeah, I know right where that is. It's closer to work than the place I'm in now."

Another nod from the Journalist. "I was only there for a few months, but the rent was cheap and it had a great view."

"How cheap?"

The Journalist glanced around. "Between you and me," he said, "I was paying five-fifty."

Nate choked on some beer. "Five-fifty a month? That's it?"

The Journalist nodded.

"Five *hundred*-fifty?"

"Yep. And that included all the utilities."

"You're shitting me."

"Nope."

"Why'd you leave?"

The Journalist smiled and gestured with his glass at his Hot Redhead Girlfriend. She was across the table and down a few seats, being talked at by a woman with jet-black hair and matching clothes. "We decided to move in together and got a bigger place. And…"

Nate raised a brow. "And what?"

"It's kind of got an odd vibe to it."

"The area or the building?"

"The building. Don't get me wrong, it's a great place. It just wasn't for me." He pulled out his phone and began brushing his fingers across the colorful screen. "I think I've still got the number for the management company if you want it."

TWO

The building was a cube of red bricks lined with gray mortar, the type of building one pictured in New York or San Francisco. Two rectangles of concrete sat in the brick at the third story, each bearing the eroded image of old heraldry. Just above the wide front door, a fire escape zigzagged up the center of the building's face. Nate knew Los Angeles had lots of old buildings like this. In fact, he worked in one of them.

It was built up on a tall foundation, sitting on top of an already-high slope. There were two flights of stairs leading to the door. Nate immediately pictured the hassle of hauling furniture up them. Two trees flanked the steps and gave some cover to the downstairs apartments. They were newer additions, not as thick and sturdy as the one sprawled by the wrought-iron gate.

A small Asian woman stood just inside the gate, an iPad tucked under her arm. She waved to him. "Nate?"

He nodded. "Toni?"

"I am. Great to meet you." She opened the gate and shook his hand.

Toni was one of those women it was impossible to pin an age on. She could've been anywhere from eighteen to thirty-five. Her skirt showed enough leg to make him think younger. Her manner and the cadence of her voice made him think older.

She smiled as she led him up the stairs. It was a fantastic smile. If it was fake, she practiced it every day. "It's a great building," she said. She gave one of the pillars by the door an affectionate pat. "Over a hundred years old. It's one of the oldest in this part of the city."

Above the wide front door, KAVACH was engraved on the concrete lintel in bold letters. Nate wasn't sure if it was a word or a name. "It looks great."

"They built them to last back then. Isn't that what people say?" She pulled open the steel security door. The main door past it was wide open. "Come on in and I'll show you the place."

The small lobby was straight out of a dozen noir films. Apartments 1 and 2 flanked the front door. A staircase with a well-worn banister curled up to the second floor. Beneath the staircase were two banks of mailboxes, and beneath them were tall stacks of phonebooks. It looked like they'd been there for a long time.

"Don't mind those," she said. "Usually Oskar, the property manager, keeps things pretty tidy."

"It's not a deal-breaker," he told her.

She gave him another smile and butterflies fluttered in his stomach. It had to be practiced. No one could naturally pack so much into curved lips and a flash of teeth.

"Let's head up," she said. She glanced at her iPad. "We'll zig-zag a bit."

She guided him up the curving staircase to the second floor and down the hall. It was all dark brown and ivory paint. They passed a narrow glass door that made him think of an old telephone booth. Toni glanced back over her shoulder and followed his gaze. "Elevator," she explained. "It's out of service right now, but they'll probably have it working by the time you move in. It's pretty small, though. You'll have to take your furniture up the stairs."

"Good thing I don't have much," he said. He glanced at the other side of the hall and glimpsed a set of padlocks on a door marked '14', but Toni's tour had already moved past it. He looked back over his shoulder, but the thick frame hid the door.

"Twenty-two units," she said as they walked toward the back. "Eight, six, and eight." They stepped through a fire door and into a large space that stretched from one side of the building to the other. There were three couches and a pair of matching chairs. The south wall held a huge flatscreen TV, at least forty inches. "The lounge area's open to everyone," she said. "There are connections for a game system or Blu ray or whatever. You might want to leave a note if you want to reserve a certain time for something."

The back of the lounge was also the landing for the rear stairwell. It was much more industrial than the front one, and switched back and forth with each short flight of steps. Toni continued up the stairs. The third floor hallway looked identical to the two below it. On either side of the landing were brown doors marked 27 and 28. She produced a key and opened 28.

The studio wasn't huge, but it was pretty big. Nate pictured clones of himself lying head-to-toe on the hardwood floor and guessed the room was about twenty by twenty. Maybe deeper than it was wide. Two long strings dangled from the ceiling fan in the center. The brick wall across from the door was filled by two huge windows, big enough for him to stand in. They were the old-fashioned, mullioned kind, with ropes and counterweights hidden in the frames.

Outside the window he could see Los Angeles. With the small hill and the tall foundation he was close to five stories up. The windows looked right over the top of the building next door. Nate could see the 101 Freeway a few blocks to the north. In the distance, up on the hillside, he could see the Griffith Park Observatory.

Toni's heels clicked on the floor. "Some view, isn't it?"

"It's amazing." He leaned his head close to the glass. Off to the left stood the tall, white letters of the Hollywood sign.

She stepped through the open doorway to the left and into the kitchen. The counter was decorated with white and blue tiles in a pattern that could almost pass for a checkerboard. The linoleum on the floor mimicked the counter. "The apartment comes with a fridge and a clawfoot tub," she said. "Laundry room is in the basement. There's a sun deck up on the roof. We start with a six-month lease but it goes month-to-month after that. Once you pass a credit check we'd need first and last month's rent."

He walked over to the kitchen and tried to play it cool. He opened a few cabinets and focused on the countertop so he wouldn't risk stupidity in the light of her smile. "And the rent is how much?" he asked. "The guy I talked with said it was on the cheaper side."

"Well, I'm afraid we just had an increase," she said, "so it's not as cheap as it used to be."

Nate looked back at the studio and pictured all his furniture lined up along one wall. "That's understandable," he said. "So how much is it?"

"Five-sixty-five," she said. "That includes utilities."

"Which ones?"

"All of them."

He risked looking at the smile. "Five hundred and sixty-five dollars total?"

"Yes," she said. "Are you interested?"

"Fuck, yes," he said. "Pardon my French."

Toni's smile wavered for a moment, and he realized a real smile had pushed through the practiced one. "Don't worry about it," she said. "I've been known to swear like a sailor when things don't go my way."

A business card and pen appeared from her pocket. She used the back of the iPad as a desk and scribbled something on the card. "Go to the Locke Management website and log on with this code," she said. "The whole application's online. Do it tonight and we can process the credit check on Monday. This time next week, this could be your place."

"That's great," he said. "Credit check shouldn't be any trouble."

"Fantastic," she said. "I'll give you a call next week and—" Her smile cracked and started to crumble. She stepped back and caught it just in time.

A cockroach had appeared on the counter. It wasn't one of the huge ones Nate saw sometimes at night out on the sidewalks, but it was big enough—half the size of his thumb. Its antennae wiggled as it followed a zigzag path across the counter.

"I'm so sorry," Toni said. She glanced at her iPad again. "We have an exterminator in every other month, but it's impossible to wipe them out, you know?"

The insect paused in a shaft of sunlight to give them a look and Nate got a good look back. Then it pressed itself behind the outlet plate and was gone. "Was that cockroach bright green?"

Toni shrugged and her smile reasserted itself. "Maybe? It's an old building. You have to expect some weirdness, y'know?"

FIRST STORY

THREE

Mandy sat at her secondhand computer and punched her information in again. She had to hunt and peck on the keyboard because she'd never learned how to type. The keyboard always confused her, anyway. Why couldn't all the letters just be in order instead of scattered everywhere? She brushed a blonde curl away from her face, then tucked it behind her ear when it fell back in front of her eyes.

The internet credit check was a first-of-the month ritual. She only had a few websites bookmarked in Firefox (a free browser, thank goodness), and almost half of them were credit agencies. The other half were articles on getting out of debt.

As she'd expected, her credit rating had gone down two more points. It was at 514 now. Over two hundred points down in just over a year. She'd never be able to get a house now. Or a car.

In a moment of weakness, in the Food4Less break room eight months ago, she'd confessed to another cashier, Bob, about her credit problems and the non-stop calls from collection agencies that wouldn't listen to her. He'd pointed out that she couldn't afford a new house or car, regardless, so what was the big deal? His advice was to ignore the calls. "After all," he'd said, "once you're at the bottom, what else can they do to you?"

The collection agencies kept calling, however, and made it clear that it was a very big deal. She believed them. They wouldn't be this mean for nothing, after all. They insulted her and refused to listen to anything she said. All the articles said to talk with creditors about payments and they made it sound so easy, but the men and women on the phone just threatened to call her parents and her grandmother and tell them what a deadbeat she'd become. Once, she had to hang up because they made her start to cry.

Her mother did not raise a deadbeat daughter. Mandy didn't want her mom thinking of her as one of *those* people. *Those* people were the ones who'd broken the economy and driven banks out of business, the liberals who thought they could spend as much as they wanted and never pay their debts. Mandy wasn't one of them. She'd just gotten careless and hit a bad patch. That's what her mom always called it. "Mike down at the store, he hit a bad patch after his wife died."

The key, of course, was that people lifted themselves out of a bad patch. She'd been trying, but there were too many fees and the interest rates were suddenly much too high. No matter what she did, things just got worse. Her bad patch had become a rough spot in the road, and the rough spot had become a hole she'd fallen into.

A week after her confession Bob "gave" her the computer as a favor. Mandy knew what it meant when a man in Los Angeles offered a "favor." One of her neighbors from downstairs, Veek, had done a bit of work on the machine and declared it internet-usable. Mandy was pretty sure the woman had added in two little green cards and done something to the memory or the processor or some computer thing. At the time Mandy worried Veek might also expect something for her "favor." After all, she was from Europe or Asia or someplace and they were a lot looser when it came to such things there. Mandy wasn't sure she could do something like that with another woman, but six months had gone by and Veek had never asked for said payment.

Mandy wasn't sure what a score of 514 was, or what was used to calculate it. But she knew it was very, very bad.

She stared at the three-digit number for a while and realized she'd spent ten minutes lost in thought. The credit score check was supposed to be a quick thing. She was going to miss her bus.

She grabbed her shirt and jeans from the bed, decided she didn't have time to change, and crammed them into the canvas shopping bag she used as a purse. Showing up in a sun dress would mean the manager leering at her and "accidentally" walking into the bathroom while she changed. She'd have to deal with it. It was her own fault for getting distracted.

She opened the door to her apartment and almost ran into a bookshelf.

It stretched across the hall at an angle. The man at one end of the bookshelf was on the thinner side of average and had a mop of brown-blond hair. He needed a haircut. The other man was stout and bald with a devil-beard.

"Sorry," said the haircut-needing man. "Just moving in. I'm your new neighbor." He balanced his end of the bookshelf on one hand, dropped his keys into it, and held out the other hand. "Nate Tucker."

Mandy ignored the hand and locked the door behind her. "Hi," she said. "Sorry, I'm late for work." She slipped past the bookshelf and dashed down the hall.

"The people here are so warm and friendly," said the bald man.

"I'm sorry," she called back over her shoulder. "I'm going to miss my bus."

She ran down the front stairs. It was an awful first impression, she knew. Her mom used to bake cookies for new neighbors. Then again, her mom had never lived in Los Angeles. Hopefully Nate Tucker wouldn't be another one of *those* neighbors.

"Hot neighbor," said Nate as her footsteps faded down the stairs. "Could make up for the parking."

Sean, his soon-to-be-former roommate, shook his head. "Believe me, even if you end up sleeping with her it won't be worth the hassle of street parking."

Nate had passed the credit check on Monday afternoon and his check cleared Thursday morning. It had wiped out his savings and meant that he was paying rent on two places at once for the month of April, but it was his. He turned the knob and opened the door of his new apartment.

"Here it is," said Nate.

"Damn." Sean stared out the window at the observatory. "That's some view."

"Tell me about it."

"You lucked out finding this place."

"I know."

"Parking still sucks, though."

They headed back down to the street where Sean's pickup held the rest of Nate's furniture. The next bookshelf went up faster now that they knew the staircase. The entertainment center was small enough to go up with no problem, despite its weight.

They moved the desk into the lobby twenty minutes later and paused to adjust their grips. As they did, a solid-looking man with dark curls came out of the hallway carrying a box of his own. He glanced at the desk. "You moving in?"

"Yeah," said Nate. He set his end back down and held out his hand. "Nate Tucker. I'm moving into number twenty-eight."

"Carl," the other man said. He tucked the box under his arm and shook the hand. "Moving out of five."

"Really?"

Carl nodded. "If I could've afforded it, I would've broken my lease months ago." He looked around at the wood and plaster walls. "Wasn't even here six weeks and I was ready to go."

"Was it the parking?" asked Sean. "I told him the parking was gonna suck."

"The parking sucks," Carl agreed, "but it's just this place. It gets on your nerves. I never felt comfortable here, no matter what I did. Never got a good night's sleep."

Nate felt his stomach sink a few inches. "Is it loud?"

"No, it's just... it's not a comfortable place, y'know? I never felt good here. Do you believe in that *feng shui* stuff?"

Nate and Sean both shook their heads.

Carl's lips twitched into a smile. "Neither do I, but it's the best way I can think of to explain it. The place just feels off. Living here was like putting your foot in the wrong shoe. It's just...wrong." He shook his head again. "Sorry. This is a shitty welcome for you."

"No," said Nate, "I'd rather hear about it now than learn it the hard way."

Carl shrugged. "There are tons of perks to staying here if you like it. The sun deck up on the roof is awesome. Check out the Mexican place up the street. The Thai place on the corner is pretty good, too, if you ask them to make stuff hot." He shifted his box back into his arms. "Good luck." He headed out through the door.

Nate and Sean got the desk up to the second floor. While they swung it around to the next flight of stairs, Sean said, "Man, I'm glad I'm moving back to the Bay."

Nate hefted his end of the desk. "Why's that?"

"I won't be here to help you move out in six months."

"He's overreacting. Some people just don't like some places."

"Like your neighbor who was running to get out of the building."

"Late for work."

"Whatever," Sean said.

The futon took two trips. They wrestled the floppy mattress up all three flights. The frame was the worst of all. It twisted just enough to hinge open, and the clang of metal was painfully loud in the stairwell. They almost lost it on the landing between the second and third story when it unfolded again.

"Thank God that's over," said Sean as they set the frame down in the center of the apartment.

"Still the boxes," said Nate.

"Didn't you say there was an elevator?"

"Yeah. Maybe they've got it fixed."

They walked out to the elevator door. Next to the frame was a pair of stubby push buttons, the type where pushing one button in levered the other one out. They'd been painted over several times, and their edges had long since become ripples in the latex. Nate tried to twist the undersized door knob, but it refused to turn. He shook it harder and the door rattled in its frame.

Sean yawned. "No elevator?"

"Guess not." Nate pressed his face against the glass and shielded his eyes from the hall lights. The space behind the glass was pitch black. There was no way to tell if he was looking at the elevator car or the shaft.

"You are ones who haff been making all the noise?"

A man stood by the stairs, half-silhouetted by the light pouring through the hallway window. He was short, bald, and round.

"Yeah," said Nate. "Sorry about that."

The man nodded once. "One of you is Mister Nathan Tucker?"

"That's me."

He nodded again. "I am Oskar Rommel." His accent turned the S into a Z and emphasized the K. "I am the building manager."

"Nice to meet you."

"Nice to meet you," he parroted. He stepped into better light and features appeared on his face. He had bushy eyebrows and a mustache like a comb. The hairy arms hanging out of his wifebeater were thick with slabs of muscle that had gone soft. Nate guessed the man was pushing sixty. "The elefator does not work."

"Ahhhh. Toni said they might have it fixed by now."

"It has neffer worked," said Oskar with a snort. "I haff been here twenty-three years, nineteen as manager. The elefator has neffer worked one day."

"Rommel," said Sean. "That's...German, isn't it?"

Oskar rolled his eyes. "Yes, I am a German named Rommel, so therefore I must be the grandson of the tank commander. And his last name is Tucker, so he must be the grandson of the man who made the car."

"Sorry," said Sean. "No offense meant."

"Don't mind him," said Nate. "Repeated testing has proved he's an idiot."

Oskar snorted again, but his lips bent into a smile. "You will like it here. It is a good building. Your room has the best view. If you need anything, I am in room twelff, downstairs in the front. Please do not knock after six except for emergencies."

"Great," said Nate. "Thanks a lot."

The manager gave another sharp nod and lumbered back down the stairwell.

"No elevator, then," said Sean. "How many boxes you got in the Bug?"

"Maybe a dozen. Nothing too heavy."

Before the unloading began, Sean went to the corner store and bought a bag of chips and a six-pack to christen the empty refrigerator. It took five more trips to empty the Volkswagen. They sat on the couch and each drank their second beer.

"I think it's going to be a nice place," said Nate.

"Yeah," said Sean, gazing out the window, "it's pretty cool. That it for today?"

"I'm gonna try to organize some of this and then maybe head back later for another load of boxes. If I can get two or three loads tomorrow, that should be everything."

"We can load up the truck again, get it all in one go."

"Nah, you've done enough, man. Besides, you haven't even started packing your own stuff."

"Yeah, about that," Sean said. "If I help you with another load, can I have your boxes?"

He chuckled. "Sure. Organizing can wait."

"You staying here tonight?"

Nate looked around the studio. "Hadn't really thought about it. But yeah, it's that or sleep on the floor back at the house." He slapped the futon twice. The bare mattress kicked up a little puff of dust. He looked at his former roommate and shrugged.

Sean sighed. "Then you're moved out."

"Guess so."

"I'm left alone with the lovebirds for another two weeks. A third wheel in my own home." He set his bottle down on the empty bookshelf and pulled out his phone. "Come on. I can have a farewell pizza waiting for us by the time we get back over there."

Nate locked up and they headed back to the stairwell.

"Hell," said Sean.

Nate looked around. "What?"

Sean pointed at the door marked 23. The door had a lock plate with a small socket above it, but there was no sign of a doorknob.

"Crap," Nate said. "Did we knock it off?"

"Maybe they're doing work in there," said Sean. "Easy way for the crew to lock it. Just take the whole doorknob."

"Maybe." Nate looked up and down the hall. "Not the best thing for my first day."

"If we did it."

"The entertainment center's pretty solid. Could've whacked it right off."

Sean shook his head. "I didn't do it, and I didn't hear you do it."

"Quietly away then?"

"I think so."

They headed for the stairwell.

FOUR

The second load went off without a hitch, although, as Sean predicted, there was no parking. Nate drove around for fifteen minutes and eventually found a place he could parallel park in, although he had to wiggle his Volkswagen back and forth five times to get flush with the sidewalk in the tiny space. They unloaded and Sean headed off at sundown with half the boxes and a promise to return next weekend for the rest of them.

Nate spent an hour setting up the entertainment system with his old DVD player and even older television. The bookshelves were stocked with his eclectic mix of books and knickknacks. He wedged the desk in a corner facing away from the window and opened up his battered laptop. The screen was coming apart at the seams, torqued open by the poorly-designed hinge, and he was holding it together with duct tape. Now that he'd emptied his savings, the tape would have to hold a little longer.

The lone closet was too small for all his clothes. Not by much, but enough that he knew it would be a constant battle if he decided to force them in there. He ended up folding some dress shirts and nicer pants and sticking them on one of the empty bookshelves. He usually stored his t-shirts there, anyway.

He dropped a cluster of clothes hangers on the closet pole. One bounced free and clattered to the floor. He bent after it and noticed the shape.

Almost invisible in the back of the closet was a panel the size of a folded newspaper. It was painted with the same latex that covered most of the vertical surfaces in the apartment, and had been coated so many times the seams around it had almost vanished. He rapped his knuckles on it and a wooden echo sounded in the closet. There was an empty space behind it.

Nate stood up and walked through his small home. Going off eyeball measurements, it looked like the panel lined up with the bathtub. Maybe a shut-off valve which hadn't been used in ages. The maintenance crew probably didn't even know it was there. Just a detail that vanished between contractors. Odds were they had to shut off the water to the whole building now to do any work.

He finished in the closet and decided to move to the kitchen. He only had three boxes to unpack in there, but he figured it'd be nice to wake up and find the coffee maker ready to go, and maybe a coffee cup somewhere nearby.

It had gotten dark while he worked in the main room of the studio. He felt the wall of the kitchen and failed to locate the light switch. It took him a minute, but he spotted it in the spill of light from the other room. A two-switch panel sat three feet from the doorway, just far enough away to be awkward.

Nate flicked the first switch and nothing happened. The second switch caused a loud growl from the sink. He flinched and the disposal rattled to a halt.

He flipped the first switch again and looked up at the fixture. A faint glimmer came from behind the frosted globe. He flipped the switch a few more times without a better response.

"Son of a bitch," he sighed.

The apartment ceilings were high. Not cathedral high, but two or three feet more than average. A moment of climbing got him balanced on the countertop. The checkered tiles were cold against his bare feet. He leaned out, unscrewed the fixture's bolts with one hand, and let the globe settle into his hands.

The bulb's filament gave out a weak glow, but no real light. He gave it a few taps with his fingernail. The filament shivered but didn't get any brighter.

In Nate's limited electrical experience, this was a power problem. A few opinions of his new home's maintenance crews stampeded through his mind. He corralled them just as quickly. No one would've been working on the apartment at night. They just didn't know it was broken.

He set the globe down on the counter and straightened up to give the bulb one last tap. As he did he noticed his hand. The base of his fingernails, the cuticles, were tinged with bright blue. It was so bright they almost glowed.

No, thought Nate, *they* are *glowing*.

It was a party bulb. The last tenant had left a black light in the kitchen fixture. It wasn't one of the cheap ones made with purple glass, so it had passed as a regular bulb. The white tiles on the checkerboard countertop had a faint gleam to them, too.

He leaned out again and set his fingertips against it. The glass was hot, but not enough to burn. A few quick twists and the bulb dropped into his hand. He let it roll back and forth, never settling against his skin for too long, and set it down on a pile of dishtowels and cloth napkins.

There were two spare bulbs in one of the boxes. It took a few minutes to find them, and he shook one against his ear, listening for the jingle of a broken filament. He switched off the fixture, set the new bulb down next to the black light, and worked his way back up onto the counter.

Nate got the new light in place without too much effort. He balanced himself against one of the kitchen cabinets and bent over to the switches. He flicked the first switch back to the on position.

Nothing.

He straightened up on the countertop. "Stupid fucker," he said. He'd fumbled around in the dark and put the black light back into the socket. His cuticles were gleaming again.

Nate stretched out his foot and used his toes to swat the light switch back to the off position. He unscrewed the bulb and went through the careful balancing act of swapping the two bulbs. Once it was in place, he reached down and turned the light on again.

The bulb gave out the dim glow of black light.

Nate wrinkled his brow. He'd swapped them this time. He was sure of it.

He flipped the switch, pulled the bulb, and hopped off the counter. He took both light bulbs into the studio where the light was good.

The one in his left hand was a General Electric. He recognized the cursive G E in the text circling the top of the glass ball. Beneath the logo were the words LONG LIFE WHITE in an arc. It was fifty-seven watts, an energy-saver. It was one of the ones he'd brought with him.

The bulb in his right hand, the one in the light to start with, didn't have a fancy logo. It was just marked K-LITE. It also was fifty-seven watts.

It also wasn't a black light.

FIVE

Nate worked at a magazine in Hollywood. Not the shining steel and glass Hollywood always seen on television, though. The part he worked in had rattling elevators, no air conditioning, and ten-year-old computers. The magazine was the same—not A list, but solidly in the Bs. He knew it had something to do with movies and celebrities, or maybe the different crew people behind the scenes, but truth be told he'd never been interested enough to pick up an issue and read it.

He'd stumbled into the data entry job and had been doing it for almost two years now. He was technically a part-time temp, but his bosses always pushed to get forty hours a week out of him. The idea of actually hiring him full-time had never been brought up by either side. This was an unspoken understanding.

It was a mindless way to earn nine twenty-five an hour. The magazine sent out thousands of mailers, flyers, and sample issues every month, and a fair share of them came back in white mail crates, bundled together in packets of a hundred or more. His job was to compare the addresses to ones in the database and determine whether they were current or flagged for non-delivery. The catch was that the database grew by a hundred names or more every week, some of which were just the same clients being listed under a new entry. Plus each week brought another crate or two of returns to his cubicle.

The cubicles defined the company in so many ways. They were bulky partitions, salvaged from the offices of a bigger company when it went belly-up. Each oversized wall and its base took up so much space that the room was a model of inefficiency. Anne and Zack, the other two semi-permanent temps, had to turn sideways to get into their cubicles. Jimmy, the office intern, had to climb over chairs to get to his. Nate only rated the cubicle by the door because nobody wanted to wrestle the mail crates into one of the others.

He reached for another bundle of returns and heard a sigh behind him. He tried not to flinch.

"I tried to call you last night," said Eddie.

Eddie was the worst sort of employer. He thought he was a generous, fair man with a firm grasp of business. He was actually a tightwad middle-manager with few good ideas who micromanaged everyone. Nate had worked in the office for two weeks when he was given a long speech about how he wasn't applying himself and meeting expected quotas. He'd countered with some very simple math and shown how Eddie's expectations were impossible for anyone to achieve. His boss had stood there, staring at him, and then wandered away. Three days later, he'd come back to moan about how he'd expected the whole project to be done the week before.

There was a shuffle of chairs as Zack and Anne leaned out to see if they were Eddie's chosen focus today. Once they realized his gaze was on Nate, they slipped back into their own cubicles.

"Sorry," said Nate. "What's up?"

"Why didn't you answer your cell phone?"

"It never rang."

"I called three times," said Eddie.

Nate felt a moment of relief and annoyance at the same time. If something was important enough to call three times on a Wednesday night, Eddie would've been down in Nate's cubicle first thing Thursday morning, not late in the afternoon. He'd called for something petty, been annoyed he couldn't get through, and only remembered his annoyance after lunch.

"I guess I was in a dead spot," said Nate. He focused on the new bundle of return slips and peeled off the rubber band.

"We're in the middle of Los Angeles and you're trying to tell me you couldn't get a cell phone signal?

"I bet it's my new place," said Nate after a moment's thought. He shrugged. "The walls are all brick and plaster. I think it doubles as a bomb shelter. When war breaks out, you can all hide out at my place."

He heard a quick snort of laughter from Anne's cubicle. She was the one bright spot in the office. She was another temp like him, with the cheekbones, eyes, and body of a model. Her hair stretched down to her waist. Anne had been at the office for eight months now.

Eddie huffed out more air to make sure Nate knew how inconvenient this was. "Make sure they get your new phone number upstairs," he said.

"As soon as I have one," said Nate.

The oversized man wandered back into the hall without ever saying what he'd called for. Nate looked back at his screen. At least the day wasn't ending on a down note.

Nate could get to work faster from his new place, but Sean had been proven right. He'd cut fifteen minutes off his travel time, but spent twenty minutes every night looking for parking when he got home. Instead of making his job more bearable, it added to the frustration he felt. He usually ended up parking almost a block and a half away.

As he walked down the hill toward his apartment, he spotted a young woman with bright blue hair leaving the building. He'd already identified a few of his neighbors. He'd seen Oskar twice, both times out on the sidewalk. The old man did most of his shopping at the two markets at the end of the street. There was also a curvy woman and a ginger-headed man close to Nate's age who walked with the practiced synchronization of a long-time couple. None of them seemed to notice him. There'd been no more sightings of the farmer's daughter blonde who lived across the hall.

He slipped through the gate and tried to find the security door key on his keyring as he walked up the steps. Something flashed sunlight in his eyes and he glanced to his left. From this angle, he could see between some of the shrubbery and the bottom of the building. At the far corner was an old fashioned cornerstone of glossy rock.

Nate stepped down the stairs and onto the small lawn. He could see the lines where rows of sod had been laid out. A few steps carried him to the corner of the building. A large shrub grew there. He bent a few branches out of the way until the symbols there were revealed.

The cornerstone was a solid block of marble, shot through with dark veins and a few flecks of sparkling stone. The numbers and letters were carved almost half an inch deep.

1894
wNA
PTK

Nate wasn't sure how much information was supposed to be on a cornerstone, but he felt let down by how little was on this one.

A few minutes later he was upstairs and tossing his bag onto the couch. He usually changed into casual clothes after work, but he had nothing clean. In fact, he'd brought a half-full hamper of dirty clothes from his old apartment.

Thursday night, it seemed, would be centered around checking out the building's laundry room. Clothes and quarters were gathered, a bottle of detergent was stuffed in the top of the hamper, and he lugged the whole thing down the back stairwell to the basement.

There were eight machines in the laundry room. Four washers stood in a line against the concrete wall opposite the door. The dryers were set in two stacks of two. Opposite the dryers was a battered couch with a man sprawled on it.

The man had his hands up covering his eyes, more in a gesture of mild frustration than any sort of protection. His solid arms and broad chest were the kind that came from constant labor, not days at the gym. He wasn't much taller than Nate. An inch or two at the most. Nate was aware, though, of the difference between being five-ten and being six feet tall. It was far more than just two inches.

As Nate shuffled in with his hamper, the man lowered his hands and revealed at least two days' worth of stubble. "Hey," he said.

"Hey," echoed Nate. "Long day?"

"They're all long," he sighed with a grin. "Forgot to do laundry over the weekend. Now I need shirts and socks and I've got an early call tomorrow."

"That sucks."

"Yeah. Don't use the washer on the left. Never spins fast enough so everything comes out wet. Really wet, not damp."

"Thanks," said Nate.

"No worries. You new?"

"Yeah. Just moved into twenty-eight last weekend."

"Right," said the man. "Saw your pickup with the desk and the shelves and stuff."

"Friend's pickup, but yeah."

"Yeah," he said. He pointed up at the edge where the wall and ceiling joined. "Roger. I live right there. Number seven."

"I'm Nate. You been here long?"

"Little over a year." The dryer chimed and went silent. Roger dragged himself off the couch and slouched to the machine with his olive-drab pillow. It unfolded into a tall rucksack.

Nate flicked his eyes to the building above them. "You like it?"

"What's not to like?" He shrugged as he shoved laundry into his bag. "Work a sixty-five, seventy hour week. Weekends I run errands or go out. This is where I sleep and keep my stuff. And it's cheap."

"Seventy hour work week?"

"Local Eighty, bro," Roger said. "Grip."

"Like in the movies?"

"Yep. Seven years."

Nate grinned. "What the hell does a grip do anyway?"

"Grips are the hammers, man. Set flags, build platforms, keep everything safe."

"Flags?"

Roger smiled. "Think of it this way. Electricians are in charge of the lights. We're in charge of the shadows." He tossed a few last t-shirts in the sack. "Have a good night, bro."

"You too."

Roger clomped up the stairs and Nate was alone in the laundry room. He packed the last of his clothes into the washer and fished two quarters out of his jeans. Fifty cents for a load of laundry was almost as surreal as his rent. Water hissed inside the machine.

He wandered back into the hall. Right across from the laundry room doorway was a door. It was rust-red with long, inset panels, not the flat faces the apartment doors had. A hasp had been screwed into the door frame, just above the knob, and a gleaming Masterlock hung from it.

He strolled down the hall. A bare bulb threw harsh light everywhere. The floor was painted the same blue as the laundry room, but just past the bulb the paint ended and it was bare concrete.

Behind the laundry room was a smaller room, maybe the size of his studio, filled with water heaters. They were squat, can-like things that reached his hip, not so much arranged in the room as shoved into it. Most of them were bone-colored, although two chalk-white ones stood against the far wall. Nate could see ENERGY EFFICIENT stickers on several of them. A faint haze of warm steam hung in the air.

He heard a rustling noise. A cockroach with a body as long as his ring finger scurried up onto one of the heaters. It was a bright green roachasaurus, the granddaddy of the one he'd seen in his apartment that first day. Its tiny claws pinged and scraped on the metal surface. It was always wrong when the pests got so big you could hear them walking.

A mental image rose up in his mind. Sigourney Weaver as Ripley, standing in a misty room of alien eggs.

Nate stepped away from the cluster of heaters.

The hall ended at a set of double doors. He looked behind him and guessed he was close to the front of the building. The elevator shaft was probably right on the other side of the doors.

Like the door across from the laundry room, these didn't match the rest of the building. These were elegant doors. The kind of doors that used to lead into ballrooms or penthouse suites in old hotels.

They had a bar across them, the way Bugs Bunny would block a door. The dusty wood just looked like a perfectly-straight two-by-four. A length of chain looped around the bar three or four times and also threaded itself twice through the door handles.

Nate stepped out of the light and peered at the padlock that held the ends of the chain. It was a huge, solid-looking block with a loop almost as thick as his finger. Lock and chain were both covered with bright orange rust, faded to dirt-brown in places. He could see a few flecks of steel gleaming through here and there. If he had to guess, he'd say no one had opened the lock in at least twenty years.

He set his finger against the left-hand door. It was warm. Warmer than the air in the hall. He gave a little push. Between the bar and the chains, the doors were locked solid. It was like pushing on the wall.

Back down the hall he heard his washer spin into high gear. *This concludes our exploration of the cellar*, he thought to himself.

SIX

Saturday was a full week in his new home. Nate wanted to mark the day and remembered the sun deck on the roof. Sitting out with a beer sounded like a great way to end his first week and start the weekend.

He headed down to the stairwell and followed it up the extra flight to the roof. There was a metal fire door with a crash bar on it. Posted on the wall next to the door was a list of rules for using the sun deck which seemed to amount to *don't be a dick about it.* A note was stuck to the metal door with a blue **X**, one of the magnetic letters kids used on the fridge.

XELA IS HERE

Nate wondered what it meant. He hit the bar and sunlight flooded the stairwell. He stepped out and let the door swing shut behind him.

A huge block of bricks dominated the front half of the roof. Nate guessed it was maybe ten feet high and even longer on the side flanking the stairwell. It was as if the architect had built one apartment for another floor and then given up. There was a weather-beaten door next to the stairs. There was no knob, but it had three half-rusted padlocks on it.

The back half of the roof was a wooden deck that looked like it should've been on a ski lodge or a Malibu beach house. It was twenty-five feet on each side and stood two feet above the tar-paper roof on short, squat legs. The planks were faded and dry, but not enough to seem dangerous.

Three wide steps led him up onto the platform. He could see downtown, the Hollywood sign, the observatory, and more. The whole city stretched around him in a vibrant panorama. It was one of those views that reminded him Los Angeles was a lot more than traffic, concrete, and graffiti.

Half a dozen deck chairs were scattered around the deck, facing all directions. On the back corner was a large mesh cabana, the kind people kept in back yards. Near the center sat a squat piece of metal. After a moment Nate realized it was a fire pit. He'd seen setups like this in movies and commercials. It was tough accepting this was his place now. He took a hit off his beer and let it soak in.

"You're the new guy, right?"

Lying on a chair he'd walked past was the woman with neon blue hair, the one he'd glimpsed before. Up close, he guessed she was a couple years younger than him. She had on a set of wayfarer sunglasses. And nothing else.

Nate's eyes flitted past her to gaze back at the fire door. "Yeah," he said. "Just moved in last weekend."

He saw her nod in his peripheral vision. "In twenty-eight, right? Far corner?"

"I guess so, yeah." He shifted his gaze from the fire door to the oversized brick structure. It didn't have any windows he could see. Just the padlocked door.

Another half-seen nod from the woman. "I'm in twenty-one. Opposite corner."

"Ahhh." He took another drink and focused on the distant observatory.

"Oh, for God's sake," she said. "They're just tits. You've seen tits before in your life, right?"

Nate made a point of looking her in the eyes. He hoped it came across a lot more casual than it felt. "Twice now," he said. "Three times if you count the internet."

She grinned. "Xela."

"What's that mean? I saw it on the sign."

"It's my name. Xela." She pronounced it so it rhymed with *Leela.* She held out her hand.

"Nate." He shook the hand. She had a solid grip.

Xela wasn't naked, he realized, just topless. Her bikini bottoms didn't hide much, though. Her body was lean, and her arms and shoulders had three or four tattoos each, or maybe one elaborate one. He didn't want to let his eyes drift down far enough to check. Her sky-colored hair dusted her shoulders. She'd gone the extra step and dyed her eyebrows, too.

"You all moved in already?"

"Yeah. I didn't have much stuff. Finished unpacking a couple days ago."

"You like it so far?"

He glanced out at the city. "Well, it's got a great view." He winced as soon as the words left his lips and tried to drown them with the bottle.

"Pathetic," she sighed. She grabbed a shirt from a pile at the foot of the deck chair and shrugged it over her shoulders. "You can look now," she said as she threaded a pair of buttons. "The awful things are hidden from your sensitive eyes."

"Sorry," he said. "It's just an odd way to meet the neighbors."

"That's why there's a sign up on the door."

"Yeah, but when I saw it, I thought 'Xela is here' might have something to do with Scientology."

"Ouch."

"Nothing personal."

"No, you're right. Most folks in the building know what it means and just leave me alone out here."

He glanced back at the door. "Sorry. Did you want privacy?"

"If I cared about privacy, Nate, would I sunbathe nude on the roof of my building? It's just a body. What's the point getting worked up over it?"

"Fair enough."

"I mean, if it makes you feel better I'm picturing you naked right now. Giving you the benefit of the doubt in a few places, too. Step towards me and to the left."

"What?"

"One step forward. Maybe a foot and a half left."

He moved and his shadow fell across her face. She smiled and pushed the sunglasses onto the top of her head. Her eyes were bright blue, too. She tapped his leg with her foot. "Thanks. That's better." She took a good look at him. "So, what do you do, Nate?"

"Do?"

"For a living. For fun. To make life interesting."

He shrugged. "I work in an office."

Xela's face fell. "I'm so sorry for you."

He took another hit off his beer. "Why say that? Maybe I love my job."

"Do you?"

"No."

"Nobody sane loves working in an office," she said. "It's against human nature to be locked up in a cubicle all day long."

"Who said anything about a cubicle?"

She grinned. It was a tight, thin smile. "If you had a big office, you'd've lied and said you loved your job."

He shrugged again and finished off the beer. "Maybe if I had a big office I really would love my job."

Xela shook her head. "You're not that messed up."

"How do you know? You just met me."

"You're uncomfortable seeing your hot neighbor topless even though I told you I was okay with it. If you were messed up, you'd've just stared."

"I wanted to stare," he told her. "I just thought it would make things awkward in the laundry room later."

"Not really. I do my laundry nude, too. That way I can clean everything at once."

"Really?"

"No, of course not. That'd be weird."

He sat down on one of the other chairs. She knocked her sunglasses back down over her eyes as he set the empty bottle down on the deck. "So what do you do, Xela? Aside from making the new guy uncomfortable?"

"Guess."

"Why?"

"Because I like to see what people say."

He looked at her hair and the tattoos peeking out of her shirt around her neck. The collar was short with little points, and he realized it was an old, plain-front tuxedo shirt. She'd only done two buttons because that's all there were. The rest of them were button holes for studs. And the shirt was dotted with pinpricks of color.

"I'm going to go with artist," he said.

"Very good. What gave me away?"

"You've got paint on your shirt. A lot on the sleeves."

"You're amazing, my dear Sherlock," she said. "Most guys just see the hair and the tits and go for stripper, although I think you would've been one of the classy ones who said 'exotic dancer'."

"Glad to know I measure up. So you're a painter?"

"Paint, sculpture, whatever the creative urge drives me to." She picked up a cell phone from the pile of clothes and glanced at the time. "Anyway, it's been nice meeting you, Nate from twenty-eight, but if you don't mind I want to get some more sun before I go to work."

"You on a deadline?"

"Sweet, but no. I've got a shift waiting tables."

"I thought you were an artist?"

"Art is what I do," she said, "but it's not my job." She unfastened one of the buttons and shooed him away. "Next time bring enough beer for the whole class."

He picked up his bottle and walked back to the fire door. The structure next to it loomed over him and he stopped at the padlocked door. "Hey," he called back.

"They're already out." She waved the shirt over her head like a flag. "I'm not covering up again."

"What is this thing, anyway?"

"What?" She sat up on the chair and gave him a flash of bare shoulder.

"This." Nate pointed at the block of bricks.

"It's the whatsit for the elevator," she said. "That's what Oskar told me."

"The elevator?"

"Yeah, all the motors and cables and stuff."

He took a few steps around the corner of the structure. It was larger than his apartment. "Kind of big, isn't it?"

Xela shrugged and vanished behind her chair again. "It's an old building," she said. "They had to make stuff bigger back then, y'know?"

SEVEN

Nate walked in the front door Tuesday after work and realized it had been ten days (not that he was counting) and he hadn't gotten his mail yet. He'd changed addresses and had things forwarded, but it had slipped his mind to actually check the mailbox. He went to the mailboxes under the stairs and located the one with 28 on it. The numbers were on red label tape, the kind where someone spun a dial and pressed the characters into the hard material until they turned white. The box was packed with junk mail with his name and bills with someone else's. As Eddie was so fond of saying at the office, he put it all in the circular file. *Circulars in the circular file*, Nate thought to himself.

The piles of phone books beneath the mailboxes had capsized. There were three different versions, most of them in bags that would've been orange or white if they weren't covered with dust. They were dated spring 2012, but he remembered them from his old place. They'd come out six months ago. There were at least two dozen of each type, so nobody had taken them. There was some brasswork behind them, hidden by a pile of alphabetical listings.

Nate tried to shove the books back into a stack, but time and gravity had rolled their spines. They'd never stand again. In a sudden burst of community spirit, he decided they all needed to go in the circular file.

No, he thought. *Recycling by the dumpster. Even better.*

He looped the plastic handles around his wrists and twisted them onto his knuckles. It took some work, but he got seven phone books on each arm. He got his heel on the door, opened it back up, and headed down the front stoop.

Nate found the first flaw in his plan when he got to the fence. He couldn't lift his arms enough to open the gate. After a few moments of struggling a man in a sweater vest and tie unlocked the gate from the other side. "Are you okay?" the stranger asked.

"Fine now," said Nate. "You got here just in time."

"Not a problem at all," said the other man. He looked at the bags Nate was holding and his head bobbed side to side for a moment. "Glad to see someone's finally getting rid of those." He stepped through and held the gate open. His dark hair was immaculately combed and parted. It reminded Nate of the plastic helmet-hair on LEGO people. "Have a wonderful day," said the man.

Nate wandered around to the side of the building where the dumpster stood. It reeked of piss, and he was careful not to step in any of the thin streams flowing down into the gutter. The blue recycling bins stood just past that. He let the bags slide off one arm, threw the lid open, and swung the other armload of phonebooks into the bin.

Two more, slightly smaller trips to the recycling bins killed off the last of Nate's community spirit and he decided the mail area looked fine with half the books gone. He spread the remainders out a bit more. As he rearranged the phone books he got a good look at the things behind them.

There was a trio of dusty plaques hidden beneath the mailboxes. The largest was a slab of brass. It was almost a square, over a foot on each side, and divided into three sections.

THE KAVACH BUILDING
HAS BEEN DESIGNATED A

NATIONAL
HISTORIC LANDMARK

THIS SITE POSSESSES NATIONAL SIGNIFICANCE IN COMMEMORATING THE HISTORY OF THE UNITED STATES OF AMERICA

1960

NATIONAL PARK SERVICE
UNITED STATES DEPARTMENT OF THE INTERIOR

Next to it was a smaller one, the size of a hardcover book, which also identified the building by name, the build date of 1894, and declared it to be **Historic-Cultural Monument No. 4** as of 1962. A large crest in the center of the plaque was labeled **City of Los Angeles**.

The last one, underneath the city plaque, was for the state of California. It was almost as big as the national one and dark with age. The California plaque was rectangular with a curvy top and a picture of a bear between two stars. It had the name and the years again, this time declaring the building a registered landmark in 1932. Other than that it was blank.

Nate wondered if landmark status granted some form of historical rent control. It might explain why everything was priced so low, although historical rents were probably closer to forty or fifty dollars a month, even in Los Angeles. He remembered something by Ray Bradbury where the author wrote about paying a miniscule amount for rent in Venice Beach back in the 1940s.

He swung back around to the stairs and just missed the farmer's daughter who lived across the hall from him. She flinched back and he stopped short. "Sorry," he said. "My mind was somewhere else."

"It's okay," she said. Today's outfit was tight jeans and a dark uniform top with a yellow logo on it. She had her hair pulled back in two stubby pigtails. A beat-up canvas shopping bag was slung over one of her shoulders.

Nate set his hand on the banister just as she put her foot on the first stair. They both stepped back. She smiled. "Sorry."

"Ladies first."

"No, it's okay."

"I insist." He took another step back and gestured her up the stairwell.

She gave a little bow of her head and started up. Her feet clacked on the steps. *She's actually wearing cowboy boots,* Nate thought, and she said, "You live across the hall from me, right?"

"Yeah," he said. "I moved in two weeks ago."

"Right. You're... Ned?"

"Nate."

"Nate. I'm sorry I was so rude to you. I was gonna be late for work and my boss kind of has it in for me."

"It's okay," he said. "I know what it's like to be running out the door and have something in your way. At my old place people used to double-park in our lot and block us in."

"Oh, that's so rude."

"Yeah, I know."

She slowed down and let him walk alongside her for the last flight of stairs. "I'm Mandy," she said. "Pleased to meet you."

"And you," he said. They tried for an awkward handshake on the move and laughed it off. At the third floor he let her take the lead again.

She glanced over her shoulder at him. "Did you get moved in okay?"

"No real problems," he said. "Still a few things to unpack. Phone just got set up yesterday. Debating if I want cable. Trying to figure out what I want to do for internet."

"Oh, talk to Veek," said Mandy.

"Vic? Is he with the rental office or something?"

"Veek," repeated Mandy. "She. It's short for something Middle Eastern or something. She's got wireless set up for the whole building. She'll let you in for five or ten bucks a month. And she works deals sometimes." Mandy shrugged in an awkward way. "She's down in fifteen."

"Good to know."

She stopped in front of her door. "What else can I tell you about this place you might not know?" She pursed her lips, pondering. "The elevator doesn't work, but you probably figured that out moving in.

Down in the laundry room, the machine on the left doesn't work well. Oh, and there's a girl who likes to lay out in the buff up on the sun deck."

"Yeah," he said. "Found most of that out already."

"Oh, I'm sorry." Mandy's voice dropped into a conspiratorial whisper as she unlocked her door. "I don't know what's up with her. She'd be a real pretty girl if she didn't do all that weird stuff to her hair."

While Nate debated if a comeback of some sort was needed, Mandy opened her apartment. He glanced in and saw homemade drapes and a broad clutter of furniture. "Hey," he said, "is your apartment bigger than mine?"

She looked over her shoulder, then past him to his door. "I don't know. I've never seen inside yours. The last guy was kind of a creep. Always talking about S-E-X, you know what I mean?"

"If by S-E-X you mean sex, then yes I do."

Her cheeks flushed. "Sorry," she said. "I know it's a silly habit."

"No problem." He nodded at her apartment. "I'd swear, it looks like your apartment is bigger than mine. Maybe you're getting more light from your kitchen window or something." He jerked his thumb to the right.

Mandy shook her head. "My kitchen's over there," she said, "behind the bathroom." She pointed left, toward the far corner.

"Your bathroom's closer to the door than your kitchen?"

"Isn't yours?"

"No. My kitchen's right here." He unlocked his door and pointed into the kitchen.

She leaned cautiously into his apartment and glanced over. "Oh, wow," she said. "You've got a real kitchen with counters and everything."

"You don't?"

Her pigtails wiggled in the air again. "Mine's just a little kitchenette, y'know, like you'd get in a motel or something." She shrugged and then took a few quick steps back to her door. "Anyways, it was nice to meet you, Nate. Again."

"You too," he said. "Thanks for all the tips."

She stepped into her oversized apartment with a meek smile, and the door closed behind her.

EIGHT

Nate wanted to look up historical landmarks at work, but a fresh crate of returned flyers and another lecture from Eddie crushed his enthusiasm for doing anything. A parking ticket the next morning—he'd forgotten the street sweeping schedule—annihilated it. It wasn't until the following Friday when Carla from accounting asked what his new place was like that he remembered the trio of plaques. Then he was ashamed to realize he couldn't remember the name of the building. He peeled a sticky note off the pad on his desk and stuck it in his wallet so he'd have a reminder and something to write on when he got home.

When he got home, though, his mind ended up focused on other things again. He'd learned weekends were the worst for parking, especially at rush hour. It didn't help that an oversized truck was blocking most of the spots in front of his building. One guy in a green Taurus sat in his car, taking up two spaces between a pair of driveways and ignoring Nate's attempts to squeeze in on either end. Nate looped around the neighborhood until he spotted a space he could wiggle his Volkswagen into on the next street over.

He walked home and inspected the truck in front of the building. It was one of the basic white ones that could be spotted all over the city. They usually had something to do with the movie industry. Then, as he approached the fence, Nate remembered it was the last Friday in April.

Toni, the woman from Locke Management, was at the top of the stairs. She had on another just-too-short skirt and held her iPad in one hand. The other hand held a phone to her ear. She saw him and her killer smile shined out across the front lawn.

Nate had almost reached the gate, which was held open with a bungee cord, when two brawny men stepped off the truck holding a couch between them. The lift gate squealed as they bounced from it to the ground.

He followed the two men up the steps. They moved like the couch was an empty box. Toni gestured for him to stop by the door and he watched the men head up the curving staircase, angling the couch so they never broke stride.

"I have to go," she told the phone. "I've got another client here." The cell snapped shut and she beamed at him. "How do you like the place so far?"

"It's great," he said. "I love the sun deck."

"I know," she said, the smile spreading further, "isn't it wonderful? I wish my apartment was this nice."

"Maybe you should get a place here."

The smile was blinding, and he knew the joke hadn't been that funny. "Speaking of which," said Toni, "you have a new neighbor. Someone just rented the apartment next to yours."

"Someone?"

"Well, I can't give out personal information," she said. "You'll probably meet him upstairs, though."

The sticky note flashed in his mind. "Actually, I've got a question for you," said Nate. He nodded toward the lobby. "I saw all the plaques under the mailboxes. What's so special about this place?"

"It's a historic landmark," she said. "Part of the reason the owners can keep rent so low is because they're exempt from certain changes and requirements, plus they get a small subsidy from the government."

"Right," he said. "I was wondering *why* it's a landmark, though."

Her smile dimmed. "Sorry?"

"What makes this place a landmark? Is there something special about the architecture or did something happen here or something?"

She stared at him for a moment. "It's very old. Did you see the cornerstone? Built in 1894." She turned and gestured at the base of the building.

Nate followed the movement to the block of marble. "That's it? It's old?"

Toni glanced at her iPad and traced patterns on the screen with her fingers. "To be honest, Mr. Tucker, I'm not sure why. It happened a little before my time, obviously." Her eyes met his and the smile went back to full power. "Oskar might know. Have you asked him?"

"No," he admitted. "I haven't seen him in a couple days."

"I'll look into it for you if you like," she said. "I can check with the office and have something for you next time I'm here." She checked her phone for the time. "If you'll pardon me, I need to get going. Another place to show in half an hour."

Nate gave her a wave as she dashed down the steps to the street, tapping her iPad the whole way. She stepped through the gate and vanished down toward Beverly Boulevard.

He headed up the stairs and passed the movers on the way down. Neither of them looked like they'd just carried a couch up three flights. Four, counting the steps from the street to the front door. They each gave him a quick grunt of acknowledgment and headed back to their truck.

Boxes sat in the hall. Nate headed down with the thought of introducing himself and being a good neighbor. Halfway there something else caught his attention.

Or, to be exact, the lack of something.

The door marked 23 still didn't have a knob. The socket sat empty on the lock plate. *Maybe they* do *take it off when people are moving in?*

Nate pushed his finger into the socket. It went into the raised flange and stopped. It didn't feel like the hole was too small. It felt like there wasn't a hole.

He crouched in front of 23 and peered at the socket. It was a dummy. Past the flange was smooth wood. The plate had just been screwed onto the face of the door.

"Hey," said a voice. "Hope my guys didn't knock that off."

It was an older guy, pushing sixty but in good shape. He stood at the door to apartment 26, holding one of the boxes. His white hair was cut bristle-short. Nate thought this was how retired drill sergeants looked before they went on to become sadistic gym teachers.

"No," he said, "it's been missing for a couple weeks now."

The man stepped forward. He was a good three inches taller than Nate and his torso was a sharp V inside his polo shirt. "How d'you get in, then?"

"It's not my place," he said. "I don't think anyone lives there. They're working on it or something and took the knob away."

The man eyed the empty socket and his gaze flitted up to examine Nate's face. Nate had the unmistakable feeling of being sized up. The sadistic gym teacher comparison reared its head again.

"Tim Farr," the man said. "I just moved in today." He shifted the box under his arm, stuck out a hand, and gave Nate's fingers a crushing shake.

"Nate Tucker," he replied. "I live next door to you. Number twenty-eight."

Tim nodded. "You a quiet neighbor?"

"I guess."

The older man smiled and showed a mouthful of small, white teeth. "I'll let you know if you're not. Is it a good building?"

Nate shrugged. "I like it," he said. "I've only been here about a month myself, but I think it's one of the best places I've ever lived."

Tim gave another sharp nod. "A little smaller than I would've liked, but it seems okay. A floor plan would've been nice."

"You didn't see it first?"

He shook his head. "Sight unseen. I was in Virginia before this."

"What brings you to L.A.?"

"Why does anyone come to California?" Tim smiled. "Trying to find myself."

Nate smiled, too. "I came for a girl."

"How'd that work out?"

He shrugged. "I've been trying to find myself for six years now."

Tim chuckled and shifted the box back into both hands. "Hey," he said, "how's that sun deck Toni told me about?"

"Pretty cool. Awesome view."

"Might as well do the whole California thing right, yeah? I was thinking of having a beer up there later and watch the sunset."

"Oh," said Nate, "as a heads up, if you see a note on the door to the roof, it means one of our neighbors is sunbathing in the nude. She probably won't be there late in the day, but just in case."

"Sad to say, I've hit that point where looking at a naked young woman makes me feel less turned on and a little more like a dirty old man."

"Yeah, well, you haven't seen her yet," said Nate.

Tim grinned and pushed the door open with his foot. It opened into a small room, half-filled with boxes. From what Nate could see, it was less than ten feet on a side.

"Hey," he said. "What the heck's up with your apartment?"

Tim nodded. "I know, right? Like I said, a floor plan would've been nice."

"You've got rooms?"

"Yeah. Not the best use of space, but I'm pretty sure I can do something with it." He set the box down on top of another and gave Nate a look. "Yours isn't like this?"

"No," said Nate with a shake of his head. "Mine's a studio. All open, but the kitchen and bathroom are separate."

"Weird," said Tim. "That would've been nice."

Footsteps clomped up the stairs. The movers were back. They were carrying a dresser between them.

"Good meeting you, Nate," said Tim. "Talk to you later."

"Yeah, you too."

Nate backed up to his door to give the movers room to get into 26, and once he was in front of his apartment it seemed silly not to go in.

The setting sun was streaming through the kitchen blinds, and he gave them a twist to cut the glare. As he did, something danced across the countertop and up the wall. Another roach appeared in the sink and circled the drain twice before moving up onto his drying rack.

He picked up a glass from the rack and flipped it over onto one of the insects. The other one scurried beneath the microwave and vanished. The prisoner was small, barely half an inch long, with brilliant patterns on its emerald shell. It had been wounded somewhere along the way and was missing a leg on one side.

"So, mister roach," Nate said. "It is down to you, me, and this glass." He considered knocking it into the sink and drowning it. He was going to need to get traps before things got too bad.

The roach's antennae brushed the inside of the glass. It skittered back, darted forward again, and hit the side of the glass with a faint but definite click. Nate watched it for a moment and then furrowed his brow. He waited for it to slow down so he could get a better look at it.

The roach wasn't missing a leg. It had an extra leg. Four on the right, three on the left. He watched it dance around the glass with the extra limb.

The mutant roach finally admitted it was trapped and stopped to await the inevitable. He watched it sit there for a moment, resigned to its fate. "Yeah, I know," he sighed. "It sucks being the guy with no options."

Nate lifted the glass and let it go on its way. It waved its antennae at him, two green threads, and then followed its partner under the microwave.

NINE

On the fourth Saturday since bringing his furniture in, Nate told himself he was unpacked. It was his apartment now in all ways. His *home*. He'd used one of the bookshelves and the couch to split the space. His desk was against the wall next to the door. Everything else was in the other section of the room, although everything else amounted to the entertainment center, now standing between the two windows, and the other bookshelf.

Now that he was unpacked, Nate came to the unavoidable conclusion that he had nothing to do. He pulled his second-to-last beer from the fridge door—he needed to go grocery shopping soon—and decided to explore the building a bit. For lack of a better plan, he figured he'd start at the top and drink his beer in the sun. He strolled down the hall and turned into the stairwell.

From the bottom of the steps he could see the blue **X** holding a note in place. For a moment, he toyed with the idea of going back and grabbing the other beer. On one level, the idea of seeing his blue-haired neighbor again—seeing *all* of her again—was appealing. On another level, there was something about her matter-of-factness that sucked a lot of joy out of the thought of hanging out and having a beer with his hot, naked neighbor. He'd heard it was a lot like that with nudity on a movie set. It was so mechanical and unnatural it didn't even seem sexy.

Nate plodded back to his apartment and opened his laptop. He still didn't have internet. He checked email and did his casual browsing at work. At his old place, Sean had a work connection set up that he let everyone share. Nate hadn't gotten around to setting anything up in his new place. He could pay to use his cell phone as a hotspot, but it'd cost him around thirty bucks a month. For now, though, hopefully someone in the area would have an open Wi-Fi connection he could use.

The area was filled with wireless signals. A few 2Wires, a Linksys, and some strings of letters he couldn't decipher. The top connection was the strongest signal. Five bars. It was WEP protected.

houseofmystery

He remembered Mandy had mentioned a woman on the second floor who had wireless setup in the building. That had been almost two weeks ago, though, and he couldn't remember the apartment number or the name that went with it.

Nate decided to walk the downstairs hall and see if one of the apartment numbers leaped out at him.

The second floor lounge was empty. He hadn't been here since Toni first showed him the apartment three weeks ago. He hadn't heard any noise from beneath his apartment, either. *Does anyone use this place?* he wondered. The idea of dragging his little DVD player down and watching a movie on the big screen crossed his mind. He could order a pizza or get Mexican food or something. There were worse ways to spend a Saturday night.

Right after the lounge was the fire door, held open by a magnetic clamp. On the other side of it were apartments 15 and 16. He looked at the door marked 15 and thought it sounded familiar. He was almost positive it was the number Mandy had told him.

He stared at the door for a moment. He took a breath and stretched his neck over his shoulder on each side. Just in case, he rehearsed an explanation for knocking on a stranger's door and hoped whoever lived here wasn't going to be too angry for the disturbance.

Then he stopped and looked to his left again.

Kitty-cornered across the hall was apartment 14. He remembered it flying past on his first whirlwind tour of the Kavach Building. At the time, he thought he'd glimpsed a pair of padlocks on it. Now that he had time to look, he could see all of them.

Four hasps had been screwed into the left side of the door frame—two above the knob, two below it. They were big, thick plates of metal, and Nate was willing to bet each one weighed a pound or two.

The padlocks were just as solid. They were heavy, riveted things. Two of them had keyholes on the front, like the locks on movie pirate chests. He didn't recognize any of the brand names engraved on them, but each one looked like it could take several hits from a hammer without loosening in the slightest.

They were old. The hasps had been painted two or three times, and paint was splattered on the locks. He could see at least four different shades and colors on the padlock just above the knob. It was the newest-looking of the four.

Even the knob was old. Beneath the layers of latex was a multi-faceted ball, like an oversized gemstone. He'd seen knobs like that before in old buildings. Nate glanced up and down the hall, then scratched the knob with his fingernails. The paint wrinkled and tore away in ragged scraps. He got a good piece pinched between his fingers and peeled away a long strip. It got wider as he pulled at it and then the edge twisted around and it tore free.

The knob was clear glass. He looked at the ribbon of latex in his hand and tried to count layers on its edge. The knob had been painted at least three times, probably more.

His eyes moved from the knob to the rest of the door. Like so many old buildings, years of rushed paint jobs had covered the metal hardware. There was also paint in the gap between the door and the frame.

Nate dug around in his wallet and pulled out a plastic card he didn't mind wrecking, a discount card for a grocery chain he rarely shopped at. He picked a spot between the uppermost hasps and tried to push the card through the paint covering the gap between the frame and the door. It was solid. There were years of sloppiness in that gap. No one had opened the door in ages, maybe decades. Probably not even in his lifetime.

He thought of the elevator buttons that were painted solid. There were decades of paint on them, too. *It's out of service right now,* Toni had told him, *but they'll probably have it working by the time you move in.*

He glanced up at the ceiling and thought of the other mystery door. Apartment 23 with its non-existent knob. The last thoughts of a wireless internet connection fled from his mind as he strode down the hall and up the staircase.

Nate stood before 23 and pulled out the grocery card again. He pushed it into the gap between the door and the frame, just above the locking plate. The card twisted around the edge of the door, sunk in half its width, and hit something solid. He worked it back and forth and mapped out the interior edge, then he swept it down alongside the lock plate.

The card slid down with no problem. No bumps or catches. No sudden stops when it hit the deadbolt. He dragged it up and down a few more times. There was nothing there. No locks or bolts of any kind.

Nate didn't have a lot of carpentry experience, but he knew this next part would be trickier. He worked the card into the other side of the door, right up at the top corner. It went in an inch and a half and stopped again.

He slid the card down and tried to feel for any snags at all. The plastic was pressed against the inside edge, so he felt confident he should sense any small edges or gaps, but there weren't any. The card made its way down to the floor. He reversed direction and dragged it back to the top. *They'd be recessed,* he thought, *sunk into the wood, but I should still feel* something *there.*

The card made it back to the top without incident.

There were no hinges on the door to 23.

He studied the card as he bent it flat again. It had no actual information on it that tied back to him. If someone found it they wouldn't be able to tell it was his.

He set it on the floor in front of 23. There was no sill, just a thin gap between the floor and the bottom of the door. He pressed his fingertips against the card and pushed it under the door.

It went in an inch and a half before it clicked against something solid.

"What are you doing?"

Nate jumped back, stumbled, and fell on his ass. The thump was very loud in the hallway. He turned to look at his accuser.

The speaker was an Arab woman, or maybe Indian, with owlish glasses and a hawk nose. Even with the loose Oxford she was wearing he could see she was slim. Her dark hair was cut short, and with her slight build it made her look like a teenager. She'd come up the back stairwell and was standing between him and the door to his apartment.

"I'm just..." He tried to think of a good answer. "I'm checking something."

She crossed her arms. She had a phone in her hand. "What?"

He glanced at the door and back to the woman. "I don't think it's a real door," he blurted out. He knew the minute the words left his mouth that he sounded like a lunatic. He wondered if she was going to call Oskar, or maybe even the police.

Instead she nodded. "You're right," she said. "It isn't a real door."

He stared at her for a moment. "How do you know?"

"Were you just downstairs?" she asked. "Did you scrape the paint off the knob to fourteen?"

All his resistance faded away. "Yeah," he admitted, "that was me." He took a breath. "I was down there looking for the person who's in charge of the wireless and I saw the door with all the padlocks and I...I got curious."

She stared down at him. He was stunned how much accusation she was able to pack into her stare. After a few moments she said, "You're the new guy. The one who moved into twenty-eight a few weeks ago."

"Yeah. Nate Tucker."

She nodded. "Mandy said you might come looking for me. I'm Veek."

The name he couldn't remember.

"You've got to be careful," she told him. "Oskar'll put up with a lot, but he gets pissed when people mess up the building," said Veek, "Things'll go a lot easier for you here if you remember that."

"You said it wasn't a real door." He glanced at 23 again.

"No, it's not," she said. "Look, just stop being stupid, okay? Scratching the paint off the knob was dumb, and I'm probably going to get blamed for it."

"What's going on here?"

Veek twisted her lips and snorted at him. "I'll get something set up for you tonight." The phone unfolded in her hand with a snap and her fingers danced on the small keypad. "Stop by my apartment tomorrow at noon and I'll give you a password."

"But what about—"

"Don't be late." The phone snapped shut. She turned, vanished back down the stairwell, and left Nate sitting on the floor in the hall.

TEN

Nate was just rising from the floor when Tim came up the front stair-well with two bags of groceries. "Hey, neighbor," he said. "What's up?"

"Oh, you know," said Nate. "Stuff."

Tim dug out his keys and waved them at 23 as he walked past. "The mystery of the missing knob still gnawing at you?"

"Kind of." Nate walked away from the door. "As one new guy to another, we have some weird neighbors."

"Besides the nudist with blue hair and the guy who sits on the floor in the hall?"

"Yeah, okay, fair enough."

Tim hefted the grocery bag. "Want a beer? I just grabbed some supplies from the store."

"You know," said Nate, "I would love one."

"It looks like the roof's open," Tim said with a nod over his shoulder. "I'll meet you up there in a couple of minutes with a six-pack."

Nate went up to the roof. Sure enough, the note and the magnetic **X** were gone. Xela'd slipped past him somehow and the sun deck was deserted. He was half frustrated, half relieved.

He dragged two chairs together across the deck. He wrestled them around to face west and Tim appeared with the promised six-pack. "Hope you don't mind light beer," he said. "I'm keeping an eye on my weight. It's easy for a man my age to go soft fast."

"No problem at all." Nate couldn't picture Tim going soft at all, let alone fast. The man was in better shape than Nate had ever been.

They clinked their bottles and sat back in the deck chairs. The sun was already making long shadows through the mesh gazebo. "Y'know," said Tim, "I couldn't tell you the last time I sat and drank a beer and watched a sunset."

"Did you ever do it before?"

The older man shrugged. "I must've. I mean, it's something everybody does at some point in high school or something, right?"

"But you can't remember?"

Tim shrugged again. "I've been busy."

The sun touched the horizon somewhere around Century City. Through the gazebo's mesh the red ball was cut up into a dozen small cells. Each one shimmered.

"So," said Nate, "trying to find yourself?"

Tim blinked twice and then grinned. "Yeah," he said. "I've been doing the same thing my whole life and now I've decided it's time for something different."

"What were you doing before?"

"Books. I ran a small publishing house back in Virginia."

Nate nodded. "Cool. Anything I might've read?"

Tim smiled. "Nothing you would've remembered. It was all technical material. Textbooks, operating manuals, stuff like that." He took a hit off his beer.

"Is there a lot of money in that?"

"God, no," said Tim. "The only reason I stayed afloat was big companies and a couple of government offices used me to print stuff for them. It was a living, but I sure wasn't going to get rich anytime soon."

The sun pressed itself down between two buildings. The horizon flared red. Nate imagined it was like watching a bomb go off in slow motion.

He sipped his beer. "That why you got out?"

Tim shook his head. "I'd been doing it for thirty-two years. Had one of those days when you suddenly wonder what you've been doing with your life, is this what you want to be doing, where'd the years go, and so on. Three weeks later someone offered to buy me out for double what I would've taken, so I said sure."

"Just like that?"

"Just like that."

A moment passed. "D'you miss it?" Nate asked.

Tim shook his head again. "Not quite yet. I'm still at the point where I spend the morning a bit confused I'm not in the office." He finished his beer and returned the empty bottle to the six pack. "What about you, Nate? What brings you to the sun deck on this fine evening?"

Nate smirked and downed the last of his own beer. "Nothing."

The older man held up the pack and they each pulled a new bottle. "Nothing?"

Nate thought about it while he twisted the cap off the beer. "You know how you got to high school and college and you thought your life's going to be *this*? But then you get out and your life ends up being *this* instead? And eventually everything settles down and you figure out what you're going to do for the rest of your life?"

Tim nodded. "Yeah."

"Well, I never figured out what I wanted to do," said Nate. "I saw all my friends and coworkers figure it out, and now they've all got homes and families and cars built in this decade."

"But not you?"

"Not me. I've had four different jobs since college. I figured it was just my restless twenties. I'd hit thirty and it'd be a wake-up call and everything would get clear." He shook his head. "I turned thirty back in 2010. Still don't know what I'm doing with my life."

The sun vanished on his last words. The sky was still lit up with streaks of orange and red.

"I wouldn't worry," said the older man. "Lots of people don't figure out what they're doing until later in life. Case in point." He raised his bottle, and the two men clinked their beers together again.

They each took a drink. "The flipside to what you're saying," continued Tim, "is that there are hundreds of thousands of people who've decided they want to do *this* despite the fact that they're no good at it. They devote all their energy toward being a doctor or a loan officer or something when they're really better suited to another career altogether. Not to mention all the folks who end up trapped in a career they don't like because they can't afford to leave it. I've met a lot of people who would've been millionaires if they figured out what they were doing wasn't what they were supposed to be doing."

"Like you?"

He shook his head. "No, I was doing what I was supposed to be doing. And I did it for a long time. Then it was time to do something else." Tim shrugged and took a long drink of beer. He turned to Nate. "One day you're just going to find the thing you're supposed to do and it's going to click. Until then, yeah, it'll be a big mystery. Speaking of which...what is that?"

Nate turned and followed Tim's gaze to the block of bricks next to the stairwell door. "It's part of the elevator," he said. "It's where all the cables and motors and stuff are."

"The machine room?"

"I guess."

"You sure?"

Nate shrugged. "It's what Xela told me. She said it's what Oskar told her."

Tim wrinkled his brow. "It's way too big for a building this size."

"Yeah, that's what I thought, too. She said it's because it's so old. Everything was bigger back then. Less miniaturization or something."

Tim shook his head again. "No," he said. "I've seen a lot of old buildings with elevators. None of them had a machine room that big." He paused. "Well, nothing this size, anyway."

"What do you mean?"

He shrugged. "The last time I saw one that big was on a tour of the Empire State Building."

ELEVEN

Nate overslept Sunday. By a lot.

He woke up and stretched under the covers. Moving had fluffed up the mattress on his futon and the past few weeks had been some of the best sleep of his life. If nothing else, the move had been worth it for that.

It was a warm day. Almost hot. He guessed it was part of the reason he'd slept so well.

He stretched again and glanced at the clock. It was twenty past twelve. Still, it wasn't like he had big plans for the day. If he could find a Target or Walmart in the area, he might get a new lamp for the kitchen, or maybe a—

Stop by my apartment tomorrow at noon and I'll give you a password. Don't be late.

"Ahhh, crap," he muttered.

A few quick sniffs of his armpits told him he could get by without a shower. He yanked a t-shirt off the bookshelf and pulled on yesterday's jeans. He stepped into the bathroom, dabbed his teeth with Crest, and swished the paste around in his mouth for a moment. Not great, but hopefully he'd make a slightly better impression this time, aside from being half an hour late.

Veek yanked open her door on the third knock. Despite the heat she was wearing another long-sleeved dress shirt, this time over a black tee. She didn't say anything.

"Yeah, sorry," he said. "My alarm didn't go off."

She glared at him through her glasses for a moment, then pushed the door open and walked back inside. He waited for an invitation, but when one didn't come he just followed her in.

Her apartment was a studio like his. Her kitchen wasn't separated by a wall, but the basic layout looked the same past that. He even saw the same blue and white tile checkered across her counters. She had a rumpled, blanket-covered twin bed shoved under the windows. The room was cool, and he understood why she had the extra layers on.

The right wall of Veek's apartment was dominated by a folding table, the kind used by caterers or hardcore yard salers. It was covered with computer components. Or maybe it was just one big computer. Everything looked connected by lots of cables.

In front of the chair were three flat screens, one of them on a long arm. A swirling blue and silver screensaver, like underwater lightning, rolled back and forth across them. The keyboard looked foreign, and he realized a beat later it was a Dvorak setup, arranged for efficiency and speed over classic training. A set of what he thought were black phone-books stood next to the tower under the table, and Nate recognized them as old Playstations just before he saw the name on one. A small cluster of external hard drives stood on the table above the towers.

She saw him studying the setup. "Got a problem?"

"Nope," he said. "This is pretty impressive."

"It's nothing great," she said. "Just some stuff I've scavenged and got secondhand."

"It all looks pretty new to me."

"I got some good deals. People throw out a lot of stuff with life left in it. If I could afford a real machine it'd be one-fourth the size."

"Must use a ton of power."

She smirked. "Well, that's not a real problem here, is it?"

"I guess not."

She dropped into the chair and tapped the mouse. The rolling screensaver vanished and the screens were filled with windows. "For now your password's just your last name spelled backwards. I got it off your mailbox. I can change it right now if you like."

"Can I just change it myself later?"

Veek shrugged. "It's all through me. I know all the passwords. If I cared to look I could tell you every email address you use and what kind of porn you download. But I don't care."

"Gotcha."

"So, do you want a new password or not?"

"Can you add one-four-four to the front of it?"

She nodded. "Twelve squared? Not bad. Easy to remember, and using it at the front instead of the end gives you a bit more security." Her fingers danced on the keys. It was an odd dance, and Nate realized he'd never seen someone use a Dvorak keyboard before.

"Done," she said. "Ten bucks a month. I'm not a hardcase about getting it on the first, but the first week'd be cool."

He fished in his wallet and pulled out his lone twenty. "Do you have change?"

"No," she said. "Tell you what, though. Give me the twenty and we'll say you paid for the first three months."

It was a good deal, but he still crunched numbers in his head to see if he could afford it. "Yeah, I guess so," he said.

He held out the bill. She plucked it from his fingers and stuffed it into her shirt pocket. "You're good to go," she said. "You should have access when you get back to your apartment. Sometimes the signal gets a little hinky going through walls. If it does, try opening your door or going out in the hall if you've got a laptop. It's usually stronger out there."

He nodded. "Thanks."

"No problem."

"So," he said, "Veek is short for...?"

"Why do you care?"

Nate shrugged. "Just trying to be polite and neighborly."

"Malavika Vishwanath. Don't try to say it, you'll just piss me off."

"Okay." He nodded at the computer. "So, seriously, what do you use it for?"

The screensaver kicked back in. "I do a lot of work from home. I'm in the office half the time, but they let me work here, too."

"What kind of work?"

Veek's eyes narrowed. "Just data entry. Nothing exciting."

He bit back a chuckle.

"What?"

"I do data entry," said Nate. "Worthless job. And it doesn't need a machine like that."

"I told you, it's not that great." She settled back in her chair. "You're all good."

He shrugged and shook his head. "Thanks." He turned to leave and saw what had been behind him the whole time.

There were five thermometers on the wall by the door. One was an old-fashioned glass rod filled with mercury. One was a dial. There was a brass, baroque thing where an arrow swung on a graded circle. The largest was a square of white plastic that gave a digital readout. The smallest was also digital, the size of a cell phone. He peered at each of them and confirmed they all said the same thing.

69

"Go on," she said.

He glanced back. "What?"

Veek nodded at the wall. She had her arms crossed again. "Get the stupid sex joke out of the way."

"I wasn't going to—"

"Just say it. I'll give you points if you can come up with something original."

"Seriously. I didn't think of—"

"You're a guy who just saw the number sixty-nine repeated five times. Don't try to tell me you didn't think of sex. Just say it so we can get it out of the way."

He stuck his hands in the pockets of his jeans and gave an awkward shrug. "You... really like sixty-nine, don't you?"

"No," she said. "It's weird and everything looks wrong. More to the point, it's not my choice."

"Sorry?"

She turned in her chair and waved her hand at the apartment. "It's always sixty-nine degrees in here. I can put the oven on high and crank the heat in the middle of summer and it'll be sixty-nine degrees in here. I can open all the windows in January and put the AC on full and it's sixty-nine degrees in here."

He looked at the wall of thermometers. "Why?"

"I don't know. It just is."

He took another step toward the door and stopped to look at her. "Yesterday," said Nate, "you told me twenty-three wasn't a real door."

Veek took off her glasses and wiped them on the corner of her shirt. "It's not."

"How do you know?"

"I've been living here for two years now. I've seen a lot of weird stuff."

"But how do you know?"

She looked at him and she smiled. It was a tight, secretive smile.

"What's up with apartment fourteen, then?" he asked. "All the padlocks?"

"I don't know," she said. "Seriously, I don't know. It's been like that the whole time I've been here. I've seen the door get painted twice, but as far as I know it's never been opened."

He studied her eyes through the large lenses. "You've tried to open it, haven't you?"

Her lips twitched. "Oskar was furious. I came *this* close to getting evicted. I even went down on the street once and tried to look in the windows with the zoom on my phone. The windows are painted black."

"What?"

"Yep. Solid black. Every inch of 'em."

Nate stared through the wall in the direction of the mystery apartment. His eyes crept across the wall of thermometers to Veek's kitchen. He cleared his throat. "Any bulb I put in my kitchen fixture lets off black light," he said.

Her eyebrows went up. "What do you mean?"

"I mean any bulb I put in the fixture lets off black light."

"You're sure it's not just one of the ones they sell at Halloween?"

He nodded. "I've traded it out four times now. Twice with bulbs I brought from my other place, twice with bulbs I bought over at Vons. Whatever I put in it becomes a black light. I think it's a voltage thing, or amperage or something."

Veek shook her head. "I don't think it works that way. You need to make the bulbs specifically."

"Are you sure?"

"No."

He shrugged. "It's the only thing I can think of."

She tapped her fingers on the arms of the chair. "Nobody stays in apartment five. They rent it and the people move out as soon as their lease expires. Some of them move out sooner."

He nodded. "There was a guy moving out the day I moved in. Craig?"

"Carl. Jerk stiffed me for two months of internet. And they never rent the apartment across the hall, sixteen."

"What's wrong with it?"

"Nothing. I've been in there a couple times. They've left it open at night once or twice when they're painting. But they never show it."

"Why not?"

"I asked one of the older tenants, Mrs. Knight down in four. She's been here for twenty-five years. Right after she moved in someone killed herself in there. A wanna-be actress. Hung herself in the closet."

"Hanged," said Nate.

"Don't be one of those people."

"So a woman kills herself and they never rent it again? That's a bit odd."

"Yeah," said Veek. She looked at him. It was a look he remembered from college, when he had a few less pounds around the waist. He was being *considered.* She spent another moment examining his face and made a decision.

"You want to see something mind-blowing?"

He gave her a faint smile. "I don't know, I've seen some pretty wild tattoos, but go ahead."

Her smile faded. "I'm serious. I can show you something else about this place but you might lose a lot of sleep over it."

They looked at each other for a moment.

"Okay," he said. "Show me."

TWELVE

Veek led him to the back stairwell. They walked down the concrete steps and out the fire door to the small lot behind the building. She gave a sweeping wave with her arm. "What do you see?"

He glanced around. "What am I looking at?"

"It's better if you figure it out on your own."

Nate studied the back lot. There was a chain-link fence between them and the building the next street over. Two small trees grew in either corner of the lot, their trunks forced up through cracks in the concrete. A few faint outlines stood out on the ground, the shapes of things that had been spray-painted red, black, or blue.

He looked at the back of the building. There weren't any concrete decorations or decorative pillars on this side. A cinderblock propped the door open. Another fire escape clung to the brick wall, and the ladder hung a few feet above the door. He followed it up to the windows of his kitchen and Mandy's studio. "I'm still not sure what I'm supposed to see."

Veek shrugged off her Oxford shirt and tied it around her waist, leaving her in the black tee. "Okay, then," she said. "Let's go out front."

They walked back through the building, past the ever-empty room 5 and the never-functional elevator. She led him out the front stoop and down to the first landing. "Now what do you see?"

"I'm still not sure of the point of this."

"Just look," she told him. "Once you see it you're going to kick yourself for not noticing before."

He shrugged and looked at the building again. It was the same mismatched brick as the back. On this side it was broken by the two slabs of concrete and the pillars flanking the front door. "This fire escape zigzags the other way," he said. "Is that it?"

"No. Keep looking."

The stone lintel had KAVACH engraved in bold letters, but Nate couldn't see anything else on it. He squinted up at the concrete over Oskar's windows and beneath Xela's. It didn't look like there'd ever been words or numbers on them, just the image of a shield. He stepped off the landing and peered over at the cornerstone with its pair of monograms. They still didn't mean anything to him.

He counted the windows, then used his hands to make sure they lined up. He looked up at the edge of the roof for any gargoyles or angels or anything else he may have missed. After another few minutes, he shrugged. "I have no idea."

"Come on."

"Where are we going?"

"Across the street," she said, opening the gate.

"What for?"

"I told you, it's better if you figure it out on your own."

"Right," he muttered. "No one can be told what the Matrix is."

She smirked. "Something like that."

They walked across Kenmore and she guided him up the steps of another building. It was one of the brighter ones on the street, with a lot more Spanish influence. It might've been a small mansion at one point before being broken up into apartments. He glanced up at the building. "Are we going to get in trouble for being here?"

"For what? Standing on the stairs? If anyone asks, we're looking at our place." Veek gestured at the far side of the street. "Now?"

He looked at the apartment building, then at the ones on either side. The one to the north, the one his window looked down on, was more of a Victorian style, painted bright blue and white. The one to the south, higher up the hill, was another Spanish-style place. Past that was a wider brick building that looked like it might be distantly related to theirs.

"Still not seeing anything," he said.

"What's on the roof of this building?"

"This one?" Nate turned and craned his neck back. There was a small balcony with a flowerbox blocking his view. He took a step back, but the edge of the roof was still lost in the cluster of wires leading into the building. He could see the orange-red tiles of the roof, but nothing else. "I don't see anything," he told her. "Can you give me a hint what I'm..."

Nate stopped and gazed over his shoulder at their apartment building. He looked over at the quasi-Victorian and the fan of power cables and phone lines running into it. He glanced up the street at the larger brick building and the web stretching between it and the phone poles.

He crossed the street. Veek stayed a few steps behind him. He got to the gate and looked up at the Kavach Building. The bricks and concrete stared back.

"There aren't any power cables," he said. "There's nothing."

Veek pointed at the single line running from the phone pole to the corner of their roof. "Pac Bell and Comcast," she said. "The one in the middle is the phone line, the one spiraling around it is the cable."

Nate was still staring up in the air. "But where's everything else?"

"There *is* nothing else," said Veek. "There's no electrical lines running into the building at all. There's also no meters out back or in the basement. No one here notices because we're not paying for it. No one else notices because it's not their job." She nodded at the building. "We're not hooked into the L.A. power grid."

"So where's the electricity come from?"

Veek shrugged and shook her head. "I have no idea."

THIRTEEN

It took Nate half an hour to get his head back in order. He sat on the end of Veek's bed and stared up at the ceiling fan and the three bulbs mounted to it. She cracked open a can of Diet Pepsi from the fridge, swallowed a few mouthfuls, and then topped it off with generic rum. She handed him the can and he took a long drink from it.

"I get it," she said. "When I first noticed it last year I was in denial for a week."

"Have you told anyone else about it?"

"Like who?"

He took another sip of the spiked soda and shrugged. "Scientists. The news. I don't know, somebody."

"I'd get evicted."

"How do you know?"

Veek popped another can of Diet Pepsi and took a sip. "I tried asking Oskar about it when I first saw it, during my denial week. He got annoyed and told me I was being foolish. So I tried to come up with a rational explanation and couldn't. When I went back to him he gave me this whole spiel about what a great deal the apartments here are, how much the owners like it being a quiet place, can't I just be happy with it, all that sort of stuff. Then he told me if I tried to make a fuss out of this and become a disruptive influence, he'd have to ask me to move out. With deductions to my deposit, of course."

"So you didn't do anything?"

"Hey," she said, "maybe you make a million dollars a year doing data entry, but believe it or not, I only make minimum wage. And despite what some people like to think, minimum wage means poverty level. This place is a godsend. I'm not taking any stupid risks."

"Sorry."

"Whatever."

"I don't actually make a million dollars a year doing data entry."

"I figured."

"It's only about seven hundred thousand after taxes."

"Fuck you," she said, but her lips curled up a little bit on the ends. She dropped into the office chair by her desk. "I've tried looking up the builders, too," she said. "You've seen the cornerstone, right?"

He nodded.

Her fingers guided the mouse through a few quick shifts and clicks. A picture of the marble block appeared on one of her monitors. "WNA and PTK," she said. "I've been going under the assumption PTK is P.T. Kavach."

"Who's that?"

"No idea. The name doesn't show up anywhere. Kavach is a Marathi name, and you'd think a Hindu in 1890s Los Angeles would stand out, but I can't find anything. There was a Prateek Kamerkar who moved here with his family in 1898, but that's it. I've tried looking with a dozen different search engines using a bunch of different variables. Architect, building, construction, Kenmore, Los Angeles." She shrugged.

"What about WNA?"

"Also no clue. There's millions of hits. Could be anyone." She shrugged. "Heck, I'm even assuming they're both male names because it's turn of the century. Not a lot of women in construction back then, but it's not impossible, I guess."

Nate looked at the picture of the cornerstone topped with bricks. He sipped his Diet Pepsi and felt the rum slow his pulse a little more. "Do you know about the machine room up on the roof?"

"What about it?"

"I thought it looked too big when I first saw it. My next door neighbor, Tim, he agrees. He says it's probably not a machine room."

"What is it then?"

Nate shrugged. "Beats me." He looked at her. "Two years here and you never noticed the big-ass brick room on the roof?"

"I don't go up there much," Veek said. "I'll add it to my list, though."

"You have a list?"

"Of course I have a list." She had a sip of her own drink. Her face softened a bit. "Can I see your kitchen light?"

A few minutes later they were up in his kitchen. She closed the blinds, grabbed his Sprint bill, and passed the envelope back and forth under the bulb. The paper had an eerie glow in the dim kitchen.

She reached over to flip the light off. "That's pretty cool."

"Cool's one word for it."

"And you're sure it's not just a regular black light?"

"Positive."

Veek looked at him again. "You know," she said, "we could do a lot more with two of us. It'd be less risky."

"What do you mean?"

"What do you think? Want to snoop around the building sometime?"

Nate blinked. "Snoop?"

"You know, investigate," Veek said. "But not be obvious about it."

"No, I know what snoop means. I just didn't think anyone actually used that word out loud." He smiled. "Is this like *Scooby Doo* now? Do we need to wait for Fred and Daphne or should we just start tiptoeing around?"

"Look, I just thought—"

"I've got an orange sweatshirt here somewhere. You'd make a passable Velma."

"Shut up."

"Don't be mad. Everyone thought Velma was kind of hot when they got older."

"If you don't want to, you don't have to be a jackass about—"

"I'm in," he said. "Sorry. Whatever you're up for, I've got your back."

"Really?"

"Absolutely."

"Oskar will throw a fit if he finds us," she said. "Possible eviction."

"*If* he finds us. Both of us together means one person keeping watch."

"You think it's worth it?"

He looked up at the light bulb. He thought about the lack of power lines and the padlocks on apartment 14 and the ornate double doors in the basement and having no idea what he was going to do with his life.

"Yeah," said Nate. "Totally worth it."

SECOND STORY

FOURTEEN

Monday meant back to work, and Nate had a hard time concentrating. Sunday evening he'd been ready to start searching the building, but Veek commuted to Santa Monica so she had to be up early. Explorations had to wait.

He got home before Veek and spent two hours waiting for her. He walked down to her door four times to see if she'd made it home. On the fourth trip, he realized he was acting like a stalker. He turned on the television in the lounge. The only thing worth watching was *Jeopardy*, which he'd never been good at, but stumbling over the answers and questions made him feel a bit less stalker-ish.

Veek thumped up the stairs just as Alex Trebek gave the Final Jeopardy answer. She had a messenger bag slung over her shoulder. She raised an eyebrow when she saw him in the lounge. "Hey," she said. "Are you stalking me?"

"No, of course not."

"Good."

"I wanted to talk to you about a couple things." Nate made a few subtle gestures at the walls. "You know."

She shook her head. "I really don't have time right now."

"Why not?"

"I got an extra assignment. It means some overtime. I can't pass up the money."

"Ahhh," he said. "Of course."

Her lips twitched and almost formed a smile. "I've been waiting over a year for this," she told him. "Don't worry, the building'll still be here on Saturday."

He went back to his apartment and searched the web for everything he could find on black light bulbs. It led him to other pages about basic electrical wiring and pages of terms he had to look up. Three hours later he felt like he didn't know much more about UV lights than he did when he first sat down at his laptop.

Nate got up and switched on the kitchen light. His shirt and socks glowed. He held his hand out and examined the blue aura around his fingernails.

A few brilliant points of light spun and circled around his microwave. They split off and scattered across the counter. Some vanished into outlets, others raced up the wall. The green roaches were little flares under the black light.

A bright spot appeared from beneath the refrigerator. It scurried out to the middle of the floor and paused. He crouched to look at it.

It was his mutant cockroach again, the one with the extra leg. It had gotten bigger. Its body was an inch long now, and so were its antennae. They waved in the air for a moment, then it spun and dashed back under the fridge. The extra leg didn't slow it down at all.

He straightened up and saw a few more flashes of light. He leaned over the counter and two of the roaches froze. Their gleaming antennae tilted back and forth, trying to sense his intentions. He looked at the gleaming patterns on their shells and the way their—

Nate blinked and squinted at the bugs. Both of the roaches had an extra leg. Four on the right, three on the left.

He looked over at one of the others. The glow made it easy to pick out details. It dashed under the toaster as soon as it sensed his attention, but not before he saw its bonus leg. He stretched his head back and tried to focus on the one by the light. Seven legs scurried across the ceiling and the roach vanished into the fixture. He saw its tiny shadow for a moment inside the light and then it was gone.

Tuesday was a band-aid peeled off as slowly as possible. Another crate of returns showed up. He was halfway through sorting the bundles of cards and magazines when Eddie showed up. "Staff meeting."

Nate looked around. Zack and Anne returned his baffled look. He looked back at Eddie. "And?"

"Staff meeting," repeated Eddie. "The boss wants everyone there."

"I'm just the data entry guy," Nate said.

"And I'm only a temp," said Anne.

The heavy man shrugged. "They want you to feel included here."

Nate tried to think of one time in the past two years he'd felt included during work hours. "I'm pretty sure she didn't mean me," he said. "And I've got a bunch of new work." He tapped the mail crate with his foot. "I'd get way behind."

"She wants everyone there. That's what she said."

The meeting he didn't need to be at ended two hours later, and Nate had forty minutes to kill at his computer before the day was over. He spent most of it sorting the new returns into rough stacks and figuring out how much work didn't get done while he was at the meeting. It was useful information to have later in the week when Eddie complained how far behind Nate was getting.

The workday ended. He struggled through Los Angeles's famous rush hour traffic and then spent close to an hour trying to find a parking space. Wednesday morning was street sweeping for half the streets in the neighborhood; people were already jockeying for next-day positions.

Near the top of Kenmore's small hill was a section of curb between two driveways. Two cars could fit there, but someone had parked a green Taurus in the middle of it. He grumbled for a minute and then noticed the driver behind the wheel. The man was staring at a laptop, mooching wireless from someone's open signal.

Nate revved his engine, then revved it again. When it got no response, he tapped the horn. The man glanced up and gave him a cold stare.

"Hey," called Nate, "could you pull forward a bit? I only need two or three feet and I could fit behind you."

The man turned his attention back to his computer.

"Hey!" Nate hit the horn again. The man looked him in the eyes. "We all need to park here. Don't be a jerk about it."

The driver's eyes hardened, and for a minute Nate had the sinking feeling he'd picked the wrong guy to berate for his parking skills. Then, as slowly as possible, the man set his laptop down in the passenger seat and started the Taurus. He pulled forward five feet and stopped.

Nate's Volkswagen moved forward, back, and parallel parked. He was careful not to get too close to the other car's bumper. He didn't want to be hanging in the driveway behind him, but he was even more certain he didn't want to bump the Taurus.

He grabbed his bag, locked his car, and headed down the hill. "Thanks," he said as he passed the Taurus. He tried to make it sound as sincere as possible.

The man ignored him. He was focused on his laptop, watching a YouTube video or streaming porn or something.

Nate stopped at his mailbox, tossed some junk mail in the trash, and headed up to his apartment. He tossed his tie on the desk and pulled a beer from the fridge. While he drank it, he stared up at the kitchen light.

It was close to eight when he went down to see Veek.

"You're getting kind of creepy," she said, "and I'm saying this as someone mildly obsessed with this place."

"Sorry," he said. "I've just got a lot of ideas."

"I don't have a lot of time, though. Trying to finish up this other assignment."

"Just one thing."

"Seriously," she sighed, "I have to get this done. It's worth five hundred bucks to me."

"Have you ever tried looking up all the plaques?"

"Plaques?"

"All the ones under the stairs." He tipped his head toward the stairwell.

She shrugged. "It's an old building on the edge of Hollywood. I didn't think they were anything special."

"What?"

"They try to make everything sound special around here. It probably just means Humphrey Bogart lived here for a week or something."

"You think this place is a national historic landmark because Humphrey Bogart lived here?"

She blinked.

"And no matter what they're for, there's probably a ton of information about the building itself. Leads, at least."

She stared at him for a moment. "I'm an idiot," she muttered.

"I'll remind you of it later," he assured her.

FIFTEEN

"Department of the Interior," said the man. "How may I direct your call?"

"Hi," said Nate. "I was wondering who I could talk to about national landmarks?"

"There's a full list of all registered sites and national historical landmarks on the Department's website. W-W-W-dot—"

"No, I mean I have specific questions regarding a certain landmark. Is there someone there I could speak to?"

Like any good receptionist, the man's sigh was quick and almost silent. "One moment please," he said.

Nate glanced over his shoulder. He could've made the call on his cell, but if Eddie decided to walk in and he was on his own phone it'd be grounds for a speech. With the land line he could try to keep the illusion of a business call and wave away interruptions.

After an agonizing two minutes, during which he was assured his call was very important, the line picked up again. "Records," said a woman.

"Hi," he said. "My name's Nate Tucker. I've got a couple questions regarding a specific national landmark. I was hoping someone there could help me."

"What kind of questions?"

"Well, I've got a national historic landmark near me and there's no mention on the plaque of why it's a landmark. I was hoping someone there might know."

"Did you check the internet? We have a full list of the landmarks up on our website with links to—"

"Yeah, I checked. It's not on your list." Which was true. He'd spent another hour online the night before. The building wasn't on any lists—federal, state, or city.

There was a brief pause. "Sorry?"

"It's not on your list. I was wondering if it might be under a different name or something, maybe?"

"Are you sure it's a landmark?"

"There's a big brass plaque down in the lobby. Three of them in fact." He tapped a few keys and pulled up a picture of the plaque Veek had emailed him.

"It's in a lobby?"

"Yeah. The landmark's a building. I live there, actually."

He could almost hear the woman frown on the other end of the phone. "If it's a building it could be on the registry, but it shouldn't be a historic landmark. You're not living in Monticello, are you?"

"Nope. An old brownstone in Los Angeles."

"And you're sure it's a historical landmark plaque?"

Nate described the slab of brass and read the words off it.

He heard the frown again and the tapping of computer keys. "You said you're in Los Angeles?"

"Yep."

"Address?"

He told her and there was more tapping, followed by rapid clicks from a mouse. "You said the date on the plaque was 1960?"

"Yes."

She blew some annoyed air onto the phone and the mouse clicked again. "The Kavach Building?"

"Yes!" He sat up in his chair and glanced back at the door. Zack peered around the cubicle wall and Nate waved him away. "Yeah, that's it. Do you know why it's a landmark?"

He heard a few more taps. "Okay," she said. "This is weird."

"What?"

"The Kavach Building was one of the original ninety-two sites named as national historic landmarks in 1960 by Secretary Seaton. It's the third to last on the list. But that's pretty much it."

There was a pause. "What do you mean?" asked Nate.

"There's no links, no cross-files, nothing." Her mouse went click-click-click. "It's listed if I break down landmarks by year and by state, but nowhere else. I can tell you it's in Los Angeles, California, and it was one of the first national landmarks. That's it."

"How's that possible?" he asked. "That you don't have anything else?"

"If you'd asked me half an hour ago, I would've said it's impossible," she told him. "I should have an encyclopedia's worth of history, photos, annual reports by assigned agents... There has to be some sort of glitch."

The door opened behind Nate. He glanced over his shoulder and saw Eddie standing in the door. He held up a finger and the fat man raised an eyebrow. "Could I call you back later?" Nate asked. "Would that be better?"

"Yeah," said the woman. "My name's Elaine, extension eight-twenty-three. I'll try to see what I can find."

"Thanks. You've been a great help."

"Thank you," Elaine chuckled. "This is the most excitement I've had here in six years. You take care now."

"Yeah, you too," he said. "Goodbye."

He set the phone down, took a breath to steady his stomach, and spun his chair to face Eddie. "What's up?"

"Who was that?"

He blinked. "Who was who?"

"On the phone."

Nate glanced over his shoulder. "Oh," he said, as if he'd already forgotten the call. "I was following up on a change of address. There was a number on file. I just caught her at a bad time. She said I could call back later."

"Why were you calling at all? No one ever told you to do that."

He shrugged and his mind raced. "Well," he said, "according to the file she'd been a subscriber for a long time. I...I just didn't want to see us lose a client over a bad change of address form."

Eddie stared at him for a moment. It was his blank look, famous in the office. Nate couldn't tell if he was considering the facts or if his mind was somewhere else altogether.

"You got lucky," Eddie said.

He tried to look calm. "Yeah?"

"Yeah. Usually if you give someone the option of ending the call that'll be the end of it. It's a good thing she said you could call back."

"Yeah, I guess so," said Nate.

"We'll let it slide this time," said the slack-faced man. "But from now on just leave contacting people to the subscription department. Or collections."

"Sure thing. Sorry." He steeled himself against the next part, but knew he needed to change the topic. "Was there something you needed from me?"

"Yeah," said Eddie, "I wanted to see how far you were in this batch. Do you think you'll be done soon?"

Nate closed his eyes and sighed. He managed to make it look like a yawn.

SIXTEEN

The rest of the week crawled by like a dying man in the desert. Nate came home Friday and dropped his bag in the kitchen. He flopped on the couch and wrestled the knot of his tie open a few more inches.

A moment later there was a knock at the door. It was Tim. "I saw you come in," said the older man. He held up a fresh six-pack. It was just starting to bead with sweat. "You look like you need a beer."

"God, yes."

"Sundeck?"

"Yeah, just let me burn this tie."

Five minutes later they were leaning back on the deck chairs watching the sky turn orange. Nate held out his beer and they clinked bottles. "Thanks," he said. "You have no idea how bad I needed this."

Tim nodded. "It's a lot better to deal with stress a little at a time than let it build up and go on a bender that'd need serious clean up and recovery time. Took me ten years to figure that out."

"Is that what these evenings are about? You trying to save me from years of stress?"

Tim chuckled. "Mind if I sound pathetic for a moment?"

"I do it all the time. Go ahead."

He stared at the sky for a moment and swallowed a mouthful of beer. "I don't think I've had a real friend in years," he said. "I've had lots of co-workers and colleagues and folks working on the same project. People I liked and trusted. But I don't think I'd call any of them friends. Didn't really have time for friends."

"So now you just want to sit on the roof and drink beer?"

"Isn't that how everybody imagines the good life? Kicking back, shooting the shit, drinking a beer or three while you watch the sunset."

Nate shrugged. "I guess so. Never thought about it."

"You never thought about the good life?"

He leaned his head back and guzzled the last of his beer. "Not for a while. I mean, in college it seemed pretty simple. Meet the right girl, find a job you love, a place to live, done." He shrugged again. "Turns out there's a lot more to it than that."

Tim shook his head. "There's nothing more to it than that. Trust me."

Nate put his dead soldier in its grave and pulled out a fresh one. "In the spirit of fairness, mind if I ask you a question?"

"Sure."

"It's an odd one."

"I'll tell you now," said Tim, "you're a nice guy, but I'm not interested."

Nate laughed into his beer and banged the rim of his bottle on his front tooth. "Bastard."

"Just wanted to nip it in the bud now so your feelings didn't get hurt later."

"You've been here, what, two weeks now?"

"Exactly, yeah."

Nate passed his bottle from hand to hand. "Have you noticed anything odd in your apartment?"

"Odd how?"

"Just, I don't know, weird. Something that doesn't make sense or you can't quite figure out."

"Besides the crap layout?"

Nate dipped his head. "The layout's kind of weird, yeah. Have you noticed anything else?"

"Why?"

"I'm just trying to figure out a couple things in this place. The rental company doesn't seem to know anything about it and I'm curious."

"You know what they say about curiosity and cats."

"Yep. Good thing I'm an ape with delusions of grandeur."

Tim mulled it over. "Actually," he said, "I don't think it's the sort of thing you're looking for, but you know what the weirdest thing about this place is?"

"What?"

"I sleep great here."

"Huh?"

The older man nodded. "Like a baby. Eight hours, solid, every night."

"That's weird?"

"It is for me. I don't think I've had a good night's sleep in years. Granted, for years I was doing six-hour nights, but even if I got my six hours, it was usually all bad dreams or waking up rattled."

"And now you sleep okay?"

Tim nodded. "Since the day I moved in. My eyes close and they open eight hours later. No tossing and turning, no dreams, nothing."

"No dreams?"

"Yeah. It's great. I used to have major anxiety dreams all the time, the ones where you wake up feeling tense. Teeth falling out, losing your hair, all those."

"Hate to tell you but the hair one wasn't a dream."

"Watch your mouth or there'll be no more beer."

Nate took a long sip. "It's just funny you mention it," he said. "I don't think I've had a dream since I moved in here, either."

"Did you have a lot before?" asked Tim.

"Some. I mean, I don't think any more or less than anyone else. Sometimes work dreams, scrambled memories. Every now and then the embarrassing naked-in-class type dream, y'know? But nothing since I got a place here."

"Sleeping better, though?"

"Yeah. Sleeping great."

Tim shrugged. "Might be some weird *feng shui*, psychological thing. Something about this place is calming somehow, on a subliminal level."

"I tell people the place was an opium den right after they built it," said a voice. "Residual drugs just knock everyone out."

They peered over their shoulders and saw Xela striding across the roof. She wore bright red chucks and another tuxedo shirt, one at least three sizes too big for her, with the cuffs rolled up to her elbows. Nate wasn't sure she had anything else on.

She walked between them and grabbed a beer from the six pack. "You remembered to bring more," she said. "Good man."

Xela dropped down on Nate's deck chair by his feet. She set the neck of the bottle against the edge of the chair and popped the cap off with a quick strike from her hand. She toasted Tim and said, "You're the other new guy, right?"

"Tim Farr," he said. He held out his hand.

"Xela."

"So I've heard."

She sighed dramatically and turned to Nate. "You can't keep anything just between us, can you?"

"Not so far."

She took a sip of her beer and looked at the sun. "So what are you guys up to?"

"Just taking in the sunset," said Nate.

"And discussing weird apartments," added Tim.

"Ahhhh," she said. "More people in the cult of Kavach."

Nate looked at her. She was almost silhouetted by the sunset. It turned her hair into threads of black. "What's that supposed to mean?"

Xela shrugged and took another hit off her beer. "Every time people move in they get caught up in all these 'mysteries' of the building. Most everybody forgets about it after a month or two."

"Or they move out," said Nate.

She smiled at him. "You've been talking to Veek, haven't you?"

"Maybe."

"She's cool, don't get me wrong, but she really needs to get out more. It's just an old place. It's got a few quirks, that's all."

Nate tipped his bottle back and swallowed the last of his beer. "I could show you something in my apartment that might change your mind."

Xela batted her eyes at him. "Oh, if only you knew how many times I've heard that one."

Tim laughed.

"So there's nothing strange in your apartment?" asked Nate.

"Aside from my bathroom being a cave? Nothing."

"A cave?"

She nodded. "You ever see those high-end Vegas hotels where the shower isn't a little stall, it's just one whole corner of the room? The water gets isolated by all the space."

Tim nodded. "I guess," said Nate.

"That's what I've got. I don't even have a bathroom door. It's just this big open space with a showerhead and a drain and a toilet about that far away." She pointed over at the firepit.

"Let me ask you something, then," said Tim. He set his empty bottle down in the six pack. "You joked about drugs knocking people out. Should I take that to mean you sleep great, too."

"When I sleep," she grinned.

"No, seriously," he said. "You sleep great?"

She raised a blue eyebrow at him. “Fine. You provided the beer.” She leaned her head forward in thought. “Yes, I sleep great. Never a bad night.”

“Do you ever dream?”

“Ahhhh,” she said. “One beer, one straight answer.”

“Xela,” said Nate. “Do you ever dream?”

Her smile flattened out, and she took a long hit off the bottle. She swallowed it and looked between them. “No,” she said. “I haven’t had a dream in a year now. I’m the most uninspired artist in the world. Happy?”

SEVENTEEN

Veek tilted her head at Nate as they headed down the back stairwell. “So none of you have had any dreams since you moved in here?”

He shook his head. “Not me, not Tim, and not Xela. She thinks she’s having an artistic slump or something.”

Veek made a noise in her throat that might’ve been agreement.

“So?”

She glanced at him. “So what?”

“Have you stopped having dreams since you moved in?”

“I don’t know if I count. I sleep great here, but I’ve never had dreams.”

“Never?”

She shook her head as they turned onto the last landing. “Nope.”

“Not once in your life? You never had nightmares as a kid or sex fantasies when you hit puberty or anything?”

“Getting a little personal,” she said.

They reached the basement. “Sorry.”

“But, no,” Veek said, “nothing.”

They stood in the short hall between the door to the laundry room and the first padlocked door. Nate glanced into the laundry room at the silent machines. There was no sign of any other tenants.

“So,” she said, “how do you want to do this?”

“Have you looked down here at all before?”

She nodded. “A couple of times. I was just never sure what I was looking for.”

He nodded at the double doors. “I bet whatever we’re looking for is in there.”

They walked down the hall. "I've never seen it open," Veek said. "I even tried to make a point of being down here whenever they'd replace a water heater or one of the washers or dryers."

"Just hanging out in the cellar?"

"I'd pull all the sheets off my bed and do laundry."

"Clever." Nate poked at the padlock securing the bar across the door. It squeaked when it rocked on the end of the chains. He set his hand on the door. "How old do you think these are?"

"The chains?"

"The doors."

"On a guess, I'd say they went in with the building."

"Me, too." He squinted at the crack between the doors. It was a seam of black. Nate wasn't sure if he was seeing a darkness beyond the doors or just half an inch into the gap between them. "I should've brought a flashlight."

"We'll have to work on our mystery gang kit."

He pulled out his battered grocery card and pushed it into the crack. It caught for a moment but slid deeper when he wiggled it. He held the card by the last quarter inch. "I'm either through or these are really thick doors."

"Do they have any give at all?"

Nate grabbed the two handles. It was tough with the chains wrapped around them, but he wiggled his fingers until he had a good grip. He leaned back and put his weight on the handles.

The doors didn't budge.

He glanced over his shoulder and Veek took a step back to be closer to the stairs. She gave him a nod. He took a breath and threw himself back, heaving against the handles.

The doors shifted. It wasn't even a quarter of an inch, but they moved and he felt them catch on the beam. A few links of the chain rattled. It was loud in the hall.

Nate shook his hands out. "Well," he said, "they're definitely locked."

"Wow," said Veek, "we've learned so much."

"We learned they're not solid like the door to twenty-three," he said. He traced the outline. "These've been painted too, but whoever did it was a lot more careful."

Veek examined the walls. So many years of paint covered the bricks they were just soft shapes. Nate studied the chains wrapped around the wooden beam.

A shuffling came from behind them, someone's feet slapping on the stairs. They spun and took a few quick steps to the laundry room. Just as they did, Xela appeared on the landing and bounced down the last flight of steps. She had a pillowcase slung over each shoulder and wore a t-shirt with a glittering Batman logo. "Wow," she said. "Could you two look any more guilty?"

"We thought you were Oskar," said Nate.

She smirked. "What are you up to?"

"Nothing," Veek replied. She crossed her arms.

"Sex in the laundry room? You must not've gotten far."

"We were checking out the doors," Nate said. "Trying to figure out if there was any way to get them open or see what's past them."

"Y'know," said Xela, "there may be a reason they're locked. Maybe it's not safe in there." She walked into the laundry room and tossed her pillowcases on top of the washers.

He stood in the doorway and shrugged. "Maybe."

"If it isn't safe we've got a right to know," said Veek. "What if there's a bunch of toxic chemicals in there? Or what if half the foundation's crumbled and they just don't want us to see because then they'd have to replace it."

"Or maybe it's something spooky and mysterious, right?" Xela grinned at them.

"Either way," said Nate, "wouldn't it be cool to know for sure?"

She stuffed an armful of mixed clothes into one of the washers. "Did you think about making a hole? They're just wooden doors, right?"

"I think Oskar might notice if we started drilling holes down here," said Veek.

Another armful of clothes went into the machine, followed by the pillowcase they'd been in. "Did you look for one?"

"What?"

"Did you look for a hole?" Xela shrugged and fished some coins out of her shorts. "It's an old building. There must be a hole somewhere from old pipes or a brick that fell out or something."

Nate and Veek exchanged looks and slipped back down the hall.

"Nothing," Veek muttered.

"The boiler room," said Nate. He stepped back to the doorway and compared the brick wall behind the boilers to the one at the end of the hall. "It looks like they line up. And the wall doesn't look like it's gotten as much love in here."

He squeezed into the room. There wasn't much space between the thigh-high water heaters. There also wasn't much light. "Okay," he said. "I'm going to go get a flashlight."

"Hang on," said Veek. Her phone came out, she tapped the screen, and it glared white. She swept it back and forth between the squat tanks.

A handful of green shapes fled from the stark light. The roaches vanished between the heaters. Veek yelped and took a step back.

Xela leaned out of the laundry room. "You okay?"

"I have a bug thing," said Veek.

The blue-haired woman stepped into the room after Nate. He leaned over one of the heaters and Veek panned the light across the wall. Xela followed the beam with her eyes. Veek tried to watch from the door.

Nate shifted his leg between two of the heaters and leaned deeper in. There was no room to move between them. He found himself wondering how the maintenance crew got them out if they needed to replace one.

"Wait," said Xela. "Sweep it back the other way. Closer to the corner and down."

Veek angled the phone's light as best she could. They all craned their necks to look.

At the base of the farthest tank was a hole in the wall, just visible between two heaters. Red chips and dust were scattered on the floor where a brick had been shattered. Some of the mortar had come away, too. One of the emerald roaches dashed through the hole and was gone.

"Good eye," said Veek. "How'd you spot that?"

"I didn't," Xela admitted. "I just saw the pieces of brick and thought we might get lucky."

"Only thing is," said Nate, "I don't know how we're going to look through." He peered down at the rectangular hole and glanced back at Veek. "I could lower you over the heaters," he said. "You could lean down and—"

"Nope." She shook her head. "Bug thing, remember? I'm not putting my hair down with the cockroaches. I'll never sleep again."

He looked at Xela. "You up for taking a look?"

She smiled and gestured at Veek's phone. "Just use the camera. If you can reach the hole you can take a picture through it."

Veek shook her head. "Does your phone have a flash? It's a dark room on the other side of the wall."

"How do you know?"

"There's no light coming through the hole."

"I couldn't reach it, anyway," said Nate. "Not without crawling over two or three heaters and standing on my head. Maybe if I lay across them and reach down..." He shrugged, "It's a two-person job, to be safe. And quiet."

Xela twisted her lip, then smiled. "Wait here." She dashed down the hall and up the stairs.

Veek sighed.

"What's the big deal?" asked Nate.

"She's scatterbrained and she doesn't take anything seriously. She's going to get us caught."

"You don't know that."

She snorted and turned her attention back to the double doors.

A moment later Xela tromped back down the stairs. One of her tuxedo smocks hung over her Batman shirt. In one hand was a bright red flashlight. In the other was a mid-range, solid-looking digital camera. "You don't think there's anything bad in there, do you?"

"We don't know what's in there," Veek said. "That's why we want to look."

"But it's safe to look, right?"

"No," said Veek, "it's incredibly dangerous. I'm almost positive there's a crossbow on the other side of the wall waiting to shoot anyone in the eye the moment they look through."

"Bitch," said Xela. It wasn't an insult, just a statement. "You hold the flashlight. You hold me," she said to Nate. "I take the pictures."

"Works for me."

Veek shined the flashlight over the heaters. "I'm fine with it."

Xela squeezed in next to Nate and climbed onto one of the heaters. He held out his arm for balance and she grabbed his wrist. She stepped to the next heater and it rocked under her foot. The noise sounded like a drum in the small room.

"Careful," said Veek. She flicked the light down briefly to the base of the heater and the shadows in the room went mad.

"Keep the light steady," snapped Xela. Without letting go of Nate's arm, she took a quick step to the third water heater. He leaned forward to stay with her. The second heater rumbled to a halt beneath their arms.

"You okay?" asked Nate.

"Fine," said Xela. "Just fine." She lowered herself to her knees and then slid onto her ass. She stretched her legs back toward him, setting her sneakers against the wobbly heater. "I think I can lean down from here and get the camera by the hole."

"Let me shift my grip." He twisted his arm and they seized each other's wrist.

"Much better," she said.

"All set?"

"I think so. Hey," she said, glancing back at him, "isn't the boiler room where Freddy Kruger always hung out?"

"Yeah, I think so," said Nate. "Why would a nubile, young exhibitionist like yourself be worried about that?"

"Bastard."

"Down you go."

She leaned to the side and stretched her arm down between the farthest heaters. Her head and shoulders vanished between the tanks. Veek saw a glimpse of blue hair between two of the tanks and shined the light at it.

"Not quite close enough," Xela called back. "Can you get three or four inches closer?"

Nate forced himself into the gap between the heaters by him. A pipe tugged at his jeans. He leaned forward a little more and let his other leg rise up to balance him.

Xela's grip loosened and she let her fingers slide from his wrist to his palm. "Got it," she said. "Just give me a minute."

There was a faint click and a burst of light came from between the water heaters. There was a faint scrape and a grunt from Xela. Nate felt her shift on his arm. Then there was another click and a more subdued flash. She set the camera off four more times and then her fingers tightened on his. "Up," she called.

He pulled and she swung back up into view. There were cobwebs in her hair and the tuxedo shirt was streaked with dust and grime. She let Nate guide her back over the wobbly heater and she jumped down next to him.

"Well," she grinned, "was it good for you, too?"

"You tell me." He nodded at the camera as they stepped out into the hall.

"Can we see them now?" asked Veek.

"See what?"

Oskar was in the hall, staring at them. His eyes shifted to each of them in turn. They stayed on Veek the longest. After a long moment of silence, he asked, "What were you doing in there?"

Nate tried to think of something, but his mind was blank. He glanced at Veek and saw she was busy returning Oskar's stare. He raced through ideas again and found the list was pathetically small.

Xela cleared her throat. "I was doing laundry and I saw a rat," she said. She pointed back into the laundry room with both hands. They were empty.

Oskar's brows went up. "A what?"

"A rat."

"There are no rats in our building."

She shrugged. "I ran upstairs to get you and found Veek and Nate in the lounge."

"There are no rats in our building," repeated Oskar.

"There was one," said Nate. Now that Xela'd planted the seed his brain was working again. "We chased it out of the laundry room and in here."

Oskar looked at Veek. "And you were chasing this rat, too?"

"No," she said. "No rats, no bugs. I was just giving moral support."

"It got away behind the water heaters," said Nate. "Do you have any traps or anything?"

"We do not haff traps," said Oskar, "because there are no rats."

"Well, we saw one," said Xela. "And if you see one brave one out and about, it means there are ninety-nine cowards in the walls."

The manager snorted. "I will look for rats," he said. "If I find any, you will be told. Next time you see one, come find me first."

"I will," she said. "I was just, you know, panicking a bit."

His face wrinkled into a smile. "I understand. I am sorry it scared you." He gave them each a nod and pushed past to look in the boiler room.

They walked back past the laundry room and headed for the stairwell.

"Where's the camera?" whispered Nate.

"Wedged in my buttcrack," said Xela. "I hope he didn't notice the bulge in the back of my shirt." They turned the corner at the landing and she yanked the camera out from behind her.

Nate grinned. "Welcome to the Mystery Gang, Daphne."

EIGHTEEN

Xela's apartment looked like every clichéd artist's apartment. Nothing matched, and the furniture gave off a certain vibe Nate was familiar with. It was all secondhand at best, maybe even scavenged from alleys.

Her desk was made from several milk crates and what looked like an old door. An oversized laptop sat on one end. A large lump of clay sat on the other end, half-formed into something that could've been either a fertility goddess or a lumpy vase.

She threw herself into a chair in front of the laptop. The camera connected to a USB cable and the computer hummed to life. "Just a sec," she told them. A progress bar zipped by and she opened a file.

The first picture was dark with a brightly-lit brick on the left side. "I had it positioned bad," said Xela. "The flash just went off against the wall."

The second photo was a blur of colors. "Tapped the camera," she muttered.

The next three seemed workable, although they all showed different details and shadows. She began clicking on different filters and tools. "Give me a minute."

Veek and Nate turned away and spent a minute looking around. Every wall was covered with photos or paintings of one kind or another. Canvases were stacked up on a wooden chair. An easel near the center of the room held a painting of the Griffith Park Observatory as seen from the roof. Next to the desk was a mattress on the floor, piled high with pillows and blankets. An old-fashioned folding screen with four panels stood next to the wall, like something out of a Wild West bordello. It looked like it had been made from large window shutters.

Nate peeked behind the screen. Just as Xela had said, her bathroom was an open space the size of Nate's kitchen. The floor, walls, and ceiling were all covered with the blue and white tile. In one corner was the showerhead and controls. In the other was a toilet, sink, and medicine cabinet. It reminded him of a locker room.

Veek was studying the painting of the observatory. There was a photograph of the same view clipped to the edge of the canvas. She pushed her glasses higher on her nose and looked between the two.

"This is the best one," said Xela. She'd cleaned up one photo and filled the screen with it. "There's a bit more in some of the others, but this seems to be the best overall." She leaned back to give them a clear view.

The flash lit up most of the room. Because of the angle, the bottom half the picture was concrete floor. It was rough and unpainted. The bright light highlighted some dust bunnies and cobwebs in the foreground.

The walls were bare brick and mortar with a few horizontal pipes running along them. One of the few vertical pipes ran down into the ground, and there was a stack of what looked like newspapers at the base of it. In the far corner he could see a glimpse of the roof and several thick wooden beams connected to an exposed I-beam. A few coils of thick rope hung on the wall. Something hung at the top edge, and the reflections on it made them all confident it was a bare light bulb peeking into frame.

"So," said Nate, "all that for a big empty room."

Veek squinted through her glasses. She reached out to point at the picture. "Do you have a better shot of that rope?"

"Maybe." Xela switched back to the two other shots. "I haven't cleaned these up, but if you give me a minute I can try to—"

"There!" Veek jabbed a finger at the monitor. "See that?"

Nate and Xela peered at the image. It was darker than the clean one, and not as sharp. The objects in the background were just shadows, highlights, and reflections. The coils of rope gleamed in the image

"It's shiny," said Veek. "It's not rope, it's cable."

"Could be," Xela said. She skipped to another picture, then back to the clean version. The enhancement and years of dust made the coils look like rope, but there were a few pinpricks of light reflecting off them.

"It is," said Veek. She looked at Nate. "I'll bet it's copper cable."

"Doesn't look like copper," Xela said.

"That's a big leap," said Nate.

"Not really. Not if we assume whatever's in there has something to do with the power mystery."

Xela turned from the screen. "Power mystery?"

Nate and Veek exchanged a glance. "The building isn't on the L.A. power grid," he said.

She blinked. "What?"

"It looks like we're getting our electricity from somewhere else," said Nate. "We just don't know where."

"Somewhere in there," said Veek.

"Except," countered Nate, "there's nothing in there."

"We can't see half the room," she said. "There could be a ton of stuff in there just out of frame."

"Something that could power a building?"

Veek glared at him. "Whose side are you on?"

Nate put up a hand. "I just want the facts. No jumping to conclusions."

"Hold on," said Xela. She flicked back and forth between a few of the lesser photos again and came back to the clean one. "Look at those shadows."

Veek leaned in. "What about them?"

She traced the shadows the pipes had cast when the flash went off. "They're too big. Too wide."

Nate tried to pull some hidden meaning from the photo. "What do you mean, too wide?"

"If the pipes were on the wall," Xela explained, "they'd cast narrow shadows. Not much wider than the pipes themselves, because there wouldn't be much distance for them to spread. We probably wouldn't even be able to see them."

"They're not on the wall," said Veek. "They're out in the middle of the room."

"Yep," said Xela. "Those aren't water pipes."

Nate thought of optical illusions, and how the whole perspective of a picture would switch once you knew the trick to it. "It's a railing," he said. "The safety railing around a staircase."

He and Veek exchanged a glance.

"One going down below the basement," said Veek.

NINETEEN

Xela had to go back to throw her laundry in the dryer and said she'd check on Oskar. Nate and Veek stood in the hall by the stairwell.

"Finding out there's a sub-basement's good," said Nate, "but her bathroom was interesting, too."

Veek gave him a look. "Why? She have something naughty drying in there?"

"It's set up like a locker room," he said. "She told me the other day but I didn't think she was serious."

"So?"

"So every single apartment I've seen in this building has a different layout. I mean, seriously different."

She smirked. "You have no idea."

"What's that supposed to mean?"

She walked past him to the stairwell and set her hand on the ornate banister. "Come on," she said. "Let's see if I can show you another oddity of the Kavach Building."

They walked downstairs. Veek stopped at 13, across from the padlocked 14, and rapped a few times. Nate shuffled through the tenants he'd met and tried to remember who lived there.

As it turned out, the woman who answered the door was no one he knew, but he did recognize her. She was the curvy half of the couple he'd seen walking in and out of the building a few times. Up close he could see a light sprinkle of freckles on her cheeks. "Hey, Veek," she said. "What's up?"

"Favor to ask you." She cocked her head back at him. "This is Nate. He moved into twenty-eight a few months ago. Do you mind if he takes a look at your place?"

The woman smiled. "Of course not." She held out her hand to Nate. "I'm Debbie. I've seen you a couple of times."

He shook the hand. "Nate. I've seen you, too. You and your...boyfriend?"

"Husband," she said. "Clive. He's at a job right now but he should be back in a few hours." The smile never cracked. She reminded Nate of a teacher he'd had way back in second or third grade.

She stepped aside and let Veek enter the apartment. Debbie glanced back at him. "Would you guys like a drink or something? We've got milk, water, orange juice."

He walked in and looked up.

And up.

"I've got half a pot of coffee," Debbie added, "but I could make some fresh stuff. Or I've got tea if you like. The water's already on."

The brick wall across from him was at least twenty feet tall. It had two of the huge windows his apartment had, and then two more a yard or so above them. Then his eyes came off the bricks and windows and found the chandelier. It was a forest of long crystal shards, a hundred icicles in concentric rings. A brass chain bolted it to the hardwood ceiling.

And now Nate saw the rest of the apartment. The ceiling and walls were rich, dark hardwood. They looked like the floors but without a century of wear and tear on them. He looked closer and saw each one was a single plank, floor to ceiling. It was like being in the private library of a mansion, or maybe a castle.

"Wow," he said.

"Yep," said Debbie. "We get that a lot."

"You guys did all this yourself?"

She smiled again. "No. Clive's a wonderful carpenter, don't get me wrong, but it was like this when we moved in. He made the loft, though, and our table and chairs."

Nate looked up again and tried not to get distracted. In the corner opposite the windows was a platform, maybe ten feet on a side. It stood on tall legs of doubled-up two-by-fours. He could see a railing at the top. The whole thing was as high as the next floor, and a staircase ran alongside it. "That's apartment twenty-three," he said. "There's no door because there's no apartment."

"You're a fast one," said Veek.

"Why the hell do you have a cathedral ceiling?"

Debbie shrugged. "Like I said, it was like this when we moved in."

"No, I mean...I mean why would anyone do this? Why put a two-story room in the middle of an apartment building?" He looked at Veek. "Maybe we should put the cellar on hold for a while."

"What? Seriously?"

Debbie stepped back from the kitchen area. "What's so special about the cellar?"

They sat at the table and told her about the photos and the railing. Debbie made tea for herself and poured them both water from a Brita filter on the counter. She reminded Nate of every cute mom in old black-and-white television shows. Debbie was a modern day June Cleaver, with her manners and smiles and cheerful hosting duties.

She blew on her tea, two polite little puffs, and looked down at the floor. "So you think whatever's in this sub-basement has to do with the electricity-from-nowhere?"

"Yeah," said Veek. "That's why I think we need to get in there."

Nate was looking around the cathedral apartment again, examining each plank on the wall. "I think we should take some measurements. All these different layouts have to mean something."

"Like what?"

He shrugged. "I have no idea. It just seems to be the most blatantly weird thing about this place. Apartments are usually symmetrical, but this place is as unsymmetrical as it can be. There has to be a reason for it. Maybe if we can make up some actual blueprints we'll catch something we've been missing."

"Or we could just see what's in the basement," said Veek.

"Yeah, but that's going to be tough. If he is hiding something, Oskar's going to be suspicious right now. We need to wait a couple of weeks for him to forget he found us there. And we might as well use those weeks checking out some of the stuff we can do without raising suspicion."

Debbie set her mug down. "He's got a good point."

"Fine," sighed Veek. She tapped her fingers against her glass. "It'll be tough," she said. "I only know maybe half the people in the building, and I'm maybe on speaking terms with half of them."

"Between the three of us and the public spaces, we could get a lot of it though," said Debbie. "Maybe enough to help us get a sense of the place. Clive's got tomorrow off, so he could help."

"Would he be up for it?" asked Nate.

She nodded. "He's just as fascinated by this place as Veek. He just never has time to do anything. If you've got a plan ready to go, he'll lunge at it."

Veek got up to refill her glass and flinched away from the counter. Nate glanced over and saw a hint of green vanish into the sink. He glanced at Debbie. "You've got 'em, too?"

"Yep," she said. "They're fascinating, aren't they?"

He sipped his water. "I guess. I've never seen green cockroaches before living here."

"Normally they're only in the Caribbean and along the gulf coast," she said. "But these aren't *panchlora nivea*. I'm studying biochemistry, and we do tons of work with roaches in the lab. The guys in this building are unique. They might be a whole new species."

"Oh, joy," said Veek.

Debbie gave her a look that should've been condescending, but she somehow made it seem cute and motherly. "If you actually looked at them sometime you'd find them fascinating, too. Besides, if you're looking for mysteries, they're little enigmas, believe me."

Nate perked up. "How so?"

Debbie smiled. Again, all the smiles should've been creepy, but she made them work somehow. They were so ridiculously sincere. "There's something lurking in their DNA if I can just figure out how to study it," she said. "I mean, I could do my graduate thesis just on their physical mutations if I can figure out how to get them and the equipment in the same place."

Veek set her glass on the table. "UCLA won't let you borrow stuff?"

"Not the stuff I need."

"So the extra leg counts as a full-on mutation?" asked Nate. "They're not just some freaks or something?"

"The extra leg's a pretty big thing," Debbie said. "A stable mutation along those lines that's fully functioning is pretty rare. They've also got a weird mandible arrangement and the green carapace. That's not even the weirdest bit. As far as I can tell, they don't eat."

"Don't eat what?"

"Anything," said Debbie. "You can leave food on the counter and they won't touch it. They walk around it. They also ignore poison and bait traps, which is why you can't get rid of them. I've got a tank of about a hundred in the bathroom and I've never fed them once." She put her hands up. "So what are they living off?"

Veek gave the bathroom an uneasy look and she and Nate both shook their heads. "And you can't study them in your lab because...?"

"Because I can't get them there."

"No car?" asked Nate.

Debbie shook her head. "I've tried to take some in. My first thought was to start a colony there and do some work on them." She shook her head. "Thing is, they die if you take them away from the building."

Nate's glass stopped halfway to his mouth. "Die?"

Debbie nodded. "I thought the first time was a fluke. Then it happened again so I ran some tests. I haven't done enough to draw viable conclusions, but it looks like they die once they get thirty-one feet, seven inches outside the building. They can't even get to the end of the block."

"What happens?" asked Veek. "Do they get sick or something or...something?"

Debbie shook her head again. "It's like flipping a switch. They cross the line and they drop dead. I even had it marked with chalk a few months back."

"I remember that," Veek said. "The big green arc in the street. I thought it was kids playing a game."

"Nope, just me. Once they get about ninety feet out they shrivel up like they've been dead for weeks. I can't be exact because I don't have a tape measure long enough. So I'm stuck working on them here with whatever I've got." She had a sip of her tea. "Weird, huh?"

TWENTY

Clive loved being a carpenter because at the end of the day he could stand back and see all the things he'd accomplished. There was physical evidence of progress. Even the grueling days ended well because he could see he'd gotten a lot done. For a guy who was never expected to do anything, the constant reminders were a good thing.

So he was already in a good mood before he got home. He found parking with no problem, walked past the liquor store without a pause, and went home to his lovely wife. They'd talked about having a quiet night in, and they'd gotten the last disc of *Middleman* from Netflix.

He opened the door to the apartment, called out to Debbie, and saw a man he didn't know sitting at their table. Veek was visiting with one of the new guys he'd seen a couple times around the building. Clive liked Veek. They shared the same fascination with the oddities of the Kavach Building. Plus he got the sense she had a few demons of her own.

He gave his lovely lady a kiss, shook hands with Nate, and joined them at the table. When they explained what they wanted to do, Clive squeezed Debbie's hand. "I'm in," he told them. "And I think Nate's right. Let's start with the basics. Measure everything we can."

"I still think we should try to get into the basement," said Veek.

"How, though?" asked Debbie. "We'd have to steal the keys or break the lock."

"We could pick the lock," said Veek.

Nate raised a doubting eyebrow. "You know how to do that?"

She sighed. "No."

Clive got up and went to his tool chest. It was a wooden case the size of a small dresser, built from two-by-fours and plywood and mounted on heavy casters. The double doors held four large shelves in place. He'd built it himself after getting his first regular studio job. It was bright blue, and on the left door he'd meticulously painted a white sign covered with instructions for the "Police Telephone" inside. He pawed through the second drawer and pulled out two neon tape measures and then a large one like a reel. "I think I've got everything we'd need."

Nate nodded and Veek made a sound of grudging agreement. "Do you want to be in charge of this?" asked Nate. "You've probably got the best idea how to do it."

Clive stopped and felt himself shrink back from the idea. Debbie met his eyes and gave him a reassuring nod. "Are you sure?" he asked. "I don't want to step on your toes or anything."

Nate shook his head. "Don't worry about it. We'll meet up tomorrow and you can tell us all what we're doing."

When Nate showed up the next morning, Clive had their plan of attack ready. He'd even drawn up a set of preliminary blueprints on a legal pad. They were ready to have measurements put in.

The redheaded man gestured at the walls and patted the reel. "We measure the outside of the building with the hundred-footer. We do the back wall and this side, so we're never near Oskar's apartment." He tapped the inside of his diagram. "We measure the distance from door to door everywhere we can. Then we measure inside the apartments from the door to the shared wall. That'll tell us how thick the inside walls are."

"We can do between you and Veek," said Nate, "and probably between me and Tim. Do you know who lives next door to Mandy?"

"That's Andrew," said Debbie. "He's a bit high and mighty, but I think he'll be okay."

"High and mighty?"

Clive snorted. "His faith is stronger, his church is better, his God can kick your God's ass. Just ask him, he'll be glad to give you the two-hour lecture on how inferior you are."

Debbie tapped him gently on the head. "Don't disrespect the man's beliefs."

"Sorry, hon."

Debbie looked at Nate. "Where is Veek, anyway?"

"Sleeping in, I think," Nate said. "She told me she was going to be up all night doing final tweaks on her big bonus project. I figured we'd hold off waking her until we got started."

Clive nodded and tapped the diagram. "We can do the same measurements going across an apartment, across the hall, and across another apartment. If we can get two doors open across from each other, we can go from outside wall to outside wall. That'll give us the depths of all four of those walls."

"Sounds good," said Nate. "Is sixteen open? Veek said it gets left unlocked sometimes."

"It might be," said Debbie. "I thought I saw them cleaning in there last week. They almost never lock it. Nobody's going to spend much time in there."

"We could do that as soon as she's up."

"Sounds great," said Clive. "We can do the outside right now and then start in here."

Nate and Clive snuck out to measure the building's walls. Then they measured Clive and Debbie's apartment. Clive ran his measuring tape across the hall while Nate checked 16 to see if it was open. The knob was stiff, but it turned and the door opened. It moved on its hinges like the door to a bank vault.

"You want to wake up Veek?" he asked Debbie. "We'll measure this and be ready for her in a couple minutes."

"Done."

Clive recorded his hall measurement in a small notepad. The tape rewound with a metallic hiss. Nate pushed open the door and they stepped into apartment 16.

The wall between the kitchen and the main room had a huge opening, and the counter spread out there to form a table, like the counter at a diner. Against the far wall were two pillars, one in each corner. They flanked the wall the apartment shared with 14.

The room was still. The air didn't move. There were none of the usual noises associated with an inhabited building. Nate wondered if the walls were soundproofed.

"Let's do this and get out of here," said Clive. "This room always gives me the willies."

"You been in here before?"

He nodded. "Right after we moved in they left the door open. They'd just repainted it. Debbie wanted to see if any other apartments were as cool as ours. We didn't know about it then. What happened here."

"Right," said Nate. He took one end of the tape and walked to the far wall.

Clive walked the tape to the opposite wall. "We were in here maybe ten, fifteen minutes and it just started getting to us, y'know? It's just...wrong in here. Like there's a noise you don't register or the temperature's off or something." He jotted numbers down in his notebook and gestured for Nate to go between the pillars.

Nate walked over and the measuring tape chimed and rustled. He pressed his end against the wall and his eyes went wide. "Whoa," he said. "Feel this."

Clive scribbled numbers. "What?"

"The wall's cold."

"Like Veek's place?"

"Colder." Nate put his hand against the painted plaster. "Maybe just a couple degrees over freezing. Check it out."

Clive set his own palm against the wall. "Okay," he said, "that's creepy."

"What do you think it means?"

"Whatever's next door is really cold? I've got a better one for you. Why isn't it cooling this whole room?"

Nate blinked and pulled his hand off the wall. It warmed up immediately. He touched the wall with his fingertips and a chill shot through them.

"Hey." Veek stood at the door, dressed in red and blue sweats. She gave Nate a quick wave and then sent one at Clive. She looked around the apartment and yawned.

"Good morning," said Nate.

"Morning. You guys almost done in here?"

"All done except for measuring across the hallway," said Clive. He ducked into the hall.

Nate looked at Veek. "How'd the project go?"

"Shitty," she said, "but it does what it's supposed to and they'll pay me for it."

"What's it supposed to do?"

"It writes 'none of your business' on the screen in big letters."

"Ahhhh. Well, as long as you're getting paid for it."

Her eyes roamed around the empty apartment. "Anything neat in here?"

"You've never been in here before?"

She shrugged. "A couple times, but maybe you spotted something I missed."

"D'you know about the wall?" He pointed at the surface between the two pillars.

"What about it?"

"Touch it."

Veek walked to the wall and peered at it through her glasses. She set her fingers against the plaster and yanked them back. "Wow."

"Weird, huh?"

She reached out again and pressed her hand against the wall. "Yeah," she said. "I've probably been in here four or five times and I never caught this." She lifted her palm away and wiggled her fingers in the air inches from the wall.

Clive came back. "Ready?"

"Oh, yeah," Nate said.

"Here," said Veek. "I'll walk it in. That way I can make a last check for what I left laying out." She grabbed the end of the tape and walked across the hall into her apartment.

Clive waved him toward the door. "Stand in the hall and make sure no one walks into the tape or anything."

Nate stepped out and joined Debbie. She smiled and they tried to look casual while they kept an eye out for Oskar.

"You good?" called Clive.

"Yep," Veek yelled back.

He made another note in his little book and gave the tape a tug. Veek let it go and he rolled it up with a little crank that folded out of the side of the ring. He glanced around 16 and looked at Nate. "Enough in here for one day."

"I agree."

They headed out into the hall and pulled the door closed behind them.

TWENTY ONE

Nate and Clive ran the long tape across the lounge while Debbie helped Veek measure her room. They headed upstairs and the two men began to work in Nate's apartment while Debbie and Veek knocked on Mandy's door. It took a little bit of work to convince her, but not too much. Tim was all for it.

"We can go do Xela's place," Debbie said while Clive jotted down all the numbers. "You guys want to talk to Andrew?"

"Not really," said Clive. She gave him a look and he cleared his throat. "I mean, of course, dear."

"Watch it, mister." She shook a mocking finger at him and headed down the hall.

Nate followed Clive over to apartment 25. "We might be lucky," said Clive in a low voice. "Sunday before two, there's a good chance he'll be at church."

"Why's that good?"

"Because I don't like dealing with him." He set his jaw and knocked.

Nate recognized the man who answered the door. He had LEGO-perfect hair, wide eyes, and was wearing a tie and sweater vest with a short-sleeve shirt. Clive nodded his head in greeting. "Hey, Andrew."

"Clive." The man with plastic hair looked at Nate. "Hello," he said. "I'm afraid I don't know your name, but I've seen you around."

"Nate Tucker." He held out his hand. "I live right over there. I think you held the gate for me once."

"That's right. You cleaned up some of the phone books." Andrew shook Nate's hand as if he was worried it might break.

"So, this is a little odd," said Clive, "but we were wondering if we could take a couple measurements of your apartment."

Andrew's head tipped to the side, went straight, and swung to the other side. "What for?"

"We're just trying to figure out something. How thick the walls are."

"Why do you need to know?"

"It's just a little bet," said Nate. He sensed Clive tense up next to him. "Nothing important."

Andrew bit his lip. "Oh," he said, "I don't know if I can condone gambling." He took in his breath as if he had more to say but just stood there.

Clive cleared his throat. "It's just a figure of speech."

"The Book has some very specific things to say about gambling and other distractions."

"But we're not," said Nate. "Sorry, bad choice of words. I apologize."

Andrew looked back and forth between them. "I have your word this is not some form of wager? It would look bad for me if it was."

"Absolutely not," said Clive. "It's just to satisfy curiosity. Nothing more."

Andrew took another breath and twisted the bottom of his sweater vest with one hand. "I suppose it can't do any harm, then." He gestured them in.

Clive ran his tape measure from the door to the wall. It wasn't hard. The apartment looked like a monk lived in it. "I didn't think we'd catch you in," he said. "I figured you'd be at church."

"I'm surprised you're not at church yourself," Andrew said in a neutral tone.

"We're going to evening services tonight," said Clive. He checked the tape again and wrote another set of numbers in his notebook.

Andrew dipped his head forward, then forward again. "We're having starlight services tonight as well," he said. "Out at Zuma Beach."

"That's quite a drive," said Nate. "What is that, forty-five minutes away? And on a Sunday night."

"Prayer with good fellows is always worth it," said Andrew. "And the sound of the waves makes it especially invigorating."

"Cold, though," said Nate with a smile.

"I've never noticed. The Lord warms us with his presence. What church do you attend, Nate?"

He felt the mine under his foot and sensed others nearby. "I don't have one at the moment," he said. "Still looking for somewhere since I moved."

"Our congregation is selective, but I'd be honored to sponsor you for membership if you'd be interested."

He tried to find a safe path. "That might be nice," he said. "Can I get back to you about it later?"

Andrew's head moved side to side again. "You're not interested now?"

"I don't know anything about it now."

The other man weighed this, as if the thought had never occurred to him. "I suppose," he said, "although it is a wonderful church. We have so much fun it almost doesn't feel like worship."

"Well," said Clive, "I think I've got everything. Thanks, Andrew. We'll get out of your hair."

"It was no problem at all," he said. "Have a wonderful day." They stepped out and he closed the door after them.

The two of them headed back to Debbie and Clive's apartment. Debbie had decided to make an early dinner for everyone. Xela had followed the women down after her apartment had been measured, and Debbie had drafted her to set the table. Xela seemed to find being domestic funny as hell. Veek stood off to the side, typing on her phone. "Got everything?" she asked when they walked in.

"I guess we'll see," said Nate. He glanced at Debbie and the pots. "You didn't have to do all this."

She waved him off. "We've got this huge table and we've never had enough guests to fill it. It's fine."

Clive walked past them to the table. He flipped open his notebook and copied numbers down onto his legal pad blueprints. Math got sketched out in the margins while they passed around spaghetti and sauce. He got up to wash his hands and then came back shaking his head. "This doesn't make any sense."

"No kidding," murmured Xela. She peered over at the mess of lines and numbers.

He shook his head again. "No, I mean, this makes no sense at all." He flipped between pages of the legal pad and held it up for everyone to see. "Okay," he said, "the exterior walls are just brick. They're three and a half inches thick everywhere we measured. I'm going to say that's probably standard throughout the building."

He traced a line on his blueprints. "The interior walls are another story. They're anywhere from fourteen to twenty-six inches thick, depending on which ones you're talking about."

"Is that normal for an old building?" asked Veek.

"For a pueblo, maybe. Not for anything like this. There's more, though." Clive looked across the table at Nate. "You were right about the layouts. There's something weird going on."

"I was bound to be right someday," Nate said, spinning spaghetti onto his fork. "Law of averages."

Clive pointed across the studio. "Our kitchen and bathroom are over there. Xela's bathroom is right above ours, so they share the same wall. So that wall has all our pipes in it. Make sense?"

They nodded.

"My bathroom's different from yours, though," Xela said through a mouthful of pasta.

"Right, but from a construction point of view there's no real difference. There's water pipes and drain pipes. What happens inside the room doesn't matter. The thing is how stuff gets to and from the room."

"Okay."

"Now, here's where it gets weird," he said. "Xela's kitchen is against the opposite wall of her apartment—the outside wall of the building. Same with Veek. You'd think she'd be against the far west wall, the same wall Mandy and Andrew's apartments use above her. But she's here," he pointed at their handmade blueprints and gestured to the far side of the studio, "against this wall. And her kitchen's against the outside wall of the building."

Nate looked over at the blueprints. "So what's the problem?"

"It's not really a problem," said Clive, "it's just weird. You want to minimize the number of walls with pipes in them. That way if something goes wrong you don't have to make as many holes. Plus, you don't need to run as many pipes so it's cheaper, too. All the drains feed into a shared line, all the water branches off a shared line."

"And that's not what we've got?" asked Veek.

He shook his head. "As near as I can figure, there's one of two things going on here. One, every apartment has its own set of plumbing running through the walls. Maybe two in some cases, because the bathrooms and kitchens are so far apart. In a building this old, that means there's more metal in our walls than wood."

Nate looked at the paneled walls. "And option two?"

"Two is that there are shared lines, but they're criss-crossing back and forth under the floors to reach different apartments. It's like trying to go from LA to New York with layovers in Tokyo and London. It's just exceptionally bad planning." He shrugged. "I've done some plumbing work. Not a ton, but this has to be the most inefficient, expensive way to set up a building I can think of. It's like they made tons of space inside the walls, then made the plumbing two or three times more complicated than it needed to be so they'd have something to fill it."

They all looked at each other across the table.

"Or," said Debbie, "they were making space in the walls for something else."

TWENTY TWO

"What if we break open a wall and see what's inside?" said Veek.

Nate shook his head. "And how are you going to explain that to Oskar?"

"We don't," she said. "We keep it quiet, knock out a wall between two apartments so no one in the hallway ever sees anything."

"It's not that simple," said Clive. He used a piece of bread to mop up the last bits of sauce on his plate. "We'd need a way to muffle the noise, even if we just do it with hand tools. And we'd need a way to haul out all the plaster, wood, bricks, and whatever else we find in there."

"Assuming there is anything in the wall we pick," said Nate.

"Plus, you'd want a way to hide it if Oskar stops by for something," added Xela. "It'll be pretty tough for him not to notice a wall is missing."

"Anything that falls into the wall would make a racket," continued Clive. "Some of it might fall all the way to the basement. And then we'd have to get all the supplies to rebuild it past Oskar."

"Not to mention this place is a national historic landmark," said Nate. "I think you can get jail time for vandalizing it."

"Really?"

He shrugged. "I don't know. Sounds likely though, doesn't it? Heck, what two apartments would we do it between?" He looked around Clive and Debbie's cathedral room. "It's not like we could afford to replace all this woodwork if we did it here."

"Definitely not," said Debbie.

The five of them sat around the table and stared at each other for a few moments.

Veek held her finger and thumb a fraction of an inch apart. "We could just make a little hole and shine a light in."

"You still wouldn't see anything," said Xela. "Not unless you were lucky enough to hit a spot where something was."

"Then we could put a camera in the hole and look around. A fiber-optics one."

"Now you're just being silly," said Nate.

She sighed. "It's just frustrating."

"Well," said Clive, "it's about to get more frustrating. I've got a five a.m. call tomorrow over at Paramount and I can't be late."

"Six more days and he's in the union," said Debbie.

"This was awesome though," Clive said. "Are we going to do more next weekend?"

Their gazes settled on Nate.

"I don't know," he said. "We should be careful, though. Oskar's not going to be happy if he thinks we're snooping around where we're not supposed to be."

"That's so cute," said Debbie. "Snooping around."

Veek sighed.

"Anyway," said Debbie, "thanks so much for coming over, but everyone get out. My hubby needs his sleep."

"Did you just call him your hubby?" Xela asked with a grin.

"Yep, now get out."

"I'll help you clean up," Veek offered.

"Out. See you all later."

Clive nodded at Nate. "Thanks again."

"Thank *you*," said Nate.

"Thanks for dinner," said Xela.

Debbie shooed them all out with a smile and closed the door behind them.

"I should go, too," Xela told them. "I've got classes tomorrow." She headed over to the staircase. "It was fun. Count me in for next time."

Veek walked down the hall to her apartment. "So," she said, "what are we doing next weekend?

Nate shrugged. "Why are you all asking me?"

"Because you've taken the lead."

"Hardly."

She looked up at him. The hall light caught her glasses and turned the lenses into white circles on her face. "Are you Fred or Shaggy?"

"Sorry?"

"If I'm Velma, and Xela gets to be Daphne, who's that make you?"

"I hadn't thought about it. I think I took a quiz on Facebook once that said I was Scooby."

"Scooby's a wuss-out answer," she said. "Are you the guy in charge or the guy who follows orders and stumbles into stuff?"

"What's it matter?"

She shrugged. "I just want to know where we all stand. You brought Xela in on what we were doing and handed things over to Clive pretty quickly."

"Did that bug you? I didn't think this was supposed to be our own secret investigation."

Veek shook her head. "No, we all live here. Whatever's going on, it affects all of us."

He nodded. "Clive knows way more about construction than I do. He knew what we needed to do and how we needed to do it. It would've been stupid not to let him run that whole thing."

"So you're delegating," she said. "Sounds like you're Fred to me."

He shook his head. "If anyone's in charge it's you. You're the one who started all this."

"I started it, but you've done more in the past week than I have in almost a year."

"I've just been building off what you started. Speaking of which, I was going to go look some stuff up before I hit the sack."

"Work tomorrow?"

"Pretty much always. Longest-employed temp in my office."

"Any benefits at all?"

"They pay me on time. That's about it."

"Why're you still there?"

Nate shrugged. "Nowhere else to go. It's not like there are tons of jobs, and I don't have enough in the bank to live off while I look for one." He shrugged again. "Something better'll show up. I just try not to think about it."

"Now you're sounding like Shaggy."

He smiled. "Whatever. G'night."

"Goodnight."

"I'll swing by tomorrow or Tuesday, we can figure out what we're going to do this weekend."

He was halfway across the lounge when her voice caught up with him. "Fred always went off with Daphne," she said. "Shaggy always went with Velma."

"Definitely sticking with Scooby for now, then."

"Wuss."

TWENTY THREE

On Monday Nate managed to spend half the day on the website for the Los Angeles Department of Public Works. He filled out online forms and wrote several emails. In between, he did some data entry and rearranged the bundles in his latest mail crate to make it look like he'd done two or three of them.

On Tuesday he worked his way through pages and pages of old pictures of Los Angeles. There were dozens of sepia-toned photos posted on the web by historical groups and preservation societies. He checked them one after another, watching for anything that looked like his neighborhood or the Kavach Building.

He'd opened, on a guess, his three hundredth tab when Eddie shuffled in. A quick mouse click brought the database back up on his screen. Nate glanced over at his supervisor as if he'd just noticed him. "Hey," he said. "What's up?"

"Don't come in tomorrow."

Anne and Zack peeked around their cubicle walls. Nate's stomach dropped. "Is there a problem?"

One corner of Eddie's mouth twisted into some indecipherable expression and he shook his head. "They want to make extra money so they're doing a big issue. The budget's tight, and they want us all to cut costs." He patted his thighs with his hands. "All of you are getting your hours cut."

Zack groaned. Nate thought about his still-withered bank balance. "Cut by how much?"

"Maybe a day a week."

Zack groaned again. A twenty percent pay cut. "For how long?" asked Anne.

"Five or six weeks, tops." Eddie gave a lopsided shrug they all knew meant *I have no real idea.*

Nate poked the tub of returned magazines and flyers with his toe. "These are going to fall really far behind," he said. "I'm barely holding my own as it is." He gave it another small kick and one of the bundles tipped over and fell into the hole he'd created in the middle of the crate.

Eddie stared at the tub. "Wow," he said in his flat voice. "You're kind of behind now. This tub showed up last Wednesday, didn't it?"

Nate clenched his jaw. The worst part of the blossoming lecture was that, for once, it was well deserved. He'd barely done any work in the past couple of days.

And he was struck by how much Eddie's flat delivery reminded him of his neighbor Andrew, the church-loving man who lived straight across from Tim, between timid Mandy and the mysterious door 23, which was not so mysterious anymore. It was just a cathedral-ceilinged room in the middle of an apartment building that wasn't on the L.A. power grid.

Eddie wasn't talking. He hadn't been for a few moments. Nate's brain shifted and he could feel the gears grind because he didn't get the clutch down fast enough.

"Sorry," he said, "my brain was somewhere else. Worried about finances now that I'm losing a day. What did you say?"

The heavy man wore his blank look. He stared at Nate for another moment, and Nate wondered if he'd just zoned off into the blank look. It wouldn't be the first time.

Eddie popped back to life. "Why do you think you're so far behind?"

"Well, I'm not *that* far behind."

"I was pretty sure you'd have this done by now. It usually only takes you a day or two."

Nate sighed. "It's never taken me two days, Eddie. The quickest I've ever done one was three days, and that was because it was all magazines."

"Are you sure?"

"Yes, I'm sure."

"I was pretty sure you'd done them in one or two days."

"Never."

Right on cue, Eddie put on his questioning face, like he suspected he was the victim of a scam. Nate saw it at least once every other month. He'd also seen it at the pizza place downstairs. Eddie didn't believe they'd always served Pepsi, never Coca-Cola.

"Anyway," Eddie said, "take tomorrow off, Nate. You want to have every Wednesday off?"

"I don't suppose I could make it Monday or Friday?"

Eddie snorted. "Yeah," he said, "like we'll be giving you a month of three-day weekends."

TWENTY FOUR

Nate woke up Wednesday with nothing to do.

He thought about exploring some more, but snuffed the idea just as quickly. The cleaning crews were in. They swept and mopped the halls, cleaned the lounge, and dusted all the corners. Oskar walked from floor to floor and back, checking on each small team.

Nate considered continuing his study of online photos, but decided to go for a long walk. It seemed wrong to take his day off from staring at a computer screen and spend it staring at a computer screen. He pulled on his best sneakers, headed out the front gate, and walked north.

Most of the neighborhood's architecture was from the sixties and seventies—low, wide apartment buildings with long balconies, all centered around a courtyard of some sort. It made him more aware of how old the Kavach Building was. He turned around and walked backward for a few steps. He was a little over a block from the building, but the bend in the street put it right in front of him. If he had a pair of binoculars he'd be able to look right through his own windows. Or Tim's. He could even see the black windows of 14 peeking out above the Victorian next door.

He turned back and noticed the man across the street had a pair of high-end binoculars. Nate almost asked if he could use them when something clicked in his mind. The man was leaning against a green Taurus.

And he was pointing his binoculars at the Kavach building.

Nate's mouth reacted before his brain did. "Hey," he called out. "What are you doing?"

The binoculars came down and the man looked at Nate. His expression was like Eddie's blank look, except this was the blank look's mean, older, don't-mess-with-me brother. The man tossed the binoculars through the Taurus's open window and stared for a moment.

Nate took a step back.

The man opened the car door, slid behind the wheel, and started the engine. It was an amazingly fluid action, as if he practiced getting into his car for hours every day. The Taurus pulled out and drove away. It reached the intersection and turned east, toward the freeway.

Nate watched him go. Either he'd just been very unlucky and a puzzle piece had gotten away from him, or he'd been very lucky the man had driven away. He wasn't sure which. He walked to the end of the block and looked east. There was no sign of the green Taurus.

He decided to keep walking.

Another few blocks took him beneath an overpass and the Hollywood Freeway thundered over his head. It was remarkably clean aside from a splattering of pigeon poop. He continued north on Kenmore as it jogged back and forth. He'd noticed a few times on the nights he circled for parking that his neighborhood had lots of odd roads that didn't line up.

Half an hour of walking brought him out somewhere on Vermont. Nate recognized a McDonalds he'd passed once or twice, the Braille

Institute, and the entrance to L.A. City College. He went another few blocks and saw a little coffee shop with big windows and a faded awning. He decided it was as good a stopping point as any. He considered the few bills in his wallet, the pitiful balance in his checking account, and the news he'd gotten the day before. In the end, a coffee and a muffin wasn't going to kill him, especially if he counted it as lunch.

The prices at the shop were cheaper than at Starbucks, which helped ease the pain of parting with his last five-dollar bill. The coffee was good, the muffin was sweet, and he settled onto a long bench below the window with a three-week-old issue of *TIME* he found abandoned on a nearby table. He paged through an article on the rise of end-of-the-world groups since the start of 2012. There was a sidebar mentioning the May 21st predictions of the year before, the Y2K paranoia of 2000, and how similar cults had sprung up in the late 19th Century, predicting the end would come in 1900. There was even a piece about the original Rapture predictions from William Miller in 1844.

He finished the muffin, balled up the paper bag it had been served in, and tossed it on the table. He glanced around for a moment and went back to the doomsday article. Then his mind registered what he'd seen.

Toni from the rental company stood in line. Her smart suit was gone, replaced by a teal tank top and a pair of shorts that showed off her legs. She had a backpack slung over her shoulder and an open textbook balanced on one hand.

"Toni?" he called out.

She kept reading.

He straightened up and raised his voice another notch. "Toni?"

A few people looked. She was one of the last. Mild disinterest filled her eyes, then confusion. And then, just for a moment, panic. She glanced around the coffee shop like a cornered animal looking for an escape route.

Then the killer smile spread across her face.

He stood up and went to join her in line. She looked away to place her order, slipped the book into her backpack, and turned to him. "Hi," she said. "Fancy meeting you here."

"Yeah," he said. "It's kind of lucky, actually. Do you have a minute?"

"Ummmmm...sure."

He glanced at her outfit. "Is this your day off or something? I could just call you later."

Toni shook her head. "No, it's no problem, I just..." Her voice dropped a few decibels. "I don't have any of the material with me. I can wing something if you think that'd be okay."

"Sorry?"

"Or just give me five minutes," she said. "I can run to my place, grab my props and stuff, get some better clothes on. I'd be ready to go." She gave a more honest smile, a faint one, and gestured at her outfit.

He frowned. "I think you're confusing me with someone else. I'm Nate Tucker. You rented me an apartment in the building on Kenmore about two months ago."

"No, right," she nodded, her voice still low. "I just...I thought everything was supposed to happen there. I'm not prepared for this."

"Prepared?"

"Normally I've got time to go over stuff, y'know?" Her head bobbed side to side. She looked very young in these clothes. "I mean, I'm not method, but I think it's still better if you've got some time to get your head in the right place."

Nate wrinkled his brow. "What are you talking about?"

Toni stared into his eyes. "You're not here for extra material?"

"Well, sort of," he said. "I was hoping you'd know something about the history of the building."

She sighed and looked around again. "This wasn't planned, was it?"

He shook his head. "I was just killing time and saw you in line. I had some questions about the apartment building and—"

They called a name and Toni raised her hand. The clerk handed her a tall cup of coffee. "No, I mean, this wasn't *scheduled*," she said. "You weren't told to come find me."

"Look," said Nate, "I'm feeling lost here. Are we talking about the same thing?"

She nodded. "The building, yeah." They sat at a table and she shot another glance at the door. "Look, this is a really sweet gig for me, so you've got to promise you're not trying to mess it up. If I get fired because of this I will sue your ass, clear?"

"Not in the slightest, no."

She shook her head. "My name's Kathy. I'm a theater arts grad student." She used her cup to gesture toward the campus across the street.

Nate felt his eyes twitch. "A what?"

"An actress. Trying to be, anyway. The Locke Management gig is still the best thing I've had, though."

"So..." He closed his eyes for a moment. "So the company hired you to pretend you're one of their managers?"

Toni-Kathy shook her head again and her bangs swished back and forth. "No, you don't get it. There is no company."

She pulled a sleek, high-end cell phone from her backpack. "This is the number you called. It's got sweet noise-reduction so you can't tell if I'm outside or in a hall or what. It just makes me sound like I'm in an office somewhere. I get texts telling me if someone passed their background checks or not so I can make the follow-up calls." She handed him the phone.

It was deep green, with a touch-sensitive screen that shifted up to reveal a keyboard. Nate had never owned a phone with so many features, but it didn't take him long to find the basics. He flipped from MESSAGES to INBOX. There were only three texts, dating back just over eleven months.

All of them were from **Caller ID Unavailable**.

The middle message was dated April fifth. He remembered that day. He remembered getting the follow-up call at work. Nate tapped the line and it expanded into the full message.

Nathan Tucker has been accepted for apartment #28.

He stared at the phone. He looked up at her and handed it back. "Can you start again? From the top? Just tell me everything."

She nodded. "Okay, every couple of years someone puts an ad in the campus paper for an acting job. It's like a campus urban legend or something at this point. You play a manager for a real estate firm. They give you all the props, enough background to answer questions, and then you do ad-lib scenes with people at the location."

"Who? Who hired you?"

Toni-now-Kathy shrugged. "Don't know. You send in your resume, a headshot, and they just pick from that."

"Who pays you?"

Another shrug. "All done through PayPal. A grand a month. Sometimes I don't even do anything. You were the first person I'd even shown an apartment to in three months."

"And how long has this been going on?"

She sipped her coffee. "I've been doing it for a year now. The girl before me did it for a year and a half. She said the girl before her did it for almost three years."

He juggled everything in his head. "None of this seemed weird to you?"

"It's LA," she said. "This isn't the weirdest acting job I've ever had. Once I was in full animal makeup, like in *Cats*, and they wanted me to—"

He waved her to silence. "Sorry," he said, "this is kind of important. What's going on over there?"

"At your building? Isn't it obvious?"

He shook his head.

"It's some reality show like *Big Brother* or something," she said. "There's probably cameras all over the place. They're filming you and making a show out of it."

"Filming us doing what?"

"Whatever. Having sex, getting dressed, all that voyeuristic stuff."

He shook his head. "That doesn't make any sense. When they do those shows they stir things up. They set people against each other, create fake conflicts, stuff like that. I don't think I've even met half the people in the building."

She shrugged again and took another hit off her coffee.

"Besides," he said, "wouldn't they need us to sign something before they could do anything? Release forms for using us in their show or whatever it is? And have you ever even heard of a show like this?"

"I figured it just hadn't aired yet. They were waiting to get enough footage or something."

He glanced at the phone. "People were doing it for years before you even started. How much footage do you think they need?"

Kathy shifted in her seat. "Maybe it's for the BBC or Australia or somewhere."

It was clear she'd never thought about it much at all. Nate wondered if it was deliberate. He'd met some pretty clueless wanna-be actors since moving to Los Angeles. He'd also met a lot of people who just kept their heads down and didn't ask questions.

"Can you do me a favor?" he asked.

She crossed her legs. "Maybe. It depends."

"You said they gave you some background information on the building?"

She nodded. "Oh, yeah. There's a document on the iPad that's like thirty or forty pages long."

"Could you send me that? There's something going on over there, and it's not a television show. A couple of us are trying to figure out what."

Kathy frowned. "I don't want to lose this gig."

"You won't, I promise. Just email me the file. It's just background information to give out anyway, right?"

"I suppose so."

He pulled out a pen and scribbled his email address down on his napkin. "Just make up some reason why you'd have to send it to me. Most rental places keep documents on their properties, right? You've just got one that's a lot better than most."

Nate pushed the napkin across the table. She stared at it for a moment. "Okay," she said. "But I swear, if you fuck this up for me I will kill you. And I know where you live."

TWENTY FIVE

Thursday Nate was back in the office and focused on making up for the three days he hadn't been doing his job. Another crate had arrived on his day off and he guessed there were close to two thousand names and addresses to input now. He checked his email every other hour, but there was nothing from Kathy-who-had-been-Toni.

At the end of the day, Anne leaned into his cubicle. "Drinks tonight," she said. "Down at the Cat and the Fiddle."

He shook his head. "Love to," said Nate, "but there are no outings in my future. Especially to places with expensive drinks."

She nodded. "That's the whole point. Editor Dave is taking us all out and buying the first round. It's his way of saying sorry."

"Dave's not responsible."

"Yeah, but he's a good guy."

He looked at the screen. His inbox was still empty. He pictured the search for a parking space in his neighborhood after hours. "I don't know," he said. "I'm still feeling tight with the hours getting cut. Plus, I'm working on a couple projects at home."

Anne shrugged. "It's a free drink. Thought you'd want to know." She slipped past him and out the door.

Her hips made a convincing argument for going out.

It went like every other time out, of course. He made small talk with Dave and Zack. He flirted with Anne even though they both knew she was out of his league. He listened to Jimmy the intern explain how he was going to make it big and change Hollywood and not play studio games. The Journalist was there, without his Hot Redhead Girlfriend, chatting with Dave and another editor whose name Nate could never remember.

Once his free drink was gone, Nate considered having another. There were four beers in the fridge at home, though, and his wallet was very thin. And for the past ten minutes he'd been leaning back in his chair not talking to anyone and the conversations were still going on all around him. Plus, thinking of home reminded him that Veek still didn't know about Kathy the actress.

He got up, thanked Dave, said a few goodbyes, and headed for his car. It was late enough he only caught the tail end of rush hour. In a record-breaking ten minutes he found a space only a block from his apartment.

He was cutting across the parking lot for the corner liquor store when a familiar figure stepped out. Oskar had a plastic bag slung around each wrist. They almost dragged on the ground. His face had a slumped expression Nate knew all too well. The look of someone who'd accepted his place in life and stopped striving for anything else.

"Hey, Oskar," he called out.

The man glanced up. It took a moment for him to process Nate out of context. Then his lips twisted into a tight smile. "Mr. Tucker," he said. "Forgiff me for not greeting you. My mind was elsewhere."

"No problem," he said. "How are you?"

Oskar waited for Nate to come alongside him and then the two men walked down the street together. "I am well, thank you. Haff you seen any more rats?"

Nate caught himself before he furrowed his brow. "Just that one," he said. "You were right. It must've been a fluke."

The older man gave a sharp nod. "The Kavach Building would not allow rats within its walls," he said.

"Sorry?"

"It is too dignified a building for pests." He tried to raise one of his burdened arms to reach the crosswalk button. Nate reached past him and hit the large yellow button. "It is a wonderful place. I am glad to liff here with such good tenants."

The glowing red hand became a white figure in mid-stride. They crossed Kenmore and headed up the block to the building. "By the way," said Nate, "I wanted to ask, what's the address for the main office?"

Oskar stopped. "The what?"

"The main office. Locke Management. Where are they?"

The older man shook his head. "Do not waste your time with them. Whateffer you need, talk to me."

"I don't want to bother you."

"It is not a bother. It is my job. I am glad to do it."

"Still," said Nate, "I'd love to get it from you. Just for my records and stuff."

Oskar stared up at him for a moment. "What is this about, Mr. Tucker?"

Nate feigned innocence. He wasn't sure if he did a good job at it. "About?" he echoed. "It's not about anything."

"Do you haff a problem with how I haff been doing my job here?"

"No. No, of course not."

"Why do you wish to work around me, then?"

"I'm not trying to work around you," said Nate. "I just wanted to know where the office is. Is it out of state or something?"

Oskar's brow furrowed. "Why do you say that?"

"Say what?"

"Why do you ask if the office is out of state?"

"Because you're being really difficult about giving out the address. I thought maybe it was far away."

He considered this. "It is," he said. "Forgiff me for being suspicious. After so long here, I dread the thought of losing this job. I am comfortable." He gestured with his head and continued up the hill to the building.

Nate fell in alongside him. "What about...whatshername? Toni? Who does she work for, then, if there's no local office?"

Oskar gave a theatrical glance over either shoulder. "Honest truth?"

"Yeah, sure."

"She works for another office. Locke hires her to be their local face because she is attractiff, but they will not open an office here. It is a tax thing. I do not know the details."

"Ahhhh."

They reached the fence and Nate held the gate open for Oskar. The older man swung his broad shoulders to fit through with his bags and they both trudged up the steps.

"So, anyway," said Nate at the first landing, "could I get that address?"

This time Oskar didn't stop. "What address?"

"The main office."

"I told you," he said, prying the door open with his heel, "you do not need it. Whateffer you need, talk to me."

"But what if somewhere down the line I'm applying to live somewhere else? I need my rental history. They'll want to talk to the people in the office."

"Are you going to moof out?"

"Well...no. But if I do someday—"

Oskar shook his head as they stepped into the lobby. "Just haff them call me. I deal with all such things."

"Yeah, but I can't just assume you're going to be here."

"I haff been here twenty-three years, nineteen as manager. I haff no plans to moof."

"Yeah, but—"

"Mr. Tucker," he said. "My job is to make things run smoothly. That means making sure there are no disturbances here. It also means making sure there are no disturbances for the people at the main office. They do not want to be getting phone calls at all hours from tenants with silly questions or worries about rats."

"This isn't about the—"

"So you will let me deal with such things. And we will stop with the idea of contacting the main office, yes?" Oskar's face had lost the cheer and humor that had filled it outside. "And also with the measuring of walls and hallways."

They stood in the lobby for a moment and stared at each other. Then the older man turned away. He raised his bags and started up the stairs.

"What is this place?" asked Nate.

Oskar didn't turn back. "This is the Kavach Building. It is my home. It is your home. It is a good home. What more do you need to know?"

Oskar trudged up to the landing and around the corner. Nate heard him thump down the hall to his apartment. A moment later a door closed hard enough to be called a slam.

TWENTY SIX

"Nate," called Tim. "Do you know my new best friend, Roger?"

Tim and the man from the laundry room were sprawled on the deck chairs in front of Friday's sunset. Between them was a twelve pack of beer and half a bag of ice. Trails of water snaked out of the case to form small puddles and drip between the planks of the deck.

"I've been replaced?"

"Well, Roger brought a half case with ice," said Tim. "What do you have?"

"I could go get chips or something."

"Save it for next time, bro," chuckled Roger. He pulled a bottle from the ice-filled box. "Want one?"

"It's why I'm here."

He popped the cap off and held it out to Nate. "Enjoy."

Nate took a long pull off the bottle while he found a seat. He grabbed a chair from the table under the cabana.

"Long week?" Tim asked.

"Too long."

Tim held out his bottle and they clinked the necks. "Tell Doctor Farr all about it."

"I don't know if I can afford your rates."

"That's okay. I work with a lot of charity cases like you."

Roger laughed and coughed up some beer.

"You want to hear the bad news or the weird news?"

"No good news?" asked Tim.

Nate shrugged. "I suppose some of the weird news could be good, in that confirmation kind of way."

"Let's go with weird, then."

Nate went back to the start of the week and explained what their measurements had revealed. Then he told them about the chance meeting with the woman they'd all known as Toni, and his encounter with Oskar. Neither of them interrupted him. By the time he was done, he'd started his second beer and the sun had touched the horizon.

"Lemme get this straight," said Roger. "Hottie Asian chick was just an actress?"

"Looks like," said Nate.

"And we're on some British reality show?"

Tim shook his head. "I think Nate was dead-on. There's no television show going on here."

"But she's an actress?"

"Yeah," said Nate. He looked at Tim. "What do you think?"

Tim drummed his fingers on the arm of the deck chair. He took a drink of beer. "I've got to be honest, Nate. When you told me your ideas about hidden secrets, I thought you were overreacting a bit." He had another sip of beer. "If you hire an uninformed third party to conduct your business, though, you're trying to protect yourself."

Roger set his empty bottle on the deck. "From what?"

"On a guess, either they don't want to be in the public eye or they don't want it known they own this building. Possibly a little of both."

Nate took another hit off his beer, but before he could say anything a throat cleared behind them. He glanced over his shoulder. Tim and Roger looked, too.

Andrew stood by the fire door. He had on another sweater vest, this time over a pink polo shirt. "I'm sorry," he said. "I didn't mean to interrupt your party. I just didn't want you to think I was eavesdropping."

"No problem," said Nate. He glanced at his drinking buddies. "Do you guys know Andrew?"

Andrew walked over and thrust his hand at Tim. "I don't think we've been introduced. I live across the hall from you. I'm Andrew."

"So I heard." He shifted his bottle to the other hand and wrapped his fingers around the offered palm. "Tim Farr. Would you like to join us for a beer?"

Andrew's head shake could've been a twitch. "Intoxication goes against the Lord's wishes."

"Not getting intoxicated, bro," said Roger. "Just having a beer or three at the end of the week."

"You're not in my congregation, so please don't call me brother," said Andrew.

Roger's eyes widened and rolled. "Sorry," he said. "Didn't mean anything by it."

"I know it seems like careless fun now," Andrew said, "but when your soul is tallied, these are the little things which add up. The Lord asks for focus and devotion. He has a plan and it doesn't involve alcohol."

Roger bit back most of his chuckle.

"You laugh now," said Andrew, "but in the end we shall see who—"

"Stop," said Tim. There was an edge to his voice. Nate remembered his first impression, of drill sergeants and gym teachers.

The word even made Andrew pause for a moment. He looked confused. "When the key to salvation is found and you—"

"I said stop." Tim took his sunglasses off and stared at Andrew. Nate could see the curve of his eyes and found himself grateful he wasn't the focus of that stare.

Andrew flinched. He cleared his throat and tried again. "When salvation—"

"I respect your beliefs, Andrew, and I'm glad they make you happy. But I'm not up here to be lectured at or spoken down to. Clear?"

Andrew's lips twisted and his head wobbled like it had come loose from his neck. They saw his jaw moving, getting ready to talk again. His nose flared as he took in a breath. "My apologies," he said. "I was only trying to help prepare your souls for—"

Tim raised a warning finger.

Andrew's mouth slapped shut. He gave them a schoolteacher's glare and marched back to the fire door. He yanked it open and stomped down the stairs.

"Bro," said Roger, "that was unbelievably awesome."

"It wasn't," said Tim. "I just hate bullies." He pushed his sunglasses back on and took a hit off his beer.

The door clicked open again and Veek stepped out onto the roof. "Hey," she said. "Which one of you pissed off Andrew?"

Nate and Roger pointed at Tim. "I apologize if he's a friend of yours," said the older man.

She shook her head. "I don't think I've ever seen him so worked up," she said. "He didn't even say hello on the stairs."

"Tim used a Jedi mind trick on him," said Roger. "It was awesome."

"Are you looking for a new apprentice?" she asked. "There's a bunch of people at work who need a good Jedi mind trick. Or a lightsaber up their ass."

"Sounds like the lady needs some relief," said Tim. He rooted around in the ice and pulled a beer free. Roger popped the cap and handed it off to her. She raised her bottle and they all returned the toast. She had a long drink.

Nate shifted aside to let her share his chair. "Big project didn't go over so well?"

"No," she said, shaking her head, "that was an outside project. This is just the mindless day job. Emphasis on mindless." She had another drink and turned to Nate. "I got your email. About your day off."

"No need to be cryptic," said Nate. He waved his bottle at the others. "We're all on the same page here."

She looked at Tim and Roger. "You guys are in?"

They both nodded. Tim pulled one knee up to his chest. "Just before Andrew joined us," he said, "I was telling Nate I think there might be a real mystery here."

"You could *so* be our Fred," said Veek.

"Want to hear really weird?" said Roger. "Have you guys noticed there're no power lines running to this place?"

Nate and Veek grinned. The four of them drank their beers, watched the last shreds of sunset, and discussed the accumulated oddness of their home.

"So," said Veek as the streetlights flickered on below them, "you figure out what we're doing this weekend?"

Nate shrugged. "I'm not sure. After running into Toni—or Kathy—it just seems like there's a ton of little things that are all worth following."

"The bigger problem," said Tim, "is that it sounds like Oskar knows you're up to something. Whatever you decide to do, you need to work around him."

"True that," said Roger. "Whatever's going on, s'not worth losing your place over."

Nate nodded. "I think a lot of people have said that. It's probably why no one's ever made all this weirdness public."

Veek set her bottle down and turned to Nate again. "So you're saying we should keep our snooping low-key for another week or so?"

"Maybe." He finished off the last of his beer and stuck his finger in the empty bottle. It swung back and forth on his knuckle. "Maybe something we won't draw too much attention with."

"Like what?" said Roger.

Nate let the beer bottle tap against his knees. "I'm thinking maybe we should pool our resources."

TWENTY SEVEN

They gathered in the lounge Saturday evening. Veek kicked the fire door shut, blocking them off from the hall. Roger set his BluRay player on a chair while he hooked it up to the flatscreen. The others dragged two of the couches over in front of the television.

Clive glanced at the movie next to the player. "*The Incredible Hulk*?"

"The Hulk rocks," said Roger as he pushed a last cable into place.

Nate flipped it over and read the fine print on the back. "Is this the good one or the bad one?"

"They were both bad," said Veek.

"Oh, don't mess with his superheroes," said Debbie.

"It's the good one," Clive announced. He glared at Veek in mock anger.

Nate handed the movie to Roger, who dropped the disc into the loading tray.

"We're not really watching it, anyway," said Veek. "What's the big deal?"

"Could watch it when we're done," said Roger. "Love it when he punts Tim Roth across the field."

"I'd be up for that," said Clive.

"Me, too," said Xela.

"Anyway," Nate said, "let's talk mysteries first." He sat down on the arm of a chair near the television and faced the group. Xela, Veek, and Tim sat on the couch closest to him. Debbie, Clive, and Mandy were on the one behind them. Roger straddled one of the smaller folding chairs and rested his chin on his arms.

"So, we've all noticed weird stuff here," said Nate. "I was thinking if we all compared notes we might start to see some sort of bigger pattern or something."

"Something like what?" asked Tim.

Nate shrugged. "If I knew, it wouldn't be a mystery."

Roger put up two fingers. "What do we get out of it?"

"I don't know. Answers?"

"It'd be cool if there was a bunch of Nazi gold buried here or something," said Veek, "but I wouldn't hold your breath."

They all chuckled. Mandy raised her hand. "Is Oskar okay with all this?"

Nate shifted on the arm of the chair. "To be honest," he said, "no. A couple of us have tried to talk to him about it, but he seems pretty dead-set on keeping things in the dark. He kind of implied if we dug around too much we could get evicted."

"He didn't imply," said Veek. "He openly told me."

Mandy's eyes went wide. She stood up. "I can't be part of that," she said. "I can't get evicted."

Nate put up a hand. "We're just talking," he assured her. "He can't evict us for talking. It's just the more active stuff."

"You sure?"

"As sure as I can be."

She sat back down, but she didn't look relaxed anymore.

Nate talked about the possible sub-basement, and about calling the Department of the Interior regarding the plaques. Then, for those who hadn't heard it, he told the story of running into Kathy the actress who had pretended to be Toni the property manager. Veek also mentioned her search for P.T. Kavach.

Roger raised his fingers again. He looked confused. "The building's named Kavach?"

Veek shook her head. "Didn't you ever notice the big letters over the door?"

He shrugged. "Never look at that stuff. None of it's ever important."

"Anyway," Nate said, "we're guessing P.T. Kavach is one of the architects or original owners or something, but we can't find anything on him."

"Where'd you get the name?" asked Tim.

"Off the cornerstone." Nate flipped though the legal pad on the chair next to him and pulled out a photo Veek had printed out. He handed it to Tim, and Xela leaned over to peer at it. Mandy peeked over the older man's shoulder. "We have no idea who WNA is. Veek thinks PTK is P.T. Kavach."

"It's not PTK, though," said Mandy.

Debbie shook her head. "Nope."

"What?"

"That's not how you read monograms," Mandy said.

"Yeah," Xela said. "The big letter in the middle, that's the last initial. It's WAN and PKT."

"I think they're right," said Tim. He handed the picture back.

Veek looked at it. "That's kind of silly."

"Didn't y'all ever have a monogrammed sweater when you were a girl?" asked Mandy. "Or a purse or schoolbag or something?"

Veek stared over her glasses at Mandy. "Do I seem like the sweater and purse type to you?"

Nate sighed. "Okay," he said, "so...now we know nothing about the people who built this place."

"Have you tried the Hall of Records?" asked Clive. "Public Works has got to have building permits or something."

"I put in a couple of requests," said Nate. "Haven't heard back yet on any of them." He shoved the photo back into the legal pad. "Has anyone noticed anything else odd about their apartments? Things that just seem a little off or unusual?"

They shifted in their seats. Clive cleared his throat. "You know how we took all those measurements last weekend?"

Nate nodded. So did everyone else.

"Well, I was looking over them and noticed something else. Not only do all of our apartments have different layouts, they're all different sizes."

"I thought your place looked bigger," Nate said to Mandy.

Clive nodded. "Mandy's is the biggest, yeah. But there's a couple inches difference between all of them."

"Isn't that just, like, a plus or minus thing?" asked Xela. "You know, some operator error with the tape measure or something?"

He shook his head. "That might change things an inch here or there at the most. I'm talking five or six inches."

Nate drummed his fingers on his thigh. "D'you still have all those numbers?"

"Yeah. I can shoot you a copy."

He nodded. "Maybe we can spot a pattern or something."

Mandy raised her hand. "Does the elevator count as a mystery? I don't think it's ever worked."

"It's never worked while we were here," said Debbie.

Nate tried to recall his moving-in day. "Oskar told me it's never worked while he was here."

"I'm not sure Oskar's a trustworthy source," said Veek.

"Maybe there is no elevator," said Xela. "It could've been removed decades ago. It might just be an empty shaft."

"Elevator's in the basement," said Roger.

Veek's eyebrows went up. "How do you know?"

"LED flashlight," he said. "Lights up the whole shaft through the window in the door. Checked it out one night right after I moved in. You can see all the cables, but no car." He shrugged. "It's not on any of these three floors, so it's in the basement."

Tim frowned. "Does the elevator go to the basement?"

"Technically, the elevator doesn't go anywhere," said Nate.

Xela smirked. "Wiseass."

"If it does, it'd be behind those big double doors," said Veek. "It's too close to the front of the building."

"I'm thinking we might try to get into there next weekend," said Nate. "We just need to figure out a way to get through the locks and chains."

"I can help with that," said Roger. "I can pick locks."

Tim raised an eyebrow.

"Seriously?" Nate asked.

Roger nodded. "Oh," he said, "Love this bit." He pointed to the screen, where Ed Norton raced through a Brazilian city with Tim Roth and a special ops team in hot pursuit.

"I've got something else," said Mandy.

"Shoot," said Nate.

"Well, it's not in the building," she said. "It's just something... I don't know. It kind of bothers me." He gestured for her to go on and she shrugged. "I think there's a guy watching the building."

Tim coughed. "What?"

"I've seen this guy hanging out a couple times. He just sits in his car. Sometimes he's using a laptop. A couple times I've caught him looking at the building with binoculars. Like a peeper."

"The guy in the green car," said Clive. "He's always hogging two spaces."

"Yeah," said Nate. "I've seen him, too."

Tim sighed. "I can answer this one," he said.

"You know him?"

"Sort of." He looked at Nate and glanced over at Roger. "I wasn't entirely honest with you guys about deciding to start a new life. A lie by omission."

Roger bent his middle finger, pressed his thumb against it, and popped the knuckle. "What'd you leave out?"

The older man drummed his fingers on the arm of the couch. "A month before I got the buyout offer, I found out my wife was sleeping around. Some guy she'd met at work."

Debbie's face fell. "Oh," she said. "That's awful."

Tim nodded. "We separated. She moved in with him. When the offer came, it seemed like a real godsend. A chance to pack up and move out. So I filed for divorce, sold the company, and here I am."

"So the guy's, what," asked Veek, "her new boyfriend?"

Tim shook his head. "He's a private detective. She knows she's fucked once we walk into divorce court—pardon my language, ladies—so she hired him to spy on me. He's been keeping tabs on me twenty-four-seven for the past month. If he can get something good, her lawyers can spin it to look like I drove her away or some bullshit."

"What a bitch," said Roger.

"Yeah," he agreed. "Anyway, just ignore the guy. I'm hoping he'll hurry up and get lost sometime soon. And no random displays of affection, please. That's all I need is for her to pull out pictures of me getting hugged by a sexy young thing. They'd have a field day with that."

"Our love will remain a secret," Xela promised. "And I'll stop hanging my underwear in your window." She blew him a big kiss across the room.

"Well," said Nate, "that's solved. Next?"

"I can tell you two things I noticed, once Nate got me looking," said Tim.

"Yeah?"

He nodded. "There's a subsonic hum in my apartment."

Veek raised her eyebrows. "And you know this how?"

"I've got some recording equipment. It messes up the microphones. Makes their diaphragms vibrate all the time, like a white noise generator."

Nate scribbled it down on the legal pad. "Is recording another hobby of yours?"

He smiled. "I play some guitar now and then."

"What's number two?"

Tim pushed his hips into the air and pulled something out of his pocket. It looked like a credit card made of clear plastic. When he held it up to the light Nate could see some concentric circles and dozens of fine lines. The inside of the circles blurred in the light like a cheap hologram effect.

"I found this in the back of my briefcase," he said. "I used to go hiking a lot when I lived back east, when I was younger. Ended up carrying it with me when I started spending more time at the office."

He handed it off to Veek. She set it flat on her palm and Nate realized it was a compass. Her eyes went wide. So did Clive's. "Holy crap," he said.

Veek handed it to Xela. Debbie and Roger leaned in to get a look. Nate stepped forward and looked over her shoulder. The blur wasn't a hologram.

The needle of the compass spun. It wasn't moving at Cuisinart speeds, but it wasn't slow. Xela tilted it while he watched. The needle showed no sign of slowing down.

"It stops spinning if you move it outside," said Tim. "You can just hold it out a window and it stops."

Xela dashed for the window on the other side of the lounge. Roger went with her.

"That doesn't make sense," said Veek. "If there was a magnetic field that strong here, half our electronics wouldn't work.

"Would it need to be that strong, though?" asked Clive. "It doesn't take much to move a compass needle."

"Not much when you're close to it," Tim said. "The whole reason compasses work is because the entire planet's one big magnet. Compared to that, see how close you need to get to a fridge magnet to do anything."

"It stopped," called Xela from the window. "Works fine outside."

"Anything else?" Nate looked at them.

"Mutant cockroaches," said Debbie.

"Noted," said Nate. "If you have green cockroaches, count their legs. We've got a weird mutation here."

"Actually," said Debbie, "has anyone ever seen a normal cockroach in their apartment? Or anywhere in the building?"

They shook their heads. Debbie's lip twisted. She looked at Nate and shrugged.

"Okay," said Nate, "I guess the only other question is...who wants to help us figure all this stuff out?"

Tim's hand went up. So did Xela's. Roger raised two fingers as soon as he saw Xela's go up. "I've got a gig starting this week," he said, "but I'll help where I can."

"You know we're in," said Debbie. She and Clive smiled.

Nate looked at Mandy. She shook her head. "I'm sorry," she said. "I won't tell on all y'all or anything, but I can't get evicted. I'll never get another place."

"It's okay," he said. "Believe me, I get it."

"I like hanging out and talking about all this, but I just can't do anything else."

"So," said Roger, "we got a couple weird rooms, mutant bugs in the walls, and our power's coming out of the air or something."

"That's about it, yeah," said Nate.

Roger nodded. "Cool. Anyone want to get a pizza or three? I'm starved."

"If you get pizza," said Tim, "I'll buy the beer."

"I'm in," said Xela. "Can we get one with no meat?"

Roger raised his eyebrow. "You a vegan?"

"Vegetarian," she said. "Don't worry. Order your burnt cow and pig, I won't give you a hard time about it."

Clive grabbed the remote for the BluRay player and restarted the film. He glanced at Veek. "Really think this film's as bad as the Ang Lee one?"

She shrugged. "I never saw it, to be honest. I just heard a lot of people didn't like this one, either."

"Yeah, well, a lot of people are stupid. This movie's just action and fun."

TWENTY EIGHT

Monday, Nate tried to concentrate on returned mail and addresses. His work dragged until he realized he was comparing the name on each form to the monograms on the cornerstone. He tried to focus and got two bundles done by the end of the day. It was slightly more than the days when he'd completely blown off work.

On Tuesday he got two bundles of returns sorted, cross-referenced, and updated before lunch. He felt so productive he spent the first hour of the afternoon sending follow-up emails to the office of Public Works. He also scribbled down the address in case he decided to go look things up in person. After that he plowed through a stack of returned issues of the magazine. Then he spent half an hour Googling his home address, looking at more old pictures of the neighborhood. The Kavach Building was in all of them. It looked the same.

At 4:35 Nate accepted he wasn't going to get anything else done before the end of the day, which meant he was done until Thursday morning. He shifted the bundles left in the mail tote and tried to make it look like as much work had been done as possible. He added to the illusion by moving a bundle into each of the other return crates. He adjusted the pens and loose return slips on his desk to maximize the appearance of work in progress.

While killing the last ten minutes of the work day, he found a pack of index cards in the top drawer of his desk. The plastic wrap was still sealed and a generic price tag was stamped onto it. The tag was crooked, and one corner hung over the edge just enough to collect dust and hair on its sticky backside. The cards came in an assortment of colors, divided between white, blue, yellow, pale green, and pink. The colored cards struck a chord.

Nate had listened to Jimmy talk about screenwriting dozens of times. It was a topic that came up at least every other week since the intern was one of Hollywood's great unsung geniuses. Jimmy read two different screenwriting magazines, frequented several websites, and had spent hundreds of dollars on books and seminars. He read at least two screenplays a week by people with names like Haggis, Black, Payne, and a pair named Kurtzman and something—all of whom were apparently hacks of the highest order, even though Jimmy was always eager to read their stuff. One wall of his apartment, he claimed, was covered with colored note cards representing character elements, story beats, redemptive moments, and other terms that meant nothing to Nate.

To the best of Nate's knowledge, the only thing Jimmy hadn't done was actually write something.

The idea of color-coded note cards stuck with Nate, though, when all the other talk of changing how Hollywood worked had faded into a pleasant background hum. It was a visual way to organize information. A cheap, easy way to do it, too.

He slipped the cards into his backpack, then added a roll of tape and a pair of Sharpie markers. When he waved goodbye to Eddie in the hall he found he felt remarkably good about stealing office supplies.

Nate spent most of Wednesday afternoon scribbling on index cards. Yellow cards would be for history-related mysteries, he decided, while pink ones would be for modern ones like Oskar and Toni-Kathy. Blue would be unexplained phenomena like the lack of power lines, the magnetic field, and apartment 14 with all its padlocks. Things that were just odd about the construction would go on white cards.

Green he saved for a class of mystery they hadn't discovered yet.

Nate stood by the window and used the entertainment center as his tabletop. He wrote out phrases like COLD WALL, SUICIDE ROOM, SUB-BASEMENT, and NO ONE DREAMS. In an hour he'd burned through half the blue cards. An hour after that half the package was gone.

It was after sundown when he started taping them to the wall. The only area big enough to work on was the section between the kitchen and his closet door. The paint felt tacky in the early-summer heat. The cards almost stuck without tape.

It was random at first. He just slapped them on the wall with loops of scotch tape. Then he gathered them by color. When 14 PADLOCKED 4X ended up next to SUICIDE ROOM he rearranged them all in the same layout as the apartments. He wrote up six more blue cards marked MUTANT GREEN COCKROACH and stuck them everywhere he'd seen one of the bugs.

There was a pattern here. He was sure there was.

He wanted to show the index card array to Veek, but it was after midnight. She was probably asleep. He should be getting to bed, too.

He also knew he couldn't risk leaving it up for Oskar to see. *If I was smart,* he thought, *I wouldn't've done it on the wall in front of the door.* Of course, there wasn't much other wall space in his apartment with furniture in there.

His phone didn't have a great camera, but it was good enough. He turned on all the lights and took a dozen photos of the arranged cards. Once he felt safe, he pulled them down.

He pulled at the blue card marked MYSTERIOUS HUM and it clung to the wall. The tape had bonded with the latex. He gave it a jerk and the card released its grip with a *pop.* Then he frowned.

Where the card had been, the paint had stretched out and formed a bubble the size of a grape. It was like a blister on the wall. Nate looked around and realized he'd made four or five puckers in the paint while he pulled cards off the wall.

Nate poked at a bubble. It sank back into the wall but left a circle of wrinkles in its place. He tried to press them flat against the underlying plaster. Some of them faded into the texture of the wall, others got even more prominent. He rubbed his finger back and forth to see if he could smooth out the larger wrinkles.

One of the folds tore and rolled up under his finger. He bit back a swear. The blister of paint became a loose triangle surrounded by a saggy circle. There were so many layers of paint in the triangle he could feel the thickness to it, like a heavy trash bag. Beneath it was raw plaster, like a wall of chalk.

He tugged at the triangle. Rather than breaking off, it grew. The rubbery paint peeled away and the patch of plaster doubled in size. It was the size of his palm.

Nate was split between panic and the fascination of watching the paint come away in such a perfect sheet of latex. He gave a gentle pull and the triangle of plaster grew again. It was four inches on each side now. He shifted the tension and tried to guide the tearing edges back in on themselves. Instead, the gap in the paint curved in a wide arc to swallow up one of the other blisters. He now held a piece of latex the size of a phone book. The edges left on the wall had pulled up, too.

"Shit," he said.

He pressed his hand against the wall and pulled the triangle up. Most of it tore off against the edge of his palm. One strip, almost three inches wide, peeled away up along the wall. He was taking in a breath to swear again when he saw what was on the plaster.

1,528,

It was written in paint, or maybe ink. Whatever it was, it was thick enough he could see the edge of it raised ever-so-slightly above the surface of the plaster. Where the latex had stretched up he could see the edge of another number, just past the eight.

The numbers were on the plaster. Under fifty or sixty years of paint. Maybe more. They could've been written when the building was still under construction.

Nate looked at the jagged hole in the paint. There was still a chance he could fix it if he stopped now. At least one of the paint cans he'd seen down under the cellar stairs would have some of the beige that coated every room. Enough to patch a hole a little bigger than a phone book, at least.

Probably not enough to do half a wall.

He pinched the loose edge of paint by the last number. It eased away from the wall. He pressed his head close to the gap.

Past the comma was what looked like another two, or maybe a three.

Nate's fingers closed on the flap and pulled. The latex came away with a faint sucking sound as air rushed in between the plaster and paint. The first piece was the size of a t-shirt when it broke away under its own weight. He grabbed at the loose edges on the wall and the paint peeled away in a wide arc. The gap opened up until the leading edge hit the door frame for the closet. Then it followed the boards down to the molding. This piece was the size and shape of his leg. He pulled in the other direction and the paint came off the wall in a wide swath.

It took him twenty minutes to tear all the paint off the wall between the kitchen and the closet. One strip had curved up toward the front door. There were some odd shapes left around the power outlet. He'd been surprised when some of the paint had come away to reveal the plate around the outlet was made of wood.

From three feet up the wall was covered with numbers.

It looked like one big equation. Not a particularly complex one, from Nate's limited knowledge of mathematics, although there were a few symbols he didn't recognize. It was all large numbers, though. He followed it as best he could down to the final figure.

1,528,326,500 ± 5000

TWENTY NINE

Veek answered her door with a plaid robe wrapped over her sweatpants. Her glasses were on, but her eyes blinked away sleep behind them. "What do you want?"

"You have to come see this," Nate told her.

"See what? It's two in the morning."

"You won't believe me if I just tell you."

She scowled. "Just tell me."

He took a breath. "You know what you said about the power lines? How I just needed to see it for myself?"

Her face softened. A little. "Yeah."

"You have to come see this."

Nate had peeled the rest of the paint off his studio walls. He'd dragged his shelves into the center of the room to expose as much wall as possible. His trashcan stood near them, filled with scraps of old latex.

In a few places the plaster had fallen away, too, to show wooden planks or bricks.

"Oh my God," she said. Her voice was half amazement, half sadness. "What did you do?"

He set his hand on her shoulder and turned her to the wall of numbers. Her eyes widened. "Oh my God," she said again. The tone was different this time. "What is this?"

"It was under the paint," he said. "Look over here."

There was another equation on the wall above his desk. This one had more symbols in it and fewer numbers. Veek stared at it. "What does it mean?"

"Not a clue," he said, "except I'm pretty sure it doesn't have to do with bricks or plumbing."

She stepped closer and pointed at one symbol, an upside-down **y**. "I've seen that before, I think." She tilted her head. "Damn, I wish I'd paid more attention in math class."

"I don't think this is math," said Nate. "I mean, it's math, yeah, but I think this is all physics or something. I'm just not sure what it is. I remember some basic stuff. Mass times velocity equals force, that kind of stuff."

"It's mass times acceleration."

"Same thing, right?"

"Yeah, you've proved your point. This is way beyond us." She frowned.

"What's wrong?"

She looked at the walls again, then looked at him. "What are the odds of this?"

"What do you mean?"

"I mean, think about it. Isn't it sort of stupid-convenient that Scooby's looking for weird stuff about the building, peels the paint off his walls, and finds weird stuff?"

He blinked. "You think they're fake?"

"No," she said. "No, I believe you. Doesn't it just strike you as a crazy coincidence, though? It's like...it's like reaching into a jar of marbles and pulling out the one blue one without even looking."

"Ahhh. Yeah, I see what you're getting at." They studied the walls for a moment and Nate's mouth opened. "Unless..."

"Unless what?"

He rolled his hand in front of him. "That's assuming there's only one blue marble," he said. "If all the marbles are blue, then it's not a coincidence at all."

She looked at the walls. "You think?"

"Only one way to know for sure."

A few minutes later they were in Veek's apartment, attacking the wall across from her massive computer. Nate slit the paint across the wall with a kitchen knife. They worked the gash with their fingernails until the latex came up and they could pull it away. The paint was more brittle in her apartment because of the cool air, and they couldn't peel off a piece larger than a paperback before it snapped off in their hands. Veek grabbed her kitchen trashcan and they started to fill it.

They tore at the wall's skin for twenty minutes. More than half the paint was gone. There was nothing but bare plaster.

"Damn it," said Veek.

"Hold on," he said. "There was only stuff on two of my walls."

"Yeah." She looked at the wall by her door. "I guess I can kiss my security deposit goodbye."

Nate carved a large X into the wall and they peeled the paint away. A circle of plaster grew. It was the size of her computer monitor when she gasped.

Numbers stretched across the plaster, written in the same black paint. They pinched and tugged at the paint until they'd revealed a line of figures.

66–16–9—4—1—89

He glanced at her. "What do you think it means?"

"Maybe there's a computer down in the basement," she said, "and we need to keep punching the numbers in."

"Very funny," said Nate. "Is it math? Sixty-six minus sixteen minus..."

She shook her head. "I don't think so. It's not like yours." Veek tilted her head, as if it would give her a different view of the numbers. "Those were equations, but I think this is some kind of code."

"Maybe. You think it's numbers for letters?"

"Not unless you know what the sixty-sixth letter of the alphabet is." She pulled at another loose edge of paint and a section the size of her hand came away. There was nothing beneath it, or under the next piece she peeled off. "I think that's all there is."

Nate turned his head. "The wall behind your computer?"

Veek looked at the wide desk and her lips twisted up. Then she nodded. "Give me a minute to shut everything down and get it unplugged."

Half an hour later her trash can overflowed with latex scraps and they were looking at another set of equations. This one was so complex they couldn't even follow it. At the bottom, however, it broke down to something they could understand.

$$\sigma = \underline{0}$$

"So," Nate said, "is zero good or bad?"

"No clue."

"Any idea what that symbol means?"

"I'd look it up, but we unplugged the computer and the wireless server."

He stared at the equation and tried to force his brain to understand it. There were too many symbols and even the numbers seemed huge and alien. It reminded him of old sci-fi movies, when the genius professor would have a chalkboard covered with some gigantic calculation. Just like when he watched those movies, he had no idea what the equations meant.

"We need to look at other apartments," he said. "I bet there's something in every one of them."

She looked at the clock. "Yeah, but who else is going to be up at three in the morning?"

Xela answered the door almost immediately. She wore one of her paint-splattered tuxedo shirts and hid her blue hair under a backwards baseball cap. "Hey," she said. "I was about to crash. What are you guys doing up this late?"

"We want to peel your walls," said Nate.

"Never heard it called that before." She looked at them and managed a tired smile. "Normally I'd say buy me a drink and you're on, but—"

Veek whacked her on the arm. "There's something written on the walls," she said, "under the paint."

Xela's eyes got wide. "No way."

"Yes way," said Nate.

She led them into her apartment. A fresh painting stood on her easel in the center of the room. "Where do you want to start?"

It took close to an hour to strip all the pictures and photos from Xela's walls. Half an hour later they'd flayed the inside of her apartment. The skin of paint came away even faster than it had up in Nate's studio. They filled half a dozen plastic grocery bags with old latex.

Xela's apartment wore complex math on two walls. "It's one long problem," said Veek. She pointed from the bottom of one wall to the top of the next. "It's the same line of the equation here and there."

Nate stared at the math. "What the hell is it? I mean, I took some science courses and I don't ever remember anything this big up on the chalkboard."

"Maybe it's just thorough," said Veek. "You know, when you do something with Einstein's formulas, you assume everyone already knows what the individual letters are and how you reached them. Maybe this is covering everything."

"It's India ink," said Xela. She had her head close to one of the lines of numbers. "Heavy stuff. It lasts forever."

"So somebody wanted to make sure all of this was here for a long time," said Nate.

Xela shrugged and bit back a yawn. "Or it's just what they had handy. It's not hard to come by."

"Next room," he said. He glanced at the Xela's alarm clock. "It's getting close to five. People are starting to wake up. Maybe Debbie and Clive?"

Veek shook her head. "They don't have painted walls, remember? All wood."

"Damn. I wonder if Tim's up?"

"He might be," said Xela. "He wakes up pretty early."

Nate's head twitched.

"Oh, get your mind out of the gutter," she said. "I stayed up one night working on a painting and saw him go out running."

"Roger, maybe?"

"Gah," said Veek. "We're idiots. I bet sixteen's still unlocked."

It was. The three of them stood in front of the broad wall between the pillars. The cold wall.

Nate looked at Veek. "You sure this is a good idea?"

"If Oskar finds it, he can't prove it was us," she said. "Besides, they never rent this place anyway."

"I actually just meant cutting into this one." He nodded at the cold wall. Xela kept touching it and pulling her hand away.

"You think it's dangerous?"

Nate shrugged. "Not a clue. It's one of the more...tangible things we've found."

Xela slashed the wall with her matte knife. "Only one way to find out," the blue-haired woman said.

It took a few minutes for the three of them to strip the wall down to the plaster. A large **X** was painted across the center of the wall. There were four words, one in each of the four triangles it made, each in foot-tall letters. The one on top looked like Russian. Nate thought the left one was French. He couldn't even recognize the letters of the bottom one. The word on the right was in English.

DANGER

Xela coughed. "I don't suppose 'danger' is German for 'free beer' or something?"

"Not as I recall," said Nate.

"I don't think we should do anything else in here," said Veek.

"I agree," said Xela.

They pulled open the door and jumped.

Tim stood there in a t-shirt and running shorts, his hand posed to push the door open. He furrowed his brow. "What the hell are you doing?"

Nate let out the breath he'd sucked in. "How did you know we were here?"

Tim pointed up. "I live right there, remember? I got back from my run and you guys were making a hell of a racket."

"Told you," said Xela.

Nate guided the other man inside and closed the door. He gestured at the bare wall and Tim's eyes widened. They gave him a quick summary of their night.

Tim touched the naked plaster above the French word and pulled his fingers away. "Every room you've checked so far, huh?"

Veek nodded. "All three of ours and in here."

He looked at Nate. "Let me see."

They went up to Nate's apartment and Tim inspected the walls. Nate watched his expression. "Does it mean anything to you?"

"Not a thing. I was hoping it was just random scribbles but..." Tim shook his head. "I've seen enough of this sort of thing to recognize heavy-duty math."

"Yeah?"

Tim nodded. "One of the advantages of publishing a lot of technical books."

Veek crossed her arms. "So now what?"

"Give me ten minutes to wash off my run and get changed," said Tim. "Then we'll do my place. Maybe you should change, too." He dipped his head at Veek and Xela. Veek was still in her robe and sweats. Xela wore her flimsy tuxedo shirt.

"Yeah," said Veek. "Ten minutes would be good."

"I need some coffee if we're going to keep at this," said Xela.

"Get changed," said Nate. "I'll have coffee ready."

By quarter of six they were drinking coffee and tearing the paint off Tim's walls. Nate was worried the multiple rooms in apartment 26 would mean any messages would've been destroyed when the extra walls were added. Instead, they were a treasure trove. Every wall was covered with elaborate patterns of lines and shapes.

They stared for a few minutes and then Veek snapped her fingers. "They're wiring schematics."

Nate looked from her back to the wall. "What?"

Veek nodded. "Some of the symbols are sort of archaic, but I'd bet big money that's what they are." She pointed at the diagram. "That's a switch. I'm pretty sure that's a fuse." She tilted her head. Nate decided it was her thinking pose. She drew a circle around several items with her finger. "No idea what any of that stuff is," she said.

Tim rubbed his chin. "I think you're on to something."

"But what's it for?" said Xela. "What the heck does all this make?"

Nate looked at Veek. "What do you think?"

She stared at the walls.

"Veek?"

She blinked and glanced at him. "You know what this means?" She tapped the walls. "These were always here. Being set up like this is part of the original design."

"Or at least as far back as all this was painted," Tim pointed out. "They could—"

"*What in God's name haff you been doing?!*"

Oskar stood in the doorway with his fists clenched.

THIRTY

Oskar's nostrils flared. "Haff you lost your minds?" he growled. "Apartment sixteen is ruined!"

Nate opened his mouth and glanced at Veek. She was already looking at him. He decided it was better to keep his mouth shut and pushed his lips together.

Oskar glared at Tim's walls and clenched his fists even tighter. Then he took three slow, deliberate breaths. His jaw relaxed a bit and his hands opened up. "Haff you fandalized all your apartments?"

Nate kept his lips sealed and nodded.

Oskar focused on Veek. "I warned you about your crazy ideas, Miss Fishwanath." He shook his head. "I am going to haff to call the painters in."

"No!" said Veek. She gestured at the walls. "Look at this, Oskar. Aren't you curious? Don't you want to know what—"

Oskar dismissed her with a wave. "I do not," he snapped. "You haff made things bad for everyone now. Do you haff any idea how much this is going to cost to repair? The owners will be furious. You will all be efficted."

"No we won't," said Tim.

Oskar's eyes locked onto Tim's.

"We've redecorated," Tim said. "What we've done in our own apartments is within our rights as outlined in the lease. It's not specified what counts as 'damage,' so at the best you'll be able to deduct the expense from our security deposits."

"You think I cannot—"

"Try anything else and I'll take you to court."

The stout man sucked in a breath and held it.

"I'm going to go out on a limb and guess the owners wouldn't like the publicity of a court case," Tim continued. "Even a minor one. So no matter how angry you are, I suggest you take a few moments to calm down."

Oskar let out his breath. "Apartment sixteen—"

"—was my responsibility. No one else was there. First offense of a new tenant. I'm sure it can be excused, especially since I'm offering to pay for it."

Oskar's jaw moved back and forth. His eyes shifted off Tim to Nate, then to Xela, and settled on Veek again.

"I haff run out of patience," he said. "This is the last warning for all of you." He looked at the math-covered walls again. "I am going to call the painters. All your apartments will be painted."

Nate glanced at the walls and bit his tongue.

Oskar gave them a last glare. "And it is coming out of your security deposits." He turned and marched back into the hall. They heard him stomp down the hall and into the stairwell.

Veek let out a sigh of relief.

"You just saved our asses," Xela said to Tim.

He glanced at her and smirked. "Well, how could I let such a fine ass go to waste?"

"Okay," said Nate, "we need to take photos. Get all of this documented before the painters get here." He looked at Xela. "Your camera can do high-resolution pictures, right?"

"It can, yeah," she said, "but I can't."

"Don't tell me you're chickening out."

Xela shook her head. "No, I just...I've got class in two hours. I need to get showered and get over to campus." She shrugged. "Sorry."

Veek nodded. "I've got to get ready for work," she said. She looked at Nate. "So do you, don't you?"

He bit his lip and looked at the wall. "I could call in sick."

Tim raised an eyebrow. "Weren't you just complaining your hours had been cut?"

"We can't lose all this," said Nate.

"We also can't lose you," said Veek. "If you can't pay rent, this little investigation of ours is over."

He looked at Tim. "What about you? Could you start taking pictures?"

"A couple, but I've got a meeting at ten in Santa Monica." The older man shook his head. "Oskar probably can't get painters here until tomorrow at best. We can meet up tonight and get everything photographed."

Xela yawned and stretched. "But we are going to sleep at some point, right?"

"At some point," said Nate with a nod.

❖

It was the longest day of work in human history.

Once the excitement of discovery wore off and his regular life resumed, Nate was exhausted. He poured a cup of coffee and drank it in the break room. He took the second one back to his desk with him. The morning was an ongoing fight to stay awake. It was a relief when another mail crate arrived and he had to get up and walk around.

He ran timetables in his head while he stared at the addresses on his computer. When would Oskar call the painters? How many would there be? When would they get there? How long would it take them to paint an apartment? Would they scrape the walls first or just layer the paint on over the bare spots?

He skipped lunch and stretched out in his office chair. In one of the timetables he'd come up with all the walls had been painted by now. His head leaned back against the top of the chair and his eyes closed.

The faint hum of his computer blended with the rattle of the air conditioner and the rumble of traffic out on the streets of Hollywood.

Then he was on the roof of the Kavach Building with Veek and Xela. Veek wore a baggy orange sweatshirt and her dark hair was cut in a retro bob. Xela was naked, because they'd come up there when she was sunbathing. She'd changed her hair from blue to bright green. He tried not to stare at the small patch of emerald fuzz between her legs. "I wash it with cockroaches," she explained.

Veek nodded. "I would too, but I've got a bug thing."

"It looks totally different under black light," Xela said. "You should take a look."

Roger stood by the oversized machine room. He shook the top padlock on the door and it made a noise like the decked-in-chains ghost from *A Christmas Carol*. "Waste of time," Roger said. "Elevator's in the basement."

"All the cool stuff is in the basement," agreed Veek.

Xela grabbed Nate by the shoulders and shook him hard. He turned and looked, but all he could see was her green hair. He tried to twist away, lost his balance, and almost fell out of his chair.

"Easy, tiger," said Anne. She stood next to his desk. "Just thought you should wake up before Eddie makes his afternoon appearance."

He blinked a couple of times and glanced around. "I slept through lunch?"

She smiled. "You were out cold. It's almost two-thirty."

"Shit." In two of his timetables the equations were painted over by now. In one of them the workers were just getting started.

"You looked like you needed it," she said.

"Yeah, kind of. Nobody saw me?"

Anne shrugged. "New schedules, remember? It's just you and me today. We could have wild cubicle sex and no one would know."

He nodded and rubbed his eyes.

"Wow," she said. "You really are tired, aren't you?"

He looked up at her. "Sorry?"

"Never mind. You'll be kicking yourself later, though."

He blinked again. She patted him on the shoulder and walked back to her own cubicle.

Nate tossed one of the bundles of returned flyers into the bottom drawer of his desk. There was already one in there. Part of him acknowledged he was falling very far behind and needed to get caught up sometime soon. Most of him watched the clock and wondered how fast he could get home.

Eddie stopped by and lamented the amount of work getting done. Nate nodded, but didn't bother to argue. He processed a few dozen more returns and then started packing his bag an hour early. Anne peeked in at him. "Somewhere to be?"

"Yeah," he said. He tried to think of something more believable than the truth. "I'm trying to get home before my landlord goes into my apartment for some repairs."

Her face twisted up. "Oh, I hate that," she said. "People in your place with all your stuff."

He nodded and paused. "Would you mind if I...?"

"Go," she said. "I'll cover for you. Again."

"You rock." He slung his backpack over his shoulder. "Thank you."

"Get some sleep," she called after him.

THIRTY ONE

Nate fought rush hour and skimmed through three yellow lights before he made himself slow down. It took him over half an hour to get home. He drove up to the Kavach Building and was stunned to find an empty parking space.Tim and Xela waited for him on the steps. "Calm down," she said. "Nothing happened. They didn't paint anything."

Nate stopped. A wave of exhaustion made him sway for a moment. "You're sure?'

"Oh yeah," said Xela. She gestured at the building. "I've been home all afternoon and Oskar's growled at me three times about it."

Tim hopped down the steps and opened the gate. "They'll be here first thing in the morning, though," he said. "Roger got the paint off his walls and there's more math there. We tried to talk Mandy into it but she's just too scared of getting evicted."

"Roger's okay with it?"

"I've got him wrapped around my finger," Xela said, smiling. "I think I'm going to ask him to rob a bank for me." She held up her camera. "I've already got my room photographed. Veek isn't back from work yet. I was just going to start Tim's and we realized it was about time for you to get home."

"They're good pictures?"

"I took triples to be safe. Already checked on my computer. High resolution, perfect detail. You can see everything."

"Awesome." He hefted his pack and nodded to Tim. "Let me dump this and I'll meet you guys in your place."

Xela's camera was on a tripod when he walked next door to apartment 26. Two poster-sized pieces of white foamcore bounced extra light onto the walls. "Don't move around too much," she said. "Long exposures. Don't want to shake the camera or mess up the lights." She looked from the camera's small screen to the wall and back, then tapped the button. A moment later the camera chirped, the electronic sound of a shutter. Xela took two more shots and moved the tripod to the next wall.

There was a knock at the door. "Hey," said Veek. "Looks like we dodged a bullet."

Xela finished the fourth wall and carried the tripod into Tim's small living room. The others shifted back into the kitchen and helped move her bounce boards. "I'll have to go download these when I'm done in here," she said. "They're really huge at this setting."

Nate nodded.

Veek gazed around the apartment. "This is sort of...claustrophobic, isn't it?" she asked Tim. "The whole space divided up like this?"

Tim looked at the tiny kitchen they were clustered in. "Not much worse than a college dorm room," he said.

"It's a lot smaller than mine was."

"But I've got four of them," he said. "I've grown to like it. It appeals to my compartmentalized nature."

"What about downstairs?" Nate asked him. He pointed a finger at the floor. "Sixteen?"

"Locked up tight," said Tim. "I think Oskar made sure of that."

"We could ask Roger to pick the lock," Xela called from the other room. "That's what I figured we'd do."

Veek wrinkled her brow. "Do you really think he can do it?"

Tim shrugged. "We can let him try. I think the real question is, do we need to get in there? It wasn't math on the walls. It looked pretty simple and straightforward. 'Stay the hell out of this room.'"

"I think we'd rather have it than not," said Nate.

"If Oskar steps out, he'll see us," said Veek. "Straight shot down the hall."

"We'll save it for last," said Nate. "Maybe he crashes early."

"Second to last," said Xela. She picked up the tripod and shuffled through into the next tiny room of the apartment. "I promised Roger I'd do his last and have a drink with him."

Nate gave her a look. "Are you okay with that?"

"Don't worry, oh-captain-my-captain. Roger's kind of cute, but he's not one-drink cute."

"Does he know that?" asked Veek.

Xela nodded. "He's just laying the foundation."

They moved to Nate's room in time to catch the last of the sunset through his kitchen window. They held the foamcore and she got shots of the equation between the closet and the doorway to the kitchen. They shifted everything around to get the one above the desk.

"Mind if I grab some water?" asked Xela.

"All I've got is the tap," Nate said. "Sorry."

"Tap's fine," she said. "My last place was down by the toy district. The water there always came out brown." Xela flipped switches in the kitchen until her shirt gleamed. Her blue hair lit up under the kitchen's unusual bulb, shimmering like a special effect.

It looks totally different under black light.

"Where to next?" asked Tim.

Nate looked at Veek. "Want to get your place out of the way next?"

"Okay," she said. "I'm going to duck down and make sure I haven't left out a bra or anything."

Xela turned back to the doorway with her glass. She stopped to look at the other side of the kitchen. Her irises were black pools against the gleaming white of her eyes. "I'm guessing you want all this, too," she said.

They exchanged glances and she gestured at the stove.

Nate stepped into the kitchen and followed her gaze. He'd peeled the walls in there when he did the rest of his apartment and found nothing but bare plaster. He was so used to the oddities of his home he'd just worked by the half-light from the rest of the apartment. He'd never thought of turning the kitchen light on.

The wall above the stove was covered with phosphorescent letters. Each one was an inch tall, written in a thin, slanting hand. The letters were blurred and arranged in some sort of code.

"Son of a bitch," said Nate.

Xela blinked. "You didn't know this was here?"

THIRTY TWO

The letters aren't blurred, Nate thought. *It's a different alphabet. Cyrillic or one of those.* The text wasn't a code, just a language he couldn't recognize. As he examined it more closely, he could see maybe two hundred words arranged in four paragraph breaks and a header. The block of text ended with a closing of some sort, perhaps a name, and a date in Arabic numerals.

1895

Veek was next to him. She tilted her head to her shoulder and back. "What is that? Russian?"

"Nope," said Tim, shaking his head. He looked at the glowing letters through the doorway. "Not Russian."

"You can speak Russian?"

He shrugged. "I can read it better than I can speak it."

"What sort of publishing company were you running?" asked Veek.

"One that published some Russian stuff." He glanced up at the light. "Must be some kind of invisible ink," he said. "A pretty good one to have held up for a hundred and twenty five years."

"It was sealed under the latex," said Xela. "Shrink-wrapped, pretty much."

Nate turned his head toward Xela, but his eyes stayed on the letters. "Can you get photos of this?"

Her lips twisted. "Maybe? It's a weird lighting set up. I've never done anything like this before."

"Please," he said. "I think it's important."

Her mouth straightened out into a faint smile. Her teeth gleamed white in the blacklight. "It might take a couple tries, but I'll get it."

He looked at Tim. "You're sure it's not Russian?"

"Positive."

"Any idea what it might be?"

He shrugged. "There's a couple of different languages that use the Cyrillic alphabet. Could be any of them. I just know it's not Russian."

Xela shooed them out of the kitchen so she could work. She asked Tim to run to her apartment for a few sheets of foamcore they could use as reflectors to get as much of the black light on the words as possible. Once he came back she handed a white panel to each of them and posed them around the kitchen. The camera clicked again and again and she made minor adjustments each time.

"Okay," she said, "if I don't have it now, I can't get it. There's got to be a good shot in there."

Nate lowered his sheet of foamcore. "Are you sure?"

She nodded. "Sure as I can be. I can go look and give you a definite."

He nodded. Xela unscrewed the camera from the tripod and vanished out the door.

Tim stepped back into the living room and studied the equation for a moment. Then he peered at the words over the stove. "Written by the same person," he said.

Veek tilted her head. "What makes you say that?"

Tim pointed at the date on the Cyrillic message. "They write their numbers the same way. Whoever it is does their eights so they form a wide X at the center. They also put a seraph and a base on their ones."

"Doesn't mean it's the same person," said Nate.

"No," agreed Tim. "Neither of these would count as a handwriting sample. But I don't think it's just a coincidence."

Xela knocked at the door. "We're good," she said. "I've got two usable ones. On one the top half is perfect."

Nate's shoulders relaxed. "Still readable, though?"

She shrugged. "I can make out all the letters. I can't read it, so I guess so."

Nate's stomach gave a little twitch as he shut off the kitchen light. They headed down to Veek's apartment. Her desk still stood near the middle of the room. She'd left the computer unplugged.

"That's some setup," Tim remarked while Xela set up her camera.

"Scavenged," Veek said. "It's not as impressive as it looks."

He studied the computer. "You could've fooled me," he said. "Are those Playstations hooked into the system?"

Veek stiffened ever-so-slightly. If Nate hadn't been looking right at her, he wouldn't have noticed it. She didn't look at Tim when she answered. "You know a lot about computers?"

Tim shrugged. It was the practiced shrug of a man who didn't care one way or the other. "I proofed a lot of technical manuals," he said. "I know a lot more than some, but a lot less than the experts."

She nodded. "A friend set it up for me," she said. "I don't really know how they're wired."

"Sure," he said with a nod.

Roger got home from work a little after nine-thirty and joined them. A shiny leather case rested in his hand. "How do you want to do this?"

"Xela's going to need to download again," said Nate. "You open sixteen while she's doing that. She gets back, snaps her photos, and we lock the door behind us."

Roger nodded.

Veek looked at him. "You can do this?"

"Yeah. Pretty sure."

"Pretty sure?"

"Yeah."

"How is it you know how to pick locks, anyway?" asked Tim.

"Did this show a few years back and the best boy was always losing his keys," said Roger. "Useless guy. Had to cut the locks off the grip truck twice and I kept one of them. Just for the heck of it. Saw this movie about Houdini and it got me thinking. So I practiced on it and pretty soon I could unlock it." He shrugged.

Veek looked at her door and the switch on the back of the knob. "Think you can open those?"

"Lock's a lock," he said. "They all open the same way."

Tim raised an eyebrow. "How long does it take you?"

Roger shrugged. "Five, maybe six minutes."

Tim said nothing but gave a slow nod of his head.

"Done in here," said Xela. She twisted a knob and the camera came away from the tripod. "Give me a couple minutes to clear these out."

"Looks like you're up," Nate told Roger.

They opened Veek's door. The blank face of 16 stared at them from across the hall. Xela headed down toward the stairwell. Nate stood in the middle of the hall while Veek leaned in her doorway. Roger crouched in front of the door. He had a thin metal band inserted in the knob and was working a second one in. Tim stood next to him and watched.

There was a click as the second pick slid into the lock. Roger held the knob with his left hand and worked the pick back and forth with his right. His eyes closed as he focused. The faint rasp of metal on metal whispered in the hall.

"Use the prybar," said Tim after a minute. "That's what it's for. Put pressure on it."

"Bro, don't distract me," said Roger. "I know what I'm doing."

Another minute slipped by. Nate crouched by Roger. "How's it going?"

Roger didn't open his eyes. "Going as fast as I can," he said. "Told you, this could take some time."

"It'd take less time if you used the prybar the way you're supposed to," said Tim.

One eye opened for a glare, then closed to concentrate again. The pick shifted and sank a little deeper into the lock. Roger shifted his grip and tweaked the handle.

There were footsteps in the stairwell. Xela was back, clutching the camera. "You're not in yet?" she whispered.

"Just give me another couple of minutes," said Roger. "Maybe a little more."

Veek looked at Nate and rolled her eyes.

"Tick-tock, tick-tock," said Tim.

"You think you can do better, you're welcome to try," muttered Roger. His hands shifted on the pick again and a minute later there was a click as the lock opened.

"Finally," murmured Veek.

Roger turned the knob and pushed. The door to apartment 16 swung open. "Told you," he said to Tim. "Just under five minutes."

Tim smiled and bowed his head. "I stand corrected."

THIRTY THREE

After they finished photographing the wall in 16, Xela headed down to Roger's apartment and promised the others she'd have all the photos set up soon. Tim announced it was too late for an old man to be up and headed back upstairs.

"Just you and me, Velma," Nate told Veek.

She shook her head. "Just you, Scooby. I'm still exhausted from last night and I've got another project I need to work on."

"Seriously?"

"Yep."

"You must be raking in the cash with all this extra work."

She drummed her fingers on the door frame. "I lose a lot of it to taxes," she said after a moment.

Nate looked at her. "You freaked out when Tim asked about your computer. Just like you did when we first met and I asked about it."

"Speaking of freaking out, what happened in your kitchen?"

He smirked. "A pathetic attempt to change the subject."

"Your eyes bugged when you saw those words on your wall."

"You didn't think it was weird?"

"Weird, yeah," she said, "but in this place not weird enough to make you go all wide-eyed like Andrew."

Nate twisted his lips in thought. "Okay," he said, "this is going to sound crazy, but I think I dreamed about it."

She smirked. "What?"

"I had this dream with you and Xela—"

"Typical man."

"Not like that."

"Did we have clothes on?"

He paused and debated. "You did."

"Should I be relieved or insulted?"

"Hey, if you want to hang out naked I'm sure I'll picture you that way, too."

"Don't count on it."

"Anyway," he said, "Xela's hair was green, not blue, and she told me to look at it under the black light. She said it would look different." He shrugged. "And then I came home and we found all this stuff under the black light."

"Sounds sort of thin," Veek said after a moment.

"What?"

She shrugged.

"You don't think it means something that I have a dream about how things look under black light and then six hours later we find a message that's hidden except under black light?"

Veek shrugged again. "You also dreamed about your hot neighbor naked. What's the meaning there?"

"You're a lot more focused on that than I am."

"Yeah, so you say. Know what else?"

"What?"

"This blows your whole 'no dreams' idea out of the water."

Nate considered it. "No," he said. "It's just a new twist. I had the dream at work. I still haven't had a dream here."

Veek rolled her tongue across her teeth. It made her lips ripple. "You really think something about this place keeps people from dreaming?"

"Maybe."

"Again, it'd have more credibility without all the skin."

"Are you jealous or something?"

"You wish," she said. "What are we doing this weekend, investigation-wise?"

He glanced down the hall. "Maybe we should lay low this weekend. Give Oskar some time to cool down. We can all meet up to talk, but we probably shouldn't do anything, y'know?"

She nodded. "Sounds good. I might not have a lot of time, anyway."

"Okay."

Veek tipped her head back at her door. "I've got to get to work. Maybe I'll see you on the roof tomorrow for Friday sunset."

"Is that what we're calling it now?"

"That's what I'm calling it. G'night, Nate."

"Night, Veek."

Five minutes later, Nate was alone in his apartment. Not entirely alone. There were two big math equations on the wall. Equations he'd helped save from Oskar's uncaring maintenance.

He looked at the numbers painted above his computer. He still had no idea what they meant. It was like staring at a wall of Arabic or Japanese. There was something there, something people had written down for a reason. He just needed to learn what that reason was.

He went to the kitchen and looked at the gleaming paragraphs over the sink. There was no doubt in his mind it was a message. Not necessarily for him personally, but someone like him. Someone who would unravel all the mysteries of this place.

It had been a long time since Nate felt excited by anything. His life had been such a dull, repetitive echo of life that he'd forgotten what it was like when things were bright and interesting and new. Stupid as it sounded, he felt alive.

Anne was making a pass at me, he realized.

Nate stared at the glittering words in his kitchen for another moment. Four paragraphs of light, frozen on the bare plaster. Then he turned and reached for the switch.

And froze.

Just for a moment, on the far side of the apartment, he'd seen a flicker on the wall facing the kitchen. It was in the space next to his desk. On the wall that didn't have any math on it.

Nate stepped out of the door, but the flickering shadow didn't return. He glanced up at the bulb—the LONG LIFE WHITE bulb—to make sure it was still working. All the words in the kitchen were still there.

He looked at the far wall again, then drew a line back and forth with his eyes. The space where he'd seen the shadow was just too high. The bulb couldn't shine on it. He looked around for a moment and his gaze dropped. His white shirt had acted as a reflector. A weak one, but enough for him to glimpse another secret.

Damn lucky, he thought. The crowd in the kitchen earlier had blocked all the light. Whatever was on that wall would've been painted over and none of them ever would've known they missed a clue. He leaned back and tried to angle his stomach in a way that would bounce the ultraviolet rays across the apartment. The bare plaster shimmered. Not enough to read, but he could glimpse lines and patterns.

Nate looked around the kitchen for something reflective to shine the light across the apartment. He checked the living room. One of Xela's foamcore sheets leaned against a bookshelf.

He carried it back to the kitchen and stood under the black light. He angled the white panel at the far wall. The plaster rippled as thc ultraviolet rays washed over it and revealed a set of thick, messy lines. A moment later his mind turned the lines into words.

THEY HAVE FOUND US

THIRD STORY

THIRTY FOUR

"It's almost definitely blood," said Tim. "You can tell by the color. It turns jet black under ultraviolet light." He stepped back and looked at the full message they'd revealed with the foamcore bounce board.

THEY HAVE FOUND US

HURT MUST HIDE

PROTECT KAVACH

PROTECT THE WORLD

The words were low to the ground. The highest line was chest height. The bottom one was only two feet above the floor.

Nate stood in the kitchen, staring at the letters while he held the foamcore steady. He'd woken Tim up and dragged the older man over to his apartment. "Someone wrote in blood on my wall?"

Tim nodded. "Looks like it."

"Why?"

"On a guess," said Tim, "whoever it was knew the message would stay even if they cleaned up most of it."

"No, I mean why in blood?"

The older man pointed at the word **HURT**. "I think it was what they had to work with."

A cold chill raced through Nate. He glanced back at the kitchen window to make sure it was still closed. "If it's blood why can't we see it?"

Tim waved his hand in front of the wall and his shadow erased the words for a moment. "Whoever cleaned it up wasn't quick enough. A lot of it sank into the plaster. Then it got painted ten or twenty times and vanished."

"And it's still there?"

He shrugged. "Like Xela said, it was pretty much shrink-wrapped in paint. Even if most of the moisture is gone, all the key chemicals are there to set off a reaction."

Nate let the foamcore drop. The words vanished. "Son of a bitch."

Tim glanced at him. "If it's any consolation, I think we can say this was written over a hundred years ago. Probably around the same time as the rest of this stuff." He gestured at the math on the other walls.

"You think someone got murdered here?"

"If they were murdered, I don't think they would've had time to write anything." He shrugged again. "Unless maybe they murdered the other person. That doesn't fit with writing in blood, though."

"You're taking this really well," said Nate.

"It's not my apartment," said Tim. "And I'm not wigged out by the thought of someone dying over a hundred years ago."

Nate took a slow breath and nodded. "I should get Xela," he said. "We need photos of this."

Tim glanced at his watch. "It's past midnight. You sure she'll be up?"

He nodded. "She's a night owl."

"I'll wait."

Nate slipped down the hall to Xela's apartment. He knocked lightly on the door twice. When he didn't hear anything, he knocked again, harder. He paced back and forth while he waited.

A shadow flickered in the peephole lens. "Just a minute," called Xela.

He paced some more and glanced out the hallway window. It looked out over the building's front lawn and Kenmore. The street was still and silent. If the man across the street hadn't moved, Nate wouldn't have noticed him.

He looked down at the man leaning against the green Taurus. The private detective hired to watch Tim. The man stared back up at him with a dead expression.

Xela opened her door and Nate forgot the detective. "Please tell me you're not checking up on me because of the whole Roger thing," she said.

He shook his head and his eyes flitted up and down her body before he could help himself. Her hair was wet, making it an even darker shade of blue. She had on an oversized t-shirt that hung off one shoulder. It was soaked through in enough places that he could tell she wasn't wearing anything else.

When his eyes got back to her face she was giving him a look. "I've got a meeting with my advisor in the morning, so what's up?"

"I need you to take a few more pictures. It's important."

"Pictures of what?"

"There's more in my apartment."

"More words?"

"They're written in blood."

Her face went blank. "Let me grab some pants," she said. She ducked back into her apartment and left the door open. She grabbed a pair of paint-splattered jeans and yanked them up over her legs. Nate turned away, but not before she hiked the t-shirt up to her waist and flashed her ass. A moment later the collapsed tripod was in her hand, the camera still mounted on it.

Tim had his cheek against the wall when they entered Nate's apartment. He was looking along the wall where the letters were. There was no sign of them without the black light. "Definitely cleaned," he said. "You can just see the marks where they scoured it. Sloppy job. I'd say it was just as much a rush as the message was."

"Wow," said Xela. "You're a regular Sherlock, aren't you?"

He smiled. "Too many forensics shows," he said.

She glanced around the apartment. "Veek isn't here?"

Nate shook his head. "She's working on another side project."

"And you didn't tell her about this?"

"I figured I'd tell her tomorrow."

Xela shook her head and her lips made a tight smile. "She's going to be pissed."

She set up the tripod while Nate got the foamcore in position to reflect the blacklight on the wall. The shadowy letters wavered and faded like smoke.

"Oh my God," murmured Xela. The color drained out of her face. "That's blood?"

"Yeah," said Tim.

She looked at each of them. "What the hell's going on here?"

The two men shook their heads.

"Who are 'they'?"

Nate shrugged. "No clue."

"'Protect Kavach, protect the world,'" she recited. Her gaze flitted between them. "Protect the *world*?"

He nodded. "Whoever Kavach was, somebody thought he was important."

"Important enough to kill for," said Tim. "Or die for."

Xela took a deep breath and bent to her camera. She snapped two dozen photos before running back to download them to her computer. When she came back she gave Nate a thumbs-up. "Almost perfect," she said. "The darker letters photograph better than the phosphorescent ones. I got three great shots. They're even better than the glowing letters." She jerked her thumb at the kitchen.

Nate nodded. "Okay then."

She glanced at the other walls. "Are there any more?"

He shook his head. "I tried shining the light around the room. If there's anything else I can't find it."

"Something else to share with everyone Saturday," mused Tim.

They headed out and left Nate with a wall covered in dried blood.

Nate looked at the plaster. Without something reflecting the light, the words were hidden. He wondered about the person who had written them. He pictured someone in old-time clothes—a pinstripe vest and a bowler hat and wingtip shoes, maybe with a wide mustache—kneeling on the floor in front of the short bookshelf. In the mental hologram he created, the mystery man had a wounded arm, although the image flickered once or twice to a bleeding leg. The man dabbed his fingers on the wound and smeared blood on the wall. Were there footsteps in the hall? Was someone pounding on the door as he wrote his message?

Did he die writing it?

Who was Kavach? His boss? His friend?

Nate grabbed the bottom edge of his futon couch and flipped it flat. He spread the blanket across the mattress. Normally he set his pillow by the bookshelf, but tonight he tossed it at the other end.

His jeans and shirt landed on the desk chair. He folded the pillow in half, leaned back, and gazed at the wall. He closed his eyes and fell into a dreamless sleep.

He woke to someone knocking on his door. It was Oskar. And the painters.

THIRTY FIVE

When Nate got home from work, a heavy smell hung in the air of his apartment. The walls were smooth and unmarked again. All the words and numbers were gone, hidden under a thick coat of paint—maybe two coats—that probably had an innocent name like Antique White or Eggshell or Birchbark.

He looked at the blank walls and sighed. At least they'd gotten plenty of pictures. His bag landed on the futon and he spent a few minutes pulling open the windows. Competing scents of fresh air, sidewalk urine, and the bakery down at the corner all fought with the paint smell and overwhelmed it.

After half an hour the expanse of Eggshell was too much for him. It was like a blank banner reminding him what he'd lost. He left the windows open and headed up to watch the sunset.

He walked out onto the roof and Tim saluted him with a beer. "Did you get any sleep last night?"

"Some," Nate said. "Three or four hours."

"You look like you're doing pretty well."

He shrugged. "I got some sleep at work. It's not like I'm doing anything important there."

Tim grinned. "I could never sleep at work. I snore if I try to sleep upright."

Nate pulled a beer from the ice-filled cardboard. "You look like you're doing pretty good, too. Did you still wake up early to run?"

"Always."

"Freak."

"Force of habit."

Nate settled into the deck chair next to him. After a moment's thought, he used his heels and toes to pry off his sneakers and let them drop to the wooden deck. He wiggled his toes inside his socks.

"Feels good?"

"Oh yeah," said Nate. They clinked their bottles together.

"Where's Veek?"

"She's coming from Santa Monica."

Tim nodded. "That's right."

They sat in silence for a few more minutes. The clouds changed from white to gold as the sun settled down toward Century City.

"They painted my place," Nate said.

Tim nodded. "Mine, too."

"They were waiting for me when I woke up. They stood in the hall while I got dressed for work."

"I saw them," Tim nodded. "They finished your place just after nine-thirty, then they came over to mine. It took them two hours. All those extra walls and not much room for their rollers." From his position on the chair, he mimed a man trying to work with a long pole in a small space.

"Oskar?"

"Stood there the whole time but didn't say anything to me. He's calmed down a bit, but he's still pretty angry."

Nate swallowed some more beer. "Joy."

"It's a setback, yeah, but you'll get past it."

He looked over at Tim. "Can I ask you a question?"

"Sure."

"How did I become the guy in charge? Veek's been into this for over a year now. So's Clive. You've got a lot more experience being the boss. Why is everyone looking at me?"

Tim shrugged. "Because you're the guy in charge."

"That's not an answer."

"What do you want me to say? We secretly met and pulled your name out of a hat?" He shrugged again. "Sometimes everyone just understands who's in charge. Not often, but it happens. In business, in the military, in politics, all the people involved just get it. *This* is the person we all listen to. And that's you."

Nate drank his beer.

"I'm going to play grown up for a minute," said Tim. "Do you mind?"

"Somebody around here ought to. Might as well be the old guy."

"The old guy can still kick your ass," Tim said, gesturing with the neck of his beer. "Keep that in mind."

"Sorry."

"I dealt with a ton of different professionals over the years. Big guys and little guys. Every one of them thought they were the top of the world. The best at what they did. And some of them were. You know what made the difference?"

"Is this going to be about suits and power ties?"

Tim pointed with the bottle again. "The only thing that really mattered to them was achieving their goals. If they were going to get something, then they got it. If they needed to eliminate the competition, they annihilated them. They're the ones who succeeded, the ones everyone else looked to as an example."

Nate took a hit off his beer. "Are you telling me I have the eye of the tiger?"

"That's one way of looking at it, yeah. Somehow, solving the riddles of this place became important to you. And that importance—that enthusiasm—spilled over to the rest of us."

"Veek was interested, too. She was interested first."

"She was interested," said Tim with a nod, "but you *want* it. Getting the answers here matters to you."

Nate swallowed some more beer and looked at his friend. "Was that how you did things? Annihilating the competition?"

Tim took a hit off his beer as the sun approached the buildings of Century City. "For a while," he said. "For a long time. Thirty years or so. And then one day I realized there was more to life than grinding your opponents into the dirt."

"And hearing the lamentations of their women?"

The older man glanced at him and grinned. "Something like that."

"Sounds like getting out of publishing was a good move."

"You have no idea."

They heard the clomp of footfalls on the stairs. Roger stepped out into the sunlight. A six-pack of beer swung from one hand, a small bag of ice from the other. "Bro," he said. "Told you I was buying this week."

"You are," said Tim. "I figured we'd have extra people."

Roger nodded. "Saw Veek. Said she'll be up in a couple minutes." He set the six-pack down next to Tim's case, pulled one free, and twisted the cap off.

"Cheers," said Tim. He held out his bottle. The glass chimed.

Roger tapped Nate's bottle. "My apartment got painted. Sorry, bro."

"Not your fault," said Nate.

"Learn anything about all the math?"

Nate shook his head. "We found some other stuff, though."

"Yeah? Like what?"

They told him about the words written in old blood, revealed by the black light and now hidden again under a blanket of fresh Eggshell. Roger drank half his beer while they talked. "That," he said when they were done, "is some grade-A fucked up shit."

"Hey," said Veek from the fire door. She wore an untucked blue shirt and a loose necktie. With her glasses, the look was somehow less working professional and more uniformed schoolgirl. Nate glanced over and could tell the thought had crossed Roger's mind, too.

"I was starting to think you weren't going to make it," said Tim. He turned to the west, where the sun grazed the rooftops of tall office buildings.

She pushed Nate's legs off to the side and sat alongside his knees on the deck chair. The ice shifted as she grabbed a beer. She wrapped the tails of her shirt around the cap and twisted it off. It left a dark spot on her shirt. "You know," she said, "I've been looking forward to this all week."

Nate glanced at her. "Sitting up on the roof with a beer?"

"Sitting up here with everyone." Veek took a long drink and they watched the sky turn orange as the sun slipped between buildings. "They painted my walls."

"Yeah," said Nate, "they got everyone's, it sounds like."

"We could peel them all again," she said. "Just be more careful."

Tim shook his head. "No real point to it," he said. "We've documented everything in all our apartments. If we were going to do it again, we'd have to do it in other apartments."

"So," said Roger, "why d'you think somebody wrote in blood?"

Veek gave him a look. "Blood?"

"Yeah," said Roger. He dipped his head at Nate. "The words on his wall."

Her mouth fell open for a moment. "They were written in blood?"

"Not those," said Nate. "I found more."

She blinked. "What did it say?"

They told the story again.

Veek shook her head. "Why didn't you come get me?"

"You said you were busy, remember? I didn't want to bother you."

"You woke up Xela."

"I didn't wake her up," Nate said.

"But you went and got her."

"She's got the best camera."

Veek bit her lip and took a hit off her beer. "I thought we were in this together."

"I'm sorry," Nate told her. "You said you didn't have time, so I just figured it meant...well, you didn't have time."

"Bro," said Roger, cracking open a new bottle, "don't you know anything about dealing with women? They never say what they mean. No offense," he added to Veek.

"No," she muttered, "I said I didn't have any time."

"Right. Which meant you wanted to spend more time with him."

She lowered her bottle. "No, it means I was busy and didn't have time."

Roger gave her a wink and nodded.

"I have a job, y'know," she growled.

Someone cleared their throat. It was a prissy sound. "Pardon me."

Andrew stood back by the rooftop door. He was wearing his usual khakis with a polo shirt and a sweater vest. *Everything the man owns must be tan or pastel*, thought Nate.

"I've...I've heard a few things," he said. "I understand a few of you are looking at some of the oddities of our building."

Veek's eyebrows went up behind her glasses. "What do you mean?"

Andrew put his hands behind his back and scuffed at the tarpaper roof with his shoes. "I've lived here for almost three years," he said. "I try not to complain, and our Lord tells us to be patient, but I can't help but notice how many questions are never answered regarding our home." He looked up and his lofty tone reasserted itself. "I'd like to help. I want to find what's been hidden here."

Tim coughed. Roger and Veek looked at Nate.

"Tomorrow," Nate said. "We're all meeting up in the lounge to talk about stuff. You're welcome to join us."

"What time?"

"Around four."

Andrew nodded. "I'll be there."

"Bring snacks," added Veek with a straight face.

"Sweets encourage gluttony," said Andrew.

"Then you can bring chips," she said. "Or crackers. Something crunchy."

He thought for a minute and gave another nod. "I will. Have a wonderful evening," he said to them before heading back downstairs.

They all looked at her. "What?" said Veek. "The guy's never helped with anything and he's lectured me half a dozen times about being a single woman living alone. And it's Memorial Day weekend. He can bring chips."

THIRTY SIX

The lounge was full of people by the time Nate came down the back stairwell. Debbie and Clive sat on a couch, talking with Tim. Mandy stood nearby and listened without saying much. Xela and Roger chatted by the fire door. Veek stood up front with a gleaming Toshiba laptop on top of a stack of milk crates. She double-checked a cable running from the computer to the flatscreen.

Andrew had a plate of celery sticks. It sat on a low table and he stood next to it like a bodyguard. There was a small cup of white stuff in the middle of the plate. Nate thought it might be sour cream. Or maybe mayonnaise.

Sitting in the center of the couch opposite Andrew was a woman with too-black hair pulled back in a tight bun. On a guess, she was pushing eighty. She had a straight back and a few spots on her thin hands. An aluminum cane lay across her lap. It stuck out just enough on either side to make it uncomfortable for anyone else to sit on the couch. Nate wasn't sure if she'd done it deliberately or not.

Most of them waved or greeted him on the way over to see Veek. She looked up and smiled. "Hey," she said. "A couple of us were thinking of going over to get Thai food afterwards. You in?"

"Ahhh," he said, "I don't think so. I'm kind of tight since they cut my hours."

Her smile shifted. Not in a bad way. "Don't worry about it," she said. "I've got you."

"Thanks." He twitched his head in a look-behind-me gesture. "Who's the old woman?"

"That's Mrs. Knight from number four," said Veek. "She's the one who told me about the suicide in apartment sixteen."

"Right," said Nate. "Okay."

"I don't think she's as mean as she looks. Or sounds."

"Great."

"Check this out," she said. The computer screen had a dozen or so large thumbnails on it. "Xela's laptop and pictures, my know-how. Just click on any picture and it'll come up on the TV." She slid the cursor over a few pictures of the building and they snapped up on the big flatscreen one after another.

"Is this PowerPoint or something?"

"Not even that complicated. It's just a photo viewing program I ran through the television. And if you drag the mouse anywhere on this side..." She slid the little arrow to the right side of the screen and the pictures were replaced by the menu screen for a movie. It took Nate a moment to recognize *The Dark Knight*. "The movie plays underneath. If Oskar comes in, just act like you got up to adjust something."

"Aren't you the clever one," he said.

"Thanks, Shaggy."

He smiled at her and glanced over his shoulder. The others had closed in when he moved up front. "Hey," he said. "We must have half the building here now, yeah?"

They all glanced around. Ten people in the lounge was impressive.

"Mrs. Knight," he said, "Andrew, I'm going to go ahead with new stuff and maybe we can fill you guys in afterwards. Is that okay?"

Andrew gave a serene nod. He sat with his back straight and his fingers laced in his lap. Mrs. Knight looked less than pleased, but gave a little grunt that sounded affirmative. One of her hands settled on her cane, as if she wanted to be ready to lash out at Nate if he offended her with any other decisions.

"So," he said, not looking at the cane, "I think everyone's heard about the messages we found the other night. The other nights, really."

He glanced at the computer, tapped the mousepad, and the glowing letters appeared on the flatscreen behind him. "This was in my apartment, in the kitchen. Even with the paint removed, it was only visible under the black light bulb in there." He looked at his assembled neighbors. "I don't suppose any of you are fluent in...whatever language this is?"

"It looks like Russian," said Mrs. Knight. Her voice echoed in the lounge. It sounded like her vocal cords were made from the same pale rawhide used for dog toys.

"It's not Russian," Nate told her. "We know that much."

She put her palm on the center of her cane and rolled it back and forth on her thighs. "But it does look like Russian," she said.

He nodded. "I know. Same alphabet. But it's not." He looked at the rest of them. "I'll take the silence as a group no," he said. "If anybody knows anyone who speaks an eastern European language, see if they can read it, too. This is probably a name that could help us a lot." He pointed at the cluster of words above the date.

"Get to the blood letters," said Roger.

Nate slid his finger across the trackpad and tapped. The message appeared up on the flatscreen. "This was in my apartment, too," he said. "Tim's pretty sure it's written in blood. From what I've been able to read online about UV lights, I think he's right."

Mandy shivered. "Is it human blood?"

Nate shrugged. "We don't know for sure, but we think so."

Clive pointed at the screen. "Do you think 'must hide' means he needs to hide, or he's telling someone else to hide?"

"I don't know," said Nate.

"I read it like they were hurt and were going to hide from whoever hurt them," said Xela.

Clive shrugged. "I don't know. If you read it straight through it sounds like they're saying to hide Kavach."

"And we still don't know who that is," said Veek.

"What if they were talking about the building?" Roger tossed out.

Clive smirked. "How could you hide a building?"

"You could put sunglasses and a hat on it," chuckled Xela.

"In a forest," said Mandy.

Nate looked at her. "What?"

"It's something I heard once on a TV show when I was little," she said. "Where do you hide a tree? You hide it in a forest. So where do you hide a building?"

They all looked at her.

"In a city," said Tim. He rubbed his chin.

"But how do you hide a building?" asked Veek. "It's not like the building could go somewhere else when you're not looking. It's always right here."

"Not the building," said Andrew. He still sat with his hands in his lap. "Something in the building."

"Something or someone," said Debbie.

"If it's someone, I think we're at case closed," said Tim. "We're talking about something that happened a hundred and twenty years ago."

"I have a question," said Mrs. Knight. Nate nodded at her and she continued. "Does this have something to do with apartment sixteen?

"How so?" asked Nate.

She raised her eyebrow and her hand shifted on the cane. Nate took a half-step back. "You know what's happened in there?" the old woman asked.

"You told me about the suicide," said Veek. "The actress who killed herself."

Mrs. Knight nodded. "Andrea, in August of 1987. She'd just done a bit part in a Roger Corman movie. She was the last of them. I remember she had long blonde hair. Just gorgeous. Mine was very short back then."

"Hold on," said Tim. "The last of them?"

The old woman nodded again. "The deaths. That's why I thought your blood-words were connected. Isn't that what this is all about?"

An uneasy shudder passed through the room. Debbie and Clive clenched hands. Andrew threaded his fingers together and squeezed. Mrs. Knight didn't seem to notice. If she did, her only reaction was to relax her grip on the cane.

"Mrs. Knight," Nate said, "what exactly happened in room sixteen?"

She gave him a glance that made it clear her opinion of him had dropped a few notches. "The girl hung herself in the archway between the kitchen and the main room."

"Hanged," said Nate.

"I thought it was in the closet," said Xela.

Mrs. Knight shook her head. "The archway. I saw her up there after the police arrived, just for a moment."

Tim cleared his throat. "Why did you call her the last of them?" he asked again. "You said there were deaths. Plural."

The old woman nodded and her hands tightened on the cane again. "I was new in the building at the time, but there was all sorts of talk when it happened. Apparently the man who'd lived in the apartment before Andrea had shot himself seven months earlier. Same thing—it just came out of nowhere. A year before that another man had shot himself in there. And before him was a couple who drank poison together. That was in December of '84."

Nate blinked. "What are you saying? Everybody who lives there dies?"

Mrs. Knight sighed and he watched her opinion drop another notch. "No," she said. "Everyone who lives there has killed themselves. Usually in a year or less."

"Everyone?" asked Veek.

The old woman nodded. "I considered myself a bit of an Angela Lansbury at the time," she said. "I spent some time going over old crime logs one week. There've been twenty-six recorded suicides in this building in the space of thirty years, as far back as I checked. And all of them were in apartment sixteen."

THIRTY SEVEN

"I also have another question," continued Mrs. Knight. "You're saying someone wrote a message in blood and you could see it because of the black light in your kitchen."

"Right," Nate said.

"Did the person who wrote it know about the light? Is it just a coincidence they wrote it in your room and not another one or out in the hall?"

Nate blinked. "I never thought of it that way."

"Damn good question," said Tim.

"Actually," said Veek, staring up at the screen, "I just thought of something."

"Shoot," said Nate.

"It's in English."

"They spoke English here a hundred years ago," said Mrs. Knight.

"Right," Veek said, "but the other message is in Russia-stani or whatever. They might've been written by different people."

"Or," said Tim, "maybe the same person leaving a message for different people."

"Say what?"

He pointed at the image on the flatscreen. "Whoever wrote this thought it meant life or death. It was *urgent* their message be understood. They weren't going to write in a language the recipient wouldn't understand."

Debbie cleared her throat. It was a husky, mannish sound that seemed to catch her off-guard, too. "We're still kind of dodging the elephant in the room, aren't we?"

"How so?"

"'Protect Kavach, protect the *world*.' What's that supposed to mean?"

They all kept their mouths shut and stared at the flatscreen.

Mrs. Knight let out a cough that sounded more like a snort. "I think it's unlikely there was a threat to the world that somehow centered around this building."

"It could just be a figure of speech," said Veek. "Maybe it's just something important to whoever built this place."

"World's pretty important," said Roger.

"And again," said Tim, "it's an important message. You're not going to waste time with metaphors or figures of speech if you're leaving messages in your own blood."

There was a moment of silence.

"It doesn't say 'save,'" Nate said, "it says 'protect'."

"You're nitpicking," said Veek.

He shook his head. "No, think about it. Like Tim said, whoever wrote this was delivering a specific message. If I say 'save' it means the problem's already begun. You don't need to save someone from a burning building if the building isn't on fire yet. 'Protect' implies the problem, the threat, is only possible. It isn't actually here yet."

"I think the dark girl is right," said Mrs. Knight. "You're nitpicking."

"Hey," snapped Veek.

"I don't mean anything by it, dear," she said. "What's the proper term these days? Hindi?"

Veek bristled and Debbie set a hand on her arm.

"Anyway," Nate said loudly, "I think we can agree there was a threat of some kind, but we don't know enough to say who or what was being threatened."

"'cept the world," said Roger. "Sounds like the world was being threatened."

"Yeah," said Nate, "except for that."

They all murmured and looked at the warning again. Even Andrew shifted on his chair. He looked annoyed.

"Let me show you a few other things," said Nate. He peered at the computer. Xela had sorted the pictures by apartment owners, so it didn't take him long to find what he wanted. A click and one of the equations he'd uncovered filled the screen behind him. "Okay, these are some of the original things that got us peeling the paint off in the first place. A couple of us have gone over them, but they're way too advanced for us." He tapped the pad again and the second equation from his apartment appeared, the one with the long number at the end.

Mandy raised her hand. "Are they written by the same person?"

Nate looked at Tim and he nodded. "We think so," the older man said. "It looks like two different people wrote the math. One of them makes their fours with a triangle, the other one makes them open on top." He sketched two different fours in the air as he spoke. "The person who made the triangle fours also had eights with more of an X in the middle of them. We think that's who left the message over Nate's stove."

Mandy nodded.

Debbie leaned forward. Her eyes flitted back and forth over the big equation. Her lips moved. Nate looked at her. "Does this mean anything to you?"

One corner of her mouth pulled up for a minute, then relaxed. "I'm not a hundred percent sure," she said, "but part of that looks like a population growth equation."

"What?"

"Population growth," Debbie repeated. She walked to the television and sketched circles around a few figures with her finger. "It's more elaborate than your basic Malthusian model, but here's your birth rate, death rate, initial population..." She shrugged. "Not really sure what the rest of this is, though."

Nate looked at the numbers. "So you think this is a population?" He reached up and tapped the big number—**1,528,326,500 ± 5000**. His fingers left a small smudge on the flatscreen.

She shrugged. "Maybe. I'm just saying it looks like a growth equation."

Veek tilted her head. "World population?"

"Don't be silly," said Mrs. Knight. "The world passed that before I was born. I remember hearing about three billion just before I turned twenty."

Nate frowned. He glanced over at Veek. She was tapping away at her phone. "Got anything?"

She took in a breath. "Yeah," she said. "The world population hit one-point-six billion a few years after this place was built."

A low murmur swept through the room.

"Could be a coincidence," said Clive. "I mean, it didn't happen at the same time."

"It could also be what they were scared of," said Xela.

THIRTY EIGHT

"Nate," said Eddie, "I'd like to talk to you for a few minutes."

It was Tuesday after the holiday weekend. With the new schedule, only Zack and Nate were there, but Zack was out having lunch with a friend. Nate had hoped to do some more web searching for the Kavach Building, but Eddie talking for "a few minutes" could mean half of Nate's afternoon was about to vanish.

"Sure," he said. "What's up?"

Eddie moved into the cubicle and settled his swollen ass against the corner of Nate's desk, filling most of the space as he did. The scent of oil and pepperoni hung around him. He'd had the two-slice special at the pizza shop down on the corner for lunch. "This is kind of off the record," Eddie said. "Nobody knows we're having this talk."

Nate didn't let his mental groan show on his face. The only thing worse than one of Eddie's lectures was one of his man-to-man talks. The guy didn't even have enough empathy to realize how fake his attempts at empathy came across.

"You know things are tight right now," Eddie said. "They cut the hours and they're on me to cut back even more. I'm fighting to keep everybody here. You know that, right?"

"Yeah, of course."

Eddie nodded. He looked past Nate's shoulder to the stack of mail crates. There were three of them now. One straddled the other two to make a short step-pyramid of returned issues and bundled flyers. Nate had spent most of the morning looking up suicides and population predictions.

"You're falling way behind," Eddie said. "It doesn't help that you've never gone as fast as some folks upstairs think you could."

Nate was confident that most of the people in the upstairs office thought this job was done by a machine or farmed out to another company. He doubted anyone past Eddie and the accountant even knew his name. "I've tried to explain," he said, "that *their* estimates for how fast this can be done are impossible."

Eddie put his hands up. "Hey," he said, "I'm on your side. And normally it's no big deal if you're slow. But this is getting kind of extreme, don't you agree?"

Nate sighed and nodded. In all fairness, he'd done maybe ten hours of work in the past week. "Yeah," he said. "Yeah, it's getting a bit out of hand."

"I'm fighting to keep you and Anne and Zack on the payroll. But that means I need a hundred and ten percent from you guys, you know?" He waved a pizza-scented hand at the step-pyramid. "If someone came down and saw all this, they'd tell me to get rid of you."

"Right," said Nate. "Sorry."

"What's the problem? If it's something I can help with, just let me know."

Nate saw the potential minefield ahead of him. "It's not a problem," he said after a long three seconds. "I just haven't been getting a lot of sleep."

Eddie gave a sage nod. "Trouble at home?"

"No," he said, "nothing like that."

Eddie's brow wrinkled up for a moment. Then his face split into a wide grin. "Ahhh," he said. "Not getting any sleep *that* way."

A grenade landed in the middle of the minefield.

"No," said Nate. "No, that's not it at all."

"You dog," said Eddie. He gave Nate a punch in the shoulder that landed too hard. "What's her name?"

"Veek," he said without thinking.

"She hot?"

"I..." An image from his dream appeared in his mind. Veek in her horn rims and an orange sweatshirt, next to Xela, naked with green hair. He pushed the picture away as fast as it had appeared and nodded for Eddie's benefit. "Yeah. Yeah, she's hot."

"Man, I remember those days," said the heavy man. "Working all day, going home and being up all night." He put deliberate emphasis on *up*.

Nate tried very hard to keep an image of Eddie having sex from forming in his mind. It was like not thinking about a pink elephant. Or, in this case, a sunlight-deprived elephant that smelled like greasy pizza.

"Yeah," he said. "I'm a little obsessed. In a good way."

"Power to you, man," said Eddie. "Where'd you meet her? At one of those nights out the editors organize?"

"No," said Nate. He thought of marching straight ahead. Surely there couldn't be any mines left after that last blast. "She lives in my building."

Eddie's eyebrows went up. "Really?"

Nate nodded.

"Kind of risky, don't you think? I mean, if she's hot and willing it's sweet but if things go wrong, well, she's always right there."

"Yeah, it's not like that," said Nate. "We're both in it for the same thing, y'know?" He found religion and began praying he could get out of the conversation without creating any more details of his imaginary sex life.

Eddie grinned and nodded again. "Cool," he said. "Between you and me, I think it's great. But, y'know, I can't tell them that." He looked at the ceiling, then back to the pyramid of returned mail. "You've got to tell her no for a couple nights and start banging things out here at the office." He snickered. "Banging things out. That's pretty funny."

Nate nodded. "Pretty funny."

Eddie nodded again and his face went slack. The grin was gone as quickly as it had appeared. "Okay, then," he said. He leaned forward until his ass came away from the desk. It was like watching an avalanche in slow motion. "If you can get most of these done by next week, that'd be great."

"I'll try," said Nate. "It'd be a lot easier if I could have my hours back."

"Nah. Just work around them."

There was a corkboard by the Kavach Building's curving staircase. Normally it was decorated with rows of business cards or sheets of pizza coupons. When Nate got home all those things had been swept away and a fresh sheet of white paper was centered there. The handwriting was crisp and precise.

To All Tenants:

A family crisis requires that I leave town for a long weekend. I will be leaving Friday morning and will return the following Tuesday.

Under normal circumstances I would not be gone for such a long period, especially not with the recent bout of vandalism. However, I have spoken with Toni from the management company and assured her there will be no problems on par with the ones which occurred last week.

Please respect your fellow tenants. If there are emergencies, please contact Toni directly on her cell phone.

Oskar Rommell
Property Manager

He doesn't know, thought Nate. Toni-slash-Kathy's secret identity was still safe from the people behind Locke Management. Probably, he realized, because she'd never sent him anything about the building's history.

Oskar gone for almost five days. They'd have lots of time to investigate.

It was close to ten when someone banged on his door. Nate stood at the wall across from his kitchen, his arm stretched out to where the warning was written in blood. His eyes went to the door and he thought it was Oskar, here to grumble that Nate was thinking about the words under the paint.

The knock came again. Three quick, solid thumps. He squinted through the peephole and saw a fish-eye view of Roger. He looked excited.

Roger pushed his way in as soon as the door opened. "Bro," he said, "you're not going to believe this."

"What's up?"

"Okay, remember I told you I'm doing this low budget indie thing?"

Nate didn't remember, but he nodded anyway.

"Met the lead actress the other day. Smokin' hot lady. She's pretty cool, been talking with her and guess what? She speaks, like six different languages. One of 'em's Russian."

The picture Roger was trying to draw got a lot clearer.

"Okay," said Nate, "but it's not Russian."

"Yeah, but she speaks a bunch of those languages," Roger explained. "Russian, French, Italian. Figure I could ask her if she could help us out."

"I'm pretty sure it's not French or Italian, either."

"Bro, why not let her look and see?"

Nate considered it. "Do you think she would?"

"She's pretty cool, and it's not like we're asking for anything big. Just to look at a couple paragraphs and translate 'em, right?"

"Right." Nate gestured Roger into the apartment. He had hard copies of all the photos posted around his desk, and he pulled down an image of the glowing words. "You want a couple copies? I've got two versions of it."

Roger shook his head. "This is perfect," he said. "One piece of paper, nice and casual, no big deal. I can ask her tomorrow and we could know what it means by the weekend."

THIRTY NINE

The next knock came just before three the following afternoon. Nate opened his door to find Veek and Tim standing there. A large backpack hung from one of Tim's shoulders. Nate looked at Veek. "Shouldn't you be at work?

"I called in sick," she said with a sly grin. "Ready for adventure?"

"What do you mean?"

"Veek and I had a talk," said Tim. "We know there was a threat involving this building. Possibly a murder, too. It's time to get a bit more active."

"Meaning what?" asked Nate.

"We're going into the cellar," said Veek.

"Sorry?"

"The big room," she said, "and the sub-basement. We need to see what's in there."

"What about Oskar?"

"Oskar is being a perfect old-world gentleman and driving Mandy out to the Food 4 Less in Van Nuys," said Tim. "Their staff got hit with a bug and they're short on cashiers. She had a chance to get an extra shift if she could be out there by four."

"With rush hour on the 101, he's going to be gone for at least an hour and a half," said Veek.

"How much of that is true?"

"Enough that Mandy went along with it," said Tim. "The clock's ticking. Are you coming?"

The three of them made their way down the back staircase and into the basement. Nate stopped in front of the first padlocked door, the one across from the laundry room. "Want to start here?"

Tim nodded. "Get the small problems out of the way first," he said.

"So how are we getting in?" asked Veek. "We never went over that."

Tim pulled a worn leather checkbook from his back pocket and flipped it open to reveal an array of lock picks. They had the dull gleam that came from years of use. The picks slid into the padlock and his fingers adjusted them. It was a smooth and practiced technique.

Veek's eyes bugged behind her glasses.

"So," Nate said, "you know how to pick locks, too?"

"I published a book on it a few years back," Tim said. "One of those how-to things they used to sell in *Soldier of Fortune* and *Writer's Digest* and magazines like that. It seemed like a useful skill, so I played around with it."

"Y'know," said Veek, "there's only so many times you can fall back on the 'I published a book about it' thing and we're going to buy it."

He smiled. "It is a great catch-all excuse, though, isn't it?"

"How do you know how to do all this stuff?"

The pick gave a sharp twist and the padlock popped open. "Tell you what," said Tim. "You want to tell us what you're doing with that brute-force computer up in your apartment? You go first, I'll spill all my secrets next."

Her smile faded. "I don't know what you're talking about."

"Good call," he said. "I'm just a retired publisher. You would've been pissed."

The door opened and they looked in. A bucket filled with hand tools sat near the door. A very broken weed-whacker stood in one corner. A plastic rake leaned over it.

Three metal-framed shelves stood against the walls, filled with boxes. Half of them were labeled, either with the original packaging or with fat swipes of a magic marker. Halogen bulbs, hallway lights, pipe fittings, several boxes of fuses with different watts and amperages. Others had random codes on them or phrases like KATIE'S BED-ROOM that told Nate they'd been recycled from previous uses.

"Wow," said Veek. "A dirty storeroom."

"But now we know," said Tim.

"And knowing is half the battle," said Nate.

They all smiled. Tim pulled the door shut and snapped the lock shut on the hasp.

The ornate double doors stood at the end of the hall. The bar stretched across them, and the chain wrapped around it. "How do you want to do this?" asked Nate.

Tim swung the pack off his shoulder and pulled out a long, metal flashlight. It was one of the black ones policemen used. He handed it to Nate. "The easy way," he said. He turned to Veek. "Do you have your phone?"

"Yeah, of course."

"Get photos of the chain," he said. "How it loops around the bar and the handles. We want to be able to put it back the same way."

Nate aimed the light at the first bracket on the left, where the chain looped under the steel L and around the bar. Veek's phone clicked and Nate moved the light to the next crisscross of links.

Tim waited until they were done and the light settled on the bulky padlock. The picks slid into the lock and shifted beneath his fingertips. A moment later it popped open.

The chain clattered on the bar and handles as they unwound it. Tim pulled a pillowcase from his backpack, slung the chain into it with the padlock, and dropped it in the corner. He wiped some rust on his jeans and set his hands on one side of the wooden beam. Nate nodded from the other end. Dust streamed down as they lifted the bar out of the brackets. Tim stood it against the wall next to the pillowcase.

Nate's hand settled on a handle. Veek closed her fingers on the other one. "Ready?"

"For about a year now," she said. A smile spread across her face.

They pulled the doors open. The hinges were smooth and took the weight and movement without a single sound. Light from the hallway spilled into the room.

It wasn't that different from what they'd seen in Xela's photograph. The floor was a single slab of concrete. There were two long cracks in it. One had been patched, one hadn't. A few green roaches scuttled away from the light and vanished into the dark corners of the room. They left thin paths in the dust behind them. Nate could see thousands of trails the bugs had traced over time.

He glanced at Veek. "You going to be okay?"

"I'll be fine." She stomped her feet and sent ripples out through the carpet of dust. Nate noticed her pants were tucked into her boots.

"Light switch," said Tim. He was walking the perimeter of the room. "You want to risk it?"

Nate looked around. "I don't think this place is wired for high security," he said. "Go ahead."

The switch clicked and the room exploded with brilliance. An oversized bulb in the center of the room drove back the shadows and the last few brave roaches.

The room covered the front half of the building's foundation. Its ceiling was wooden beams strung with a few decades of dusty cobwebs, made even brighter by the light bulb they surrounded. The walls were brick all the way around the room, and cast-iron pipes ran up each one into the building.

At the center or the room was the railing. It was made of pipes held together by oversized flanges. There were two horizontal bars. The whole thing was seven or eight feet long and three feet wide.

Between the pipes was a staircase. The steps were made of steel splattered with dots of orange rust. They led down into darkness.

Tim finished walking the perimeter. There were some tools in one corner—a shovel and a pair of push brooms—that had all faded to the same shade of gray.

"Nothing," he said. "It's pretty much just a big empty room. And the elevator shaft." He pointed in the corner behind the door. There was a steel cage with a wooden frame built around it. The door looked like a screen door made with heavier mesh. There was no sign of the elevator. The shaft was empty except for a pair of cables running up into the building and down into the sub-basement.

Veek snapped pictures with her phone. She photographed the coil on the wall and then tapped it. The coil swung and tore loose a few ancient cobwebs. They drifted in the air in slow motion. "It's cable," she said. "I told you so."

"Not copper though," said Nate, looking over her shoulder. "Maybe it's for the elevator."

She shrugged.

Nate crouched by the stack of newspapers at the base of the railing. The top page was a haze marked with a few roach trails. He blew on it and words and pictures appeared from beneath years of dust.

Tim stood next to him. "What's the good news?"

"Planes are safe again. It looks like President Carter's hoping we can all pull together and get through the energy crisis." Nate smiled. "Oh, and Governor Brown cut three hundred million from the state budget by saying no to raises for state employees." He blew more dust off the paper's banner. "*L.A. Times.* July fourteenth, 1979."

"Is that important?" asked Veek. "The date?"

Nate thumbed through the stack of papers. They were yellow and stiff, but not too fragile. "Doesn't look like it. I think it's just a stack of newspapers somebody dumped in here."

"It does give us a sense of time, though," said Tim. "Going off the rust on the lock and all the dust, I think it's safe to say no one's been in here since those got stacked there."

Veek tilted her head. "Thirty-three years," she said. "That's ten years before Oskar was even living in the building. He may never have been in here." She glanced around the room.

"Maybe he doesn't have the key," said Nate.

Tim moved to stand next to them. He peered over the railing into the darkness and checked his watch. "Tick-tock," he said. "Fifteen minutes gone. We've got an hour left if we want to play it safe. Ready to move on?"

Nate looked at Veek. She nodded. "Yeah."

"Want me to go first?"

Nate took a breath and lifted the flashlight. "I'm supposed to be in charge, right?"

Tim gave a thin smile. "Doesn't mean you can't delegate."

"I've got it." He switched on the light and aimed it down into the shadows. The bottom of the stairs was about fifteen feet away.

He set his foot on the first step. The metal creaked but didn't budge. He went down another step and Veek put her hand on his shoulder. She gave it a squeeze. He reached up with his free hand to squeeze back.

They descended into the darkness.

FORTY

Going down several steps into a pitch black hole with only a flashlight took a lot more nerve than Nate thought. Every step made the circle of light shake and waver, plunging the stairs into darkness for an instant before he directed the beam again. It was a scene out of dozens of horror movies. He kept waiting for the light to reveal a skeleton, a blood stain, or an albino creature that had been locked in the sub-basement for years. Veek's grip on his shoulder kept him calm. It got tighter with each step. By the tenth he was sure she was leaving marks.

"I think we're there," he said after the eighteenth step. He let the flashlight trace wide circles around his feet to make sure he wasn't on a landing. It would suck to slip and break the flashlight. Or his neck.

The stairs came out along a wall. The floor was metal. It looked like he was standing on the hull of a battleship. Some of the rivets were ringed with bright orange circles. All of it was covered in dust.

He felt Veek step onto the floor behind him, and sensed Tim a moment later. "Everyone here?"

"Yep."

"Yeah," said Tim. "Do you see a light switch? There might be one down here, too."

Nate shifted the light to the wall and found a push-button switch right where he would've reached for it. The lower button was in, the higher one was out. He pressed the higher one and it clicked into place.

Six china-hat lights blossomed across the room, hung in two rows of three. The one closest to them flickered for a moment, flared, and died. The explorers blinked. A few small spots of green, the only bright color in the room, skittered away. It took a moment to resolve the dust-coated shapes around them. They spread out to look at everything.

They were in a rectangular chamber a little bigger than the lounge three stories above them. The walls were wooden planks, shrunken and warped with age. The ceiling was steel beams and concrete.

A desk and a long table dominated the half of the room closest to the stairs. There were overlapping carpets laid out under them, covering the steel floor.

Six chairs were pushed in around the table. A few small jars were gathered at the center of it. Tim blew the dust off them. There was a white mass in one he thought was salt, which meant the jar of black and gray particles was probably coarse pepper.

Nate examined the desk. It was a large, solid piece of wood, the type of thing found in New England universities. He glanced over his shoulder at the staircase and wondered if they'd had to disassemble it to get it down into the sub-basement.

An ancient blotter covered the desktop. The edges around the pigeonholes were carved to resemble scrolling vines and leaves. A brass hook, brown with age, protruded above one pigeonhole. A ring bearing a trio of keys hung from it. They all had long shafts and blocky teeth.

There were a few papers in a box marked OUT and none in the box marked IN. Time had faded the ink and turned the paper to brittle sheets. A few of them had already crumbled on the edges under their own weight. A few more papers had been curled and inserted into specific pigeonholes, but most of them had cracked into fragments.

There was a calendar on the wall above the desk, hung by a nail. Like the papers, it had faded, but its ink had been thicker. Nate couldn't make out the notes written on some of the days, but the calendar itself was open to November of 1898.

"I think that far wall's just under the laundry room," Tim said.

"No elevator here, either," said Veek. She was standing at another steel-cage shaft a few feet from the stairs. The cables ran down into more darkness. She gave the gate a tug, but it was latched solid. She shook it and a cloud of dust formed in the air.

"Easy," said Tim. "Kick up too much and you'll choke us all."

She snorted and snapped some pictures of the frame around the shaft with her phone. Then she dug into her pocket and pulled something out.

Nate tipped his head to her. "What've you got?"

"A nickel," Veek said. "Call it."

She tossed the coin through the gate into the shaft. It vanished. A moment later they heard a faint ping. Then silence.

"I think that was just it hitting the side," she said.

Tim stepped closer and held up his finger for quiet.

"It didn't hit bottom," she said.

"How can you tell if you were talking over it?" growled Tim.

"It didn't hit," she repeated. "I think it's still falling."

Nate shook his head. "Can't be."

Tim pulled a quarter from his own pocket and silenced them both with a glare. He reached his hand through the gate and let the coin drop straight down. He cocked his head to the shaft and closed his eyes. Nate counted fifteen Mississippis before Tim opened his eyes again. There hadn't been a sound.

"That's disturbing," said Veek.

Tim nodded in agreement.

"What are all those?" said Nate. There were three bundles leaning against the wall, like sheets of canvas wrapped around long boards. Each one was fastened with what looked like a pair of thin belts.

"I think they're cots," said Tim. He ran his finger along one and the canvas frayed at his touch. "Old camp beds."

Veek walked past them to glance at the desk. She took pictures of the desk and the keys and the calendar. Then she moved to the back half of the room. It was separated from the front half by two concrete pillars sunk into the walls, almost making it a room of its own.

There were no carpets or wood plank walls in this section. The metal floor was a gong under her heels. A little further down the wall from the desk was what looked like a tool bench. Across from it was a row of lockers. Veek counted six of them. They were made of wood, but looked like every set of gym lockers she'd ever seen.

Her eyes followed the edge of the room and stopped at the back wall. The pattern of rivets was different there. They doubled up and traced a large rectangle on the wall. If she hadn't been this close, she never would've seen it. Inside the line of rivets was a stubby handle, maybe six inches long, almost lost in the dust and cobwebs coating everything. She took a step closer and saw a dark blister at the center of the rectangle. It might have been painted black, but the thick layer of dust made it hard to tell.

Veek stepped to the wall. She crouched, took in a deep breath, and blew at the blister. The dust scattered and leapt into the air. A lot of it bounced back in her face. It revealed enough that she swept the rest away with her fingers.

"Oh," she coughed, "wow."

Nate looked over at her. "What's that?"

"Come see." She wiped the dust from her face and raised her phone. The camera clicked. She bent to blow another puff of air at the line of rivets.

Nate and Tim walked into the back half of the room. "Well, well, well," said Tim.

Set in the back wall of the room was a vault door. It was tall enough for Tim to walk through without ducking his head. Veek had cleaned most of the dust from the combination dial. It was black with white numbers and lines, set into a silver ring. The squat handle was made of dull steel and still draped with cobwebs. As Nate studied the door he could see the recessed hinges along the opposite side. They'd been hidden by a century of dust.

Tim crouched to examine the dial. It was reset so the **0** was at the twelve o'clock position, just below the small arrow marking the position of the dial. To the left of **0** were four white lines and then a **95**. "One hundred digits," he said. "A million possible combinations, assuming there's only three numbers."

Nate glanced from the dial to Tim. "There could be more?"

He nodded. "There's different classes of combination locks, depending on how the wheelhouse inside them is built. Nowadays you've got class twos, which are your basic combination padlock or gym locker,"—he glanced over his shoulder at the row of wooden lockers—"or you've got class ones, which are the things on bank vaults, big safes, and so on. One as old as this doesn't follow the actual classifications, but the technology really hasn't changed much since Houdini was breaking out of them." He reached out a hand and rapped his knuckles on the door. It was the dead sound of thick, solid metal. "The combination for this thing could have three digits, or four, or five..." He shrugged.

Veek had turned to snap pictures of the room from the other direction. "You know what this place reminds me of?"

"What?" asked Nate.

"A break room." She tipped her head to the lockers. "There's a place to hang your work clothes or your non-work clothes. A place to put your tools away." She gestured at the other half of the room with her phone. "Have lunch, maybe get a quick nap. Somewhere for the boss to sit and get caught up on stuff."

"You know what gets me?" said Nate. "This place is so neat."

Tim smirked and puffed another cloud of dust off the combination dial.

Nate shrugged. "It hasn't been used in a while, but look at it." He gestured at the table. "All the chairs are pushed in. The table's cleaned off. Everything's filed away on the desk. Whoever was working here didn't leave in a rush. They took their time when they were done here."

"Not like the message on your wall," Veek said.

"Right."

"What are you thinking?" asked Tim.

Nate looked around the room. "I'm wondering if whatever was going on here wasn't just a brief thing. What if it was going on for years? The date on the calendar's four years after the date on the cornerstone." He gestured at the lockers and the desk. "You don't set up all this for a weekend project. Probably not even for something you're going to spend a few months on. I think people were *working* here. All this...this was somebody's full-time job. They had time to clean up, and they expected to come back. Son of a bitch."

Veek tilted her head at him. "Yeah?"

He glanced at her, the vault door, and then at Tim. "Could that lock have six numbers?"

Tim nodded. "Class ones can still be set to six digits today. It doesn't even change the mechanism that—shit. Do you have a picture of it?"

They looked at Veek. She tapped and swooshed at the screen of her phone, then held it up. On it was one of the images from her wall.

66–16–9—4—1—89

"Read them off to me," said Tim. They tried it once, but the handle refused to budge. He spun the dial a few times to reset it and started again. This time he turned in the opposite direction for each number. The dial settled on the line next to **90** and he gripped the handle again.

The dull steel resisted for a moment, then swung up. They felt the vibration as bolts that had rested for decades shifted inside the door. The clang echoed through the room and made the floor tremble.

"Not ominous at all," said Veek.

Tim pulled the handle. The vault door drifted forward inch by inch. The hinges groaned and sent another vibration through the floor. Nate and Veek added their weight. A foot of steel swung away from the wall before musty air spilled out from behind the door. It was warm. It smelled hot.

They stepped back to look at what they'd revealed.

"Well," said Nate after a moment, "we should've seen that coming."

FORTY ONE

Inside the vault was a small space, not much bigger than a closet. Half the floor was a circular opening like a manhole. The edge was a smooth curve of metal, hammered over and riveted in place. Bolted to the back wall of the closet was a metal ladder leading down through the hole.

Nate leaned forward and switched the flashlight on. Veek squeezed in next to him. The beam sank into the hole and formed a circle of light a few yards below. "Looks like it doesn't go far," he called back to Tim. "Maybe twenty feet, tops."

Veek looked around. "Ahhh," she said. She straightened up and hit another pushbutton switch just inside the vault door.

Down in the hole, a light came on. They could see another dust-covered metal floor.

Nate handed her the flashlight and grabbed the rungs.

"Hang on," said Tim. "We don't know what's down there."

"That's why I'm going down," said Nate.

"Just take your time and be careful, ace. Just because we're on a time limit doesn't mean we should rush. This has all been here for over a hundred years. It's not going anywhere."

Veek looked at him. "What are you worried about?"

"I'm worried that a ladder's damned easy to booby trap. Whoever built this place wanted to protect it."

"I don't think we need to worry about traps," Nate replied. "Like I said, I think people were working here. You don't booby trap the office if you're expecting to come back the next day."

"Depends on the office," said Tim.

Nate smiled and swung out onto the ladder. It was flecked with rust but took his weight without a sound. He looked over his shoulder and locked eyes with Veek.

"Right behind you," she said.

He climbed down through the manhole. The inside was a circular tunnel of steel. He paused on the ladder to glance over his shoulder and saw a line of shadows he was pretty sure were rivets. He had a brief moment of claustrophobia, but a moment later the shaft opened up into the next level. His feet touched the floor and the first bead of sweat ran down his temple. It was warm down below, and the temperature shift was like stepping out of an air-conditioned store on a hot day.

The lower room was the size and shape of Nate's kitchen. The metal tube he'd climbed down through extended a foot and a half through the ceiling. The walls were bare metal. A single bulb lit the room, connected to two thin wires twisted into one. The bulb looked swollen and had an odd shape to it. The glass was clear and he could see the filament glaring inside of it.

The entrance to a wrought-iron spiral staircase filled the other half of the room. It sank down into the floor and out of sight.

Veek came down out of the tube. "Oh my God it's hot."

Nate dabbed at his forehead. "I don't think it's that bad," he said. "I think it's just the sudden change."

She shook her head as she stepped off the ladder. "It's that bad," she said. "I hate the heat."

Tim let go of the rungs and dropped the last few feet to the floor. "Been worse places," he said, looking around the room. He squinted at the light. "That's not a standard bulb."

Nate shook his head. "If upstairs was old, I'm guessing this is older. No one's opened that door in a hundred years, I bet."

They gathered around the staircase. With its steep curves, the bottom was nowhere in sight. Nate stretched his neck out and looked as far as he could. There was light shining around the phone-pole-like center of the stairs. "It's made of rock," he said. "This isn't a finished tunnel, it's just cut into the ground."

Veek looked around the room. "We're three stories down now, right? The sub-sub-basement."

Tim nodded. "We're probably about level with the base of the hill," he said. "Maybe even a little lower." He pulled something out of his pack and held it on his palm. "Compass still doesn't work."

"Well," said Nate, "do we keep going?"

They looked at Tim. The older man glanced at his watch. "We've got a little over thirty-five minutes left," he said. "Going up always takes more time than going down. Let's say we've maybe got fifteen more minutes before we need to head back. Hang on a minute." He slid his pack off his shoulder and pulled out a large bottle of water. "Everyone take a hit."

Veek took the bottle, cracked the plastic seal, and chugged three big swallows.

"You really came prepared, didn't you?" Nate said. He took the bottle from Veek and let it pour down his throat.

"I was a kick-ass Boy Scout," Tim said. He wiped off the lip of the bottle with his hand and took two big swallows. "Let's see how far we can get."

Nate led them down the staircase. Veek was behind him, one hand on his shoulder again. Tim brought up the rear. It only took a few steps for Nate to realize the spiral staircase would get dizzying if they moved too fast.

A pair of twisted black wires ran along where the steps connected to the stone. Every ten steps or so the wires split off and ran up to a crude alcove chopped out of the rock just above head height. A bulb sat in each one on a ceramic base. One or two of them had frosted glass blocking the alcove. Some just had shards.

"Fifty steps," said Veek after a couple of minutes.

Tim let his foot come down heavy. "Yep."

"I'm glad you guys thought to count," Nate said.

"You're in front," said Veek. She patted his shoulder. "It's your job to block the crossbow traps."

Tim made a grunting sound that might have been a laugh. "You feel that?" he said.

Nate stopped. "What?"

Tim had his hand on the center post of the spiral staircase. He waved at them to do the same. Nate set his palm against it. Veek reached out with cautious fingers.

A vibration echoed through the post. It was low enough it didn't spread out into the air, but strong enough it couldn't be denied. Nate shifted his hand, then took another few steps and shifted it again.

"It's like high tension lines," said Veek. "The way they make the air buzz."

They exchanged looks and continued down.

A few moments later Veek called out sixty and then seventy. The thought crossed Nate's mind that one hundred was a good landmark to stop at. Maybe they'd be able to leave a mark of some kind.

He took another lopsided step around the curve of the staircase and saw the bottom in the light from the stairwell. Another two steps and he was standing on dirt and stone. Veek and Tim appeared on either side of him in the gloom.

On the wall was a square of wood. A large knife switch was mounted on it, one of the blocky, Y-shaped ones used by mad scientists to activate doomsday machines and bring monsters to life. It was in the down position.

Nate stepped past Veek and heaved the switch up. The contacts crackled. Light overthrew the darkness.

"We *are* in a Scooby Doo cartoon," murmured Veek.

They were in a mine shaft. Nate had never been in one before, but the tunnel matched every mine shaft he'd ever seen in films and television shows. The floor, walls, and ceiling were all carved out of the earth and all flowed into one another. Every seven or eight feet an arch of thick timbers braced the tunnel. He could see one place where three arches stood right next to each other.

More of the thin, twisted wires ran along the tunnel. They hung on nails in the timbers and in some places a thin spike had been hammered into the wall. Every other arch had a light bulb hanging in a small cage. Of the eight or nine Nate could see down the length of the tunnel, at least five of them were burned out.

"I counted seventy-eight steps," said Tim. "Yes?"

"Yeah," huffed Veek. She blotted her forehead with her hand. "Could I bug you for some more water?"

"It's what I brought it for." He slid the backpack off his shoulders. "Seventy-eight steps, about nine inches each," he said as he handed her the bottle. He closed his eyes and did some mental math. "That's...fifty-eight and a half feet. Another five stories down."

She swallowed some water and wiped her mouth on her arm. "Wow."

On the left side of the tunnel were several cables, each one as thick as a fire hose. They were coated in what looked like black rubber under all the dust. A length of twine was wrapped around them to form a loose bundle, or maybe just to keep them neat. Nate prodded the bundle with his foot and felt a tingle of electricity. The movement made the twine collapse into bits and one of the cables flopped onto the floor with a *thwack* of dead weight.

"They're live," said Nate.

"So that's why we're not on the grid," Veek said.

Tim looked at the cables. "Maybe. We don't know which way it's flowing. Maybe there's something at the end of the tunnel that needs a lot of power."

"Occam's razor," she said. "Going up makes more sense."

"I think Occam would've kept his mouth shut if he lived in our building," said Nate. He followed the cables back to the spiral staircase. The bundle slipped under the steps and ran into the hub. "The center post doubles as a conduit," he said.

Tim had set the water bottle down on the floor of the tunnel. Once the liquid stopped rocking he crouched to study it. He moved it a few feet and stared at it again. Then he shuffled a few feet and set it down a third time.

"Checking to see if it's level?" asked Veek. She had her phone out and was snapping photos again.

He smiled. "Clever girl," he said. "Yeah, and it's not. It's still heading down. I'd guess it's a five or six percent grade." He see-sawed his fingers in the air. "Maybe a little more, maybe a little less."

Nate stepped back to join them. "How are we doing for time?"

Tim glanced at his watch. "You've got about thirty seconds to do whatever you want."

"What if we just went a little ways?" Veek waved down the tunnel. "We could just go to the bend."

"The bend?" echoed Nate.

She held up the phone. "Digital zoom. The tunnel either stops dead or takes a turn about fifty yards ahead."

"Let's go take a look," said Nate.

"Let's not," said Tim. He tapped his watch. "We're pushing it now. We should be heading back, not walking downhill."

"It's just a fifty yards," said Veek. She wheezed as she spoke.

"Fifty yards downhill," Tim said.

"You're right," said Nate. "We don't want Oskar finding out what we're doing. We should go back and wait. He's going to be gone for almost five days."

Veek frowned. "What if he's not?"

"He will be," Nate promised her. "Besides, you're not looking that great."

"Thanks. I've been thinking you're pretty butt-ugly too."

"He's right," said Tim. "You're all flushed."

"Mild asthma attack," she said.

"Do you have your inhaler?"

"Never needed it. It's nothing, I'll be fine. Let's just go look."

Nate shook his head. "No. He's right. We head back up."

Veek glared at them and shoved her phone back in her shirt pocket. "Fine," she muttered. She stalked past them and back to the spiral staircase.

Tim gestured with his free hand. "After you."

"Thanks," said Nate.

Tim shook his head. "I just don't want to get kicked in the face if she stays pissed."

Nate took a last look over his shoulder and reached for the knife switch. It swung down into the off position with a loud clack. The lights faded and the tunnel vanished into the darkness.

FORTY TWO

Once Anne had left for lunch on Thursday, Nate skimmed through his notes and found the number for the Department of the Interior. He punched in extension eight-twenty-three and waited while the system connected him. There was a pause, two clicks, and then a ringtone.

A man answered the phone. "Records."

"Hi," said Nate. There was an awkward pause. "I think I've got the wrong extension."

"Who did you want? I can transfer you."

"I'm trying to reach Elaine at eight-twenty-three. She was checking on some stuff for me."

The man made a noise. "This is eight-two-three," he said, "but I'm the only one at this extension."

Nate's stomach twisted into a knot. "You're the only one there?"

"Yep," he said. "I've been here for about three...Duh! You said Elaine."

"Yes! Yes I did."

"Sorry about that. I heard 'Shane' for some reason and my head was thinking of another guy."

"So Elaine's there?"

"Nope. She left three weeks ago."

"Left?"

"Yeah," said the man. "What was she helping you with?"

"What," Nate started to say, and then switched tracks. "Why did she leave?"

Nate heard the phone shift on the other end. "Don't know all the details," he said. "I think she might've gotten transferred or something. I just know it was kind of abrupt. It was a mess here for a few days. I've got this desk now. I'm Russell."

Nate's stomach collided with his intestines and pushed through to impact on his hip bones. It left ripples echoing up through his body. "Do you know where I could reach her?"

"No idea. Normally we get a memo for forwarding calls and email, but I think I got left off the list. Or maybe she got switched to another department altogether." Nate heard the distant sound of computer keys. "Anyway, if you tell me what she was helping you with, I might be able to help. I've got all her files and requests. Although...was she helping you just before she left?"

"I think so," murmured Nate.

"Yeah," said Russell, "we got hit with a virus right around then. Some jackass browsing porn at work or something. We lost two weeks' worth of requisitions and searches."

Nate felt a drop of sweat run down his back, tracing a line between his skin and his shirt. "No kidding?"

"Yeah. If you were in there, you're back to square one. I can help you start over, though. If it was just before she left, she couldn't've gotten far."

"Yeah," said Nate, thinking that Elaine may have gotten far enough, "it's not a big deal. Thanks anyway."

"Hey, it's not a problem," Russell said. "Are you sure I can't—"

Nate hung up.

Nate got home and found a spot on Kenmore in less than ten minutes. He double-checked the street-sweeping signs to make sure it was real and not just a trick of parking enforcement. He saw the days and times, felt his shoulders relax a little, and someone grabbed his arm. He twisted away and brought his arms up in something like a defensive pose, even though he still held his backpack.

Debbie had her briefcase slung over her shoulder, the handle hooked on her fingers. Her other arm was still out. "Sorry," she said. "Didn't mean to scare you. I just saw you parking."

"No, sorry," he said. "Long day. I didn't even see you there."

They started walking toward the building. "It's funny, I was just thinking about you. I thought I'd have to go knock on your door later."

"I won't tell Clive," said Nate. He smiled at her.

She rolled her eyes but smiled back. "He already knows. I called him from the lab." She glanced around. "Are you guys still heading into the tunnels tomorrow?"

"Yeah," he said. "I dropped a few hints about feeling sick at work. I'll call my boss later tonight and tell him I can't make it in."

"I don't think Clive and I are going to be able to do it," she said. "He's got a gig he can't get out of. And we can't afford for him to leave it."

Nate nodded as he unlocked the front gate. "No problem. What about you?"

She gave him a weak smile. "It'd be weird to go without him."

They climbed the steps and Debbie stopped to look at the engraved name on the lintel. "Veek is sure this is Indian?"

"Pretty sure, yeah," he said. "Martha-something. Why?"

Debbie shook her head. "Just had a thought on the tip of my brain, y'know."

Nate glanced up at the letters. "About Kavach?"

"I thought I remembered something about Indian names but it's gone." She looked at him and shrugged. "Sorry."

FORTY THREE

After some discussion Thursday night, it was decided that Nate, Xela, and Roger would be the ones to head down into the tunnels. They'd all managed to get the day off and Veek grudgingly admitted she'd slow them down if she had another asthma attack. Tim was worried if he vanished for too long the detective might cause problems. They agreed amongst themselves there was no point asking Mandy or Andrew.

Oskar left Friday at ten in the morning. He spoke to no one and they had no idea where he was actually going. "I feel kind of bad," said Debbie as the cab whisked the building manager away. "It's like we're taking advantage of him while he's dealing with a problem."

Nate and Veek showed the sub-basement to the others while Tim brought down the packs he'd assembled. He'd gone out to Target and bought new ones, despite everyone's protests. "We're not doing this half-assed," he said. "We don't know how far you're going, but it's going to be like hiking a mountain or the Grand Canyon. Up takes twice as long as down."

They had food, flashlights, and extra batteries. Xela had her camera and two extra memory cards. They'd all chipped in to buy the third one.

The packs had water bottles on either side in web sleeves and sleeping pads tied across the bottom. There was also a whistle tied to each one. "Phones aren't going to work a hundred feet underground," Tim explained. "That's your long-range communication. We'll keep someone down in the break room to listen for you in case you need help."

They all nodded.

"One last present for you," Tim said to Nate. He held out what looked like a pager made of translucent orange plastic. "Pedometer. It'll keep track of how far you've gone. If you keep a pretty steady pace and I figured the angle more or less right, every ninety feet you go is about another ten feet down."

"More or less?" echoed Roger.

"I don't have any surveying equipment," Tim said. "We're going to have to make do with 'more or less' and what I remember from tenth grade geometry."

"Cool," said Nate. "I'll try to keep track of it."

Tim spun the dial on the vault door and heaved it open. The ladder-tube wasn't wide enough, so Roger climbed down into the tiny spiral staircase room and they dropped the packs down to him. They went down the ladder. Veek squeezed in after them.

Xela glanced at her phone. "I've already lost reception," she said. "How about you guys?"

Nate glanced at his phone. "Me, too."

"Flickering half-bar," said Roger.

"So we're cut off," said Nate. He swung the backpack onto his shoulder and batted the whistle hanging from the strap. "We figured on that anyway."

"Figuring it's one thing," said Xela. "Knowing it's another."

"You guys be safe," said Veek. She gave Nate a crooked smile. "Don't do anything too stupid, Shaggy."

"Like going down into a hundred-year-old mine shaft?"

"Yeah," she said. "That'd pretty much max out the stupid-meter."

He smiled back at her. "This is new territory, isn't it? I don't think Shaggy ever went off with Fred and Daphne and left Velma alone."

"I won't be alone," she said. "We'll be busy here going over the break room."

"Who's Fred and Daphne?" asked Roger. "Thought it was just going to be the three of us."

Veek shook her head and the others chuckled. They walked down the spiral staircase and passed from sight. A moment later Roger's voice echoed back up. "Right," he said, "like *Scooby-Doo*. That's funny."

They'd gone twenty steps when Xela paused to examine one of the small light alcoves with intact glass. There wasn't enough room on the staircase to pass one another, so they had to wait for her. Roger discovered the tingle of the central post, and Nate explained the power cables down below. Even with the pauses, it felt like a quicker trip down the staircase to Nate. *Probably because I know what's there this time,* he thought.

After a few minutes they stepped out into the tunnel. Nate found the knife switch and turned on the lights. The bulbs glowed for a moment before illumination burst along the length of the tunnel.

"Whoa," said Roger. "You weren't kidding about this place."

"It's not as hot as I thought it was going to be," said Xela. "Veek made it sound like an oven."

Nate slid his pack off his shoulders and dug through the pouch. He'd brought along a few things to let him make as many observations as possible. One of them a small thermometer from Veek's apartment wall. He propped it up as straight as he could against his backpack and had a sip of water.

Roger and Xela spent a minute examining the wooden arches and the cables running along the wall. Nate had another drink and checked his pedometer. A few clicks reset it to zero. He slid the bottle back into its sleeve on the backpack and picked up the thermometer. "Ninety-four degrees," he said, jotting it down in his notebook. "What was it up top? High eighties?"

Xela nodded. "Think so, yeah."

"Saw eighty-five on the news," Roger said.

Nate looked around the tunnel. "So it's almost ten degrees hotter down here," he said. He slung the pack back onto his shoulder. "Wonder what it's going to be like deeper down?"

"Only one way to find out," smiled Xela.

FORTY FOUR

According to the pedometer, it was two hundred-seventeen feet to the bend. They'd already dropped another twenty feet. The tunnel made a hairpin turn marked by half a dozen wooden beams and supports. The cables stayed tight against the wall and wrapped around the corner.

Xela stopped, closed her eyes, and turned back and forth for a moment.

"What's up?" asked Roger.

"I'm trying to figure out where we are," she said. "The spiral staircase kind of screws things a bit, but I think this tunnel points northwest."

Nate looked from the stone walls to Xela and back. "You sure?"

"Spatial relations," she said. "It's what I do." She glanced back down the tunnel towards the spiral staircase, then looked up. "I think we're under the road right now. That T-intersection on Beverly where Kenmore does that little jog, between the garage and the store. We're maybe thirty, thirty-five feet under it."

Roger nodded. "Yeah, I think you're right. Listen, you can hear the cars."

Nate looked down the next leg of the tunnel. "So we're heading back toward the building now?"

"I think so, yeah."

They started walking again. Every fifty or sixty yards the tunnel would switch back in the other direction, sending them deeper and deeper into the earth. The wooden arches counted off ten-foot sections. The dust-covered bulbs lit the way with sepia light. There weren't any landmarks or signs, and the tunnel legs began to blend into each other.

"So, Xela," said Roger after an hour, "how'd you get into art?"

She glanced over at him. "What?"

"Art," he said. "You always like art as a kid or did it happen at college or what?"

"Why do you need to know?"

He shrugged. "Just figured we could talk about something or we'd all go nuts."

"It's pretty boring," she said.

"That's okay," he said. He slowed his pace and dropped back a few feet. "I can just hang here and watch your ass for a few hours."

Xela chuckled. "Oh, my," she cooed, "my shoe's untied." She bent over and thrust her hips back at Roger. With the backpack, she overbalanced and staggered forward. Nate grabbed her arm before she sprawled on the sloping floor.

They all laughed. "That's very entertaining," said Nate. "If you keep doing that we don't need to talk."

"Only one show per customer," she said. She adjusted her pack, tugged at her jeans, and continued down the tunnel. "I believe we were talking about art?"

Roger grinned. "Think so, yeah."

"The short answer," she said, "according to several psychologists, is childhood rebellion."

"Psychologists?" echoed Nate.

"Oh, yeah," said Xela. "I mean, for someone to keep ignoring her parents and wasting time on pointless things, there has to be something wrong with them, right? Probably something the nanny did."

"You had a nanny?"

"No, but you know how it goes. 'How our kid turned out is everyone's problem but ours'." She shook her head. "You sure you want to hear this? I swear, it's like a bad sitcom plot."

"Sitcoms are cool," said Roger.

Nate nodded. "As long as they don't have a laugh track."

"Oh, no laugh track, I assure you." They walked another yard or so while she juggled things in her mind. "Okay, I loved coloring books when I was little. I mean, I *loved* them. My mom would buy them by the dozen and I would do every single page. I'd even color the mazes and word problems and stuff. When I got a little older she bought me some colored pencils and the cheap watercolors in the long tray. They could give me a ream of paper and I was good for a week.

"Anyway, this was all good until I was eight and then it was time to buckle down. My dad's a doctor and he'd already decided I was going to follow in his footsteps. He was diagnostic, but I was going to be a surgeon. Maybe a cardiologist or a neurologist."

"Hold on," said Roger. "Seriously? Your dad wanted you to be a doctor?"

She shook her head. "Oh, he didn't want it. He *knew* I was going to be a doctor the same way you know you're wearing shoes. It was just a fact of life."

"That's fucked up."

"Told you it was a bad sitcom."

The tunnel took another hairpin turn. The bulb there flickered, its filament pulsing but never quite igniting. Nate blew the dust off the glass and gave it a gentle twist with his fingertips. It blossomed, spilling white light across the tunnel. He blinked a few times and shook his fingers out.

"Hey," said Roger, "that's a lot better." As they walked past the next bulb he leaned over and blew on it. A cloud of dust and grit scattered, and the tunnel brightened a little more. He looked at Xela. "So, your dad's fucked up?"

She smirked. "He's not really a bad guy. He's just inflexible. If he thinks this is the way things are, that's how they are. No question, no doubt. Him thinking I was going to be a doctor was like most parents thinking their kid's going to grow up and get a job."

"He have you studying anatomy when you were ten?"

"Nothing that bad," said Xela. "But it was all about grades and curriculum and after-school activities. Everything designed to make me the perfect med school candidate. They'd even go in to talk to my guidance counselors and make sure I was taking the best classes. I took violin lessons for two years to show I was well-rounded."

"You couldn't just take art classes?" asked Nate.

She shook her head. "Art's too flighty," she explained. She deepened her voice and straightened her back. "'Violin is precise and mathematical and involves a measurable quantity of manual dexterity.'"

Nate puffed dust off another bulb as they went around another turn. "What's that even mean?"

Xela shrugged and put on a lopsided grin. "I don't know, but I heard it once a week for two years. I even started to go along with it. I just figured everyone else's parents were doing the same thing.

"Anyway, sophomore year the school got a new guidance counselor. Mr. Woodley. He was maybe ten years older than me. I think he'd just gotten out of school himself, so he was still all excited to shape kids' lives. He called me into his office, asked if I was happy with my course load, and what I wanted to go to college for. I said medicine and he asked me if I wanted to be a doctor." She shrugged. "No one had ever actually asked me. Dad said it was true, Mom said it was true, so I just accepted it. So did everyone else."

Roger nodded. "What'd you tell him?"

"I told him, yeah, of course I wanted to be a doctor. I didn't know what else to say. But I think he got it. He pulled out my schedule, told me some class had been overbooked, and he'd have to stick me in a painting class instead of Russian history. It was just sheer luck. I think he pulled art out of a hat. I might've ended up in the marching band or something."

Nate looked at her. "You had Russian history class in high school?"

"Private school," she said. "Custom-made for churning out little professionals."

"Ahhh."

"Anyway, once I had a brush in my hand it was like I was six again. All the colors and the textures and the images. I think I went kind of crazy. I tried to keep it secret, but Mom found some paint on my sleeve a few weeks later and that was that. I got dragged into a meeting with my parents and Mr. Woodley and the principal. Dad went nuts and accused Mr. Woodley of sabotaging my future. I found out later he pulled some strings and got him fired.

"Then we got home and I got a whole lecture about not getting distracted and staying focused. But it was too late. I started skipping study hall to audit art classes. I think it scared some of the teachers after what happened to Mr. Woodley, but they figured they were safe since I wasn't actually in their class.

"Every now and then my parents would catch me with paint or colored pencils or something and there'd be a lecture. Then the lectures became therapy sessions. And some of those morphed into actual psychologists and psychiatrists. One of them recommended Ritalin or one of those drugs. Thank God, Dad finally put his foot down.

"I graduated, ended up at Yale, which annoyed Dad because he'd been pushing for Harvard. As soon as I got there I changed my whole schedule to a bunch of art classes. The first semester was just fantastic."

Nate gave her a look. "And then Dad saw your course listings?"

She nodded. "Christmas was awesome, believe me. I thought he was going to have an aneurysm. He just kept going on and on about how all 'our' plans were getting screwed up and how art was for lazy people with no goals." Her voice dropped an octave again. "'You're throwing away your *life!* Do you think this will *lead* somewhere, Alexis? I can't believe you'd stab your mother and me in the back like this after *all* we've done for you. You've going to have to repeat this whole semester, Alexis, and that's *not* going to look good on a grad school appli—'"

"Wait a minute," said Roger. "Who's Alexis?"

The tunnel floor was clean, but Xela stumbled over something and caught herself. For a moment the only sound was their feet crunching on the dirt.

"Oh my God," said Nate. "You *are* a bad sitcom."

"No," she insisted, "that's the only non-sitcom part about it. A real artist can't be carrying around useless baggage."

"Thought that was the whole point of being an artist," said Roger. He managed to say it with a straight face.

"Comments like that are not going to get you a real date," Xela warned him. She tipped her head back to swallow some water and gave him an exaggerated glare. "Anyway, Dad said to cut it out or he'd stop paying for medical school. I said fine, I never wanted to go anyway. After that was a very uncomfortable five months when I lived at home and took community college art classes. At the end of the next semester a bunch of us decided we'd move to Los Angeles and get inspired by all the creativity out here."

"Didn't know anything about LA, did you?" said Roger, again with a straight face.

Xela smirked. "We drove cross country with all this talk about forming an art commune in a big warehouse loft somewhere, like Andy Warhol's Factory. That lasted for three months, until it was clear the guys both thought 'commune' meant 'harem.' Plus, it turns out big warehouse lofts are really expensive, even when you're splitting rent five ways.

"Mom paid for me to live out of a hotel for two months. I got a waitressing job and one of the bartenders brought up this place. I signed up for some night classes, and haven't felt inspired since. And so here we are." She turned in a circle with her arms wide. "Thus comes to a close the sad story of she who was once Alexis Thorne."

"It wasn't that sad," said Nate.

"Oh, and my cat died when I was eleven."

"Ah, well."

She pointed at Roger. "Your turn, wiseass."

He tossed out his hands. "Open book. What d'you want to know?"

"How'd you end up a grip?" asked Nate. "Did you go to film school or something?"

Roger shook his head. "Just fell into it. Same way everyone gets in, I guess."

"Oh, come on," said Xela. "I share my birth name and life in the harem to you and 'I just fell into it' is the best you can offer back?"

He shrugged. "Graduated San Diego State with a degree in engineering. Got pissed at the world when I found out the only job I could get was at Target. And to do that I had to lie my ass off on their stupid job application computers."

"I hate those things," said Nate. "I tried to get a part-time job over the holidays and it's just some stupid multiple-choice quiz to guess what answers they want."

Roger nodded in agreement. "Anyway, spent a year wearing a red shirt and being pissed at the world, then a year not caring. Then a friend gave me a call about a film job. There were always a couple TV shows or something shooting down there, and one of 'em just needed a body for a few days—three days that were going to pay as good as two weeks at Target. Called in sick, worked for two bills a day, and learned everything I could. They asked me to come in the week after that and then hired me on full time for the last week." He shrugged. "Quit Target, moved up to LA. Did the couch trip for a few months while I got my days. Once I had 'em my folks loaned me some money and I joined the union. That's it."

"So," said Xela, "where do you go from being a grip?"

"What d'you mean?"

"Are there, I don't know, grip ranks? Promotions?"

He shrugged. "You can work up to being a best boy for someone. Some guys specialize on the camera dolly or rigging." He shrugged again. "Eventually you get a job keying a show."

"Is that what you're going for?"

"Don't know," said Roger. "A lot of the guys who've been doing this for twenty or thirty years, they're all just...tired, y'know? Great guys, really smart, getting good money, but they all seem..." He struggled for the right word and gave up. "Tired."

Nate nodded. "Not for you?"

"No. Don't know what I want to be doing in ten years, but I want to at least be happy doing it. Just figured I'd do it for eight or nine years and sock away a ton of money. When I heard about this place, figured it was perfect, y'know?"

Nate stopped. They were at yet another turn in the tunnel. "What?"

"What what?"

"You heard about this place from someone?" He glanced between Xela and Roger. "You didn't see an ad on Westside Rentals or something?"

Roger shook his head. "Why? That how you found it?"

"No," said Nate, "it was recommended to me, too. Some guy at a bar I barely knew. I mentioned I was looking for an apartment, he told me about this place."

"So?"

Nate shrugged. "It's just kind of odd, don't you think? None of us found this place on our own. It was recommended to all of us."

They made it to the next turn and Xela stretched her arms back. "How long have we been walking?"

Nate flipped his phone into his hand. "Two hours. Want to take a break?"

"Seconded," said Roger.

"The ayes have it," Xela said. She slumped against the nearest arch and lowered herself to the floor.

Packs came off and water bottles came out. Nate wiped his brow and propped the thermometer up against his pack. Roger kicked off his boots and flexed his toes. "Calves are killing me," he said. He reached down and kneaded his foot.

"All the downhill walking," said Nate. "We're only working our muscles one way. Don't worry, we'll use a whole different set on the way back."

"Awesome."

Xela eyed the pedometer. "How far have we gone?"

He popped the device off his belt. "A little over five miles," he said. "So I think we're like...two thousand feet down."

"Two *thousand*?"

Nate shrugged. "That's if this thing's dead on and Tim's guesstimate on the slope of the tunnel is right."

"What's the deepest cave in the world?" asked Roger.

"Seven thousand feet," Xela said. "It's in Georgia. Asia-Georgia, not down south."

Roger grinned. "Smart women are damn sexy."

She blew him a kiss. "I looked it up this morning before we started. And you're still in the shithouse for the art comment."

"Temperature's gone up to ninety-nine," said Nate.

"That's weird," said Xela. "When I was researching caves it sounded like most of them got cooler once you were away from the entrance, like fifties and sixties, because all the heat went into the ground." She slapped her backpack. "I brought another shirt and a sweatshirt."

"That doesn't make sense," said Roger. "Getting closer to the core with all the lava and stuff. It should get hotter."

"We're nowhere near the core," said Nate with a wry smile. "That's like saying North Hollywood should be cooler because it's closer to the Arctic Circle."

Xela stared down the next leg of the tunnel. "So what's going on?"

Nate shrugged. "Beats me."

FORTY FIVE

The sloping tunnel stretched on and on. The trio would walk in one direction for a hundred yards, then the tunnel would twist back on itself and drop them even lower. On one leg all the lights had burnt out and they inched through the darkness with two flashlights making circles of light on the floor of the tunnel. The scattered bulbs resumed after they rounded the next turn.

"How'd they do this?" Nate wondered aloud. His current estimate had them about three thousand feet below ground. "I mean, they would've had to move hundreds of tons of rock to make these tunnels."

"Money," said Roger. "Got enough money, you can do anything."

Xela had gotten ahead of them. She glanced back. "How do you know they had money?"

He pointed at the bundle of cable on the floor. "All that," he said. "Cable's expensive 'cause of all the copper. That's why people steal it out of houses and stuff. This is all one piece of cable. All the way from the spiral staircase to here. No connectors, no splices, nothing." He gestured at Nate's belt. "How far we been walking now?"

He checked. "About seven miles."

"Nine pieces of cable," said Roger. "Each one more'n seven miles long. That's some serious money, even a hundred years ago."

They turned another corner and walked in silence for a few minutes. Xela stopped to brush the dust from one of the bulbs. Nate and Roger walked past her and she puffed away a few last bits of accumulated grit.

They reached the corner and Nate glanced back. Xela was examining one of the burnt-out bulbs. She looked up and met his eyes. "You guys go ahead," she said. "I'll catch up in a minute."

"Something wrong?"

She shook her head. "No, nothing," she said. "I'll catch up in a minute or two."

"We shouldn't split up."

Xela raised an eyebrow. "It's not like I can get lost and accidentally start walking the other way. I'll be right with you."

"Why? What's the problem?"

"Nothing."

"So let's stick together."

She sighed. "I have to piss, okay?"

Nate smirked. "So there *are* some things you're shy about."

"Look, just walk around the bend and I'll be there in two minutes, okay?"

"You sure you're okay with us just leaving you here?"

"Yes. Will you please go? I've been holding it for an hour now."

"Go away from the cables," said Roger. "Rubber's pretty crumbly in places. You don't want to get a shock."

"Important safety tip," she said. "Thanks, Egon." When he gave her a blank look, she just smiled and waved him around the corner. "Talk amongst yourselves," she called to them.

Roger looked at Nate. "That's a movie quote, right?"

"Yeah, *Ghostbusters*, I think," said Nate

"You sure?"

"Yes, it's *Ghostbusters*, you philistines," Xela shouted around the corner. "How can you not immediately know that?"

"I think I was four when *Ghostbusters* came out," Roger called back.

"It's an American classic!"

"You always talk this much when you're taking a piss?"

She laughed. "What if I do? That a real turn-off for you?"

Nate cleared his throat. "Y'know, I'd leave you two alone but there's nowhere for me to go."

They stopped for another break at the four-hour mark. All three of them were sweating. Roger's face looked pink. Nate broke out the thermometer again. Roger gestured at it as he kicked his shoes off. "How hot is it now?"

"One hundred and two," Nate said. He angled the thermometer towards the light. "Maybe a hundred and three. It's flickering."

"Okay," said Roger. His pack slid off his shoulders. He reached up, grabbed a handful of t-shirt, and yanked it over his broad shoulders. "Too damned hot."

Nate nodded. "Yeah, I think so, too." He pulled his shirt off and tucked it through one of the straps of his backpack.

They glanced at Xela. "Don't get your hopes up," she smirked.

Roger shook his head. "Just wanted to make sure you were cool with—"

She peeled her shirt off, baring her tattoos. Her bra was bright green—

cockroach green

—with little white skulls on it. "I meant, don't get your hopes up, I'm not going topless," she said. "But thanks for the display of manly nipples and chest hair." She used the t-shirt to wipe her forehead.

"Any time," said Roger.

They slid out water bottles and drank. Roger splashed some in his hand and plastered his hair with it.

"Don't go crazy," said Nate. "Remember, this might have to last us another two and a half days."

Roger shook his head. "Gets much hotter, we'll have to turn back anyway."

"Good point," said Xela. She raised her bottle and poured a few drops on her head. Nate shrugged and did the same.

Roger padded across the tunnel in his socks. He put his hands against one of the wooden supports and pushed back against his heel. He closed his eyes and grunted as his Achilles stretched out. His feet shuffled and he stretched the other leg.

A trickle of dust and sand drifted down from the top of the arch. There was enough that it rattled when it hit the floor of the tunnel.

"Hey," said Nate. "Stop it."

Roger kept his eyes closed. "Just stretching my—"

"You're shifting the arch," snapped Xela. A small rock dropped and accented her words. It hit a stone on the floor with a loud *crack*. One the size of a basketball dropped next to it and missed Roger's shoulder by inches.

He leaped away from the beam and another stone hit the floor. Then a third. They stared at the arch. A haze of dust floated around it, but nothing else fell.

Xela rapped on the walls. "It's all sedimentary rock, isn't it? Not really solid."

"Thus all the beams and supports," said Nate.

"Sorry," mumbled Roger. "Didn't even think."

"Don't worry about it," said Nate. "Let's just make sure none of us push on anything else."

Xela studied the roof of the tunnel. "How much do you think it'd cave in?"

Roger shrugged. "Enough to kill us?"

"No, I mean if this tunnel collapses, the one above it will probably go, too. And then the one above that and the one above that. Maybe all the way up to the sub-basement and the foundation. You could've brought the whole building down."

"Cool," he sighed. "Got it."

"I didn't mean it like that," she said. "Sorry."

Nate shouldered his pack and took a few steps. "C'mon," he said. "Let's see if we can hit bottom before we've got to turn back."

They walked for another twenty minutes, around four more turns, and Roger stopped. His brow furrowed and he looked at the air around him. He took a few more steps and stopped again.

Nate glanced back. "What's up?"

"You feel that?"

Xela looked around. "Feel what?"

Roger stopped walking for a moment and crouched down. He set his palm against the ground and closed his eyes. For a moment Nate pictured the tanned, bare-chested man with a feather in his hair and cheesy warpaint.

Xela closed her eyes and rolled her head in a slow circle. "A tingle in the ground," she said.

"Feels like an engine," said Roger. His eyes opened and he looked up at them. "A big one."

"We're about forty-five hundred feet down," said Nate. "Maybe we're getting close."

After the next hairpin turn Nate could feel it, too. It reminded him of big trucks and buses driving by on the street outside his office, or the tiny earthquakes that shook Los Angeles for a few seconds every month or so, the ones people only noticed after years in California. This wasn't a brief tremor, though. It was constant. The longer he focused on it, the more he could feel it working its way through the soles of his shoes and into his bones. He was sure if he waited he'd feel it vibrate his teeth.

The trio went around two more turns and they could hear it. A low, rolling rumble. Roger was right. It sounded like an engine.

After the next turn they could see dust hanging in the air. The sound shook the beams. Halfway down the tunnel a trickle of sand fell in a steady stream. They could see a pile on the ground the size of a big bag of dog food.

"What do you think, boss?" said Xela.

"I think we're safe," said Nate. "If all this stuff has stood for a hundred years, it'd be real stupid for it to collapse the day we show up."

"Yeah," said Roger, "and nothing stupid ever happens in real life."

They marched down three more legs of the tunnel. The rumble got louder but the vibrations didn't seem to get any stronger. Then Roger staggered.

He took a few quick steps, as if he was trying to get his balance, then set his front foot down hard. Xela stumbled and caught herself. Nate felt his legs get rubbery and stopped moving.

"It's the ground," said Xela. "The ground's level."

They looked at one another. Roger grinned. They had a quick toast with their water bottles.

Their unbalanced muscles protested for a few more yards. Over five hours of walking downhill had messed them up. Nate was sure the real pain would start later, probably on the way back up.

The level tunnel stretched out for a few hundred feet. Up ahead Nate could see a wooden crate covered with a century of dust. There was a pile of spikes near it. He guessed they were the same ones holding the arches together.

The passage turned to the left. Instead of a hairpin turn, there was a small chamber carved out of the rock. The supports here were steel, the riveted I-beams that made up the insides of buildings.

A series of thinner beams descended between two of the supports. Strips of metal had been riveted back and forth across them to create a simple cage. Sitting in the cage was a wooden box the size of a phone booth. A heavy cable ran from its roof up into the shaft above it. Its cage door was propped open by a crumbling cardboard box and what looked like a wooden broom handle, also withered from years in the heat.

Something shiny sat in the dust near the broom handle. Roger crouched, plucked it off the ground, and held up a 2003 nickel for them to see. They scanned the dust for a few moments and Xela found the quarter a few feet away. "Finders keepers," she said with a grin, tucking it in her pocket.

Across the chamber was a pair of doors coated with dust and grit. The heat had made their paint fade and peel. Nate glanced at Xela and she nodded back at him. She recognized them, too. This set didn't have a bar stretched across them.

Roger gave the handles a quick tap, then a more lingering one. He turned and gave Nate a nod. The two men wrapped their fingers around each handle.

The doors were heavy. The hinges gave a low groan that became a squeal as they continued to open. They might have been oiled once, but now they were coated with a hundred years of neglect.

The noise level jumped up a few decibels. The rumble was a steady roar on the other side of the doors, like a truck stop parking lot with all the engines running. A wave of heat washed out at them. It was close to painful, like standing in front of an open oven. The hot air rushed down their throats and scalded their lungs.

Nate squinted his eyes against the heat.

"Holy shit," said Xela over his shoulder.

FORTY SIX

During his years in the industry, Roger had seen a lot of film stages. Some of them had been on the big studio lots like Warner or Paramount. Some had been at the smaller stages that cropped up all over Los Angeles, like Lacey Street or Ren-Mar or Raleigh. Most of the time the stages held multiple sets. A few of them had been filled by a single, enormous construction project. And a few had been empty. Seen like that, stages looked a lot like airplane hangars. They had enormous floors and ceilings two or three stories high.

The room on the other side of the double doors was as big as any stage Roger had ever seen or heard of. It could've been the size of a small stadium. He'd never sat on the ground level of a stadium so it was hard to be sure.

Once the blast of heat had faded, they stepped inside. The room was rough stone, and Roger felt sure it was natural, not something dug out like the tunnel. Steel girders framed the whole thing, extending up in a dome fifty or sixty feet high. Heavy buttresses reached out to brace the walls and his eyes followed them up. It was some serious construction work.

Hanging from the center of the dome was a makeshift chandelier. Three big metal rings sat one inside the other, and dozens of light bulbs hung from them at different heights. At least half of them were burned out. What was left bathed the room in a light somewhere between yellow and orange, like an ongoing sunset.

Six huge cylinders of black metal dominated one side of the room. Each one was fifteen feet high on their round face and maybe twenty long. Heat rippled around them and they flickered like mirages. Roger got a little closer and could see vents. Something reddish-gold was whirling in there, racing around the inside of each cylinder at blurring speeds. They were the source of most of the noise echoing in the chamber.

"Holy shit," he said over the roar of the machines. "They're generators."

Roger saw the bundle of cables they'd followed back and forth for ten miles. The cables split off and ran to—ran *from,* he corrected himself—the different generators. Behind the big machines he could see some huge pipes running down into a ditch. They were as big as air conditioner ducts, and it looked like there were two of them for each of the generators. Nate walked past them and crouched down to look in the ditch. Whatever he saw must've been pretty cool because he kept shaking his head and looking at it again.

Xela was standing halfway between Roger and Nate. She was turning around in a slow circle, looking at everything. Her hands were fumbling with her backpack, trying to pull out her camera. It would've been quicker to look, but she couldn't tear her eyes away from the huge room. Her skin was gold in the yellow-orange light.

Roger tried to picture laying out track for a camera dolly if the big chamber was a film set. The track came in ten-foot sections and he guessed he'd need at least twenty of them to go across the room. Going from the door to the back wall was trickier, across the ditch, but he guessed it would take fifteen pieces of track to run between them.

Not as big as he first thought, but still a big room.

He glanced over at Xela. Her camera was finally out and she pointed it at one thing after another. He waved to get her attention and pointed up at the chandelier.

She looked up and grinned. Her head tipped back. The camera went up. Her stomach went taut and her tits pushed against the green bra.

Roger glanced over at Nate. He was still staring into the ditch. It didn't look like he'd moved. Roger waved to get Xela's attention again and pointed at Nate. She glanced between them and called something to Roger. He could hear her voice, but couldn't understand her over the noise of the generators.

Xela turned and moved next to Nate. She looked down into the ditch. Her camera hung from her hand at her side.

Roger took a few steps toward them. It was enough of a shift to give him a better view of the ditch. It was deeper than he thought, and it looked natural. It was a crack in the ground, and its sides were rough and uneven.

Another few steps and he realized he'd misjudged how wide the crack-ditch was, too. It was at least fifteen or twenty feet across. It was hard to be sure with all the heat ripples in the room. The big chamber was closer to round than he'd calculated. And it looked like the other side was a few feet higher than their side.

Roger noticed one of the tattoos on Xela's bare shoulder—an elaborate oval filled with hieroglyphs—and glanced down. The far side of the crack was still going down. What he'd thought was a ditch looked to be a canyon in the floor.

Then he was next to her. Xela reached out and grabbed his hand. She had a strong grip for such a slim woman. It made a number of thoughts dance through his head for a moment.

And then he was looking down, down, down, down...

Nate stared into the abyss. He didn't know if it stared back, but he was pretty sure it had singed his eyebrows. As it was, he closed his eyes and saw the red after-image of the bright, jagged line he'd seen far below.

"I'm not crazy, right?" he said to them. The words rasped at his overheated throat, but his friends were close enough to hear him. "Is this what I think it is?"

"Holy fuck," said Roger. "Holy fuck."

The canyon went down for miles. Nate had climbed to the top of the Hollywood Hills once or twice and looked out ten miles or so to the Pacific. Now he looked straight down at least that far. It was a wound in the Earth, a cut deep enough to draw blood. Not just a swell of red but the bright, pulsing blood that only came with serious injuries. They could all see it shifting and writhing far below, the filament of a hundred-thousand-watt bulb.

The heat rose up at them, an ongoing stream of air that made him squint. It smelled like fire. His eyes watered from it. Out of the corner of his eye he could see it rippling Xela's hair across her scalp.

"Is this..." She paused to rub her eyes with the heel of her hand. Then she raised her voice to be heard over the rumbling generators. "Is this a volcano or something?"

Nate let his eyes drift up to the edges of the huge crack. "I think it's a fault line," he said.

Roger shook his head. "Those are miles underground."

"*We're* miles underground," said Nate. "At least a mile, maybe more."

"Doesn't make any fucking sense." Roger shook his head again. "It can't be a fault line."

"It's just a little one, I think,"said Xela. She looked across the canyon. "It's only twenty feet or so."

"And a hundred miles down," Roger said.

Nate gazed past Roger. A dozen metal pipes hung over the edge of the canyon, each one at least four feet across. They reached down for the distant fire and disappeared into the distance. It was far enough that the huge pipes couldn't be picked out against the canyon walls. He was sure they kept going all the way down.

He closed his eyes for a moment and then looked over his shoulder. A red rope of light burned across his vision. He blinked a few times and wondered if he'd damaged his eyes somehow.

The pipes ran across the ground, held up on squat brackets. They almost formed a platform behind the generators. In fact, Nate could see some low catwalks stretching back and forth across them. There were tanks and valves and huge wheels to spin. It all led into the generators.

"They're geothermal," said Nate. "They run off the heat of the earth. The magma and all that."

Roger dragged his eyes from the chasm to look at Nate. "What's that mean?"

Xela squeezed his hand. "It means they'll run forever."

FORTY SEVEN

It took another ten minutes before they could drag themselves away from the fault. Nate had heard of people hypnotized by the sheer scale of the Grand Canyon when they saw it in person. All the movies and television specials in the world couldn't prepare someone for the sight of a solid object that went from horizon to horizon. Seeing an exposed fault line had the same effect.

They wandered to the generators. There was a battered desk set up a few yards past them. The discolored wood blended into the stone wall. A few yards beyond that was a wooden shed, its boards just as bleached as the desk.

Nate could feel the heat coming off the generators. They weren't red-hot, but he thought they'd still burn his fingers. Each of the big turbines was coated with years of dust and dirt that had cooked into soot. He wrapped his hand in his shirt and took a few swipes at the hot metal. The steel gleamed beneath the grime.

"Check this out," said Xela. She'd used her own shirt to clear a big patch on the next generator in line. A strip of silver and black was riveted on the dull metal. She gave it another wipe with the shirt. Nate and Roger looked over her shoulders at the curling letters.

Westinghouse Electric and Manufacturing Co.

Roger glanced at them. "That's a real company, isn't it? They make kitchen appliances and stuff?"

"I think they used to do everything electric," said Nate. "How much power do you think these put out?"

Roger shrugged. "Generators on set are half this size. Think they put out something like fifteen or sixteen hundred amps."

Xela gazed up at the steel cylinder. "Does twice as big mean twice as much power?"

He shrugged again. "Not my thing. Might mean more power. Might just mean they're older."

Nate walked along the row of generators. Each one had the Westinghouse label, hidden by the layer of dust and silt. He recognized it by shape. There was a heavy plaque marked with a Roman numeral at the base of each generator. He was standing in front of **IV**, and Xela had just cleaned **V**. The one closest to the fault line was **VI**. He took a few more steps, passed **III**, and approached **II**.

Xela had her camera up again and was getting photos of each plaque. "Did you notice the base?" She pointed at the floor. The generators sat on a raised platform carved out of the rock. It was fitted with steel straps that wrapped back and forth across it. "These things are solid."

The desk was warped and cracked. It reminded Nate of pictures of house fires, where some of the furniture had been in the home and exposed to the heat but hadn't caught fire. In front of the desk stood a charred-white framework of wood that might have been a chair a hundred years earlier. A windswept pile of rags between the legs was all that was left of a seat cushion.

The desk itself was barren, and warm to the touch. There was a black fountain pen and a cracked ink bottle. A newspaper stuck out of one of the desk's pigeonholes. Nate touched it and the edge crumbled away. He yanked his fingers back and tried to read what he could of the fragile headline.

"Anything?" asked Roger.

Nate shook his head. "I wrecked some of the date. I think it's the twentieth of some month in 1894, but that's all I've got." He angled his head. "It looks like there's a dozen little articles all on the front page."

Xela pushed him gently aside and lined up her camera. It clicked once. "You know what bugs me?" She dipped her head at the rolled-up paper in the pigeonhole and the camera clicked again. "In the movies, when people find some dusty old chamber or something, there's always a newspaper with some big banner headline that nails the date. 'Titanic Sinks' or 'Japanese Attack Pearl Harbor' or something like that. It always knocks me out of the movie." The camera clicked again.

Nate smirked. "You think it's more believable that this is a crap daily paper?"

"Don't you?"

"I'm not having a lot of trouble believing all this."

"I am," muttered Roger. "Still doesn't make sense."

They left Nate to study the desk and moved to the shed. Xela pried open the door and barked out a laugh. "Oh, of course there's a bathroom here," she said.

"Yeah," said Roger, "if only you could've held it for another three hours."

She peered down the hole of the outhouse. "Not too sure I'd feel safe sitting there anyway."

"Worried something'd grab you?"

"Worried I'd fall through," she said.

Nate crouched between the desk and the outhouse. The ground was covered with papers. They fluttered in the constant breeze coming out of the chasm. Most of them danced near the desk and pressed themselves in the rough corner where the floor and ceiling ran together. Some of them were trapped further out on the floor, pinned by random eddies and air currents. They were singed on the edges or burned black.

Nate reached to touch one and it collapsed into ash that was swept away on the constant breezes. He squinted his eyes at the next one and tried to make out the faded ink lines. "Can you get photos of these?" he called over his shoulder.

Xela looked back. "Which ones?"

"All of them. As many as you can."

She nodded and bent to the closest page.

Roger crouched next to her. "Drink some water."

"I'm not thirsty."

"Ain't about being thirsty," he said, "it's about staying hydrated on the job, y'know? You're not sweating that much."

Her lips formed a quick grin. "You're watching me sweat. That's not too creepy."

"Damn hot in here. Suck to get heatstroke at the bottom of those tunnels."

She pulled a bottle from her pack and he did the same. "We could ride the elevator back." She washed the words down with a double mouthful of water.

He took three deep swallows from his own bottle and wet his head again. "Don't know about you," Roger said, "but I'm not too keen on getting in a hundred-year-old wooden elevator with a cable a mile long."

She smiled again and went back to taking photos.

Nate took a few steps and his eyes slid around the room. Generators. Cables. Pipes. Supports. Chandelier. Roger joined him and held out a water bottle. "Whatcha thinking?"

He took the bottle, tipped his head back, and poured it into his mouth. "I'm thinking we're missing something," he said, wiping his mouth on his arm.

Roger looked at him. "Whaddya mean?"

Nate waved his arm at the row of generators. "Okay, you said movie generators are half this size and put out fifteen hundred amps, right?"

"Think so, yeah, but it's not really my thing, y'know?"

Nate nodded. "So even if these aren't any more powerful, there's still six of them. So they're putting out at least nine thousand amps. Maybe twice that."

Roger nodded.

"If all this is going up to the building," said Nate, "what's using it all? It's not like we're using all this to power a couple dozen refrigerators and computers."

"Flatscreens suck up a lot of power," said Roger.

"Not that much," said Nate. "Heck, I think a subway only uses a couple hundred to push a train. So what's using all the power from six big generators like this?"

"Guys," called Xela, "take a look at this."

Xela was crouched in front of a piece of paper. As they got closer, Nate could see the brittle edges where more of it had crumbled away. Going off what was left, the original could've been the size of a large poster. Then he saw the lines, faded but still clear enough.

"You see what I see?" Xela pointed at the drawing.

The image was a large rectangle. It was divided into multiple levels, and the top three were subdivided by more layered lines, so each of the top three sections had two large squares separated by a narrow rectangle. It took Nate a moment to realize he was looking at a cross-section of a building. The Kavach Building.

On the second floor, the right-hand square was marked with a thick X that filled most of the box. The mark was so heavy it had lasted a century. Four words were written outside the large rectangle next to the marked square. They were some of the only words on the sheet that hadn't faded to a blur. Nate recognized all of them. He understood the bottom one.

DANGER

Across from the marked square was a different shape. It was another rectangle extending up to the top floor. There were four words next to Clive and Debbie's apartment, right on the brittle edge of the paper. Half of the top two had crumbled away, but they could just read the bottom word.

CONTROL

FORTY EIGHT

Veek sat at the far end of the break room table. In front of her was a collection of all their notes and photographs, all printed out and labeled. More than half of it was information she'd learned months ago, long before she'd met Nate. Now that they'd discovered so much more, though, there was a chance of spotting something new or seeing a fresh angle on things.

For the fourth or fifth time, she wished she had a working laptop she could've brought down. Something with a screen larger than her phone. The Wi-Fi didn't penetrate this deep, but it still would've been easier than dealing with so much paper.

She glanced over at the vault door. It was propped all the way open. Clive had found a small latch to lock it in position.

She'd been in the sub-basement break room for four hours. Tim had split the watch up into three-hour shifts, but Veek had offered to take Debbie's so she could spend the evening with Clive before he went off to work.

In another eighteen minutes it'd be twenty-seven hours since she said goodbye to Nate and the others in the room below the vault door. "The airlock," Tim called it. One way or another, the explorers should be headed back soon.

Assuming nothing had gone wrong.

They'd spent yesterday and this morning searching the big room. Every piece of furniture examined, every drawer and locker opened. They'd found some clothes that had fed generations of moths and a pair of reading glasses—spectacles, really—with gold frames. They'd also discovered a few silver notes Andrew guessed might be worth twenty or thirty dollars each from collectors. This assessment came with a lecture on material possessions which Tim put a quick end to.

Debbie had pointed out that they were leaving trails in the dust. It was hard not to notice someone had been in the room at this point. This worried them at first, but it was agreed the room had stood untouched for so long it didn't make sense someone would be looking at it in the near future. With that decision made, she started to clean while the others searched. Veek's college roommate had been the same way. In the face of crisis and uncertainty, the best thing for some people to do was break out the Dustbuster. It was amazing what a can of wood polish and two rolls of paper towels had accomplished. The sub-basement wasn't sparkling, but no one would've objected to eating a meal at the table.

Veek picked up a pile of pictures and shuffled the top one to the back. She tapped them on the table to straighten the stack. She looked at the new top photo. It was a low shot, looking up at the front face of the building.

"Fuck," she said to no one in particular.

It wasn't even loud enough to echo against the hard walls of the room. She pushed her glasses up onto the bridge of her nose and considered saying it again.

She was angry about not being down there with Nate. She'd been angry for four days, since they'd first explored the sub-basement with Tim.

Eight years! She hadn't had an asthma attack in just over eight years. She'd biked to work three times last summer and never felt a twinge in her lungs. Hell, she'd tried a kickboxing course two years ago and never felt short of breath once. Half the time she didn't even carry her inhaler, and when she did it always felt like a useless gesture. It was like carrying a condom in her bag in college when she knew she was going to be the last one having unexpected sex.

But down there in the tunnels it had kicked in. She was close to doing something amazing with her life, and her lungs had tightened up on her. She'd felt the straps settle around her ribs and known they were getting ready to bind her chest. It had taken all her will to force warm air into her lungs.

And now he was down there with Roger and the slut. Which was unfair, but it was how she found herself thinking of Xela more and more. *How's that old joke go?* she thought. *The difference between a nymph and a slut? A nymph sleeps with everyone. A slut sleeps with everyone except you.*

Not that she wanted to sleep with Xela. Or thought she was a slut. She just wondered who Xela wanted to sleep with. Because experience had taught Veek that women with Xela's looks and attitude tended to get a lot more guys than women who looked like...

Well, like Veek.

The metal staircase creaked. She looked over her shoulder and saw Andrew coming down the steps. A brown and white sweater vest wrapped his torso and clashed with his sky-colored tie. "Ahhh," he said. "I didn't realize anyone was here."

"Someone's always keeping watch here until they're back," she said. "You heard Tim say so."

Andrew gazed at a spot in the air for a moment. He studied it for a moment and then shook his head. "No," he said. "No, my mind must've been elsewhere."

"Right," said Veek. "Good thing you're not volunteering." He'd been pretty useless during the search of the sub-basement and the airlock.

"Now I remember," he said. "Timothy wanted me to work on Sunday."

She turned her head toward the vault door so Andrew wouldn't see her roll her eyes. "Change your mind?"

"No." He walked past her to glance through the vault doors, his arms and hands close to his side. He leaned back and turned his head to her. "They're still not back?"

Veek set her photos down on the table. "No."

"No word on if they found anything?"

"I just said they're not back yet."

His chin went up and then dropped down. "Ahhh."

"So what's up, Andrew?"

"Nothing," he said in his sing-song voice. "I just wanted to look around some more and see if there was anything else to find."

"We went over the place pretty good yesterday," Veek reminded him. "Tim and I did some more this morning."

"And you didn't find anything interesting?"

She twisted around to look at him. "More interesting than a bunch of underground rooms and tunnels?"

Andrew's head dipped to one side, then the other, then back. His shoulders swayed as he did. "I was just wondering about our meeting in the lounge. About what was hidden here."

"All this was hidden here." She gestured around her.

His side-to-side swaying became a nod. "Yes," he said, "this was here, but it wasn't hidden. We don't think the message on Nathan's wall was about protecting a kitchen table, do we?" He bared his teeth at her. She almost flinched before she realized he'd spread a smile across his face.

"Maybe we'll find out," Veek said.

"Maybe we will," said Andrew. "If our Lord is willing."

It crossed her mind that she was two stories underground and there was a good chance no one would hear her if she started screaming. Andrew's smile encouraged that sort of thought. Then again, he'd always given her the creeps on some level.

They stared at each other for a moment, and then Andrew's smile faded. "Well, I shan't take up any more of your time," he said. "You looked quite deep in thought when I came down the stairs."

"Yeah," she said. She gathered up the ream of notes. "We've got a lot of stuff to go over at this point. Don't want to miss anything."

He gave another nod. "Yes," he agreed, "that would be bad."

Veek kept adjusting the photos in her hand. She didn't want to look at them until Andrew turned, because she had a gnawing feeling he might just stand there and stare at her for a while. So she shifted them again while she stared at the vault and watched him out of the corner of her eye.

Andrew's head bobbed side to side again. Then he turned and walked back to the stairs. "Have a wonderful evening," he said.

"You, too," she answered. She counted out all eighteen steps as he headed back up to the basement. To be safe, she even listened for his footsteps across the floor and down the hall to the laundry room. She knew he was more annoying than dangerous, but sometimes he managed to blur the line.

Veek settled back into her chair. A picture of the cornerstone topped the stack, brought up by her shuffling. It had printed in landscape format, so she was looking at it sideways, and just for a moment something about seeing the block at this angle made sense. She glimpsed something that vanished the instant she focused on it.

And then, before she could retrace her mental steps, a faint sound echoed out of the vault door.

"Holy shit," said Roger. "We there?"

"I think so," Nate said.

The trio had spent last night ten tunnel-legs up from the generator room. Today had been twelve hours of marching back up through the tunnels. They'd trudged along like the walking wounded for the last hour. Xela leaned on Roger. Nate's shoes had turned to concrete sometime around lunch.

But they came around the corner and there was the spiral staircase at the top of the last leg of the tunnel. The wrought iron looked like a slanted shadow. They stopped for a moment and felt their muscles tremble. Nate's calf stiffened and he forced his toes up to fight off the Charley horse.

"Come on," he said. "Let's not get caught up in the moment."

"Damn straight," said Roger. "I need a beer."

"Oh, dear God," Xela said. "I'm going to wash all this dust off me and then sleep for at least a day."

Nate glanced at her. "What about all the photos? You're going to pull them all off the camera, right?"

She sighed. "Maybe?"

"This doesn't get priority over cleaning up?"

"Nate, my dearest," she smiled, "nothing personal, but fuck you."

"Typical woman," said Roger. "Coolest thing in her life and she's more concerned with her looks."

She reached up and gave him a gentle slap in the back of the head. "Sorry," she said. "What I meant to say was fuck you both."

"Doesn't look like you've got the strength," said Roger.

"Oh, I could do it," she assured him. "You're just not worth the effort when you stink like this."

They laughed. It took some effort so they had to stop walking to do it. Then they plodded toward the spiral staircase. It took them five minutes to walk the last two hundred feet.

"Thank God," Roger said. "Stairs. Was worried I couldn't go uphill anymore."

The steps clanged under their feet. Nate counted them out loud and after a few minutes Xela and Roger joined him. They followed the twisting path up the stairs and tried to make a song out of the numbers.

They rounded the bend on the seventy-fifth step and saw Veek in the little room waiting for them.

"Hey," she said. Her smile was a tight curve beneath her glasses. "Welcome back to the surface world."

"We, the Morlocks, accept your welcome," said Xela. She threw up a power salute with a weak fist. "Take us to your showers."

Veek and Nate looked at each other for a moment and then she gave him an awkward hug. He wrapped his arms around her and hugged her back.

"Tell me you found something cool," she said.

"Unbelievably cool," said Nate.

FORTY NINE

Nate wanted to go to Debbie and Clive's apartment right away, but he changed his mind after climbing the ladder and the two sets of steps that got him to ground level. Veek pulled his arm across her shoulders and helped him walk. He told her about the generators, the fault line, and the cutaway diagram they'd found.

Roger and Xela stopped at the first floor and both gave him ragged salutes and smiles. "Conquering heroes," said Roger. Nate returned the salutes before continuing up the back stairwell with Veek. His legs were trembling.

"So," she said as they stepped onto the lounge landing, "Xela's not going up to her apartment."

"Doesn't look like," he agreed.

They went up a few more steps. "Her and Roger," said Veek.

He glanced at her. "I wouldn't've pegged you as the jealous type, Velma."

"Jealous?" She thought about it and snorted back a laugh. "Oh, yeah. That's what calls to me. A guy who shaves once a week and doesn't use articles or pronouns half the time."

Nate had a follow-up question but exhaustion settled on him like a lead apron. He'd been eager to get back and see Veek's face light up when he told her about the generator room. With that done, his body was shutting down. Every step took a major effort.

Tim was waiting for them at the top landing. "Didn't think we'd see you so soon," he said. "What've you got for us?"

"Big stuff," said Nate. "Tons of pictures."

"There's a bunch of generators down there," said Veek, "running off a fault line."

Tim's eyebrows went up. "How deep down are we talking?"

"About a mile," said Nate. He tried to say something else and yawned.

"Dead on your feet," said Tim with a nod. "Let's talk about it tomorrow."

Nate had a response for that, too, but couldn't remember what it was. He relented to the terrible weight of his eyelids for a moment. When he opened them he was in his apartment and his sneaker was trying to get off his foot. Veek sat on his steamer trunk with his right foot in her lap. The laces were undone and she tugged on the sole. It popped off in her hand.

"Oh, God," she said, wrinkling her nose. "You've been walking for two days, that's for sure." She tugged off the sock with two fingers, held it like a dirty diaper, and set his bare foot down on the floor. The sock flew toward the bathroom and she picked up the other sneaker. The knot fell apart under her fingers and Nate realized he was stretched out on his couch with a pillow under his head.

"Just go back to sleep," said Veek. She dragged a thin blanket over him. "Like Tim said, we can talk about it tomorrow."

He was going to answer this time for sure. He even had a clever joke about her pulling his clothes off. And then he was asleep.

❖

"This room was marked 'control,'" said Nate the next morning. He'd been out for ten hours straight. He hadn't slept that many hours in a row since college.

He turned in a slow circle. He looked at the towering walls and window of Clive and Debbie's apartment. "It's the control room."

Tim looked up at the high ceiling. "Controlling what, though?"

"The building," said Veek.

"Yeah, but what does that mean?" said Tim. "Is there something in here that controls the temperature or the water pressure or the power usage or..." He shrugged. "How do you control a building?"

"It's got to have something to do with the walls in here," said Nate.

Clive looked around his apartment. "Thc fact that they're two stories tall or the fact that they're wood?"

Nate eyed the tall planks. "I don't know," he said. "Yes? Both? This is the only place with walls that aren't painted, so we know there wasn't something written here. But we know it's a special room because it's built different than all the rest."

"But they're all different," said Tim.

Veek nodded. "Right, but this is seriously different. It's like apples and oranges and a cinderblock. So what's in here that makes it special?"

"It's got a chandelier," said Tim.

"I've helped Oskar change bulbs on it twice," said Clive. "If it was the big secret, I don't think he would've let me get that close to it."

"Unless he doesn't know it's the secret," said Nate.

"I have a question," said Debbie.

"Sure," Nate said.

"Did the diagram say 'control room' or did it just say 'control'? There's a difference."

"How so?" asked Tim.

"Well if it's just 'control' then it might mean like a control *group*," she said. "The one you don't do anything to so you've got a baseline."

"Like an experiment," Tim said.

Debbie nodded.

Nate wished he had Xela's pictures. "I think it was just 'control,'" he said.

"Well, that's a pleasant thought," murmured Clive.

Veek's lip twisted up. "What are you worried about? If that's right, we're the lab rats and you're the one getting sugar pills."

"Yeah," said Debbie, "but all the rats get dissected at the end of the trials. That's just the way it goes."

Nate stood by the couch and studied the walls. "There's got to be something else," he said. "You haven't noticed anything else? Anything at all."

"Nope," said Debbie.

"Nothing's attached to them," said Clive.

"Oh," Debbie said. "Yeah, there's that."

Nate looked at them. "What do you mean?"

Clive gestured at their kitchen area. "Nothing's attached to the walls. Anywhere. The counter, the sink, the cabinets—it's all a big free-standing piece, like an entertainment center or something. There's a five-inch gap between the counters and the wall." He pointed down. "The outlets aren't even in the walls. They're all in the floor."

"You never told me that," said Veek.

Debbie shrugged. "With all the things you've found, it just seemed like minor weirdness."

Nate went to the counters, and stretched his arm in the space behind them. His fingertips parted cobwebs and brushed something that whisked away. The wood was lacquer-smooth behind the counter, too.

"There's nothing there," said Debbie. "I've dropped a dozen forks and spoons back there and had to go after them."

"And a spatula," said Clive. "It ended up dead center in the middle. Took forever to get that damned thing out."

"Language," said Debbie. "And I told you to just leave it."

"Yeah, but then we wouldn't have a spatula."

"We could've got one at the Ninety-Nine Cents store."

Veek leaned over Nate and her phone shined white light into the space. He glanced up at her. "High-tech to the rescue?"

"Velma's the smart one," she said. "I don't see anything."

"Neither do I."

"Told you," said Debbie.

Nate slid his arm out and tapped his fingers on the counter. "If there was something to find," he said after a moment, "if you were going to hide something, you wouldn't put it down low."

Tim nodded. "You wouldn't want somebody stumbling across it by accident."

"Right," said Nate. "So you'd put it where someone could only find it if they were looking for it." He pointed above his head. "And who's going to stumble across something twelve or thirteen feet up?"

Veek already had eyes on the loft platform. "Can I look?"

"I'll go with you," said Debbie. They climbed the staircase and started to pore over boards around the bed.

"I looked at the walls a lot when I built the loft," said Clive. "I'm pretty sure there's nothing up there."

"How sure?" asked Nate.

The other man shrugged. "I thought it was pretty amazing, all this hardwood," he said. "And I know I checked it again when we moved the furniture up there. The guy I asked to help was a little rambunctious and kept hitting the walls. I was freaking out about how much it would cost to repair them if one of the boards got gouged or cracked."

"And you never saw anything at all?" asked Tim.

Clive shook his head and shrugged again. "Not up there. And we've been up there every night for two years. Debbie even studies up there sometimes."

The women took another ten minutes. "Nope," Debbie called down. "We can't find anything."

"We've got to get out there and check out the rest of it," said Veek. She gestured at the high walls. "We need a ladder."

FIFTY

Roger had a collapsible ladder in his truck. He unfolded it in Debbie and Clive's apartment until it formed an A-frame eight feet tall. It stood against the wall near their loft. "What am I looking for?"

Nate shrugged. "A hidden panel or switch or something," he said. "Maybe something between the boards. Something that looks like it could be some type of control."

"So...something weird?"

Nate smirked. "Yeah."

"Yeah. Getting sick of that word."

Over the next hour, Roger worked his way across two walls with the ladder. Tim took over for the other two. When they got to the end they reconfigured the ladder into a straight length and leaned it back up against the walls. It went up sixteen feet, well into the next floor of the building.

Veek looked up the ladder. "Not for me," she said. "I've got a thing about heights."

Nate glanced at her. "I thought you had a thing about bugs."

"I've got more than one thing. It's allowed."

"You were okay up in the loft," said Debbie.

"Because the loft is a nice big space with guard rails," Veek said. "A ladder's a flagpole with delusions of grandeur."

"S'okay," said Roger. "I'll do the high stuff. I'm fine on a ladder."

Veek coughed once. "So where's Xela?"

"Working on something for a class tomorrow. A painting. She was excited about the big hike and forgot it was due."

"When'd she remember?"

"Early this morning," said Roger. "One of those things where she just opened her eyes and said, 'Shit, I've got to do this thing.'"

Veek pursed her lips and nodded.

Roger caught himself halfway up the ladder and gave her a wry smile. "Didn't hear that from me, though."

Clive snorted out a laugh.

"Hey," said Nate. He gestured at the walls. "Less bragging, more climbing."

Roger went up a few more rungs and balanced on one near the top. He examined the seams between the planks. Nate felt pretty sure the rung below Roger's feet said something along the lines of DO NOT STAND ON OR ABOVE.

Veek leaned next to him against the couch. "So," she murmured. "Xela and Roger."

Nate glanced at her. "For someone who's not jealous," he said quietly, "you keep bringing this up a lot."

"I'm just thinking of you," she said. "You're not jealous?"

"Why?" said Nate.

"Single guy," she said, "pretty neighbor..." She shrugged.

He shook his head. "A little envious, maybe, in that basic guy kind of way, but hey, good for them."

Veek nodded. "Good. I don't want you all mooning and heartbroken and distracted when we're getting close."

"Nope. Don't worry about it."

"Good."

"Hey, check this out," called Roger. He balanced on his left and leaned out past the ladder. His finger touched a black spot on one of the planks.

Nate tried to focus on it. Against the dark wood it was almost invisible. "What d'you got?"

"This isn't a knot," said Roger. "It's a hole. A drilled hole. Looks like a coffin lock or something." He leaned a little further and squinted at the spot.

"Seriously?" asked Clive.

Roger nodded. "Yeah, I can see the socket in there. Got an Allen wrench set?"

"Yeah." Clive stepped away towards the oversized tool chest.

Nate tapped the ladder. "What's a coffin lock?"

"Special latch," said Roger. "Use 'em when you want to have a low-profile connection you can undo real easy."

"They use them in theaters to hold sections of the deck together," added Clive. He held up a small silver rectangle for Roger to see and then lobbed it underhand up alongside the ladder. Roger snagged it in mid-air.

"The deck?" asked Tim.

"The stage floor," Clive explained. "It's called a deck."

"Learn something every day," said Tim.

"What," said Veek, "that wasn't in one of those books you published?"

Roger unfolded the Allen wrench set and slid one of the thicker arms into the small hole. "Not good," he said. "Might be metric. Maybe custom, knowing this place." He aimed a small flashlight into the opening. "Yeah, it's kinda funky. Looks like two of the sides are longer. Diamond-shaped, like a jewel or something."

"Can you make it work?" asked Veek.

Roger nodded. "Think so." His face bent into a look of concentration as he worked the Allen wrench with his left hand and hung onto the ladder with his right. "Wrench is biting, but the lock's stiff," he told them. "Feels like it might be rusted or something."

"Careful," said Nate. "You don't want to break it."

He shook his head. "Doesn't feel weak," he said. "Just stiff. Ahhh!" He grinned. "Got it loose."

Roger twisted his hand and the lock turned.

A series of clanks came from inside the walls. They banged out one after another. It was the sound of chains and giant clocks grinding to life.

A second noise, a shrill sound, started up behind the long wooden planks. All around the apartment, they trembled in time with the sounds. A deep rattle echoed out, and Nate realized all the sounds had become much clearer.

"Fuck!" shouted Roger.

Clive lunged at the ladder as all the walls in the room became hazy. The boards puffed out years of dust along their entire lengths. The tremble became a blur. A beat later Nate realized why Roger had shouted.

The planks turned like a monstrous set of vertical blinds. The ladder shifted with them and almost toppled before Clive leaped onto the bottom rung to balance it. Nate and Tim dove in to help. Roger slid down, almost fell on top of Clive, and a loud crack echoed in the room. The rotating boards forced the loft away from the walls. The side of the wooden steps splintered as the outer edge of the platform refused to budge.

The ladder fell against the kitchen counter and crashed to the floor.

The planks kicked up more dust as they swung open to reveal the dark space inside the walls. Sounds echoed out and shook the glass in the windows. The boards pointed straight out from the wall and slid back into narrow slots.

The noises stopped. There was a beat of silence.

"You okay?" Nate asked Roger. His eyes stared past the man to the new walls.

"Oh, yeah," he said. He stared over his own shoulder. "That big wet spot's just a drink I spilled in my lap."

Tim chuckled and batted his hand at the air.

Debbie coughed out some dust. "Oh my God."

The walls behind the planks were brass and wood. In places they were steel. A faint hum drifted from them, felt on the air more than heard. In a few spots there were tall cylinders. Veek pointed at the wall by the apartment door. It held racks and racks of horizontal glass tubes, each one strung with a series of glowing wires. A second row was visible behind the framework holding them. "Are those fuses," Veek asked, "or vacuum tubes?"

"Christ," said Tim. "It's all World War One high tech."

"Forget World War One," murmured Clive. He and Debbie clenched their shaking hands together. "It's all steampunk."

What had been the space between the kitchen and the loft was now a large panel of switches and pushbuttons, levers and knobs. They were grouped in rows and in small rectangles. A handful of large gauges clustered above the controls, like six brass portholes.

"What the fuck is all this?" murmured Roger.

Nate glanced at Tim. "You were right," he said. "You don't control a building. You control a machine."

FIFTY ONE

Veek walked up to the control panel and shook her head. "I think I can say a Victorian super-computer was one of the last things I expected to find in this place."

Clive and Debbie looked at the wall of fuses. Half of it was hidden by their loft. He reached out to touch one of the glass tubes and she jerked his hand back. She glanced back at the others. "Do you think it all still works?"

There was a crackle of energy from one of the tubes. Debbie stepped back as it flared a brilliant orange and then faded. Tim leaned past them and peered at it.

"Power surge," he announced. "Almost blew the fuse, but not quite."

"So it's a fuse?" asked Roger.

Tim shrugged. "Maybe. Just a figure of speech, I guess."

Clive inspected the edge of one of the boards. An inch of it still stuck out between the banks of glass tubes. He pinched it between his fingers and slid his hand down its length. "They're covered with rubber inside," he said. "Electrical insulation. It probably soundproofed the apartment a bit, too."

"So this is what all the power's for," said Nate. "Whatever the hell this is."

"It's a *Koturovic*," said Veek.

"Sorry?"

She pointed next to the kitchen counter. There was a brass plaque on a dusty wooden panel. The word was engraved across the plaque in tall letters. "*Koturovic*," she repeated.

"What the hell's a co-turravitch?" said Roger.

"Is it the machine," asked Tim, "or the creator?"

"Or someone they dedicated it to?" said Clive. "Maybe someone who died while they were building it. It could be a memorial."

Debbie's face lit up. "K is one of the letters on the cornerstone, isn't it?"

Veek gave a half shrug. "It is, but it's a middle initial. Kinda weird to just use your middle name on a plaque."

"Koturovic's a surname," said Tim. "A patronymic. Not a middle name."

"Know what?" said Roger. He was standing by the gauges and switches. "These controls are all fucked up."

Nate looked up from the plaque. "What makes you say that?"

"Everything's at zero."

"So?"

He gestured at the wall of tubes. "Power's on right? Things are glowing, tubes are sparking, all that?"

"Flux capacitor is fluxing," nodded Clive.

"Should be reading something, then, right?"

"Maybe zero is what you're reading," said Nate.

Roger shook his head. "If zero's normal what do the needles do when the power shuts off?"

"Maybe the power isn't really on," said Debbie. "Maybe this is all...I don't know, in sleep mode or something." She gestured at the kitchen counter. Behind it was an array of brass cylinders like a pipe organ. "You can have power running to the microwave even when it's not doing anything."

Roger shook his head again. "It's old and it's busted."

Tim walked over and peered at the brass-ringed dials. "Zero's in the middle," he said, "not at the end."

"So?"

"So it means the needles can go either way," said Tim. "They're not at an extreme, they're at a midpoint." He tapped one of the dials. "These tell you if it's in balance."

"If what's in balance?" asked Nate.

"Beats the shit outta me," said Roger.

"Question," said Veek. "Do you think this is all one thing, one machine, or is this a bunch of stuff that's just all controlled here?"

"Kinda the same thing, isn't it?" asked Clive.

Nate shook his head. "You can have a universal remote that controls a bunch of stuff."

"Right," said Clive, "but it's a bunch of stuff that's all part of the same system."

Nate got close to the wall of tubes. He could feel Debbie's hand hovering near his arm, ready to pull him back if something happened. There was another rack of glass fuses—if they *were* fuses—past the first one. Behind those he could see more wires and cables and something like a tire wrapped in copper wire. He stepped back and looked over at the panel of switches and buttons. It looked like the controls for a Victorian jumbo jet.

"So a hundred and twenty years ago," he said, "someone built a big machine in the middle of Los Angeles and disguised it as a building. Why?"

"Not even in the middle," said Veek. "There's a great map on the Library of Congress website from 1909. A hundred years ago this wasn't even the suburbs. Hollywood was still a big field. Heck, the official roads ended over at Temple Street."

Nate looked at the banks of machinery and instruments. "So they built it far away from everything," he said. "On the far coast of the country, on the outskirts of a city that was only a few thousand people. They probably never dreamed it would get this big, that Kavach would end up dead in the middle of everything."

Something clicked. It echoed through the apartment. Roger's hand hovered by the controls.

They all closed in on him. "What'd you do?" said Nate.

"Flipped a switch," he said. "Don't worry, bro, I've got my hand over it."

"You idiot," snapped Veek. "We don't know what this thing does."

"Only way to find out is to do something," said Roger. He nodded at the six large dials. "Check it out."

The first dial hadn't budged, but the needle on the second one had shifted over by four thin lines. The next needle was still moving, creeping across the round face. Two of the bottom ones hadn't moved. The needle on the last dial had tilted in the opposite direction.

"You're right," Roger said to Tim. "Some kinda load-balance or something for the power lines."

"Still stupid," said Veek. "That could've been the self-destruct switch or something."

"Naaah," said Clive. "Self-destruct's always a big red button."

Roger and Debbie chuckled. The corners of Veek's mouth twitched. "Still think it was a stupid move," she said.

A big truck drove by on the street outside. It blended with the hum of the machine. The low rumble made the floor tremble.

Roger studied the dials. "Can't figure out what they're measuring, though."

"I thought you didn't know power stuff," said Nate.

"Don't, but I know the basics."

"None of us know this, though," said Tim. "We don't know what this thing does, or how much one switch affects it doing its...whatever it does."

A cloud crossed the sun and the windows grew dim. Nate glanced up at the sky. As his eyes moved he saw Debbie looking at the chandelier. Veek and Tim looked back and forth at the corners of the room.

The rumble of the truck was still going. It got louder. It swung the chandelier. It shook the floor. The loft was quivering on its legs.

"Quake!" Clive called out. "Get out from under the chandelier."

Debbie dashed to her husband. Tim took a few long strides and pressed himself against the door. Roger and Veek, California veterans, stood their ground and waited to see how bad it got.

Nate's gaze came down from the sky—a sky burned into his mind—and looked at the building next door. He could see it through the trembling panes of glass. While he watched a little girl walked by a window. She held a bright blue plastic cup at chin height with both hands.

"Roger," he said, "flip the switch back."

"What?"

Nate pointed at the panel. Roger's hand had drifted away from the switch but was still close enough to be sure which one he'd flipped. "Put it back."

The dishes in the sink began to clatter. The vase of flowers on the table toppled and water splashed to the floor.

"It's a fucking earthquake, bro."

"It's not an earthquake," shouted Nate over the rumble, "it's *the building*! Put the switch back!"

Roger's finger stretched out, settled against a tiny lever, and flexed. The switch snapped down. A small spark flashed around the rim of its base and vanished.

Two of the needles leaped to zero. The last one, the slow one, paused for a moment and then reversed its swing. It inched its way back up to its start position.

The rumble faded. The clouds cleared away outside and the sun beamed through the window. A few seconds later, the only sign of the disturbance was the creak from the swaying chandelier. Then it stopped and there was silence.

"Holy shit," muttered Tim.

Nate looked out the window again, up at the sky. The rest of them exchanged glances and took tentative steps. "Everyone okay?" asked Veek.

"Think I wet my pants for real this time," said Roger.

"You're not alone," murmured Debbie.

Veek punched Roger in the arm. "You are a fucking idiot, you know that?"

"Hey," he snapped, "how was I supposed to know it was a fucking earthquake machine? You think somebody'd label the switches for something like that."

"It wasn't an earthquake," said Nate. He was still staring out the window.

"How can you be so sure?" asked Tim.

Nate turned from the window. He looked up above the control panel. A square of polished wood, a foot on each side, still remained there. Clive's Allen wrench jutted out from the center of it. The silver steel looked out of place against all the wood and brass. "Can you reach that?" he asked Roger.

Roger glanced at the ladder, still stretched out on the floor by the kitchen. "Think so," he said. "Might be a little tricky, but I think I can use the A-frame now that I know where the keyhole is."

"Do it," said Nate. "Get these walls closed up."

"Hey," said Veek. "Hang on. What's wrong?"

"What's wrong?" echoed Nate. "Did you miss that? This thing...this *place* is *dangerous*. We shouldn't be fucking around with it." He jabbed a finger at the Allen wrenches. "Close it and forget it."

"How are we supposed to forget about it?" said Debbie. "We live here. It's all around us."

"Well, you have to," said Nate, "because we can't mess around with this thing anymore." He looked at their faces, took in a breath to say something else, and shook his head. He walked past Tim, yanked the door open, and headed down the hall toward the stairwell.

Veek chased him to the foot of the stairs. "Hey," she called out. "What the hell's your problem?"

He stopped on the landing. "I just think..." He shook his head. "We shouldn't be messing with this anymore. Whatever it is, it's way beyond us."

"That's why we're looking," she said. "To find out, remember? To learn what the hell this stuff is."

"Maybe it's better not knowing," he snapped. "Maybe this is one of those...one of those things men weren't meant to know."

She frowned up at him through her glasses. "What happened?"

"Nothing happened, I just think—"

"Nate," she said, "you're freaking out. What just happened?"

He shook his head.

"You've been through an earthquake before, right? It's sort of scary but they almost never amount to anything. Once I slept through one that—"

"It wasn't an earthquake."

She studied his face. "Why do you keep saying that?"

Nate pressed his palms against his temples and shook his head. "This is nuts," he said. "It's just...it's fucking nuts."

"What?"

He looked at her. "When he flipped the switch and the ground started shaking," he said, "you saw the sun go away?"

She nodded.

"It wasn't clouds," he said. "It was going out."

Veek blinked. She opened her mouth, shut it, then blinked again. "What?"

"Right in front of my eyes," said Nate. "It turned red, the whole sky got dark around it, and the sun started to go out."

FIFTY TWO

Nate went into the office determined to get as caught up as possible. He'd been neglecting his work for too long, as the stack of mail crates proved. A fourth one showed up first thing that morning. It was mostly issues of the magazine, so it would go fast. For the moment, though, it just added to his pile. A pile now higher than his desktop.

Halfway through the magazine crate Eddie showed up. The big man made a few clucking noises and shook his head while he made some comments about productivity. Nate tried to ignore him and kept typing in addresses.

When Zack and Jimmy filed out for a quick smoke-break, Nate switched to his browser. He checked email and saw he'd gotten a response from someone at the city's Office of Public Works about the building. It'd almost been a month since he put in a request to see the Kavach Building's blueprints. He'd given up on it. Now he was nervous about what it might say.

He looked at the news. There was no mention of anything happening to the sun. No unexpected eclipses or sudden dense cloud layers. One weather forecast said the spectacular weekend sunshine was going to last all week. There were no reports of an earthquake in Los Angeles. Not even a small one.

As far as Nate could tell, whatever happened yesterday only happened inside Kavach.

Which was insane. Grade-A insane, without a doubt.

But it hadn't been his imagination. The building had shook. He'd heard Tim talking with Mandy about it in the hall—with Biblical commentary from Andrew—after he'd retreated to his apartment. They'd all felt it. So had Mrs. Knight. He wondered if she was going to complain to Oskar about the disturbance.

Oskar, Nate thought. *Maybe we should've been listening to him all along.*

The machine in the building, the machine that *was* the building, had made the sun go dim. It made the sun change color and fade in intensity, like a candle wick sputtering in a puddle of wax. But only for people in the building.

Maybe, he thought, *it did something to the windows. Like polarizing lenses. Maybe the glass got dark and it made the sun look like it was fading.*

Except there had been the little girl in the next building. The girl with the bright blue plastic cup. She hadn't been dark. He'd expected her to look up at the thing in the sky and scream or cry or react somehow. But she hadn't seen it.

I saw it.

And that, he admitted, was the real problem. He'd lied to Veek. He hadn't told her everything, because what he *had* seen up in the sky was real madness.

The sun had waned, the sky had turned red and he'd caught a glimpse of...something else. It hadn't been just a red sun freaking him out. There'd been something moving up there, something fading *in* even as the sun was fading out. Something bigger than any plane he'd ever seen, even the ones that sometimes roared by just overhead and blotted out the sky. It had been that big and it had been far away, like a blue whale soaring in the sky.

A whale with bat-wings and a huge mass of...

It had to be a delusion of some kind. Maybe it had been a balloon. He was so out of touch, it wouldn't be hard to believe some custom blimp was flying around LA and he hadn't heard about it. Probably advertising some new tentpole movie. It could've just been a picture on the side of a blimp. He glanced around his desk for a current issue of the magazine and wondered if there were any summer movies with big dragons or space monsters that had

tentacles.

That had been the snapping point. Seeing the dozens of tentacles drifting back and forth, moving up and down in the air—and they *had* moved. It hadn't been a picture on a blimp. A blimp that vanished as soon as Roger threw the switch back.

A hand settled on his shoulder and he shuddered away from it.

"Dude," said Zack. "Chill. It's just me."

"Sorry," said Nate. "Off in my own world. What's up?"

Zack sighed. "I quit."

Nate sat up in his chair. "Sorry?"

"I'm done. Packing up. I just sent Eddie an email."

"You've got something else lined up?"

Zack leaned against the desk and shook his head. "Nothing," he said. "I just can't take this anymore, y'know?"

"I guess."

"It's a mind-numbing job with shit pay and no bennies," he said. "I think I'm losing an IQ point every week. I checked it out—if I'd been working for Jack in the Box all this time I'd've made another two thousand dollars and I'd have a health plan."

Nate had no response. He'd started working at the magazine six months before Zack.

"Jack in the Box, man! That's a better career path than this place." He shook his head again. "I want to do something with my life, y'know? Achieve something. I can't sit here doing data entry for another year and wishing something amazing would happen."

"Yeah," said Nate, "I know what you mean."

Nate paced in his apartment for an hour. Veek was going to be pissed at him. Pissed was her default setting, so he couldn't imagine dodging it. He needed to apologize and he needed to tell her about the

tentacles

thing he'd seen up in the sky. Bugs terrified her. She had to understand him getting freaked out by something with wings that dwarfed football fields.

Then Veek banged on his door. He realized he'd been pacing around without a shirt on and grabbed a nearby tee. Then he sniffed it, threw it toward the bathroom, and grabbed a clean one off the shelf. She banged again. "Hold on," he yelled.

He glanced through the peephole and saw Veek had turned into Roger. He unchained the door. "What's up?" asked Nate. "I thought you always worked late."

Roger shook his head. "Told the best boy I was sick. Started coughing and sniffling at lunch. He let me go on the Abby."

"I don't know what that means."

"Means he let me go early," said Roger. "Know you're having some issues right now, bro, but this is seriously fucked up."

Nate nodded. "I'm working past them."

"Good." Roger held up a sheet of paper. "She translated the mystery note from your wall. Said it's really authentic and creepy."

"What?"

"She thought I was writing a script or something."

Nate took the sheet. It was covered in the neat, curvy handwriting so many women mastered and men almost never did. The top half was the message, recopied in the same Cyrillic that it had been on the wall. Below it was the translation in English.

To Whomever Finds These Words,

Thirteen years ago I made a discovery of the most shocking nature. Some men would quake at the nightmarish truth I learned. Others would lose their minds to the horror of it. Indeed, I have since learned, much to my dismay, of those who accept and embrace such horror, as a drowning man will sometimes embrace another and take the poor unfortunate down with him. In the face of such a destiny, perhaps such madness is to be expected.

Yet I have chosen to resist, and I have been fortunate enough to find those men brave enough and strong enough to resist with me, and I am proud to call them my friends.

Humanity shall never lay down and die. Humanity shall conquer every challenge it is given. Kavach is a monument to what we have achieved, and to the inextinguishable spark that is man.

Do not falter. Do not doubt. Keep the needles at zero.

Your Friend in Triumph,
Aleksander Koturovic
12 August 1895

He looked up and met Roger's gaze.

"What the fuck, right?" said Roger.

"Aleksander Koturovic," said Nate. "That's the name on the machine. It's a person."

"Yeah, saw that, too."

"What language is it?"

"Serbian, but she said it's old Serbian. A lot of people just use the regular English alphabet now, not the Russian one."

"Latin and Cyrillic."

"Yeah, whatever. See what it says, though?"

"What do you mean?"

"'Keep the needles at zero,'" said Roger. "What d'you think that means? We just found a whole bunch of hidden dials and gauges and stuff."

Nate nodded. "All of them at zero."

"And everything went apeshit when I flipped a switch and made 'em move, remember?"

"Yeah," said Nate, "I remember."

"Been thinking about this all day," he said. "You get what's going on here?"

Nate tried to wrap his mind around the message and the machine. "We need to make sure the needles stay at zero."

Roger shook his head. "Think big," he said. "Machine's on and things are cool, right? Everything's cool while the needles are at zero."

"Okay," said Nate. "Right."

"That means all the shit that happened when I fucked with it—when the needles weren't at zero—that's what things are like when the machine's not working. That's what the machine's *stopping* things from being like."

Roger tapped the piece of paper and it rustled between Nate's fingers.

"That's *normal*," said Roger.

FIFTY THREE

"Okay," said Nate, "despite my little freak-out last weekend, we've learned a lot this week. I'm going to tell you my one new bit, and then I'm going to let Debbie tell you all the stuff she found."

They were gathered in the lounge for the Saturday meeting. It was a smaller group. Clive was working at a theater in North Hollywood, but he'd heard most of it already, and Andrew was at a prayer meeting. Mandy didn't want anything to do with them after the building shook. Tim had gotten her to promise she wouldn't turn them in to Oskar.

They'd dragged the couches into a rough circle. *More of a triangle, really*, thought Nate. He leaned on the arm of one couch, where Veek sat with Debbie and Tim. She was next to Nate, but still a bit cool toward him. Mrs. Knight dominated her couch, her cane ready to strike. Roger and Xela sprawled together on another couch, and her laptop covered her lap.

"I finally heard back from Public Works the other day," Nate said. "They're supposed to have all the building plans on file. The only things they don't keep are residences, which get tossed, and historical documents. Those go off to libraries or museums.

"The guy was pretty helpful. A bunch of stuff from the late 1800s had all been moved to the Getty a while back, and he'd assumed the Kavach plans, if they still existed, would've gone with it."

"And now they're missing from the Getty?" guessed Mrs. Knight.

He shook his head. "No, they never went. He checked and it turns out the Kavach plans are still considered active material and are still on file at Public Works."

"Fantastic," said Xela. "So we can go see them."

Nate shook his head. "Nope. That's where it ends. They're sealed records."

Tim's eyebrows went up. "Sealed?"

"Yep. The same way they seal plans for things like the Federal Building or parts of the state capitol or embassies. The guy emailed me to explain why he couldn't tell me anything. He even said he has to make a note in the file that I asked about them because of some Patriot Act thing."

"The Patriot Act?" coughed Veek.

Nate nodded.

Tim set his jaw. "So this isn't just something that happened a hundred and twenty years ago," he said.

Nate nodded again. "It might just be bureaucracy, but yeah. I think somebody's still trying to keep this place a secret."

"So...what's that all mean?" asked Roger. "Are we terrorists now or something?"

Tim shook his head. "Persons of interest at best."

"What's that get us?"

"Fifty years at Guantanamo Bay," scoffed Veek.

"Well, hang on," said Nate. "Debbie's got the really big stuff."

He slid off the arm and onto the couch. Veek shuffled down and Debbie stood up. She held a thin deck of index cards that she massaged with the other hand. They were bright white, but halfway through she'd marked the edges with black magic marker. She'd gone over most of them with Nate the night before. Debbie smiled nervously and then slipped a pair of reading glasses from her pocket. She skimmed the first few cards and then smiled again.

"Okay," said Debbie, "everyone ready for history 101?"

"Would've brought an apple if I'd known teacher was going to be hot," grinned Roger. Xela reached over the laptop to whack him in the arm.

Debbie blushed and massaged her cards again. "I spent the past three days at the school library looking for Aleksander Koturovic."

"I could've done that," said Veek. She shot a glance at Nate. "How long could a few web searches take?"

"I didn't use the web, though," said Debbie. "There's still a lot of older stuff that hasn't made it to the internet, so we figured it might be better to go old-school. I checked card catalogs, encyclopedias, and some newspapers and magazines on microfiche."

"Stop keeping us in suspense, dear," said Mrs. Knight. "What did you find?"

"Sorry," Debbie said. "I'm not good with public speaking."

"It's just us," said Tim. "We're not grading you." He gave a pointed look at the others. Even Mrs. Knight shifted on her couch.

Debbie glanced at her cards. "Okay," she said, "Aleksander Koturovic was a Serbian biochemist and neurophysiologist before people used those words. He also did a lot of research into evolution and wrote a few papers on Neanderthal man and extinctions. He was the Walter Bishop of his time, and most of his ideas got him labeled as a quack." She gave a little smile as she flipped an index card to the back of the pile. "To be honest, half his ideas would still get him labeled as a quack.

"This makes it tough to find a lot of solid material on him because so much of his work got discounted as irrelevant. Most of it just ends up buried in pseudo-science books. Pretty much the only place you can find him is lumped in with guys like Edgar Cayce or Immanuel Velikovsky. He believed in telepathy, shared dreaming, race memories, all that kind of stuff. The idea that people's minds can all connect on some extra-sensory level."

"So he was a nut," said Tim.

"Maybe." She flipped over another card. "At the time people thought this was real science. H. G. Wells edited this huge book, *The Science of Life*, and there's a whole section about telepathy in it. He even mentions Koturovic in passing.

"Now, this is all a bit sketchy," Debbie said. She looked up from the cards and gave an apologetic frown. "I had to piece stuff together from a few different sources and they didn't all agree. I didn't have time to cross-check all of it, so I don't know how much of this is accurate."

"Don't worry about it," said Xela.

"Okay. So, Koturovic studied the structure of the brain and how much bio-electricity it put out and what frequencies that electricity was on. He moved to London and in 1877 he attended a lecture given by a mathematician named William Clifford who was one of the first people to propose the idea of other dimensions. He noticed—"

"Wait," said Tim. "Other dimensions?"

She nodded. "I looked him up. Clifford did a lot of work with concepts like curved space and there being more to the world than just the standard three dimensions. At least a fourth, mathematically speaking, and probably a fifth, sixth, seventh, and so on."

Tim raised an eyebrow but said nothing else.

She glanced at her cards to find her place. "So, Koturovic noticed a lot of similarities between Clifford's math involving higher dimensions and his own calculations about telepathy. There were places where the numbers lined up, and he decided there might be a connection."

"I remember something like that in an astronomy course I took in college," said Nate. "There was one class where the professor showed us how geometry and trigonometry tie directly to relativity. It really blew me away."

Debbie nodded. "Right. Same idea. So this became the focus of Koturovic's research for the next ten years. He didn't write much, but he did note that he'd gotten confirmation of the 'telepathic vibrations' from a friend. He tried to present his work to the University College board in 1887 and got kicked out. It was another year before he published anything else, and even then it was more of this fringe science stuff that's gotten twisted and become unreliable."

"Just a moment," said Mrs. Knight. "First you were saying all of this was considered acceptable science. Now you're saying they called him a nut because of it."

"It's because of where he was going with it," said Debbie. "It's like people today who try to use math to prove the moon landings were faked or aliens built the pyramids. He was an embarrassment to the university, so they got rid of him."

"So what got him fired?" Roger asked.

Debbie tapped her cards. "He thought the world was going to end."

"No way," said Xela.

"Yep. He claimed there was a kind of psychic critical mass, and when it was reached...that was it."

Veek tilted her head. "Critical mass?"

Debbie nodded again and shuffled another card to the back. "Okay, remember how Koturovic was studying telepathy and got obsessed with dimensional mathematics?" She waited for enough of them to nod. "Okay, so he was convinced that once there were enough people in the world—when the population passed a key point—their combined brainwaves would sync up and achieve a sort of harmonic frequency that would break down certain dimensional barriers, like how a tuning fork can break glass."

"Let me guess," said Tim. He glanced at Nate. "Would that population be somewhere around one and a half billion?"

"One-point-five-two, according to the article I found," said Debbie. "But I think we've got the refined number."

Veek looked at Nate. "Why didn't you tell me all this?"

"I tried last night," he said. "You weren't talking to me, remember?"

She smacked his arm.

Roger frowned. "So this was gonna destroy the world? The tuning fork thing?"

Debbie shook her head. "Nope," she said. "What was in the other dimension would."

Nate blinked. "What?"

"I have no idea where this next bit comes from," said Debbie. "This is just how all the stories and articles I found go, and it's almost definitely what made University College get rid of him.

"Koturovic somehow came up with the idea there were some kind of creatures—big, smart, scary alpha predators—living in these higher dimensions. Telepathically-sensitive people sensed them all through history and that's where all our myths about demons and monsters come from. It's their presence leaking through. When the dimensional barriers were shattered, according to him, these things would come through and eat everything they could until the barriers reasserted themselves. Kind of the universe's method of population control."

Nate glanced at the sky through the lounge's big windows.

"Creepy," said Veek.

"It gets creepier," said Debbie.

"It sounds silly to me," said Mrs. Knight.

"You didn't tell me any of this the other night," Nate said to Debbie.

"I just gave you the highlights," she said. "Sorry."

"Sucks to be left out, doesn't it?" said Veek. She smacked Nate in the arm again, but it wasn't as hard this time.

"So what were these things supposed to be?" asked Tim.

"I don't know," said Debbie with a tiny shrug. "He falls back on a lot of the fancy descriptions they used back then that say a lot without saying anything. Again, he doesn't even explain how he figured this part out. He just says they're really big and really nasty."

"I'd've fired his ass, too," said Roger. "And it still doesn't tell us what all this shit is." He waved his arms around at the building.

"Seems pretty straightforward to me," Nate said. "He predicted the end of the world. Then he built this place to stop it."

FIFTY FOUR

They gazed at the blank walls of the lounge for a few moments.

Xela spoke first. "So this is...what, the anti-apocalypse machine?"

Mrs. Knight sniffed hard through her nose. It was a very dismissive sniff. "If this is supposed to stop the end of the world," she said, "why does it cause earthquakes?"

"It doesn't cause them," said Nate. "It's *preventing* them."

Roger nodded at Nate. "Like we were saying the other night. That's normal. That's what things are like if the machine stops working. If the needles aren't at zero."

Veek nodded. "Makes sense. If doomsday works off the population, it's not like the problem's gone away. If anything, it's gotten worse."

"So you think this is still going on?" Xela's eyes were wide. "The end of the world is, well, still happening?"

Nate shrugged. "It makes sense," he said.

"Not necessarily," said Tim. "If you stick with that tuning fork analogy, it only works at one pitch. If you go higher or lower, it won't work. Maybe once the population passed the critical mark it moved back into a safe zone."

"Bro, maybe you didn't notice when I flipped that switch the other day," said Roger, "but there was an earthquake."

"And the sun went out," added Veek with a nod to Nate.

"See, that doesn't make sense either," said Tim. "I felt that. I saw the shadows. But *no one else did.* We're in California. There's a dozen earthquake sensors in Los Angeles alone. You can't drop a barbell in this state without it registering somewhere. How did we have a five-point-something earthquake in our building that nobody else noticed?"

Nate and Veek exchanged a glance. She shrugged. "Beats me."

"Don't get me wrong," Tim said, "there's definitely something going on here. I just think we need to get a better grip on things before we leap to any conclusions."

Veek looked at Debbie. "You said it got creepier. So what's the creepy bit?"

"Well, Koturovic emigrated to the United States and moved here to Los Angeles," she said. "And he died here. At least, that's the official story."

Tim raised his brows again. "The official story?"

"They never found a body," said Debbie, "which apparently wasn't that rare back then. Lots of people went missing and got reported dead. He was out having dinner with two co-workers on New Year's Eve, 1898. When they left the restaurant they were attacked by a group of people with knives. The other two were killed, witnesses said Koturovic was stabbed but got away. The mob went after him and he was never seen again. The authorities declared him dead a week later."

Xela shifted on the couch. "I thought it took years to do that?"

"Depends on the circumstances," said Tim. "Even back then they could do it quick if they had good reason." He looked at Debbie. "Who were the attackers?"

She shook her head. "The main suspects were a doomsday cult that had been active in Los Angeles at the time, but the police couldn't prove it. From what I've been reading, they probably got paid off. The police, that is."

There was a moment of silence.

"Guessing everyone else is thinking this," said Roger, "but I'll say it out loud. Guy predicts the end of the world, builds a machine to stop the end of the world, and then gets killed by a group worshipping the end of the world."

"A doomsday cult?" said Mrs. Knight. She rapped her bony knuckles on her cane and shook her head. "This whole thing sounds more and more ridiculous."

"There were a lot of them back in the 1880s and '90s," said Debbie. "The same way we had people freaking out over Y2K, there were a lot of people back then who were convinced the world was going to end in 1900." She held up her index cards. "This group was called the Family of the Red Death. I don't have much on them because I didn't want to get too far off-track, but I could look on Monday."

"They have found us," said Nate.

Veek gave him a look. "What?"

"That's what it said on my wall. 'They have found us.'" He nodded as he considered the words. "'They' were the cult. It was his blood."

"Oh, shit," she said.

Tim's chin went up and down. "That fits," he said. "But if they were chasing him here you'd think they'd've found all this."

"That's the big trick, though, isn't it?" said Xela. "If they were looking for a machine, they'd search the building. But it probably wouldn't occur to them the machine *was* the building."

Nate nodded. "What was it Mandy said? If you want to hide a tree, you hide it in a forest. It's the best camouflage you could have."

Tim snapped his fingers. "Which is why they rent it out. A building that stands empty poses questions, but a building with a bunch of unconnected tenants is just another building."

"And why they screen us," said Veek. "They don't want comfortable people. They want tenants with something to lose, ones who won't ask questions or complain about some of the weirdness they come across."

"Well, I've got more on the building, too, sort of," Debbie said. A new card switched to the front. "Once I had Koturovic I could do some cross-referencing and found out a bit more about this plot of land."

"What?" said Veek. "You found more?"

Her face shifted. "I'm sorry. It's just the research bug, y'know? Once I find something I just keep going."

"I should've had you helping me a year ago," sighed Veek.

Nate waved Debbie on. "So, what've you got?"

"Okay, she said, "the land the Kavach Building is on was bought in October of 1890 by a group called the Owyhee Land and Irrigation Company. Like you were saying the other day," she said to Nate, "it was out in the middle of nowhere. A few months later, they filed permits to start construction."

She switched cards again. "Now, about a year after this the company started work on a dam out in Idaho, on a branch of the Snake River called the Bruneau. The story was that this dam was going to replace one they'd built a few years earlier which had collapsed."

"What were they really doing?" asked Tim.

Debbie smiled. "This is where it gets clever. They *were* building a dam. They'd been planning to for about four years. The president of the company was some kind of early entrepreneur-land baron. He wanted to build a town on a lake, so he needed to make a lake."

"But...?" asked Nate.

"But," she said, "there's no actual evidence of the company building the first dam. The one they said they were replacing. There are stories about its collapse and a few news articles about the replacement. Even some photos of it. But it's all kind of thin and there's nothing dated before 1890."

Roger frowned. "Somebody run off with the money?"

"I think we're living in the money," said Veek. "It all went here."

Debbie nodded. "I can't find anything certain, but reading between the lines it sure seems like the first dam was just a story they made up so they could funnel a ton of money out here to make the Kavach Building."

"Just like Locke Management," said Nate. "They didn't want anyone to know they were connected to this place."

"Who owned the company?" asked Tim.

Debbie shuffled back through her notes. "The president of the Owyhee Land and Irrigation Company was Whipple Phillips."

"Whipple?" chuckled Xela.

"Yep."

"Don't name 'em like that anymore," said Roger.

"He traveled all over Europe in the 1870s and 1880s, so it's not hard to guess he could've met Koturovic on one of his trips, heard all his theories, and gotten recruited to help save the world." Debbie stopped to straighten her cards. "The ironic thing is their dam—the real dam—collapsed about ten years later, in 1904. It bankrupted the company. Phillips died at about the same time."

Tim straightened up. "So the...the company, whatever they were called, they don't exist anymore."

"Nope."

"They didn't change their name?"

Debbie shook her head. "They changed it and reorganized a few times back then, but they were gone by 1910."

"So who the hell is Locke Management, then?"

"Wait a minute," said Veek. Her eyes were wide behind her glasses. "We're idiots."

They all looked at her. She turned around and tapped the computer in Xela's lap. "Pull up a picture of the cornerstone," she said.

Xela's fingers swiped back and forth on the mousepad. She spun the computer around and the picture filled the screen. Everyone leaned in to see.

1894
WNA
PTK

"Right there," Veek said. She pointed at the screen. "This was gnawing at me the other day and I couldn't get it. It isn't two monograms, it's three sets of initials. There's Aleksander Koturovic. There's Whippy Phillips."

"So we've got the idea guy and the money guy," said Nate. "So maybe NT is the guy who built it for them."

"What, like the foreman or something?"

Nate shook his head. "He got big letters. Probably more like the architect. Koturovic had all the theories, the raw math, but he needed someone who knew how to put them into practice." He looked at Debbie. "You said he was here in Los Angeles with his co-workers, right? Who were they?"

Debbie flipped back through the cards. "Neville Orange and Adam Taylor."

"Makes sense," muttered Roger.

"Ummmm..." Xela looked at Nate. "This sounds silly but aren't *you* NT?"

"What?"

"Nate Tucker," she said. "NT is you."

They looked at him.

"Bro," said Roger. "You're a time traveler."

"No, I'm not," said Nate.

"Not yet, but maybe in the future."

"It's not me. You really think I built this place?"

"What if you're the one who tells him about the monsters?" suggested Xela, "That's why they just come out of nowhere. He couldn't tell anybody a time traveler from the future told him about them."

"Right," said Tim, "because involving a time traveler makes the idea of giant monsters from another dimension seem foolish."

"I agree with Nathan," said Mrs. Knight. "The initials probably just belong to someone else with a name like..." She rolled her cane on her knees for a moment. "...Norman Terry or Noah Truman or something."

"Nancy Truman," said Veek. "Could be a woman."

"Nigel Tufnel," said Roger with a bad English accent.

"Nelson Tuntz," added Xela.

"Nicholas Ticklebee," giggled Debbie. Then her jaw dropped. "Oh my God."

Nate looked at her. "What's wrong?"

"Serbian scientists and Westinghouse generators," she said. She pointed at the picture of the cornerstone. "It's Nikola Tesla."

FIFTY FIVE

"No way," said Xela.

"Tesla's the electricity guy, right?" asked Roger. "The one in *The Prestige?*"

"Now this is just silly," Mrs. Knight said.

"No, it all makes sense," said Debbie. Her eyes were huge. She bounced on her toes and squeezed the index cards. "Veek, you said Kavach was Indian, right?"

"Marathi, yeah, but it's—"

Debbie bounced again. "Is that the same as Sanskrit? This was on the tip of my brain the other day. Tesla liked to give his projects Sanskrit names. What does it mean?"

"Ummm...I think it means 'armor,' or maybe 'shield.' It depends on...context." Her eyes went wide behind her glasses.

"It's silly," said Mrs. Knight again. "Tesla's a public figure. He couldn't have just snuck off to work on a secret project no one ever knew about."

"But he did," said Nate. "Didn't he move out to Colorado because Thomas Edison burned down his lab or something?"

"Maybe it wasn't Edison," said Tim. "It might've been the Family trying to get him. He went to Colorado to get away from them."

"Getting away from Edison was just a bonus," grinned Xela.

"So now we know the names on the cornerstone," said Veek. "And we know what the machine's supposed to do."

"More or less," said Tim.

"So," Nate said, "I guess that just leaves one last thing."

"Excuse me, Mr. Rommell?"

Oskar turned from the gate. "Yes, Mrs. Knight. What can I do for you?"

She stood at the top of the stairs. She wore a bright red cardigan despite the summer heat and leaned on her cane. Her eyes were hidden from the afternoon light by a wide pair of sunglasses. "Are you heading to the store?"

"I am," he said. "May I pick something up for you?"

Mrs. Knight nodded. "I was wondering if you could get some white tea for me? I'd go myself but my hip is killing me today." She held up a ten dollar bill and a small box, folded flat. "This is the brand I like."

Oskar took the box and his brows shifted. "They haff this at the corner store?"

Mrs. Knight's face dropped. "Oh," she said. "I thought you were going to the real store. The Vons over on Vermont."

"I had not planned to," he said.

"Ahhhh," said Mrs. Knight. She held out her hand for the box. "Well, never mind, then. I'm sure I'll be fine tomorrow and—"

Oskar shook his head. "Not at all," he said. "It is a nice day for a walk, and the Vons will haff better prices. Besides," he winked and patted his broad stomach, "I can always use the exercise."

"You're too kind," she said. "Thank you so much."

"You are very welcome," he said. "I will be back in an hour or so with your tea." He gave her a little bow of his head and headed out the gate.

Mrs. Knight headed inside. Nate, Veek, and Debbie watched from the second floor window as Oskar headed down the street. "He's such a gentleman," said Debbie. "I feel kind of bad tricking him like this."

"He's the one keeping secrets," said Veek.

"Y'know," said Nate, "I'm not even sure he knows."

Debbie looked over her shoulder at him. "Really?"

Nate shrugged. "Think about it. He's a middle-management guy. He's just doing the job he was hired to do. They tell him to keep people from snooping around and causing problems. It doesn't mean he knows why. Like a security guard at CIA headquarters or something."

"I don't know," Veek said. "He always seems like he's hiding a lot to me."

"Yes," said Mrs. Knight from the stairwell. "He hasn't told us our building is an earthquake-causing-apocalypse-prevention machine. That definitely makes him the bad guy."

Nate and Veek headed down the hall to join everyone else at apartment 14. Tim looked up from the padlocks. "I can have them all off in five minutes," he said. "The older ones are a different system. Haven't tried something like that in years."

Veek tilted her head. "The old ones are going to take longer than the new ones?"

He slid out his picks. "They will if you don't want it obvious they were opened."

"Let's do it," said Nate. "Time's a-wasting."

"Just waiting on you, boss," said Tim. A few quick movements and the top lock popped off.

"You'd think the modern ones would be harder," Nate said.

"Nah." Tim hooked the open loop of the lock through his belt. "The core of most modern padlocks are pretty much all the same even though they dress them up with big steel casings." His tools slid into the bottom lock and the pick did its dance. The second lock snapped open and he hung it on the opposite hip.

Xela marched down the hall with a gallon bucket hanging from her hand. A paint-streaked backpack was slung over her other shoulder. "We lucked out," she said. "This one's almost full."

Clive pushed open his door so she could hide her supplies inside his apartment. He looked at the bucket. "You're sure you can fix all this when we're done?"

"It's just paint," Xela said. "Paint's my thing. A little bit of texturing and I can make it pass. Thirty minutes, tops. Maybe a little less if we run some extension cords and I get a hair dryer or two on it."

"Are you sure?" asked Veek.

"If someone stops and studies it, yeah, it might not hold up." Xela said. "But for anything else it'll be fine. And once they slap another coat over it it'll be perfect."

Tim switched to a different tool, a thick wire he pushed into the first of the pirate padlocks. He pushed down on the handle, shifted it, and pushed again. He bit his upper lip, tweaked his grip, and applied pressure a third time. The riveted padlock swung open with a heavy *clunk*. He hung it on a belt loop and bent to the last one, just beneath the doorknob. A minute later it was on his waist. He'd hung them in order, left to right along his belt.

Nate used a screwdriver to pry the over-painted hasps off the door and fold them back. He took hold of the knob and twisted. Decades of paint stretched and twisted. Something shifted and he held a ragged latex pouch wrapped around the glass knob. He pulled it off and twisted the knob again. It was resistant, as if the inside latch was carrying a lot of weight.

The door didn't budge.

"Paint in the cracks," said Veek. "It's pretty much glued shut."

Nate studied the seams. "Don't suppose anyone's got a knife on them?"

A matte knife slapped into his hand. "Don't mess up the blade," said Xela. "It's my last one and I need it to trim off all the loose edges you're leaving."

"I'll do my best."

"Got a bigger one in my place if you need it," said Roger.

Xela beamed at him. "Are you arguing size with me now, sweetiekins?"

"Don't even," he said, shaking his head.

Nate crouched, flicked open the blade, and plunged it into the blobs of paint between the door and the frame. It was like working through half-dried gum. The knife slit some sections, stretched out others. He worked his way down the seam. He was reminded of an autopsy video, and the long incision down the torso. The paint came apart like cold flesh.

He paused to rest his hand and looked over his shoulder. Veek, Tim, Xela, and Roger leaned against the wall and watched him. Clive stood in the doorway of his apartment. "Don't everybody help all at once," Nate said.

"You're the one with the knife, Shaggy," said Veek. She held up her phone and snapped a picture of him. "For our exploration album."

"I've got another matte knife," Clive said. "Give me a minute."

Nate shook out his fingers and attacked the paint again. He'd finished the long edge from floor to ceiling by the time Clive came back. He started on the top seam. He wasn't halfway across the width of the door when his shoulders started to ache.

Clive crouched on the floor with a bright green knife. He sank the blade into the paint at the base of the door and dragged it toward the hinged edge. The paint opened up and some of it broke off in ragged clumps.

It took another few minutes for them to do the whole outline of the door. Nate handed his matte knife back to Xela. She eyed the blade and gave him a playful scowl. "This is why we can't have nice things," she said.

He smirked and looked at Veek. "How are we for time?"

"Oskar's probably halfway to the store," she said. "We've got maybe forty-five minutes, tops. Say fifteen minutes before Xela needs to start cleaning up after us."

Xela saluted.

Nate set his hand on the knob. "Okay, then," he said. "Let's call it ten minutes to see what's in here, get as many photos as we can, and get out. No matter how cool, no matter how weird, we're out in ten minutes. Agreed?"

Xela held up her camera. Veek held up her phone. A scattering of confirmations came back to him.

He turned the knob. Again, it dragged, as if someone was holding the knob on the other side and resisting. Then he felt a *click* as the latch passed the locking plate.

The door yanked open.

Nate's fingers were so tight on the knob it tugged him forward. Then he lost his balance and his grip got even tighter as he tried to stop his fall. The door swung all the way into apartment 14.

Someone—something—shoved him from behind. His feet left the ground and it took a moment to realize they weren't coming back down. Nate spun around in the air and his only constant was the doorknob. He threw his other hand up and managed to grab the knob on the other side—the inside—of the door.

The air conditioner was on full blast. The air in the dark apartment was frigid to the point it nipped at his skin and bit at his eyes. It rushed and howled around him.

Xela was next to him. She wrapped her arms around him and screamed. She slid down to his waist and a naughty thought stood out amongst all the chaos. Then he realized she was being dragged away from him.

The air wasn't rushing out of 14. It was rushing *in.*

He looked down at Xela. She had his legs in a death grip, digging into his thighs with her fingernails. He could see she was still screaming, but he couldn't hear her over the roar of air washing past them. Her legs flailed behind her. One of her sneakers flipped off her foot and spun away.

In the distance past Xela's feet he could see a brilliant shape of light, a fiery basketball with a swollen blister on it. It hurt to look at it.

Apartment 14 had no walls. It went on forever in every direction. Pinpricks of color, like distant Christmas lights, studded the expanse of darkness.

They were in space.

EAVES

FIFTY SIX

When the door swung open, Tim lunged forward. Nate plunged through the doorway and Xela stumbled after him. Tim caught himself on the frame and threw out a hand to grab his friends. It made his head spin. His balance was off.

A fierce wind picked up in the hallway. It was like the gusts in Chicago in the winter, the ones that blasted between skyscrapers and roared down streets so hard they were almost visible. Those winds had gotten inside the building and were racing past him into apartment 14.

Tim's foot slipped, the air tore at his shirt, and he realized the wind was dragging him into 14, too. And even as the words *depressurize* and *vacuum* raced across his mind and were torn away by the relentless wind, he looked through the door and saw the distant stars and the double solar discs hanging in front of him. Nate and Xela flailed in deep space, tethered to the world by a glass doorknob.

His mind rebelled for a moment, but Tim was too well-trained to let the impossible shake him for long.

He glanced over his shoulder. Clive was braced in the doorway to his apartment, clutching the frame. Veek had sunk low against the wall and scrabbled on the hardwood floor, fighting the relentless winds. Roger had ended up on the opposite side of 14's door across from Tim.

"Help me!" he yelled.

The sound of a dozen busboys dropping their trays filled the air as all four picture windows shattered in Debbie and Clive's apartment. A kaleidoscope spun behind Clive, and the younger man winced as the glass slashed at him. It skimmed across the floor and toward 14's door.

"Close your eyes," Tim shouted at Nate and Xela. "Close your eyes and look away!"

He wasn't sure if they heard him or just reacted to the endless wind, but they clenched their eyes shut. The shards whipped through the doorway and became a sparkling hail that flew out into space. One piece traced a line of red across Nate's shoulder as it whizzed by. Another gashed his forehead. Xela screamed as they cut the back of her hand and sliced her calves. She slipped a few more inches down Nate's legs. Her arms were below his knees now.

Another crash came from behind Tim, toward the front of the building. The hallway window sprayed more glass down the hallway. Debbie and Mrs. Knight shrieked. Clive looked that way and howled something.

Nate's knuckles were white on the doorknob. His desperate grip wouldn't hold much longer. Neither would Xela's.

Tim kicked his leg up and swung it around the door frame. He felt gravity shift as he let his other leg come up to fall into 14. His stomach settled on the edge. It felt like hanging off the edge of a cliff, but his body was three feet above the floor of the hallway. He slipped and caught himself on his elbows.

He looked over—up—at Clive. The other man looked dazed. Papers were whipping around him as they were sucked out of his apartment and across the hall. Blood crept around his shoulders and soaked through his shirt. "Clive," he hollered over the roar. "Anchor me!"

Clive shook his head, and for a moment Tim thought he was refusing. Then he realized Clive was clearing his head. The younger man pushed out of the doorway and slammed into the opposite wall. He threw himself flat and grabbed Tim's forearms. They twisted their hands and seized each other's wrists.

Something clunked and Tim saw Xela's can of paint sliding across the floor. Halfway across the hall it flew into the air and vanished through the impossible doorway. A paperback book flew after it.

"Go lower," screamed Veek. She was still braced across the hall, but her angle let her see through the doorway. Tim glanced over his shoulder just in time to see her glasses slip down her nose and vanish into deep space.

Something came rushing up the hall, over Clive's shoulder, and hit Tim in the side of the head. It felt like metal and he got a quick glimpse of silver spinning past him. He looked down and saw Mrs. Knight's cane whirling past Nate and Xela. It vanished into the darkness of space.

Roger had managed to move a yard or two away from the door. Now he ran forward and lunged at Clive. The winds pulled at him but his momentum carried him across the hungry maw of 14's doorway. He slid along the floor, spun on his hip, and grabbed Clive's legs in a bear hug. Past them Tim saw Debbie and Mrs. Knight trying to resist the pull of the wind. Debbie threw herself against the wall and wrapped her arms around her husband's shoulders.

A sheet billowed out of Clive and Debbie's apartment. It thrashed in the hallway for an instant, like an angry ghost, and was sucked away.

Tim looked into Clive's eyes. The other man nodded. Then Tim took a deep breath and let himself slip past the door frame.

❖

Nate looked back at the door and the wind whipped at his eyes. The wooden frame hung in space, like the mystery door at the start of the *Twilight Zone*. He could see the hallway through it, see Veek braced against the brutal wind. And if he looked past the frame he could see flecks of light and a sparkle of interstellar dust.

Nate's fingers slid on the knob. He made them into hooks on the glass ball. It didn't help. Things flew by too fast to see what they were. A few papers plastered themselves on his shoulders before leaping free and diving toward the stars.

Xela had thrashed and tried to climb his legs for a few moments. Now she squeezed his calves together so hard his legs ached. The wind pulled at her and tried to drag her off into space. He shot a glance down and saw her face pressed against his legs. She was almost silhouetted against the twin stars below her but he was sure her eyes and mouth were shut tight.

He saw flecks of ice on her eyebrows and lips. Frost formed in her blue hair. His toes were getting numb.

It's cold in space, he thought. *Even just a few feet into space.*

He looked back up at the doorway and saw a pair of legs hanging down. A dark-soled sneaker was just above the doorknob. It was too far for him to reach. He saw Veek through the rectangle of light and her mouth moved in a scream. A moment later her eyeglasses flew by.

Something long and silver whizzed by him and the legs dropped about a foot. Then they came a few more inches. The sneakers brushed his elbow.

Someone flew past the doorway up above. It might've been Roger.

Nate took the deepest breath he could as the air rushed past him. He looked down at Xela. "Hang on!"

He counted to three and flung his hands from the doorknob to the legs. He got his arms wrapped around them but slid down the pant leg. Xela shrieked and her nails bit into his calves.

Whoever was hanging through the doorway flexed his feet up to make a hook. Nate's arms caught on it and the slide jerked to a halt. Xela screamed again. She was crying. He looked down and ice sparkled around her eyes.

Something whacked him in the shoulder hard enough to make his collarbone ache. He glimpsed a steel padlock as it plunged into outer space. Nate looked up and saw three more hanging from the waist the legs were attached to.

He had a moment of wondering if they were expected to climb and then they were dragged toward the door. Tim's legs went up a few inches, then a few inches more. The older man bent at the waist, folding around the door frame. Nate realized he was above the knob, alongside the door. He turned his head and saw the number 14 sitting sideways next to his face.

He heard a distant crash, a shriek, and more things flew past him. Bigger things. He caught a flash of red and a flutter of papers and something whacked his hip. They missed Xela and flew off into space.

Tim trembled and lurched up again. Nate felt Xela slip. He tried to bend his feet up the same way Tim had, but they were so numb he couldn't tell if they moved.

He looked down. Xela's head was swaying. She looked dizzy. "Hold on!" he shouted to her.

Hands reached through the doorway and grabbed him under the shoulders. They pulled him up and he was in the hallway. His perspective swung around and he was sideways. "She's slipping," he yelled. "Grab her!"

Tim rolled over on the floor. The older man reached in—down—through the door. Nate fell to the ground on top of Clive. Roger twisted free and lunged after Tim to grab Xela. They dragged her out of the doorway.

Someone slid next to Nate and wrapped her arms around him. "Oh, thank God," cried Veek in his ear. She squeezed him tight. Either she was very warm or Nate was much colder than he realized.

He hugged her back, then leaned forward. "Tim," he shouted. "We have to close it!"

Tim nodded and waved for Clive to grab his legs. Roger was still holding Xela. She wasn't moving. He was rubbing her arms and hands, trying to warm her.

Tim lowered himself into the doorway head first. He reached down and his fingers closed on the knob. He flexed his back and tried to heave the door closed.

A trio of shapes bounced down the hall from the lounge. The couch cushions spun across the hardwood before leaping into the air and diving through the doorway. One of them whacked Tim in the arm as it passed him.

Tim heaved again and managed to get the door a few more inches up. He stretched across the hinged side of the door. The higher he went, the harder it was to keep his body out across the doorway. Clive was across Tim's legs, his feet braced across the hall. Debbie had Tim's ankles.

Nate gestured for Veek to join him and they threw themselves across the doorway. For a moment deep space pulled at him and then Nate landed on the edge of the door, right by the four empty hasps for the padlocks. Veek wrapped her arms around his waist and he stretched his fingers out for the knob. The winds roared and tried to push him back into space. He looked in—down—and saw the spinning cushions and a distant flash of red beyond them. There was a cloud of debris falling out of the Kavach Building and into the twin stars.

Tim heaved and his fingers brushed Nate's. He heaved again and their hands clasped together on the knob. Nate stretched and grabbed the edge of the door. He tried to lift but with the air pounding against it the wooden panel weighed a ton.

Roger was next to him. He reached down and grabbed Nate's wrists. "Don't let go!" he bellowed.

Nate nodded and Roger pulled. His muscles swelled and his veins pulsed under his skin. He let out a bellow of his own and the door rose another foot. It was a handful of inches away from being closed. The wind screamed through the gap.

Tim and Roger exchanged looks across the gulf. Tim let go of the knob. Roger's hands jumped from Nate's wrists to grab the ball of cut glass. He turned his head to Nate and shouted "Get clear!"

Nate let go and Veek dragged him away. The air shrieked as it made a last rush through the narrow opening. Roger worked one knee up against the door frame, took in a breath, and roared. He threw his weight back and the door slammed shut.

The latch caught with a sharp click.

The wind vanished. A few papers drifted to the floor. Silence boomed out along the length of the hallway.

Roger collapsed. The hallway tipped and shuddered, and Nate realized he'd fallen over and slid down the wall. Veek slumped against him.

Xela crawled over and fell onto Roger's lap with a smile. Her nose was bleeding. She patted his thigh.

"What the hell?" said Clive. He was holding Debbie and rocking her back and forth. Her eyes were wide and wet. "What the *HELL JUST HAPPENED?"*

Nate held up a hand to quiet him. "Everybody okay?" he called out. His throat was raw.

Veek nodded. Xela gave a tired thumbs up. Roger closed his eyes and stroked her hair. "Think we're good, bro," he said.

Clive looked up and gave a quiet nod.

Tim staggered to his feet and gave the door a tentative poke. Then he banged it with his fist. It echoed and trembled like a wooden door. He slapped the four hasps down into place and fished a padlock off his belt. The lock snapped shut on the hasp and Tim pulled the next one from his hip. He stopped and looked around the hall. "Wait," he said. "Where's Mrs. Knight?"

Veek leaned her head out away from Nate. "Did she duck into the stairwell?"

"Mrs. Knight?" called Nate.

"She slipped," whispered Debbie.

Clive looked down at his wife. She was crying. "What happened, hon? Where'd she go?"

Debbie raised her eyes. "I couldn't let go," she said. "It was dragging you all and she slipped and fell and I...I couldn't let go of you. I couldn't grab her."

Her eyes drifted away from his and settled on the door to apartment 14.

a flash of red

"Oh, no," murmured Tim.

"I'm so sorry," Debbie cried. "I'm so sorry."

FIFTY SEVEN

They heard a low rumble and Roger braced himself against the wall. They all gave each other looks. A second peal of thunder came from outside.

Clive looked from Nate to the door and back. "Should we open it back up? Maybe...maybe we can find her?"

Nate remembered the distant cloud of debris and shook his head.

Tim crouched by Debbie and took her hand. "Debbie," he said, "there's nothing you could've done."

She sniffed and her eyes flicked up to focus on him.

"We barely got Nate and Xela out. You were doing everything you could to help save them. If you hadn't, we would've lost them. And probably me." He set his hand down on her shoulder. "And maybe Clive, too."

Her arms tightened around her husband.

"What happened is awful, but we all have to stay calm for now, okay? Right now we need you to go into your apartment and see how much damage the wind caused. Check all the walls. Can you do that for us?"

Debbie sniffled and nodded.

"Good."

Clive helped her up and she shuffled across the hall. She vanished into their apartment and he stood watch at the door.

Tim looked at Nate. "What now?"

Nate gazed at the tenants slumped in the hall. His eyes fell on 14 again. "I'm not sure. How long was...how long did all that take?"

Veek pulled her phone out. "It's time for Xela to get started."

Nate blinked. "That was ten minutes?"

"Not even," said Tim, "but I think we all collapsed for a couple minutes once you were out and it was closed again."

Nate glanced over at Xela, who wiped blood from her nose. "You need to paint the door."

"What?"

"The door," he said. "You still need to paint over it and hide the seams."

"I..." She looked at the door. "I think the paint's on the other side of the galaxy with Mrs...with my brushes."

"Do you have more?"

"I do but they're good ones. I can't use them for—"

"You have to," he told her. His fingers cramped and he bit back a grunt. "Go get your other brushes, Roger will dig up some more paint for you down in the cellar." He looked at the other man and got a nod in return.

"My knife's gone, too," added Xela.

"You can have one of mine," said Clive from the doorway. "I've got two."

Roger helped Xela up. She hobbled on one shoe for a moment before kicking it off. The two of them shuffled down the hall toward the lounge and the back stairwell. "Wow," she called to them. "We made a mess of the place."

Clive glanced between Nate and Tim. "What are we going to do about... about her?" He tipped his head at the door to apartment 14.

"I don't know," said Nate. He pressed his fingers together and forced them straight. "We've got to take care of all of us first. Then we'll figure that out." Another crash of thunder rattled the building. "All your windows are gone?"

He glanced over his shoulder. "Yeah. There's glass everywhere."

"Blame it on this storm. Tell Oskar as soon as he gets back. That way he won't question it if you don't have your story straight." He pointed down the hall at the shattered front window. "We'll blame all of this on the storm. It's all broken inward so he shouldn't question it."

In their apartment Debbie lifted up a shredded quilt and started crying again. Clive went in to hold her. She broke down in his arms.

Tim snapped the last padlock into place. The bottom one was missing. Nate reached up to rub his shoulder where it had hit him. It crossed his mind that said padlock was now in deep space, headed into a star that wasn't the sun.

So is Mrs. Knight.

"We need another padlock," he said. "We'll have to pull one from somewhere."

"The cellar storeroom?" said Veek.

Tim shook his head. "Too visible. Everyone's down there at least once a week for laundry."

"The roof then," she said. "You could do your publishing-magic on one of the locks up there."

Nate nodded. "Go to the roof," he said. "Get one of the locks from the door, one that looks the most like the one we lost."

Tim nodded and headed for the staircase. He passed Xela coming back down with a collection of brushes. She'd washed the blood from her face and some of her swagger had come back. He paused to give her a quick hug and she squeezed him back.

"You should get cleaned up, too, boss," she told Nate as she got closer. "You've got a horror movie thing going on right now."

Nate dabbed under his nose. His upper lip was sticky. So was his chin and the corner of his jaw under his ears.

"Go wash up," Veek told him. "We'll get everything under control here."

Roger appeared up the back stairwell with a can of paint. It was coated with drips and small spills, but it moved like it still had some liquid in it.

"Okay," said Nate. "Everyone remember to talk to Oskar if you need to."

They had a perfect excuse to meet later in the lounge. Oskar found his own windows cracked and brought in the maintenance team for an emergency call. Men were all over the building, screwing sheets of plywood over the window frames.

Debbie had recovered, but Clive kept a reassuring arm around her. He'd changed his bloody, shredded shirt for a tee. Xela wore a heavy sweatshirt and a pair of Uggs. She wrapped Roger's arms around her as well. Veek had a pair of backup glasses with thick frames. Nate thought about making a Velma comment, but decided against it.

His hands still ached. His forehead had needed a Band-Aid and his shoulder had needed three. He'd been grateful to find an old pair of wool socks at the bottom of one of his drawers for his frozen feet.

Tim had the flatscreen on. Every channel was covering the freak thunderstorm which had formed over Los Angeles. One showed footage of planes making emergency landings at LAX. The Channel 7 meteorologist, Dallas Raines, explained how a storm of such magnitude could appear out of nowhere. He used computer models to show two high pressure fronts colliding to form a low pressure zone.

"It was supposed to be clear tonight," said Xela. "Clear for the rest of the week."

"I think we did this," said Tim. He pointed up at the screen and circled the glowing green rendering of the storm. "This low pressure zone...we made it."

Roger frowned at the television. "How?"

"What do you think all that wind was?" asked Veek. "We just funneled something like a few tons of the atmosphere off into deep space."

"Among other things," muttered Clive.

Tim mimicked the weatherman's gestures on the screen. "Air rushes in to fill that gap," he said, "high pressure hits low pressure area, and wham. Thunderstorms in July."

"We should call the police," said Debbie.

They turned to look at her.

"We need to tell them...tell someone about Mrs. Knight," she said. Her eyes were open and alert.

Roger shifted behind Xela. He shot a glance at Veek, who traded it with Tim. Clive saw it over his wife's shoulder.

Nate leaned forward on the couch. "I don't think we can tell anyone," he said quietly.

Her eyes opened a little more. "Why not?"

Tim reached over and took her hand, just like he had once they'd closed 14's door. "What would we tell them?"

"That she's dead."

"And when they ask how she died?" murmured Veek. "What then?"

"We'd tell them the..." Debbie stumbled over the words. She took in a breath to start again and let it slip out.

"You see the position we're in," said Tim. "If we tell the truth the police'll think we're lying. If we make something up, they might sense the lie from one of us. Either way, they'll assume we're involved in her disappearance."

"We *are* involved."

"He means...actively involved," said Nate. "Don't you?"

Tim nodded. "We'd all be suspects. When she never turns up, some of us might even get taken into custody."

"We could show them," she said. "We could open the door again."

"Spectacularly bad idea," said Roger with a shake of his head. "And I've heard some shitty ideas, believe me."

"Assuming Oskar even let them open it," said Nate. "He can just say he's the only one with keys to the locks. Heck, we made sure it looks like the door hasn't been disturbed in decades."

Xela had run out of paint and pronounced the door done just a few minutes after Tim snapped the replacement lock into place. It wasn't perfect. Nate could see the wrinkles of torn latex beneath the fresh coat, but Veek pointed out any irregularity could get written off as damage from the storm.

Tim let go of Debbie's hand and stood up. He looked at Nate. "May I offer a suggestion?"

"Please."

The older man straightened up. "No one say anything. Don't say anything about Mrs. Knight to anyone."

Debbie and Clive both shifted in their seats. Even Roger looked stunned. "Are you serious?" asked Veek.

Tim nodded. "Say nothing. In three or four days I'll bump into Oskar and ask if he's seen her lately. I'll tell him I loaned her a book or something. That plants the seed. In another three weeks rent's due and she won't answer her door. He'll knock, maybe he'll call. Finally he'll unlock it and she'll be gone."

Nate looked at him. "And?"

"And nothing. She'll have skipped out or vanished. I guarantee even if he calls the police they'll barely investigate. There's almost ten million people in this city. I'd guess a dozen of them vanish into thin air every week."

"But she didn't vanish," said Debbie.

"Yes, she did," Tim said. "And we all know they can search this planet for a hundred years and they will never, ever find a trace of Mrs. Knight again. Her disappearance will get handed off, someone will do a routine investigation, and that'll be it." He paused. "I've seen it happen before."

Tears ran from Debbie's eyes.

"I'm sorry," said Tim, "but that's the way it has to be."

"I think she has cats," said Clive. "Someone's going to have to feed them."

Tim twisted his lips. "It would look better," he said, "if the cats weren't fed."

Debbie's eyes blazed. "You are *not* going to starve her cats," she said.

He raised his hands. "Then there'll be a big bag of cat food. The cats will tear it open and eat like kings. I promise."

She didn't say anything, but her gaze dropped away.

Tim's eyes traveled around the room. Roger and Xela clasped hands and nodded their agreement. Nate and Veek exchanged a glance and nodded as well. Debbie stared at the couch arm, but Clive made an agreeable sound for them.

Xela cleared her throat. "Does anyone know what her first name was?"

Veek shook her head. "I only knew her last name. I knew she was a Missus because once she mentioned Mister Knight not being around anymore."

"I just knew her as Mrs. Knight," said Nate. "I met her a few weeks back at one of our meetings."

"Same," said Roger.

Debbie closed her eyes. "I think it was Linda," she said. "Or maybe Laura."

Tim nodded. "It says L. Knight on her mailbox." He sat down.

They were quiet for a moment as the conspiracy settled over them.

"I think Debbie's partially right," said Xela. She swept hair away from her face as she spoke and then jabbed a finger down the hall. The fingernail was cracked lengthwise, from tip to cuticle. "We need to tell someone about that room."

Veek sighed. "Like who?"

"I don't know. Someone. NASA? They deal with space stuff, right?"

"And what do we tell them?" asked Tim. "Hey, NASA, there's *space* in our building. A whole room full of it. Come take care of that."

Xela shook her head. "Not like that, no."

"Well, how then? It's the same problem. Think of a way we could tell anyone about it and not sound like raving lunatics."

"Y'know, forget what it is," said Clive. His head twitched with frustration. "I want to know *how*. How is there a black hole in our building? And how the *hell* is it blocked by a wooden door?"

"Language," murmured Debbie.

"I don't think it's a black hole," said Nate. "I think it's just... space. It wasn't pulling us with gravity. It was more, well, the building was depressurizing and we were getting pushed in."

Tim nodded. "Thus the weather."

"Oh," said Clive. "Awesome. Now it all makes perfect sense."

Xela snapped her fingers. "What about Torchwood? They deal with stuff like this."

Veek smirked. "You know that's just a television show, right?"

"Are you sure? I thought it was based on a real group."

Tim shook his head. "It's just a television show."

"Think I know what it is," said Roger.

Veek rolled her eyes at him. "Oh, really?"

"Yeah." He pointed across the lounge and through the wall. "Space room's there, right?"

They followed his gaze and nodded.

His finger drew a line across the room. "Clive and Debbie's place, the control room, is there, right?"

"Yeah," said Tim. "What are you getting at?"

"It's a sandbag," said Roger.

FIFTY EIGHT

Veek stared at him. Xela twisted her head around. "What the heck's that supposed to mean?" asked Nate.

Roger straightened up behind Xela. "Lot of time on set you have to put up flags or scrims for the lights and they go way out past the base of your stand," he explained. He held his hand up by his chin and mimed grabbing something stout with the other hand. "Sometimes we even use these big mambo stands 'cause the arm goes out so far to get the flag in the right place. When you do, you have to throw a ton of sandbags on the other side to balance it out."

"You're talking about a counterweight," said Veek.

"Right."

Nate mulled the idea in his head. "So you're thinking whatever the machine is in their apartment, the space-warp room is some kind of opposing force? That it's supposed to be there for the machine to work?"

Roger nodded. "Yeah," he said. "We know this thing's supposed to have something to do with bending dimensions or something, right? So if it's bending really far that way over there..." His finger traced back across the lounge to point in the direction of 14. "...it's gotta bend really far the *other* way to balance out."

"I can't believe I'm saying it," said Veek, "but that almost makes sense."

"Thanks," said Roger. "Fuck you, too."

"It does make sense," said Nate. "This isn't a brute force thing. They wanted this machine to run as long as possible. The generators show that. So it makes sense it'd be a balanced machine, something that works as efficiently as possible."

Debbie shuddered. She pushed herself off the couch and searched around until she found a spot that let her not look at anyone. "I think I need to go to bed," she whispered. "I want to see if they're done in our apartment."

Clive stood up and set his hands on her shoulders. He gave the rest of them a nod. The two of them walked off down the hall.

"She's not taking this well," said Nate.

"She's doing better than most people would in this situation," said Tim. "We all are."

"Had a while to ease into it, bro," said Roger. "Slow steps into madness."

Xela smiled at him. "How poetic of you."

"Was in a movie I worked on," he said. "Actor was an idiot. Heard that line twenty-nine times. Figured we'd all go nuts on thirty."

Down the hall, Nate saw Clive and Debbie talking with Oskar. He heard the echo of their voices, but not the words. Oskar's head bobbed up and down. He gestured at their apartment door and talked at length about something. He kept his back to 14 the whole time.

"You think they're telling him?" Veek murmured.

"No," Nate said. "Debbie's shaken up, and I think living across the hall from another solar system is a big hole in Clive's view of reality. But they're still with us."

"You sure?"

He shrugged. "I was in deep space an hour ago. I'm not too sure of anything right now."

"You and me both," said Xela. She snapped her fingers. "Y'know what? That's why the wall in sixteen says 'danger.' It's not a warning for the room, it's telling you not to mess with that wall."

Roger nodded. "Makes sense. Don't want a repair crew breaking through the wall to work on pipes and getting sucked in."

Veek's eyes opened wide. "That's what all the writing on the walls is," she said.

They looked at her. "You think it's all warnings?" asked Tim.

She shook her head. "Think about it. This building's a big, complicated machine Koturovic and his pals knew was going to be running for years after they were gone. We know the combination for the vault was in Xela's apartment—it let us get down to the generators. It looks like all the math is Koturovic's equations, maybe some of the big dimensional physics. The wiring diagrams in Tim's place are for the different circuits. There's even a note from the creator in your apartment," she said to Nate, "but set off from everything else so we know it's different." She paused and smiled. "It's an instruction manual."

Nate knew he should feel more excited, but his brain felt sluggish and his body was heavy with exhaustion. He looked at the others and saw they felt the same way.

Oskar stepped into the lounge. "The men are done," he announced. "All broken or cracked windows haff been boarded up. They will all be replaced in the next few days, starting with those apartments which lost both windows." He waited for them to acknowledge the words before moving on. "If any of you wish to stay in a hotel, Locke Management will reimburse you for the cost."

"I'm good," said Tim, "but thanks anyway."

"Same," said Xela.

Veek and Nate nodded as well.

Oskar returned the nods. He looked at Nate and his eyes flicked up to the Band- Aid across his forehead. "None of you are injured?" He gestured back down the hall. "I know Mister Holt was cut."

Nate shook his head. "It's not as bad as it looks," he said. "A piece just hit me and bounced off. I've got a hard head." He rapped his knuckles above his ear.

The manager snorted, then shifted his feet. "I cannot reimburse you for any damages to personal property," he said. "I am sorry." He bowed his head and shuffled back down the hallway.

"So," said Roger. "What d'we do now?"

They all turned to Nate.

"I don't know," he said. "Maybe we should think about calling our little investigation done."

Veek frowned. "What do you mean?"

He shrugged and one of the tendons in his shoulder popped. "We know why the building is the way it is. We know how most of this weirdness works. I'm not sure what else we can hope to find. And..."

"And what?" asked Tim.

"It's getting dangerous," Nate said. "Not just possible-eviction dangerous. If this machine is supposed to save the world—"

"It's *still* saving the world," corrected Veek.

"Right," he said. "That's my point. We shouldn't be screwing around with it. I mean, we're like kids with a nuclear bomb. With a pile of nuclear bombs."

"You think we should try to forget all this?" asked Xela.

Nate shook his head. "No, of course not. But we don't want to risk doing something awful to the world." He gestured up at the television, where the news was now about flooding in the Valley. There were shots of a Japanese garden where the water was ankle-deep. "We changed the weather tonight. We grounded planes."

"I think," Tim said, "we crashed one. No serious injuries, though."

"Aside from Mrs. Knight," murmured Veek.

Nate nodded. "And that's all just minor, side-effect stuff. What if we did something and we shut the machine off? Not just tweaked its settings for a few minutes, but maybe broke it?"

"Super-ginormous alpha predators," Xela said. "That's what's supposed to happen, right? Lions and tigers and bears? Dogs and cats living together?"

a whale with bat-wings and tentacles

"Yeah," said Nate. "Something like that."

A yawn burst out of Roger's mouth. "Sorry," he said. "Wiped."

"No worries," said Nate. "I think we all are."

Roger pulled his phone off his hip and glanced at it. "Shit," he said. "Call time's at seven-thirty tomorrow. I need to get to sleep."

Veek squeezed a handful of hair. "I need to finish a project, too."

The real world came crashing down on them.

"I guess we'll talk later," said Nate. "I mean, if anyone wants to talk about stuff anytime..."

"We know where you live," said Xela.

Veek glanced down the hall and then up at the ceiling. "What are we going to do about the lock from the roof? That door's one short now, right?"

"I'll head over to Home Depot in the morning and buy one to replace it," said Tim. "It looks like a pretty standard padlock."

"Oskar won't have a key for it," said Roger.

"A little corrosion on the lock and he won't question why his key doesn't work, assuming he ever checks it. He'll just assume it rusted inside, cut it off, and buy a replacement. Done."

"What if he tries to open this one?" Xela asked.

Tim glanced down the hall. "I feel pretty safe saying that door never gets opened except by stupid tenants."

A few of them chuckled, but the laughter died a swift death.

Xela and Roger got up, and the rest of them followed. Roger shook Nate's hand while Xela gave Tim a big hug. Roger moved on to give Veek a clumsy embrace and Xela wrapped her arms around Nate and squeezed him. "Thank you," she whispered.

He hugged her back and she squeezed him again. Then she released him and grabbed Veek. Roger and Tim had a manly handshake and exchanged punches to the shoulder. Then Roger and Xela headed down the back stairwell.

"I should go check on my friendly detective," said Tim. "I'm sure there's some way all tonight's activity could get spun against me." He gripped Nate's shoulder, smiled at Veek, and walked down the hallway.

"What about you?" asked Veek. "Don't you have work tomorrow?"

"Yeah," Nate said. "Yeah, I do. I just..."

"What?"

He looked at her. "Does this feel a lot like we all just said goodbye?"

She shrugged. "Sort of, I guess. Isn't it? Sounds like the Mystery Gang is breaking up."

Nate smiled. "You never see what they're doing the rest of the time, do you? No idea if they live in the van or they've got a home somewhere or what. Do they go to the movies or hang out with other friends or anything like that?"

Her mouth twitched. "Guess we'll never know."

"Suppose not."

Veek took a few steps toward the hallway and her apartment. "Y'know," she said, "we could go to the movies sometime."

"What do you mean? Get everyone organized for a big night out or something?"

"Yeah," she said. "Or it could just be, y'know, us. You and me."

"You'd want to be seen in public with Shaggy?"

The twitch became a smile. "Shaggy wasn't that bad. When they got older, all the girls realized he was a lot more fun than Fred."

"Where would you want to go?"

"The Arclight's nice," she said. "We could see something on the big dome screen."

"Expensive, though."

"But they have the best popcorn."

"If we're talking about getting popcorn, it's super expensive."

"I'll tell you what," she said. "It'll be my treat. I should have some extra cash after this assignment."

"Okay, then." He looked over at her. "Thanks for watching out for me."

"Everyone deserves a night out now and then. Even poor slobs like us."

"I meant...back there." He tipped his head down the hall.

"Ahhh. Well, no problem," said Veek. She looked at the floor. "You know, Xela's probably really grateful. You saved her life."

"I think it's you guys who saved our lives. Maybe with an assist from the doorknob. So thanks."

She smiled. "On behalf of the doorknob, you're welcome."

FIFTY NINE

Nate sat in his cubicle and stared at his computer. There was an address form on the screen that had been there for half an hour. It corresponded to the pink return card on the top of his stack.

He'd done six of the forms so far. Six in three and a half hours. It was below his cruising speed of one every ninety seconds. A lot lower than the mythical one every fifteen seconds Eddie kept claiming he could do.

I was in space yesterday. Hanging by a doorknob in deep space.

It occurred to him, for the third time today, that he should switch to returned magazines. More bulk meant he could wear away a larger part of the pile. Like the last two times it occurred to him, he glanced at the mail tote full of magazines and then back to the screen.

The real question is, why isn't anyone protecting this thing? If this machine is the only thing between us and the end of the world, why isn't there a Marine base built around the damned thing?

Granted, the machine had stood in plain sight for over a hundred years without being discovered. Or, at least, without being reported. If anyone had found it, they'd kept very quiet about it.

He drummed his fingers on the desk and looked down at the pink card. It was almost lunch. He stabbed at a few random keys without thinking.

He'd typed SPACE into the last field he'd been working on. There was a fifty-fifty chance ALAN SPACE would either get a kick out of his new name or call to complain. If he called, he'd speak with Eddie, who would come talk to Nate. It was a safe bet Eddie's talk would take at least five times longer than the phone call.

They have found us.

Of course, someone had discovered the machine. Or at least, where it was hidden. They'd chased Koturovic across the city back to Kavach. And he'd managed to keep it a secret, even though they killed him.

He tapped at the keys again and replaced SPACE with ALAN's real last name. A few more keystrokes and he'd updated the subscription information. Seven in just under four hours. He tossed the card in the trash and peeled another one off the rubber band-wrapped stack.

Something wasn't sitting right in his mind. He worked back through his thoughts and found himself at his mental picture of Koturovic writing his final message in blood. There was a problem with that image. Something gnawed at him. It was just out of sight, right on the tip of his—

"Hey," Anne said, "did you want to do anything for lunch?"

Koturovic disappeared in a puff of mental smoke.

Nate looked up at her. He bit his lip and tried to make note of where his thoughts had fallen.

"Sorry," she said. "Did I catch you in the middle of something?"

"Yeah. Don't worry about it."

"So," she said, "lunch?"

"I brought a sandwich," he said.

"We could just do cheap pizza downstairs."

"Then I just wasted a sandwich."

"I could get cheap pizza and you could watch me eat."

He smiled. "So you're offering to torture me."

"Hey," she grinned, "don't knock it 'til you've tried it."

"Thanks, but I think I'm still going to say no. Besides, working through lunch gives me a slim chance of getting caught up by the end of the month."

Her dark eyes fixed on him. "You know, the past couple weeks or so you've been a lot more focused."

Nate chuckled. "Not according to Eddie."

"I didn't say focused on this. I just meant you've sort of..." She tapped her fingertips on her lips. "Do you mind if I say something a bit new-age sounding?"

"Are you going to read my aura or something?"

She laughed and it turned into a snort. "No," she said. "You just seem like you finally found your purpose, y'know?"

He looked at her and thought about Aleksander Koturovic dying to protect the machine he'd helped build. The machine Nate now lived inside of. He thought of Tim, Xela and Roger, Debbie and Clive.

He thought about Mandy, too scared of the future to do anything.

He thought about Mrs. Knight, floating through space until she fell into an alien sun.

And he thought about Veek.

"I have," he said. "I think I've figured out where my life is going."

"It's working for you, whatever it is," she said. "Anyway, I'm dying for a break and if you're not up for lunch what if we just—"

dying to protect the machine

"Fuck," he said.

Anne's brows went up. "Not quite where I thought this little chat was heading," she said.

"Sorry. I've got to get out of here," Nate said.

She smiled. It flitted across his mind that Anne had a spectacular smile. Not long ago he would've been thrilled to be this close to it, let alone be the one causing it. "Fantastic," she said. "Lunch it is, then."

"No," he said, standing up. "I mean, I have to get out of here."

Nate grabbed his backpack. He snatched up a few things from the desk and stowed them. He patted himself down, located his keys, and made sure his phone was still on his hip.

Eddie's voice sounded from the door. "Everyone off to lunch?"

Anne bit back a groan and it became a quick hiss in her nose. Nate had heard it before. He'd made the same noise at least a dozen times. The dreaded Eddie's-inviting-himself-along groan, often muted to an exhalation through the nostrils.

Nate looked at his boss. "I need to leave," he said.

"For lunch?"

"For the afternoon. Personal matter."

"How much have you gotten done so far today?"

"It's a personal *crisis*," emphasized Nate.

Eddie looked at the stacks of mail totes and shook his head. "I don't know, Nate," he said. It was the lecture tone, tinged with a hint of good-buddy tone. "You're really far behind right now. Really far. I don't think you can afford to take an afternoon off and expect—"

"I quit."

The words leaped out of his mouth. For a brief moment he thought it had been Anne or someone in the hall. But Anne was behind him and she'd made a little sound that was half shock and half excitement.

Eddie blinked. His jowls flared pink and he blinked a few more times. "What?"

"I quit," repeated Nate. The phrase threw a weight from his shoulders, and Eddie seemed to shrink as he said it. "I don't have time for this." He turned back to the desk and grabbed the few personal things there. His spare phone charger. A battered paperback dictionary. Some post-it notes on the monitor with important phone numbers he'd scribbled down.

"Hold on," said Eddie. "You can't quit."

"No time." Without that weight he felt strong. He stashed the items in his backpack, zipped it shut, and threw the strap over his shoulder. He locked eyes with Anne, halfway in her own cubicle. Her mouth moved silently. *You rock.*

Eddie was still shrinking. His shoulders slumped and he looked a bit scared. "Let's take a minute and talk about this," he whined as Nate stepped past him.

"There's nothing to talk about." He checked the hat rack to make sure there wasn't anything he'd forgotten. He found a battered gray baseball cap and decided to leave it.

Nate turned to the big man. "Goodbye, Eddie," he said. He held out his hand and Eddie, flustered, shook it. Nate glanced past the big man. "Bye, Anne. Say goodbye to Jimmy for me."

She blew him a kiss. "See you around, Nate."

His former boss followed him into the hall. "You're not going to quit your job in this economy, are you?"

"I've got more important things to do."

SIXTY

He found a parking space a block away and jogged down Beverly to the intersection. A delicate framework floated in his mind, a three-dimensional outline of events. He didn't want to focus on it and risk breaking the tenuous threads, but he was nervous about letting it out of sight.

As he crossed the street, he could see someone sitting on the second set of steps leading up to Kavach. His pace quickened as much as it could without turning into a run. He looked at Veek through the gate while he flipped through his keys. She wore a battered UCLA hoodie over a tank top. For a moment he let his mental construct slide away.

"Aren't you supposed to be at work?" he asked after a moment.

"Aren't you?"

"I just quit," said Nate.

Her eyes lit up a little behind the thick frames of her glasses. "Yeah?"

"Yeah. I had an idea. Not even an idea, just...just a thought."

"And it was worth quitting over?"

He shrugged. "Data entry seemed a little pointless after going into space."

She smirked and nodded. "Are you going to be okay? Without a job?"

Nate shrugged again. "I'm good for a few weeks. After that...I'll figure something out." He opened the gate. "So what about you? Some people might think you were here waiting for me."

She stuck her tongue out at him. "You wish. Just warming up. I called in sick again."

"Isn't that going to get you in trouble?"

"Maybe. I find it really hard to care, too, y'know?"

"I do."

"So, what's your almost-idea?"

He paused. The construct leaped back to the foreground of his thoughts and he took a moment to avert his mental eyes. "I don't want to say yet. I'm still trying to get it right in my mind."

Veek nodded. "As it turns out, I do have news of my own. Want to hear something sort of creepy?"

"Do I have a choice?"

She shook her head. "First off, score one for computers over books."

"How so?"

"Debbie found so many little things, she missed one of the big ones. I found Whipple Phillips this morning. He's on Wikipedia."

Everything shook. It took Nate a moment to realize he'd come to a dead stop, one foot on the stairs, one on the first landing. "You're joking."

She shook her head.

He raised himself up to the landing. "So what's it say?"

"Pretty much just what Debbie had. He was a businessman from New England with investments in Idaho. Spent a lot of his later years taking care of his daughters and grandson. Died in 1904."

"He had a family? Are they still around?"

She shook her head again. "All gone. But you've heard of his grandson."

"Stop being melodramatic."

"H. P. Lovecraft," said Veek.

Nate's mental gears spun for a moment. The fragile framework came close to being thrashed. "Wasn't he...he's a horror writer, right?"

"The original horror writer, if you ask some folks," Veek said. "When H. P. was a little kid, according to several accounts, Grandpa Whippy told him all these weird stories about other worlds and monsters and stuff. When he got older, Lovecraft said those talks inspired a lot of his stories about Cthulhu and the Elder Gods and all that."

"You're shitting me."

"It's on Wikipedia, so it must be true."

"Cthulhu's some kind of evil god, right? The one with

tentacles

the octopus head?"

"Technically, I think he's an immortal alien," said Veek, "but he's so powerful he's a god for all intents and purposes."

"I didn't know you were into that stuff."

"I'm not. Wikipedia scores again."

Nate let it sink in. It pushed against the fragile construction and he shoved it away. He couldn't get distracted. Not even by Veek. "Can we talk about this in a little bit? I need to...I have to get this idea worked out."

"Go," she said. She stood up and brushed herself off. "I'll stop by in a while."

Nate stared at the blank wall next to his desk. Half of his apartment was in shadow, despite the midday sun. Two of his windows had plywood over them. He was low on the list to get them fixed.

He'd been staring at the wall for ten minutes. While he did, the framework in his mind grew and became more solid. The threads spun into wires, and the wires twisted into cables. He just needed to winch the cables tight and pull the little ideas into one big one.

Underneath the paint there were words written in blood. Aleksander Koturovic's blood. He'd been right there, in this apartment, one hundred and thirteen years ago. He ran there to make sure his friends and co-workers knew the Family of the Red Death was coming for them.

Nate played the scene in his mind again.

Koturovic had been stabbed by one of the Family members. Probably a fatal wound back then, and he would've been educated enough to know it. He knew he was a dead man walking. He wasn't going to make it through the night, even if he ended up at a hospital. Definitely not if the Family got him.

Koturovic had run through the night on New Year's Eve, bleeding the whole time, crazed doomsday cultists chasing him. He'd gotten into the building, run to the farthest apartment from the front door, and scribbled a warning that couldn't be washed away. And then...

What happened next?

He couldn't risk being caught. The stakes were too high. No matter how dedicated he was, there was a chance he'd talk if the Family tortured him. Especially as he got weaker from blood loss. He knew Kavach was the world's only chance. So he wouldn't let himself be taken prisoner.

Nate turned and examined the room. He tried to picture it when he'd first moved in. When Toni first showed it to him. An empty box. Kitchen, closet, bathroom.

MUST HIDE

The closet wasn't big enough to hide someone, even if it was filled with clothes. The cabinets in the kitchen were too small. Granted, everyone said people were smaller back then, but Nate couldn't even picture a child fitting inside those little boxes. The bathroom couldn't hide a cat, let alone a person.

There was a ledge outside the big windows. It was just wide enough for someone to stand on, but they'd be exposed to anyone down on the street. And Koturovic would've been too weak to risk the ledge. If the scientist fell and *didn't* die, the Family would have him.

There was always the chance he would've hidden in another room, or left the building altogether, but it didn't feel right. He would've been weak. He wouldn't have a lot of time. The Family couldn't have been far behind him. Too close to risk leaving the room and being caught once the message was written.

Maybe there'd been furniture in the apartment. A bed to crawl under. A steamer trunk or wardrobe to hide in. But the first thing anyone did was look under the bed, and any piece of furniture in plain sight big enough to hide in would've been an obvious place to search.

Ahhh, something in the back of Nate's head piped up, *but Koturovic* knew *people would be looking for him. He would've been ready. He would've had a trap door or a bolt hole or...*

Something in plain sight.

Nate walked to the closet. A sweep of his arm pushed all the clothes to one side. He dragged his laundry hamper out and kicked aside a few pairs of sneakers.

Down in the corner of the closet sat the panel he'd first seen three months ago. It was a foot tall and maybe eighteen inches across. The width made it look less like a door. He ran his fingers along the paint-covered seams and the rough stretches around it where the framing had been pulled away.

Nate bet whoever tore the framing off never even looked inside the little hatch.

He went back to the kitchen and got a knife. The blade wasn't as sharp as the razors they'd used to open 14, and Nate found himself stretching and tearing the thick latex a lot more than cutting it. A few times the paint came away in strips and he tossed them over his shoulder into his studio.

It was hot work, made even hotter by the lack of circulation. The ceiling fan's air patterns didn't extend into the closet. He grabbed a shirt from the top of his hamper—the shirt he'd worn on his unexpected trip into outer space—and blotted his forehead again and again.

It took Nate half an hour to carve around the rectangle. He pried at the panel with his fingernails but couldn't get enough leverage. After a few moments he picked up the knife and stabbed it as deep as he could into the gap. He tried to lever the little hatch open.

A tremble worked its way up through the blade. It was the slow, thick sensation of something dragged into motion after ages at rest. He felt threads of latex stretch and pop around the panel.

A line of darkness appeared at the top of the hatch. The blade slid in deeper. Nate grabbed the edge with his free hand and pulled. The smell of a hundred years rushed out to greet him in a dusty cloud.

The panel was loose, but he could feel a tug of resistance. He pulled again and something rustled behind the door. He yanked his fingers away before realizing it was his own motions making the sound. He got a grip on either side and dragged the panel away from the wall. Light spilled into the space.

The backside of the panel had a brittle loop of rope on it. The rope was attached to an elaborate lever-arm held in place with blobs of plaster. They dropped to the floor as he pulled the hatch open. The lever was wrapped in a crumbling sheath that led back to a cobweb-covered pile of dusty sticks, plaster, and fabric. A pair of neon-green roaches darted across the pile and vanished into a patch of shadows.

Nate studied the rats' nest of odds and ends. It was crammed into the space between the walls. Most of it was wedged under the bathtub's raised platform, which was recognizable even inside-out and from this odd angle. One length of wood and fabric hung down to balance the assembly against a thick electrical cable.

After a few moments his first impressions broke down into the truth. He saw the loose buttons on the sleeves, each hanging by just one or two threads. The blobs of plaster clinging to the rope became individual finger bones. A pattern emerged from the random shadows and he recognized the eye sockets and nose cavity of the sideways skull. One of the roaches felt Nate's eyes on it and skittered deeper into the building.

"Aleksander Koturovic," he murmured.

SIXTY ONE

Oskar expressed disbelief at first, then anger at the opened panel, and shock at the sight of the skeleton. It left him pale and short of breath. Right then, Nate was certain Oskar didn't know all the secrets of the Kavach Building.

An hour later six people were in Nate's apartment with a gurney, a very expensive-looking camera, some lights on tripods, and several bright orange tackle boxes. They looked and acted like the medical examiners on countless television shows except for the distinct lack of badges on their shirts or windbreakers. He asked who they were with. One man told him "the morgue," while the sole woman in the group said "the authorities."

Nate waited in the doorway with Oskar. Mandy was by her apartment across the hall, looking nervous and fascinated at the same time. Veek, Tim, Xela, and Andrew stood two doors down. They couldn't see anything, but they watched Nate and Oskar for hints or signs of what was going on.

Inside the apartment the medical examiners removed Koturovic's body in the largest pieces they could. Each part was placed in a large container that looked like industrial-strength Tupperware. There was no discussion of cutting into the wall. None of the people mentioned the odd cables or devices inside the crawlspace.

One of them, the man who said they were from "the morgue," asked a few questions. When had Nate found the body? Did he touch it? Did anyone else touch it? Could they contact him later for a full statement? He answered as best he could.

It was quarter after eleven when the last container was loaded onto the gurney. The woman spoke with Oskar, while the same man who'd asked the questions gave Nate a pat on the shoulder and told him not to think about it. The gurney was rolled down the hall, carried down the stairs, and slid into the back of an official-looking blue van. They drove off, and Nate knew he would never see either the people or Koturovic's body again.

Oskar cleared his throat. "I am so sorry I doubted you," he said for the fourth or fifth time. "It must haff been a horrible shock to discoffer that."

"Yeah," Nate answered for the fourth or fifth time. He looked at Oskar. "Any idea who it is?"

The older man shook his head. "I think you would not be shocked to know many bad things haff happened here offer the years. I can think of two or three people it could be, and I'm sure there are more from before my time." He shivered. "Again, you haff my apologies."

"Don't worry about it."

"I am going to haff that hatch sealed and your apartment cleaned. The company will coffer the cost."

"Thanks."

When Nate got back upstairs he found everyone standing around his door. He'd left it open when he went down with Oskar and the group of medical examiners. Clive was there, but no Debbie.

Mandy cleared her throat. "Are you okay, Nate?"

"All things considered...yeah, I'm okay."

"So is it true," asked Clive, "what Veek and Tim are saying?"

Nate looked at Veek and she nodded. "I guess so," he said. "It was Aleksander Koturovic."

"You found him?" said Andrew. His eyes were wide with awe. It made him look like an anime character.

Nate nodded again.

"Did they say what they're going to do with him?" asked Veek. "With his body?"

"No." Nate shook his head. "They were polite but they didn't give out a lot of answers, y'know?"

"I didn't think they would," said Tim. "They smelled like contractors."

Xela raised a blue eyebrow. "What's that supposed to mean?"

"They weren't with the city or the state," said Tim. "Not with the feds, either. Not officially, at least."

"And again," said Veek, "you know this stuff how?"

He didn't take the bait. "You sure you're okay?"

"Look, guys," said Nate, "I appreciate the concern, but right now I'm beat."

Mandy's head turned to look at something in her apartment. "It's almost midnight," she said.

"Man, you're a wuss," Xela said to Nate.

"What if we all meet up Friday on the roof?" he suggested. "We can watch the sun go down, have a few beers, and talk about...about this and yesterday and all the stuff that's happened these past couple days."

Andrew's head bobbed from one shoulder to the other. "Intoxication goes against the Lord's wishes," he said.

"Yes, we know," said Tim. "I'll bring a bottled water just for you."

"Thank you." He turned to Nate and bowed his head. "You'll be in my prayers." He slipped down the hall and vanished into his room.

"Roger'll still be at work," Xela said. "He doesn't get off until pretty late on Fridays."

"Ask him if he's okay with us doing it without him," said Nate. "He knows pretty much everything already. We can get him caught up over the weekend."

Xela nodded. She gave him a hug and a quick kiss on the cheek. Then she leaned in to whisper something in Veek's ear. Veek batted her away with an annoyed growl. Xela smirked and headed down the hall to her apartment.

"I'm going to go let Debbie know what happened," said Clive. "She'll probably bake you a banana bread or something." He rested a hand on Nate's shoulder and headed down the back stairwell.

Mandy's waved once before closing her door.

Tim angled his head toward Nate's apartment. "You going to be okay in there?"

"No," said Nate. "To be honest, I think I'm going to sleep in the lounge. Maybe forever."

"You're not sleeping in the lounge," said Veek.

He shook his head. "I know this shouldn't freak me out. I know he's been there all along, but still..."

"It's normal," said Tim. "Everybody freaks out when they see their first dead body. No matter how long it's been dead."

Nate looked at him. "You're not freaking out."

"It's not my first dead body." He walked back to his own apartment. "Get some sleep. You'll feel better in the morning."

SIXTY TWO

Nate stared at the brass 28 for a moment and then pulled his door shut. The lock clicked. He felt stupid, patted his thigh, and was relieved to feel his keys in his pocket.

"Come on," said Veek.

"What?"

"I'm not going to let you sleep in the lounge. Those couches suck."

"They're pretty comfy."

"You'll regret it in the morning."

"Thanks," he said, "but I don't want to—"

"Nate, just shut up and come to my place."

They walked down through the lounge and into her apartment. The cool air jolted him as he stepped through the door. The computer screens were all dark.

The window above her bed had been replaced and the caulk around the glass still glistened. She saw him looking at it and shook her head. "It's going to take forever to dry in here," she said, "but you get used to the smell pretty quick."

"So," he said, "how do you want to do this?"

Veek dragged one of the blankets off the bed and handed him a pillow. "You can sleep on the floor. Or in the chair. But move it away from the computer."

"I'll just sleep on the floor."

"Fine."

"I'm sure it's a lot more comfortable than those big, puffy couches in the lounge."

"You can head back out there if you want. Just leave the blanket."

"No, no, I'm good."

She vanished into the bathroom. A moment later he heard running water and the hum of an electric toothbrush. He didn't have a toothbrush. He also realized he hadn't eaten anything since breakfast.

He folded the blanket in half alongside the bed and stretched out. It wasn't much on the hardwood floor, but he could remember sleeping on worse a few times.

Veek reappeared and walked across the room. She set her glasses next to the computer keyboard and tossed her hoodie onto the chair. She pried off her sneakers by the heels, stepped past him, and climbed into bed.

"You always sleep in your clothes?" he asked.

"Only when there's a strange man next to my bed."

"Now I'm a strange man?"

She chuckled and turned out the light. The apartment went dark for a minute until his eyes adjusted. Her desk was a scattered collection of red and green lights. Each one marked a different piece of computer equipment.

"Can I ask you something, Velma?"

"No, you can't get in the bed."

He chuckled. "No," he said. "I was just wondering...what do you do?"

He heard her shift on the mattress and saw the outline of her head peer over the edge at him. "What's that supposed to mean?"

He pointed at the desk. "What're all these special projects you're always working on? Are they really part of work?"

"Sort of," she said. Her head vanished and he heard her drop back onto the pillow. "It's part of my work."

"Meaning...?"

She sighed. "Meaning I've got another job besides data entry. One that pays the rent, unlike that shitty temp job."

"So what do you do?"

She didn't answer for almost a minute. "I find stuff online for people."

"Stuff?"

"You know," she said. "Stuff. God, Shaggy, are you going to make me spell it out for you?"

"Shaggy's pretty stupid," he said. "You better spell it out."

"I get passwords to different systems and encrypted databases. Usually corporate stuff."

"So you're a hacker?"

"It's the twenty-first century. I'm a black hat." She rolled over and looked down at him again. "Does it bug you?"

Nate shrugged and then wondered if she could see it in the dark. "I don't care what you call yourself."

"I mean does it bug you what I do? That I'm helping people steal stuff?"

"Are you getting anyone killed?"

"No. I'm not good enough to get into most of those systems."

"Good. How much do you get?"

"As much as they want."

"No, I mean how much do you get paid?"

"How rude," said Veek. "You want to ask my age and weight, too?"

"I'd guess twenty-eight and a hundred and five, tops."

"Twenty-nine and one-oh-one, loser. I make five or six hundred bucks. Once I asked for a grand and got it."

"That's pretty good money for a couple nights of work."

She flopped back on the bed. "Yeah, great. With that and the temp money I'm almost at the poverty line."

"Veek?"

"What?"

"Can I get another blanket?"

"Why?"

"Because your apartment's fucking cold, remember? Especially the floor."

"No," she said. "If I give you another blanket then I don't have one."

"You've only got two blankets?"

"I don't usually need to divide them up."

He sighed. "Don't worry about it, then. I'll be okay."

"Oh, for Christ's sake, you whiner. Just get in the bed. Bring the blanket and take your shoes off."

"I already took them off."

"Whatever."

He tossed the edge of the blanket into the air and guided it down over the bed. Veek lifted the covers and he slid in next to her. "Don't get any ideas," she said.

"I won't," said Nate.

She turned her head on the pillow to face him. He could just see the gleam of her eyes in the dark room. "Are you freaked out?" she asked.

"I don't know if freaked out's the right term." He folded the pillow and put his head down to hold it in place. There were a handful of inches between their faces. "Disturbed, maybe. There was a dead body in the walls of my apartment."

"Yeah."

"A dead body that wrote on my walls in blood. Someone's dying message, written in their own blood."

"Yeah."

"I mean, I knew he had to be dead by now no matter what, but to find out he died like that. And he's been right there for all these years... Okay, yeah, I'm kind of freaked out."

Veek leaned forward and their lips brushed. She gave him a gentle kiss and retreated. "You've had a bad night," she said. "Don't read too much into it."

"I won't."

"Good."

He resettled his head on the pillow and looked at her face. "Are you nearsighted or farsighted?"

"Why?"

"I barely ever see you without your glasses on."

"Farsighted. If I was nearsighted working on the computer wouldn't be that big a deal."

"Makes sense," Nate said. He put his hand on her face and kissed her. He pulled back after a moment. "It's just the stress. Sorry."

"I figured." Her shiver made the mattress tremble. "Don't worry about it."

"Cold?"

"You're letting a draft in," she muttered. She wrapped her arms around him and pulled herself tight against his body. "I'm just trying to keep warm."

"Right."

She leaned her head back and pressed her mouth against his. Their tongues darted against each other. He rolled her onto her back and her legs wrapped around him.

"Kissing's not a big deal," she said when they pulled away to breathe. "It's just a sign of affection. Lots of friends kiss."

"They do," he agreed. He grabbed the hem of her t-shirt and pulled it over her head.

"What are you doing?"

He paused for a moment, then said, "Staying warm." He pulled his own shirt off and threw it on the floor. "Best way is to get naked with someone in a sleeping bag."

"Right," she said, tugging at his belt. "Yeah, I read that somewhere, too. We're just staying warm."

"Right." He kissed down her neck to the strap of her bra and pulled the elastic aside. His mouth closed over her and she took in a sharp breath.

"Just staying warm and reacting to stress," Veek said. She pushed his jeans over his hips, got her foot on them, and shoved them down his legs. She fumbled with his boxers.

"Nothing but." Nate grabbed the waist of her pants and underwear and yanked them both off at once. She shook them off her ankle and pulled him back down on top of her. Her thighs opened and he sank into her.

"It's just sex," she said between kisses. She pushed up at him. "We both agree this is just meaningless sex, right?"

"I think I'm in love with you."

"Oh, for Christ's sake," she gasped, grabbing his neck, "don't ruin the moment."

SIXTY THREE

Three people were already on the sun deck when Nate and Veek walked up the stairs on Friday. Tim poured ice into an open case of beer. Clive and Debbie arranged chairs into a loose semi-circle. "Hey," Tim said. "How are you feeling today?"

"Much better," said Nate. "Relaxed."

"A few good nights' sleep will do that," he said with a sage nod.

They dragged chairs around the wooden sun deck until they were all in a rough semi-circle facing toward the west. A few moments later Xela appeared with a half-case hanging on each arm. "Oh, for Christ's sake," she said. "If I'd known all the men folk were going to be up here I would've flashed a tit and had you lug all this stuff."

"I've passed sixty," said Tim. "Tits don't have quite the power over me they used to."

"They've still got power over me," said Nate. "So if you've got anything else you need moved—" Veek cuffed him on the back of the head and Clive laughed.

Tim took one of the cases from her and set it down by the cooler. "How'd the starving artist afford so much beer, anyway?"

"The starving artist has a boyfriend who happens to think her tits are fantastic. He gave her money so all their friends can drink beer without him. He's very classy that way."

"Boyfriend," echoed Debbie. Her voice had more of an edge on it than they were used to. "Doesn't sound like your kind of thing."

"I'm a very traditional girl at heart. He won me over."

Mandy appeared on the roof at six. She asked about Nate's mental state and then joined Debbie and Xela by the firepit.

Nate and Clive dragged one of the last deck chairs into the semi-circle. "So," said Clive, "have you been getting any sleep?"

Nate looked him in the eyes. The other man feigned innocence for a moment, then winked. "How?" Nate asked. "The walls are two feet thick. With soundproofing."

Clive nodded. "They are," he said, "but everyone leaves their windows open in the summer. Including Veek."

"Jeeez. Is there anyone who doesn't know?"

Clive shook his head. "Not on our side of the building, no."

Andrew stepped out onto the roof. He had a Tupperware box filled with more celery sticks and a box of Value saltines. "I brought snacks again," he announced to Veek. "Crunchy ones."

"That's awesome," she said. "Thank you, Andrew."

He stopped and his head bobbed side to side for a moment. "You're welcome," he said.

Veek dragged a chair out of the cabana and over next to the cooler to serve as a small table. Tim finished loading the cooler and cracked open the first bottle. Its hiss reached across the rooftop. Everyone started to settle in around the arc of chairs and get drinks. Clive twisted the cap off a big ginger ale. Debbie and Veek both made a point of taking some of Andrew's dry crackers, and he beamed with pleasure.

"Okay," said Nate. He took a sip of his beer. "Monday night. Short form, I had a moment of inspiration, searched my apartment, and found a body walled up in my closet. There was nothing left of it but bones." He let them all mutter for a few moments. "We're pretty sure it was Aleksander Koturovic."

"You had a skeleton in your closet?" grinned Xela.

Andrew raised his hand. "Pardon me for asking, but why are you so sure it's him?"

Nate shrugged. "We don't know for sure, but everything fits," he said. "We know Koturovic was stabbed and got away. We know he'd want to warn everyone else working here about the Family of the Red Death. We know he was never found. I'm no expert, but that body'd been in the wall for at least seventy or eighty years. And the clothes looked old, style-wise. It had a bow tie."

"Hey," Clive said, "bow ties are cool."

"So there's a dead body in your wall," said Xela, "and control panels in Debbie and Clive's. I'd hate to think what's in mine."

Mandy scratched the side of her head and ended up twirling her blonde curls. "Control panels?"

Nate nodded and Debbie cleared her throat. "Our apartment's the control room for the whole building," she said. "The walls fold away and there's switches and levers and gauges and all that kind of stuff."

Clive nodded. "It's very steampunk," he said.

"I'm sorry." Andrew had his hand up again, like a confused schoolboy. "Pardon me. I don't understand."

Nate looked at him. "Don't understand what?"

Andrew's mouth opened three or four times without making any noise. It made him look like a fish drowning in the air. "You're saying the building itself is the machine?" he got out. "There's not something hidden inside the building?"

"Right," said Veek. She tapped her foot on the wooden deck. "If you peeled off all the paint and plaster you'd see cables and frameworks and electrical stuff."

"Again," said Clive, "all very steampunk. Built by Tesla from Koturovic's theories."

"I also found out that Whippy's grandson was H. P. Lovecraft, the horror writer," said Veek.

"No way," said Clive and Xela at the same time.

Veek swallowed a mouthful of beer and nodded.

"So," said Nate, "we've got a years-ahead-of-his-time scientist who discovered a great interdimensional threat to Earth. He tells his theories to Whipple and convinces him to give them a ton of money to build this place, with help from Tesla. Whipple then goes and tells all these theories and stories to little Lovecraft, who writes it all up as his Cthulhu stories."

"Why?" said Debbie. "Do you think the stories were supposed to be some kind of warning? A way to prepare people?"

Tim shook his head. "They probably weren't anything. I think Whip just needed to get stuff off his chest and his overly-bright grandson seemed like a good target."

Nate nodded. "Smart enough to talk to, but he wouldn't tell people Whipple was mad. He'd just assume it was all stories."

"So would everyone else," said Xela.

"What about 14?" asked Clive. "Do we know anything else about that?"

Nate shook his head. "Right now Roger's idea, that it's a counterweight of sorts, is our best theory."

Debbie coughed. "What about Mrs. Knight?"

"I checked in her apartment last night," said Tim. "There's no messages on her machine. From a few things I saw, I don't think she had a job or any immediate family. No one's missing her. I don't want to sound harsh but...that's good for us."

Debbie studied a board near her feet.

"I also found a big bag of dry cat food and slashed it up with a knife. It looks like the cats got hungry and ripped into it. For the record," Tim said to Debbie, "those cats were *not* going to starve. They're both almost round, they're so fat."

She glanced up and smiled at him, but it looked forced. "Thank you," she said.

Veek tilted her head. "Are you worried about leaving fingerprints or DNA or something in there?"

"No. Even if I had, which I didn't, they won't be looking for anything like that. It's not a crime scene, just an abandoned apartment."

"Did something happen to Mrs. Knight?" asked Mandy.

Debbie looked at the board again. Tim gave Nate a small shake of the head.

"It's complicated," said Nate. "She went away for a while."

Mandy rolled the answer around in her head. "Because of what y'all were doing?"

"Yes," said Debbie. The edge on her voice was a razor now. "Because of what we were doing."

Mandy flinched a bit, but nodded. Nate got the impression she accepted the story *because* Debbie had been a little too mean with her answer. He looked over at Andrew to see if he accepted it, too.

Andrew didn't look like he'd even heard them. He was fondling his water bottle and blinking out Morse code gibberish. "I'm sorry," he said. "Pardon me again. I just want to be sure I understand you." He looked down at the planks of the sun deck and then at the oversized machine room for the elevator. "You're saying this *entire building* is Koturovic's machine? We're *living* in the machine?"

"That's right," said Tim. "It's one big machine that they disguised as a building. Renting it out to people like us is part of the trick."

"And Clive and Deborah's apartment is the control center for this machine?"

Clive nodded.

Andrew's head tipped side to side. "Fascinating," he said.

Tim smiled at this and raised his bottle. "To Aleksander Koturovic," he said. "He saved the world and no one ever knew."

"To Aleksander," said Nate.

They echoed the toast, even Debbie. Andrew looked confused for a moment and then raised his water with a wide smile.

The sky turned orange and they watched the sunset together.

SIXTY FOUR

The man named Carmichael had been watching Tim Farr for close to two months at this point. He had the three-month mark clear in sight. Hopefully they wouldn't keep him on for two pulls. Once or thrice a week it crept into his mind that Farr could be his assignment for the foreseeable future. Which could suck on a number of levels. The man was flagged for eighteen months of observation and five years of monitoring.

Some people thought observation was a sweet gig, but not Carmichael. A full year in the car would drive him nuts. He hadn't signed up to keep eyes on retired clerks and analysts who got sacked. Granted, they didn't put clerks and analysts under observation. There was a reason men like Farr rated so much attention.

Carmichael was jotting notes in the logbook when he noticed the group on the far side of the street. After six weeks, he knew all the residents of this stretch of road. He'd never seen any of the people in this group before. Four men. He could see them from across the street. They were nondescript, Mediterranean or eastern European from what he could see. One of them was a bruiser dressed in a gym-gray hoodie, pulled low enough to shadow his face. Heavy clothes for June, but he might be a tagger. There were more than a couple of them in this neighborhood.

The group stopped outside the Kavach building. A moment later two more men and two women walked down the hill and joined them. They had the same pale, vaguely Slavic look to them.

He switched to the laptop and typed in some quick notes about the group. Real-time analysts waited on the other end of the encrypted link, even at eight-forty-seven on a Friday. Anything even slightly suspicious went straight to them.

Carmichael glanced up from the computer. Someone had come out of the building. Andrew Waite, the Bible-thumper. His background check was so clean it was creepy. He waved to the group at the bottom of the steps—a group that had grown to over a dozen while Carmichael typed—and they waved back. One of them called him by name and he walked down to open the gate.

The other thing Carmichael saw was the old woman working her way around the front of his Taurus. Her round body was draped in a sun dress and oversized cardigan, and she wore a wide hat that could've been made from a small umbrella. She squeezed between his car and the truck in front of him and waddled up toward the driver's window.

He had to deal with the locals at least once a week. The old woman would ask for directions or ask him to move or offer to sell him something. Fruit or pirated movies or bedroom comforters. It was some cultural thing he couldn't wrap his head around. He set the computer down on the passenger seat and prepared to receive her.

The old woman cleared her throat. It was a wet, phlegmy sound. "Excuse me," she said in accented English. "I'm so sorry, but could I bother you for directions? I seem to be lost."

"I don't live around here," he said. He made sure the laptop was steady and then gave the woman a lazy glance. "I wish I could help you out, but you're better off asking over at the corner..."

The old woman wore a Halloween mask. Then she blinked and Carmichael thought it had to be prosthetics. By the time he admitted her face was real and fumbled for his sidearm she'd already reached in through the open window and crushed his windpipe. He struggled for a moment, got the pistol up, and she slammed his head into the steering wheel. She slammed it three more times before the airbag went off in an explosion of white streaked with bright red. It pinned Carmichael's body in place against the driver's seat.

"Auntie," called Andrew from across the street. "Are you all done? We don't want to be late."

"Coming, dearest," said the old woman. She tugged her hand free and gave it a delicate shake. "Just tidying up a bit first."

"Maybe we should move," said Debbie.

Clive found himself craving a drink. He'd wanted one since the day they opened apartment 14. To be honest, he wanted to get sloppy drunk like the good old days, before he'd met Debbie, when he could forget whole weekends.

But those days hadn't been all that good.

"What do you mean?" he asked.

Debbie shrugged. "Move. Find another place. We always wanted to someday."

"Someday when you were done with school or I had a steady gig on a show," he said. "We can't afford it right now."

"We could make it work."

Clive shook his head. "Where would we find another place like this, at this price? We'd be lucky to get a little studio, and it'd probably be way out in the valley."

"The valley's not so bad."

"You'd spend an extra two hours every day on the bus. You hate the ride as it is."

She crossed her arms. After five years together, Clive knew that wasn't a good sign. He reached out and took her hand. His fingers slipped between hers. "Come on," he said. "What's going on?"

She glared at him.

He nodded. "Mrs. Knight?"

"Mrs. Knight, the thing in our walls, the thing across the hall. All of it." She waved her hand out toward room 14 and at their loft. Everyone had helped Clive move it away from the swiveling planks and closer to the coffin-lock. He'd added a handful of new diagonals to steady it now that it was free-standing.

He rubbed her fingers with his thumb and eased her arms open. "Still," he said, "it's better than what Nate found in his walls." He gave her a little smile.

"See," she said, "that's what I'm worried about. Everyone's just making jokes about death. There's all this death here and we're all pretending it's not." A wet spot formed in the corner of her eye and threatened to become a tear. "What if it had been you?"

"Ahhh," he said.

"You reached *into* it."

He nodded. "To save our friends."

"But you could've died," said Debbie. Her grip on his hand tightened and a matching wet spot swelled by her other eye. "You could've been sucked in like she was. And if you were gone they'd all just try to hide it. They wouldn't even care."

"Hey," he said. "That's not true. You know they'd care."

"They don't care about Mrs. Knight."

He reached up and dabbed at the wet spots with his thumb, then wiped them on her nose. Her mouth formed a weak smile. "They do care," said Clive. He kissed her knuckles and looked her straight in the eyes. "I've got to say something, and it's going to sound mean, but I want you to hear me out. Okay?"

She nodded.

"We didn't know Mrs. Knight," he said. "She lived here. She wanted to learn about the place. But she was just a lady who lived down the hall."

"That doesn't mean we should—"

He set a gentle finger against her lips. "It doesn't make it any less sad. But she wasn't one of our friends and we didn't know her. None of us did. Most of us just thought she was a nasty old woman with a racist streak. So did you."

Debbie looked at the table top.

"We're all upset about what happened to her. We all wish it hadn't happened. But she was almost a stranger." He paused. "They wouldn't be like this if it had been me. They wouldn't leave you alone like her cats. They'd be here. Nate would be making a play for you because you're just too damned beautiful."

She looked up. The wet spots were back. "Language."

"Sorry."

"Nate's with Veek."

"Well, yeah. No doubt about that after this week."

She snorted out a laugh. Her free hand came up to wipe her eyes. "I love you, you know that?"

"I think it came up at the wedding."

"Please don't get killed by this place."

He kissed her knuckles again. "I won't. I promise."

Someone pounded on the door and they both jumped at the sound. Clive smiled and gave his wife's hand a squeeze. "You want to get it?"

"I've been crying," she said. "And I've been awful to everyone."

"You'll get sympathy, then," he said.

"Meanie." She wiped her eyes and whoever was in the hall pounded again. It sounded urgent. She went to the door and peered through the peephole.

Andrew stood front and center. There were a few other people with him, but because of the fish-eye view she couldn't be sure who they were.

Debbie spun the deadbolt and unhooked the safety chain. She opened the door and Andrew's eyes tracked over to her face. She got a quick look at the other people and didn't recognize any of them.

"Good evening, Deborah," said Andrew. "I'm so very sorry about this."

"What? Is there something—"

Andrew's hand cracked across her jaw. He couldn't bring himself to make a fist, but his backhand slap was still enough to send her staggering back into her apartment. He pushed the door open and moved after her. The others followed him in. An old woman in the back of the group closed the door behind them and twisted the deadbolt closed again.

Clive saw Debbie fall and leaped forward and Andrew swung another backhand. This time he made a fist. Clive's head twisted on his neck. He'd been whacked in the head by a swinging two-by-four once. It hadn't hit as hard as Andrew's casual blow.

He tried to form another thought, white spots whirled in front of his eyes, and he was on the floor near Debbie. She blinked away her own surprise. Blood dripped from her nose and from a split in her upper lip.

Clive tried to roll back to his feet but one of the men pushed him back down. The man's foot was wrong. Clive could feel the shape of it through the cheap sneaker and wondered if the man had a fake leg. Maybe a bionic fake leg.

Andrew stood over them. He held his off-color bible. He looked down on them the way someone looked down at a cat or a dog.

"To think that all this time," he said, "you were living with the key to salvation and never knew it. That may be enough to make you one of the chosen, even though you're not part of our congregation."

The squat old woman worked her way through the group until she stood next to Andrew. Something was wrong with her face. It reminded Clive of embryo pictures where the mouth was nothing but a line and the eyes were still too large and far apart for the head. She blinked and it made him realize just how big her eyes were. The dull white of her eye blurred against the gray tone of her skin.

Andrew reached over and patted the old woman on the arm like a doting son. "This is Auntie Bradbury," he said. "These are my spiritual brothers, Zebediah, Lucas, Charles, and Howard."

They each bowed their heads as they were introduced. None of them spoke. All their eyes were wide and round, like Andrew's.

"They're all members of my congregation," he explained. "You could say we're a Family."

SIXTY FIVE

Tim felt it first.

He'd noticed the hum weeks ago. It was a subtle vibration, the kind you got on a plane or large ship. A hint that there were things going on under the floor.

When he felt the change, he knew it was something that'd been going on for ten or fifteen minutes. That was a bad sign. It used to be that nothing could sneak up on him.

The hum was a little faster, a little higher pitched. Just enough he was sure it'd changed.

The vibration was different, too. Since he first noticed it, the ever-so-faint tremble had been clean and steady. It synced with the hum. Now they'd fallen apart and become two distinct elements. The vibration was slowing and becoming less steady. It was more of a low *thrum* now, like a guitar. It was as if he could feel the pulse of the building, and the building was...

Tim's mind snapped into crisis mode. He ran into his small bedroom, threw some shoes aside, and pulled a high-impact case from under the bed. Three combinations leaped to mind, a different one for each lock, and he spun the first dial.

Nate and Veek might have noticed sooner if they hadn't been distracted in the kitchen and then on the futon couch. As it was, they became aware of the change at the same moment Tim was throwing open the case from under his bed.

Nate stood to drag his pants up and paused with his hand on the zipper. "Do you feel that?" he asked. "Like a...like a throbbing, kind of?"

Veek pulled her shirt over her head and smirked. "If you're fishing for compliments, I think you got enough while we were—"

"No, seriously." He gave his fly a quick tug, buttoned the jeans, and crouched next to Veek's bare legs. She still wore her socks. He set his hand on the floor. "It feels like someone's blasting their stereo downstairs."

"I don't hear anything."

He shook his head. "Neither do I, but that sure feels like a big set of speakers."

She set her own feet down and took a few quick steps to where her jeans had landed. The lights were out but the windows were wide open. "Yeah," she said, "it does. What the heck is that?"

Nate grabbed his shirt from the kitchen floor. In his drying rack two glasses were trembling. They started to clatter against each other. "Is it an earthquake?"

"No," she said, stepping into her pant legs. "If it was an earthquake it'd..." Her voice trailed off and her eyes went wide behind her glasses. "Oh, shit."

Someone pounded on the door. Any harder and whoever it was would be trying to break the door down. They glanced at each other.

"Who is it?" shouted Nate.

"It's Tim," he hollered. "I think we've got a problem."

Xela saw it next. Her headphones were in, and the pounding voice of Jessie J was blocking out all other sounds and sensations.

She was working on another painting of the building. This was her third in as many weeks, acrylics on canvas. For such a fascinating subject, she couldn't come up with a way to picture it that didn't feel trite or overused. The canvas in front of her was a mix of architecture lines and circuit boards. She'd been shooting for an optical illusion.

It looked like crap.

A wave of despair washed over her, but she managed to get above it. Art was her destiny. She knew it for a fact. She just needed to get past this creative block.

The light in her apartment shifted as the streetlights came on. There was one right by her front window that lit up her place at night. It was crappy yellow light, though, way too diffuse and scattered to be any good.

In all truth, she knew she hadn't created anything worthwhile in months. Nothing that felt good enough, anyway. One of her teachers had told her being able to accept your work was no good was a vital step, a sign of growth and maturity in an artist.

Xela was very ready for the next vital step.

She toyed with the idea of grabbing her stubby little roller and covering the whole thing with titanium white. It'd be awesome to be able to cut canvases to shreds with a knife, or to smash their frames and burn them. Probably a great emotional release.

She couldn't afford new canvases, though. As it was she had to work with the cheapie ones from Michael's Crafts. And she had to paint over those four or five times, until they were too stiff to use.

The streetlight flared. For a moment she thought it had burned out, but then it went back to its regular levels. Then it flashed again. And a third time.

Xela glanced out the window and all thoughts of painting vanished from her mind. She yanked out her headphones and the hum assaulted her ears. She dashed into the hall just in time to see Nate and Veek following Tim down the back stairwell.

Mandy sat at her computer and checked her credit score. Someone had told her they were updated once every four or five days, but she was sure the bad news got updated more often. The news of Mrs. Knight moving out had convinced Mandy she was guilty by association. Everyone knew the banks and the government were one big socialist group, so it made sense they'd try to damage her score even more now.

While she waited for the website, the screen jumped like an old television. The image scrolled up and back so fast she could've blinked and missed it. But Mandy hadn't blinked and she'd also heard the low, distant rumble.

She looked away from the monitor and saw the summer evening had become dark and dreary. A haze of fog hung outside her window, and she heard another rumble of thunder. This one shook the building.

And the building kept shaking. Her window panes started to rattle.

She heard someone bang on the door across the hall. Nate's door. There were raised voices and running footsteps.

Her computer screen went blank and her heart sank. She should've unplugged it at the first sign of thunder. She wouldn't be able to get it fixed. Unless Veek would be willing to fix it in exchange for...well, whatever Mandy could give her that she wanted.

Then the monitor lit back up. Mandy took a relieved breath and then her heart sank again. The screen was all nonsense. Green squiggles scrolled up the screen. They looked like Chinese or Muslim or one of those languages that used chickenscratch instead of proper letters.

Her whole room was shaking and the roar of thunder wouldn't stop. Her tall lamp tipped over and a picture of her parents dropped off the wall. Out of the corner of her eyes she could see flashes of lightning through the fog.

A circle appeared on the monitor. It was filled with more squiggles. And the squiggles moved across the computer screen like little worms.

Or little tentacles.

Andrew stood before the control panel. Auntie Bradbury had given him the honor of shutting the machine down, but it didn't feel right to do it all by himself. That would be selfish. This was a joyous moment which needed to be shared with as many people as possible. He'd insisted Auntie be first. The old woman had smiled with pleasure, selected a large lever, and pulled it down.

Debbie and Clive had yelled and shouted. They still didn't understand what was going on. Clive fought to his feet but Charles grabbed his arm and Andrew punched him once in the stomach. Clive dropped back to the floor.

Zebediah and Lucas each picked a knob and gave them a hard twist. Howard set his hand across a row of switches and pushed them all down. Charles pulled another lever. And then Andrew flipped down every switch he could see.

One needle pegged itself to the far side of the dial. Another swung back and forth like an inverted pendulum. One twitched between thirty and forty.

They all heard the arcs of electricity behind the panels and saw the flashes. The machine howled and the air in the building roared back. Andrew could see the sky changing outside the windows, and for the first time in his life his faith was rewarded with the sight of one of his lords, soaring in the sky by the dying sun.

He reached out to either side and held hands with Auntie Bradbury and Brother Charles. The group formed a chain in front of the control panel. Auntie led them in a prayer.

At last, Andrew thought, *the time is right.*

Roger parked his truck and walked home down Beverly. Home before nine on a Friday. It was going to be a good weekend.

He'd expected to see midnight on set. There were ten and two-eighths pages on the call sheet for that day. The whole crew had started the day with doom hanging over them.

But the actors had their shit down today and the director had kicked serious ass. He'd minimized setups. He rearranged the call sheet so they could block-shoot three scenes. Two of the others he did as one-ers. The assistant director called the martini shot at seven-thirty, and even with a last-minute olive they'd wrapped by eight-oh-nine. A few of the guys had invited him out for drinks and Roger'd been surprised how cool it felt to tell them his woman and some friends were already waiting on him.

He pressed the button for the walk signal and glanced up Kenmore towards his home.

All thoughts of Thai food and movies and fooling around with Xela up on the sun deck under the stars vanished.

The Kavach Building was glowing. At first he thought everyone had their lights on, but it was the building itself. A flicker raced around the edges of each brick, the way static chased fingertips across an old television screen.

Roger took a moment to check traffic and then crossed the street against the light. By the time he reached the far curb he was running.

Power hung in the air. It prickled his skin and tugged at his hair. He could feel the hum in his teeth and hear glass trembling in the windows.

A few people from nearby buildings looked out windows or stood out on their stoops. There was a crowd gathered around the gate, almost two dozen men and women Roger didn't know.

He sprinted past the green Taurus, noticed its airbag had gone off, and was at the fence. Roger shoved through the crowd and the open gate. Some of them grabbed at him and he let them pull away his toolbelt and backpack. A woman yanked at his arm and he slammed his fist into her face.

He forced his way up the front steps. The air around the building was *clotted*, like old milk or blood. It felt like he was pushing through millions of invisible bees, each one letting its razor-sharp stinger brush across his skin. The air roared at him, warning him to stay back, and Roger yanked open the security door and dove into the lobby.

Just in time, he told himself. He didn't question how he knew this.

The Kavach Building shuddered and groaned. It bent in ways brick and stone and concrete weren't supposed to bend. It twisted along angles most human minds couldn't comprehend. It let out a long howl, and then, like a spinning top that built up enough speed to leap up off the ground and into the third dimension for a moment, the building shifted in space.

And it was somewhere else.

NOT ON BLUEPRINT

SIXTY SIX

Nate felt sick.

Violently sick.

He'd gotten drunk at college a few times. And while there was no denying the hangovers were bad, he knew the real pain was at night when you crossed the line. When you went from fun-drunk to horribly-sick-hugging-the-toilet-drunk.

Somewhere between the lounge fire door and Veek's door, while the building was roaring and the air had been filled with static, he'd crossed that line. But the taste in his mouth was bad milk, not booze. Gray, cloudy milk that had curdled and separated and turned rancid. Just the thought of it made his stomach churn even more.

He was on the floor outside Veek's apartment. He didn't remember sitting down or falling. Veek sat next to him. Her lips trembled and told him she felt the same thing he did.

Tim was still on his feet. The older man looked queasy, but he kept himself upright, somehow. And past Tim, Nate could see the window at the end of the hall. Something was wrong about it, but he couldn't figure out what. It nagged at the back of his whirling mind.

It was quiet. After all the noise the building had made, the quiet boomed up and down the hall like the hour after a concert.

"Are you okay?" Veek patted his arm with a clumsy hand. Her voice sounded muffled. She wrinkled her brow and he realized she'd heard it, too. She reached up and touched her ears, then closed her eyes and swallowed twice. "My ears popped," she said.

He swallowed and his stomach rumbled. For a moment he thought he was going to throw up on her, but he got it under control. He swallowed again and felt a quick rush from his ears. "Gahhhh," he said.

"Better?"

"Yeah, thanks." They struggled up to their feet.

Tim lifted his foot and slammed it into Debbie and Clive's door. There was a crack of wood, some splinters flew from the lock, and the door smashed open.

A dark-haired man none of them knew raced out of the apartment. He swung a wide punch and Tim did something fast with his hands. The dark man grunted and a knife clattered to the floor. Tim slammed his head forward into the other man's nose and drove a punch into his gut. The man tried to drag Tim down as he slumped to the floor and

Tim hit him in the face with a knee. He grabbed the man's jaw, pulled hard, and a sharp crack echoed in the hall.

Nate stepped forward, even though he had no idea how he could be helpful, and heard a roar inside the apartment. Another man charged through the door.

Tim had a large television remote in his hand. Just as Nate was registering the absurdity of that, and realized what the older man was really holding, the television remote thundered twice and spit brass out its side. The man in the apartment staggered a few more feet and Tim fired again. The man crumpled to the floor.

Tim marched into Clive and Debbie's apartment. Nate and Veek stumbled after him.

The walls were open and the controls exposed. With the wooden panels slotted away Nate could hear the whining of the machine and a sound like a grinding transmission. Electricity sparked and crackled behind the instruments.

Andrew stood in front of the controls with an older woman. A larger man, his face shadowed by a gray hoodie, stepped toward Tim. Another one crouched by Debbie and Clive, both prone on the floor and coughing. Clive had the unmistakable wetness around his mouth of someone who'd just thrown up.

The crouching man had a knife.

Tim fired once. The blade flashed and hurled itself across the room. The man howled and exposed a mouthful of crooked teeth. A second shot hit him in the side of the head and knocked him down next to Debbie. She and Clive screamed.

The larger man, the closer one, growled and reached out. Tim grabbed two of the grasping fingers and twisted them. They made a bubble-wrap noise. His other hand swung forward and pistol-whipped the large man twice, back and forth across his broad jaw.

The giant spat out a tooth and growled again. His mouth opened and it split his head in half. Nate glimpsed it from the doorway and thought the man's head had somehow been chopped off and was getting ready to tumble.

Tim fired point blank into one of the man's wide eyes. The giant dropped to the ground. The old woman howled and waddled forward.

"Auntie, no!" shouted Andrew. "It doesn't matter."

The old woman lumbered to a halt halfway across the room. Nate, Veek, and Tim could see she had the same wide mouth and swollen eyes as the giant on the floor. They were even more distorted on her face.

"Down," said Tim. "No fucking around. On the floor, now."

The old woman sighed, crouched, and lowered herself to her knees. She panted when she was done. She raised her arms awkwardly. They were too heavy to get them much above her shoulders.

Tim suddenly had another pistol in his left hand. This one stayed on the old woman while the first one shifted to cover Andrew. "Step away from the controls," he said. "On the floor."

If Nate was right, it had only been fifteen seconds since Tim kicked open the door.

Tim angled his head back without letting anyone out of his sight. "Nate, can you look in Clive's toolbox over there? He should have some rope or zip ties we can use on these people."

All four men were dead. Tim had killed all of them in fifteen seconds. He'd made it look easy.

"Nate?"

"Ummm...sure." The toolbox was by the window, and there was something wrong with the windows inside, too. Nate couldn't spare the attention to figure out why.

"Veek," Tim said, "why don't you check on our friends."

Veek made her way around the creepy old woman to Clive and Debbie. Clive looked stunned. Debbie seemed to be doing better. She looked up as Veek touched her arm. "Veek," she said. "Are you okay?"

"I'm good," she said. "I think we're all good."

Debbie squeezed her arms. "What happened?"

"Freedom has happened," said Andrew. A blissful smile spread across his face. "Freedom from a tyranny on all our souls for over a hundred years."

Tim looked down the pistol sights at Andrew. "No more talking," he said. "You don't speak unless you're spoken to. Clear?"

"If you wish. It makes no difference. The path has been made clear and soon our Lord and his fellow gods will come to reward us for—"

"Shut up, Andrew," Tim said.

The skinny man's smile got wider. His head went side to side.

"You have a gun," Debbie said to Tim.

"I've got two," he told her. "If it makes you feel better, you can hold one of them."

"Clive," said Nate. He'd gone through half the drawers in the large wooden chest. "Help me find this stuff."

Clive blinked a few times. Debbie rubbed his arms and Veek tried to clean up his face with a wad of paper towels. "M'okay," he muttered. He took a few deep breaths. "I'm okay."

"Nate could use some help, Clive," said Tim. "You know your tools better than anyone else here."

Clive stumbled to his feet with some help from Debbie. They went over to the toolbox. He pushed Nate out of the way and crouched to one of the lower drawers.

The floor creaked by the door. Tim spun, keeping one pistol on the old woman. Xela shrieked and Roger threw his hands up. "Whoa!" he shouted. "It's us, bro."

"Sorry," said Tim. "Old habits."

"Fuck me," said Roger. He spit a mouthful of stomach acid into the hall and looked at the bodies. "Look at the old man, going all Bruce Willis on us."

Clive pulled a bundle of black plastic zip-ties from one of the drawers of the chest. Each one was at least a foot long. He split the bundle and gave half to Nate.

"Are they...are they dead?" asked Xela.

"I hope so," said Tim, "but I'm not feeling confident about anything right now." He gestured at the big windows.

Weak sunlight streamed through the glass. Clive looked at the wall clock that read ten past nine. Debbie looked up at it, too, and then stepped to be near her husband. Xela and Roger moved to join them. Veek went to stand by Nate at the window.

"Guys," said Xela, "where are we?"

The brick building which stood a dozen feet to the south was gone. So was the building behind it, and the one past that. As far as they could see was rocky hillside spotted with patches of yellow grass and a few sickly palm trees. It looked like the prehistoric setting for dozens of B-movies.

Veek pressed her face to the glass and looked toward the front of the building. There was more wasteland. The same behind them. All the other buildings on the street had vanished. So had Kenmore Avenue itself, as far as she could tell.

The shrunken ball of the sun was a bright spot in the blood-colored sky. It was an ember, the last remnant of a holiday bonfire that had burned out the day before.

"Everything looks dead," said Debbie.

Tim cleared his throat. "Speaking of which..."

Clive bound Andrew as Nate cinched a zip tie on the old woman's left wrist. She had fat wrists. Her arms were so blubbery she couldn't put them together behind her back. He ended up making a chain of zip ties to hold her.

The woman's skin was pale and decorated with spots that were too dark to be freckles. She smelled damp and cold under a cloud of floral perfume that might've just been a generous coat of Lysol. Nate felt a pulse in her wrist and she yelped when the zip ties bit down, but he couldn't shake the feeling he was tying up a waterlogged corpse.

He also felt the thick muscles under her blubber, and decided to add another set of bindings, just to be safe. Maybe two more.

"So," Veek said. She stepped back from the window and looked at Tim. "You learned how to shoot because you published a book on it?"

His lip twisted in a wry smile. "Not quite."

"So, what's the deal?" asked Nate. "Are you like...a hit man or something? An assassin?"

"Let's just say 'or something.' Before I retired, I worked for an outfit best known by three letters."

"Holy shit," said Roger from the window. "You learned all this at IBM?"

Tim smirked. "Yeah, IBM's got one hell of an employee training program."

"Fuck me," Roger said.

"I'm guessing telling us this violates some rules or laws or something," said Veek.

"Tons," said Tim. "And at least one act of Congress. But like I said, I think we've got bigger prob—"

"Guys," said Xela, "what the hell are those?"

"Oh my God," said Debbie.

A quartet of green shapes soared through the air a mile or so up, in that altitude reserved for passenger planes or the occasional fighter jet. It would've been easy to call them whales, but it would've been wrong.

Wings stretched off the enormous bodies. They were thin, bony wings that let the weak sunlight through them. If they were smaller they'd be bat wings, but on this scale the unspoken, unnecessary agreement was they were the wings of a dragon.

Beneath the base of the wings sat wiry arms with talons, like a bird's legs tucked away for flight, or the small forelimbs of a dinosaur, armed with curving claws that were never used. Their bodies tapered to a reptilian tail.

Where there should've been a head, or at least some type of face, was just a mass of tentacles. At least two or three dozen ropes of muscle stretched out from each whale to pick and snatch at the air. The tentacles had to be forty or fifty feet long, although it looked like each creature had a few as long as its body.

The smallest was over two hundred feet long. The largest one, an alpha among alpha predators, was at least four times that. Even as high up as they were, its monstrous wings cast shadows across the ground. They coasted at a lazy pace, drifting on unseen winds.

Their path led them across the wasteland and towards the Kavach Building.

SIXTY SEVEN

"They're coming this way," said Veek. She managed to hide the tremor in her voice. Clive and Debbie squeezed each other's hands and turned their knuckles white. Xela still stared up at the things in the sky.

"They're coming for us," said Andrew. "Coming to reward the faithful."

Tim leveled his right-hand pistol at Andrew's eye. "I think I was very clear about you not talking," he said.

A throat cleared and Tim whipped around again.

Oskar stood at the door. Mandy lurked behind him, her eyes wide. She looked like a cornered animal and shrieked when the pistol came to rest in her direction.

The building manager muttered a string of German words Nate was pretty sure were swears. He walked into the apartment and shook his head. "I warned you," he said. "What haff you idiots done?"

Veek glared at him. "What do you mean, what did we do? Forget that. Where the hell are we?"

"We are somewhere we are not supposed to be," said Oskar.

Mandy scampered past Oskar and pushed herself into the corner between Clive's tool chest and the wall. Her eyes were wide and her cheeks were lined with tears. Clive stepped away from the window. "How did we get here?"

"How did the building move?" asked Xela.

"Do not be stupid," Oskar told her. "The building did not moof."

Nate blinked. "What?"

"It is still in Los Angeles," said Oskar. "Right at Befferly and Kenmore. If it was *not* in Los Angeles we would all be dead by now."

Roger waved his arm at the window. "If we're in Los Angeles what the fuck is all that?"

Oskar raised an eyebrow. "That is not in the building, is it? That is where we are not supposed to be."

"It's precisely where we're supposed to be," said Andrew.

"Last warning," Tim told him.

Oskar glared down at the bound man. "You are the one who did this?"

Andrew pressed his lips together in a smug smile and tipped his head at Tim.

"Yes," said Debbie. "It was him and these other people." She kept her eyes up and didn't look at either the prisoners or the bodies on her floor. "They broke in here, beat Clive and me, and opened the walls. Then they just started flipping switches and pulling levers."

She walked over and wrapped her arms around Mandy. The other woman was still wide-eyed. Her lips moved but didn't make a sound. Nate thought the farmer's daughter was deep in shock. He shot a glance at Veek and saw the same thought in her eyes.

"Is there anyone else in the building?" Nate asked.

"I think the guy across the hall from me works the night shift," said Roger. "He's probably not home."

Oskar nodded. "Mister Cook," he said. "Also Mister Brogen in apartment one and Miss Little in twenty-four. All of them work late. I am not so sure about Mr. Kamen in eleffen or Mrs. Knight in four."

Debbie and Veek both jumped at the mention of Mrs. Knight. Roger threw a look over his shoulder. "Think she's dead," he said matter-of-factly.

Oskar's brows twitched and he sighed. "That is too bad," he said. "She was a good tenant."

"Oskar," Nate said, "It's time to talk. What do you know about this place? We need to know everything."

The older man looked at their faces and sighed again. "I do not haff all the facts," he said. "Only what they told me when I was giffen the job, and some things I also figured out on my own. It is like knowing a car needs gasoline to run, but not knowing what it does with the gasoline that makes it run."

"Who gave you the job?" asked Veek.

"A man in a suit." Oskar put up his hands and shrugged. "I think he was from the government."

"Why?" asked Tim.

"My paychecks, they come from the Department of the Treasury. They haff the Statue of Liberty on them."

"What branch of the government?" asked Tim. "What office?"

Oskar shrugged again.

Nate gestured for him to continue. "What's going on? Do you know?"

Oskar's fingers fiddled in the air in front of him. "Picture a lock and a key," he said. "The key goes into the lock, so most of it is on the one side, but part of it is *between* the two sides. Does this make sense?"

A few of them nodded. Veek tilted her head in her thoughtful way.

"Go on," said Nate.

Oskar's head bobbed up and down. "This is the Kavach Building. It is a key, built to ensure a certain doorway stays locked shut. Do not ask me how or why. I do not know." He held up his hands with the palms facing each other. "Now, what many people do not consider is that a key can fit into both sides of the lock. The same part stays between the sides, but it does not matter which side the rest of the key is on." He wiggled one set of fingers, then the other. "That is what they haff done. They haff altered the balance and put us on the other side of the lock."

Andrew's mouth was a flat line.

"Question," said Veek. "You're saying we're on the other side, but is the key still in the lock? Is it still doing what it's supposed to be doing?"

Oskar nodded. "It is. If it was not, as I said, we would all be dead."

"Dead how?" asked Clive.

Oskar gestured at the window. "From them, I belief."

"Super-ginormous alpha predators," murmured Xela.

"Damn," said Roger. He was back at the window. "They're really close."

Nate followed Veek to the window. Even Tim stepped closer, still keeping a clear line to their prisoners.

The whale-things coasted a few hundred feet above the ground. It was like watching planes make their final approach to a runway.

The smaller ones led the way, wind rippling the skin of their wings. The ground swirled as their passing stirred up dust and dirt. The walls shook as they passed over the building and the air rumbled like a brief storm. Sand and stones rattled against the windows. A large rock made a spiderweb that stretched across one of the recently-replaced panes. Something solid hit the wall outside with a large *thunk*.

The chandelier chimed as it swung back and forth.

"Shit," muttered Roger. He had one arm around Xela. "Everybody okay?"

Mandy sobbed and Debbie hugged her tight.

"Everyone get away from the window," said Tim. "Now."

Nate glanced at him, then back out at the wasted hillside.

The great one, the largest of the beasts, came at them. Its tentacles writhed like a nest of worms. It was night beneath it. The beast blocked out the sky and it was still hundreds of yards away. Every sweep of its wings—each one bigger than a football field—pounded air against the ground like an artillery strike. The hill broke apart under the relentless battering and the rubble was dragged along in the monster's wake, a tidal wave of earth.

The residents of Kavach took a few steps back. Then they threw themselves behind the couch and under the table. Debbie dragged Mandy down behind the toolbox, and Clive wrapped himself around both of them.

Nate looked back over his shoulders and saw nothing but tentacles. Thick cables of muscle filled the window, each one flailing at the sky.

And deep inside the twisting mass, just for a moment, he glimpsed something else. Not shadows. Whatever he saw at the center of the tentacles gleamed like an unlit pool or a mirror of dark glass. The beast was still at least sixty or seventy yards away, so what he saw had to be huge—thirty or forty feet across, at least.

Then Veek dragged him to the floor and they covered their heads.

The window exploded as the creature flew by. Its bulk hid its speed, like a freight train or jumbo jet. Glass flew across the apartment and hit the furniture like flying blades.

Hunt You Kill You Eat You Prey Food Feed FEED

The air roared around them as a tornado smashed through the apartment. Plates and silverware whipped out of the sink to smash themselves against the walls and floor. The couch slid halfway across the room, dragging Andrew with it. Clive's tool chest swung away from the wall and rolled a few feet before it tipped over and crashed to the floor next to him and the two women in his arms. The loft creaked, leaned, and collapsed. The kitchen table threw itself against the far wall.

FOOD FOR ME MY SERVANTS MY MORTALS MY FOOD MY PREY

Veek threw her hands over her ears and Nate wrapped his arms around her head and shoulders. He wasn't sure where the words were coming from. Was he hearing them over the wind or feeling the vibration of them in his gut? There was blood on his arm. A shard of window stuck out near his elbow.

The old woman rolled back to her knees. She was laughing. Nate couldn't hear her but he could see her wide lips flapping up and down below joyful eyes. A piece of glass the size of a pizza slice appeared in her head and her lips stopped. She fell forward and the glass cracked apart as her head hit the floor.

The building rocked with earthquake force. Plaster cracked in the roof and rained down on them. The floor shuddered. One of the bookshelves, picked clean by the wind, crashed down on top of Roger and Xela.

MY FOOD MY PREY MY CATTLE MINE

The words crushed them. Blood ran out between Veek's fingers. Nate felt wetness across his lips and figured his nose was bleeding. He squeezed his eyes tight and tears rolled down his cheeks.

The roar of wind died down. The scraps of dirt and paper swirling around the room settled down to the floor. Nate released Veek and met her wide eyes. Gobs of blood were under her nose and ears. There were trails of it from her eyes and a small line along the bottom of her glasses. She'd cried blood.

Veek reached up and dabbed his cheeks. Her fingers came away red. He'd been bleeding, too. He squeezed her arm and gave her forehead a quick kiss. It was the only part of her face without gore on it.

"Is everyone okay?" he called out. A few people winced and Nate realized he was shouting after the onslaught of noise. He dropped his voice a few decibels and tried again. "Anybody hurt?"

Clive unwrapped himself from Debbie and they both stuck their thumbs up. Both of them had streaks of red coming from their nose and mouth. Mandy had pulled herself into a ball between them, but Nate saw blood on her ears.

He looked over at Tim. He looked like the monster in a hardcore vampire movie. Dark blood covered the lower half of his face and soaked the chest of his t-shirt. He'd tucked one pistol into his belt and had the other one back on Andrew. He gave Nate a nod and a thumbs up.

"More new windows," muttered Oskar. He wiped the back of his hand under his nose and smeared blood across his upper lip and cheek.

The bookshelf shifted as Roger and Xela pushed it off themselves. He had a gash on his arm and the start of a bruise across his forehead. A knife-sized piece of window glass stuck out of Xela's thigh, but it didn't seem to be bleeding much. They both had blood on their faces.

"What was that?" yelled Roger. "What *the fuck* was that?"

Andrew cleared his throat. There were a few spots of blood under his nose, but not much. "Auntie Bradbury's dead, if anyone cares."

"We don't," said Tim. "Shut up."

"We're dead," said Clive. "That thing'll come back here and—"

"Hang on," said Nate. "Let's not give up yet."

"Quiet!" snapped Oskar. "All of you!"

His volume bought him a moment of silence. It occurred to Nate that it was *too* quiet, but he wasn't sure why.

"Now, listen to me," Oskar said. "We will all be safe. There is a way to fix this, to get back to our side. We just—"

A thick tentacle smashed through the remains of the windows, wrapped around his head, and dragged him away.

SIXTY EIGHT

Mandy was screaming. Long, powerful screams that carried on even after the tentacle had vanished. In between each howl she took a raw, panting breath that told Tim she was using more air screaming than breathing, which meant she'd stop in a moment one way or another.

Oskar was short, but Tim put him at two hundred-forty pounds, easy. The only time he'd seen anyone vanish that fast before was during paratrooper training, when guys would step out the hatch and be gone before you could register it. Television and movies made skydiving look slow because there were no reference points. It was fast. Speeding on the highway fast.

The tentacle had yanked Oskar up and away that fast.

Mandy's screams broke down to a hoarse rasping that became tears. Debbie rocked her back and forth like a child.

"Did it kill him?" asked Clive. "Is he dead?"

"Didn't take him outside to hug him," said Roger.

Nate stepped toward the window. Veek grabbed his hand. She didn't hold him back, just stepped to the window with him.

Tim shot a glance at his prisoner. Andrew still looked blissed out. It was the smile and gaze of someone prepared to drink their paper cup of Kool-Aid. Tim stepped over to the window, but made sure he still had a clear shot at the man. That wasn't hard, since ninety percent of the furniture was now against the far wall. He glanced out at the wasteland.

There was no sign of the squid-whales. Nate leaned out and looked up, left, right before yanking his head back. Then he leaned out again and took his time.

"Come on," he said. "To the roof."

Roger's jaw dropped. "You nuts? You want to go outside?"

"It's not safe," said Debbie.

"Especially up high and exposed," Clive added.

Nate shrugged. "We need to see more," he said. "You with me, Velma?"

"You got it, Shaggy."

Xela straightened up, winced, and put on a brave face. "I thought I was Velma?"

"Back off, bitch," Veek said. She managed a smile. "You're Daphne. Deal with it."

"Seriously?" Roger shook his head. "You're going up?"

"Coming or staying?" asked Nate.

Roger met Xela's eyes. "I'm in."

They headed for the door. Tim pulled the pistol from his belt and offered it to Nate. "Just in case."

"In case what?" Nate asked. "Is it loaded with nukes?"

"Sorry, no. Just hollowpoints."

"Then I don't think it's going to do much good."

The fire door to the roof was wedged tight. The four of them positioned themselves on the stairs and pushed. There was a lot of weight on the other side. The door moved a few inches, then a few more. They saw bricks scattered on the rooftop. Some were still cemented together in groups of three or four.

"Looks like the machine room came apart," said Veek. "You think they hit it?"

"Wind from the big one was pretty gnarly," said Roger. "Might've just been that."

The door opened another two inches. "I think I could squeeze through," said Xela.

"Keep pushing," said Nate.

"Why?"

"Because if we need to get off the roof fast we don't want to squeeze through one at a time."

"Hey." A voice echoed up the stairwell in a bad stage whisper. It sounded like Clive. "Are you guys making the scraping noise?"

"Yeah," called Veek. "The door's stuck."

"Cool," he said. "Just making sure."

They all broke out in grim smiles and pushed again. The opening was two feet wide. Roger put his back against the door and braced his leg up against the frame. He grunted and heaved and the door moved another seven or eight inches. "Good enough?"

Nate nodded. "Works for me."

He led the way out onto the barren roof. The wooden sun deck and all its furniture was gone. In places the tar paper was torn away in broad patches. One of the air vents was shredded into long strips of metal.

They turned, scanning the skies in every direction. Roger saw them first and pointed. All of them looked north.

The squid-whale pack was two miles away. They'd gained altitude and were soaring up over a set of huge hills like desert sand dunes. One of the smaller ones swept down and plucked a palm tree from the ground with its tentacles. It was hard to tell from their angle, but it looked like the beast swallowed it whole. The pack veered off to the east and coasted across a ridge that ran from the distant hills down past the building and on to the south. They swooped down and vanished from sight.

Nate's eyes followed the ridge, waiting for them to reappear, and then he squinted. He tried to focus on a distant shape that contrasted against the endless gray of ground and sky. It was at the very top of the hill and was thinner than it was tall. "You guys see that?"

Veek peered over the top of her glasses. "I see something."

It seemed to be glossy, but Nate wasn't sure if it was just his eyes trying to focus on it. He tried to estimate the distance and height off a few lone palm trees and guessed the tower might be fifteen or twenty feet tall, which meant it was about ten feet wide.

Xela hobbled over. The blade of glass was still in her leg, but didn't seem to be bleeding much. "Looks old," she said.

"How so?" asked Nate.

She shrugged. "Just the lines of it. I might be totally wrong."

"Doesn't look like they're coming back," said Veek.

Nate glanced over his shoulder. "Assuming they're the only ones."

Roger leaned past the railing. "Found the sun deck," he said. He tipped his head at the ground below.

The broken planks and beams stood out against the bleached soil. The wood spread out in a trail starting at the base of the hill and leading north. A lone deck chair stood right side up in the middle of it all.

Nate strained his eyes. "Anyone see any sign of Oskar? Anything? Any...any parts?"

"I think," Xela said, taking her time, "if one of those things ate him, they wouldn't need to bite."

"Wouldn't need to," muttered Roger, "but they might do it for fun."

"But if we don't see anything it means he might be alive, too," said Nate. "We can't write him off yet."

They stared at the sun deck for a moment. Veek pulled off her glasses and wiped the line of blood onto her shirt. "Okay," she said, "I'll bring it up. All you guys heard those things talk, too? It wasn't just my brain crashing, right?"

"I heard it, too," said Nate.

"Almost pissed myself," Roger said with a nod.

"Me too," added Xela. She didn't smile.

"No question about how they see us," Nate said.

"Yeah, but they're smart," said Veek. "They speak *English*."

"I don't think they were," said Xela. "I mean, I don't want to sound all new-age, but they were speaking right to our minds, weren't they? Telepathically?"

Roger shrugged. "It was loud," he said. "Really loud."

"It could've been in our heads," said Nate. "That might explain all the bleeding."

Roger nodded. "Right. Getting stuff done to your brain makes your nose bleed. I read that in a book once."

"You read a book?" said Veek.

"Wait for it…" said Roger. "Annnnd...fuck you."

"What I mean is," said Xela, slapping Roger on the shoulder, "I don't think we were hearing English. I mean, I don't know about you guys but I was getting a lot of ideas and images more than actual, y'know, words."

Veek nodded. "Same here. Just lots of things like 'food' and 'prey' and—"

"Cattle," said Nate. "It called us cattle."

"We're hamburger, you mean," said Roger.

"No." Veek shook her head. "It means we're something they raised on a farm to turn into hamburger."

They all looked to the northern hills for a few moments.

Veek moved toward the back of the building. Xela limped back over to the remains of the machine room and Roger went with her. Nate followed the path of the whale-beasts with his eyes. The shattered deck made a fine guide for half a mile. He scanned the horizon in every direction. He didn't think they could sneak up on the building, but he wasn't so sure about being able to get away from them if he did see them.

Xela tossed a half-brick through one of the holes. It clattered on some of the machinery and then the sound of it faded as it fell down the elevator shaft. She looked back at them. "D'you think all the tunnels came over, too? Do they count as part of the building?"

"No clue," said Nate.

"Might be a good place to hide out."

"Good place to die," said Roger. "One of those things collapses the building or lands on it, bet you anything all those tunnels cave in." He walked back to Nate and crooked his chin up at the sky. "Don't think the sun's moved since we got here," he said.

"I think you're right."

Roger waved up at the distant dunes. "D'you notice the shape of the hills?"

Nate followed his gesture. "What do you mean?"

"There aren't any of the other buildings or anything, but the land's a lot like it is in our world. We're still halfway up that same hill. Got little mountains up ahead of us, just like the Hollywood Hills."

Nate studied the hills and realized Roger was right. They were scoured down to dirt and stone, but he could see the curves and dips that made up the view from his apartment. He could even see the small plateau where the Griffith Park Observatory would sit.

"Up there to the right, that ridge? That's where Vermont Avenue would be." Roger waved his arm in the other direction. "That's all Hollywood over there. Bet if we went a couple miles that way we'd find an ocean."

"Yeah," said Veek, from the far side of the roof, "but what'd be in it?"

"Nothing," said Nate. "That's the overriding factor here, isn't it? Everything's dead."

"Not dead," said Xela. "Killed. Eaten. Those squale-things have sucked the life out of this whole world."

Veek tilted her head. "Squale?"

"Squid whales," said Xela. "A stupid name makes them a bit more bearable."

"Squale it is, then," said Roger.

The door scraped and they all jumped. Clive stepped out onto the roof. "We've got a problem," he said. "The machine's off."

Veek's eyes went wide. "What do you mean?" asked Nate.

"I mean it's off. The sparks, the hum, it's all stopped. Ever since that big thing flew by." Clive took a moment to breathe and slow himself down. "The machine's not protecting us anymore."

SIXTY NINE

Nate wiped the blood from his face with a damp paper towel. "So, here's where we stand," he said. "We've got some bottled water, and enough in toilet tanks for anything else. We've still got power, which means everything in the tunnels came over to this side with us. That also means we don't have to worry about food for a little bit. All our refrigerators are going to keep working, so we should be good for a couple of days at least."

They were back in Clive and Debbie's apartment. They'd straightened some of the surviving furniture so people had somewhere to sit. Mandy was curled up silently on one end of the couch with her arms wrapped around her legs. The bodies of Auntie and the two men were down in the lounge, out of sight.

"And then what?" asked Xela from the other end of the couch. She'd dropped her pants so Tim could pull the glass from her thigh. She squeezed Roger's hand while it happened. Tim put a few drops of superglue on the gash and then wrapped her leg with some gauze pads and a long bandage from Clive's first aid kit. It was messy, but it wasn't getting any worse.

"By then we're not going to be here," said Nate. "There's a way to reverse what they did. Oskar was sure of it, so I'm sure of it."

"Oskar's dead," said Andrew. He knelt on the floor near the kitchen area. "He's joined the Great Ones."

"I don't think you know as much about all this as you think you do," Nate said to the bound man.

Andrew pasted on his smug look.

Nate looked back to his neighbors. "There's a chance he's out there hoping we'll rescue him. We don't know for a fact he's dead."

"We don't know that he isn't," said Clive. "Hell, even if he is alive, he could be a hundred miles from here, the way those things move."

Nate nodded. "I know, but I think we need to check. The squales flew off over a ridge out by the hills. They might have a nest or something up there."

Roger cleaned the last of the blood out of his ears. "So what's the plan?"

"I think some of us should go over all the pictures from Tim's room. Maybe we can find a connection between the circuit diagrams and the actual machine and figure out how to get it running again. The rest of us will go up to that ridge and look for a sign of Oskar. If there's nothing, we come home. If there's something, depending on what it is, we'll figure out what to do next."

"How are you going to get up there?" asked Xela. "We don't have cars and I'm pretty sure there aren't any buses."

"Thank God for the subway, then," said Veek with a smirk. A few of them chuckled.

Nate smiled. "We've got four or five bicycles in the building, right? The ground's sandy, but it looks solid enough to ride on. We could be at the ridge in an hour. Less time to come back because it's all downhill."

"We could just sit tight, too," suggested Tim. He ran a piece of white tape across Xela's bandage. "We'll all get reported missing in an hour, tops. There'll be a lot of really smart people looking for us on the other side."

"I thought it took three or four days before somebody could be declared missing," said Debbie.

"Most people aren't under twenty-four hour surveillance," said Tim. "If the guy in the green car or part of his team doesn't lay eyes on me inside of sixty minutes there's going to be a shitstorm. Pardon my language."

"Ummmm..." said Roger, "Think that guy's dead."

Tim's face dropped. "What?"

Roger angled his head towards the front of the building. "Saw it when I was running up here. Green Taurus with the airbag set off. Looked like blood on it."

"Plus, remember what Oskar was saying," said Nate. "The Kavach Building's still in Los Angeles. It's still in the lock. I bet nothing looks that unusual over there. It's just wrong for us because we were in the building when it happened."

"Were a lot of weird lights when I got home," said Roger. "People noticed that."

Nate shook his head. "I just don't think we should be counting on anyone except us. We've got food, but not enough to risk sitting around doing nothing."

"You're right," said Tim. "But I'm still not sure going out there's the best choice. No offense to Oskar."

Nate nodded. "Okay. What do you think we should do?"

"Taking care of this place, the machine, was Oskar's job," said Tim. "Let's search his apartment for schematics or an owner's manual or something. He's probably got better information than us. Hell, for all we know he's got the reset instructions posted on the back of his door."

SEVENTY

Clive wiped his hands on a towel. There wasn't much blood on the bodies. He'd expected them to be leaving rivers of blood in the hall and on the stairs. It wasn't much worse than dealing with a leaky garbage bag.

That thought bounced in his head for a moment and his empty stomach churned. He paused to get his thoughts back under control. The last thing they needed was someone else losing it. He took a few very slow breaths, thought about Debbie, and pictured how they'd rebuild their home again.

It's just like any gross job, he told himself. He'd been a dishwasher in high school and a janitor for the two years he was at college. There'd been awful stuff to deal with in both jobs. The trick was to put a little mental distance between yourself and whatever it was you had to touch.

God, a drink would be great right now.

His jaw still ached from Andrew's backhand. Clive tapped one of his molars with his tongue for the umpteenth time and felt it shift ever-so-slightly under the probe.

Moving the smaller men hadn't been a problem. None of them weighed much more than Clive, so it'd just been a matter of tying their ankles together—a tip from Tim, and it also wasn't good to wonder how Tim knew that and how many times he'd done it himself—and dragging the men across the lounge and down the stairwell. That went slowly until Clive assured himself the first man's head wasn't going to crack open as it bumped down the stairs one at a time.

The large man had been more troublesome. Aside from the extra weight, he was built wrong. He had the large eyes and over-wide mouth, but there was more to it than that. When Clive lifted the corpse's legs to tie them, they bent in the wrong place. The knees were too high, and the hips too loose. And the fingers were long. Not alien monster-long, but just long enough. It was most noticeable on his left hand, where Tim had broken two of the fingers.

There was a term some of Clive's friends used, the ones who did a lot of computer gaming—"the uncanny valley." It was a psychological threshold where things looked very human, but still weren't quite human enough. It was why some mannequins were creepy and others weren't, and CGI monsters looked better than CGI people.

The large man was in the uncanny valley. He was a living person—or had been—whose features were almost human but not quite human enough. He was creepy as hell. Andrew had said the man's name, but when Clive stopped to look at the body the name that came to mind was "Grendel."

In a way, the old woman was easier. There was no way to mistake her for a normal person. Her face looked like a frog had stretched a human mask over its head. Her skin was pale gray and slick, like an eel. When she died her body had stretched out flat and let them all see how off her proportions were.

All five bodies were in a line for now. There was a fair-sized ledge of concrete behind the building. Most of the slab had come through with them. The back fence hadn't, though, and there was a ten-foot drop to the ground below.

Clive cleaned the last of the woman's clammy slickness off his hands and tossed the towel on top of her body. The idea of Debbie touching it, or using it on dishes, made his stomach swirl again.

Oskar didn't have instructions on the back of his door. What they found was an apartment which stretched over the entire corner of the building. All three floors were connected by an ornate spiral staircase. Roger searched the top floor bedroom while Nate went through the kitchen and Veek ransacked the first floor office. Twice.

She stomped back upstairs and the wrought iron clanged under her footsteps. "Okay," Veek said to Nate, "how can he not have a computer? There are people living in mud huts who have laptops."

"Maybe he doesn't have one for a reason," said Nate. "Maybe his apartment is at some magnetic juncture or something in the machine. They might not work in here."

"Or maybe he's just an old guy who never got a computer," she sighed. "I don't think we're going to find anything."

"We've only been looking for, what, an hour?"

She nodded. "Yeah. We've been searching these three rooms for an hour and none of us have found anything besides the key ring."

Veek had found it in the unlocked top drawer of the desk with Oskar's checkbook. Most of them were for the various apartments, the numbers written on small cardboard circles wired to the keys. There were four mismatched keys bound together with yellowed tape. A manila tag on the largest was labeled 14 in blue ink. It crossed Nate's mind one of the keys fit a padlock that was still tumbling toward a pair of alien suns.

Along with Mrs. Knight.

"Maybe you're right," he said. He'd rooted through the kitchen, moved through the bookshelf, and even pulled the couch apart.

"Nothing upstairs," said Roger. He'd come down the spiral staircase. "Box under his bed with some old pictures. Lots of World War Two stuff with tanks. Went through his dresser and his closet, found a few old letters, box of tax stuff going back to the eighties." He shrugged. "Nothing like what we want, though."

"Toilet tank?" suggested Nate.

Roger shook his head. "Checked it."

"There has to be something," said Veek. "How can you be in charge of all this stuff and not have something written down somewhere?

"Might've tattooed it on his arm if it was that important," said Roger. "Who knows?"

"Or," said Nate, "maybe all he knows is 'pull this lever in case of emergency' or something like that." He shook his head. "I think this is the final nail in the coffin, though."

"Bro," said Roger, "*not* the right expression." He shook his head.

"Sorry," said Nate. "We're going to have to go out there and try to find him. And if we're lucky he'll be okay enough to tell us how to get out of here."

SEVENTY ONE

Veek, Roger, and Tim already owned bikes. Nate found one in the back of the building, chained to a drainpipe. He made a point of not looking at the bodies while he smashed the lock open with one of Clive's hammers. An hour later they stood at the base of the stairs. Nate looked up at the faded sun hanging in the sky. According to his internal clock, it was coming up on midnight.

"Go on," said Roger. "You go first."

Nate looked over at him. "What, you're scared of a three-foot drop?"

"Not scared," said Roger. "I'm just not the guy in charge."

"And you keep saying I am, so get down there and I'll hand you a bike."

Roger took another look at the ground below the last concrete step. It looked like beach sand, but there was something off about it. The grains were too large and too gray. It looked like someone had tried to make a desert from an off-the-cuff description.

"What if there's sand worms or something?"

"Sand worms?" said Nate.

"Big worms that move through the sand like it's water." Roger's level arm went up and down in a smooth wave. "Or the big thing in *Star Wars*. What if we step down there and the sand just turns into a big pit with a mouth at the bottom?"

"For the record, it's called a Sarlacc," Xela said.

Roger snorted. "Geek."

"Chicken," said Veek.

"I'm just—"

"Oh for God's sake," said Tim. He stepped off the stairs and sand puffed out from his feet as he landed. "The damned sun doesn't move and we're still going to run out of daylight before you two grow up."

Veek glanced down. "No sand worms?"

"Just give me a bike."

Nate and Roger lowered the bicycles down to Tim. Nate hopped down, then Veek, and finally Roger. Nate threw one leg over his bike and pointed to the northeast.

"I'm thinking if we head straight up to the ridge it does two things," he said. "One, it's a smoother, easier ride up to the hills than cutting across this depression. Two, it also lets us take a look at whatever's over there before we reach the tower."

"Normally I'd say being up higher makes us more visible," said Tim, "but it's not like there's anywhere else we could find cover." He gazed out at the wasteland with its occasional lone tree or half-buried boulder. "If the squales come back, we're screwed."

"Even if they don't go after us, we'll just get thrown around until we break something," said Veek. "It'll be like getting caught outside in a hurricane."

Xela crouched on top of the small ledge with her hurt leg out straight. She and Roger exchanged whispers. He slapped the pistol on his waist and went to pull it out.

"Roger," Tim growled, "don't screw around with your weapon."

Roger's hand jumped away from the pistol. "Sorry."

Tim had returned to his apartment and come back with a small arsenal. Each of them wore a black, blocky pistol clipped to their belts, and Tim's were strapped to his thighs. Upstairs, Clive had a Mossberg shotgun for watching Andrew. Tim had explained it was loaded with beanbags, so Clive shouldn't hesitate at all if he needed to shoot.

After all he'd learned about Tim in the past few hours, Nate felt a little uncomfortable with that explanation.

Xela waved them over to the ledge. "Be careful," she said. "There's something weird about this place."

"You're very perceptive," said Veek. "What gave it away?"

"Bitch," Xela said. "I'm serious. I think it'd be real easy to get lost here. The lines aren't right."

Nate looked at her. "The what?"

"The lines," she repeated. "The vanishing points. None of them match up."

Tim nodded. "I noticed that but I couldn't figure out what it was."

"Still don't know what you're talking about," said Roger.

"Vanishing points, baby," said Xela. "You know how things look smaller and closer together the farther away they are? Like how the sides of a straight road look like they come together and disappear at the horizon. That's the vanishing point."

"Okay, right," said Roger with a nod. "Sooooo...?"

She looked out at the wasteland and gestured at the hills. "The lines, the angles, the vanishing points...none of it matches up here," she said. "It's tough to be sure because there's so few reference points, but it looks like the perspectives are all wrong."

"How's that even possible?" asked Veek. "I mean, I think I understand how you could mess it up in a picture, but how can you do it in the real world?"

Xela shrugged. "I don't know. Other-dimensional geometry or something. Everything still seems okay in the building." She tipped her head at the ridge. "Just keep it in mind while you're out there." She gave Roger another kiss before heaving herself back to her feet.

They kicked off and headed across the hill toward the ridge.

They rode for fifteen minutes or so. The only noise was the *whirr* of bicycle chains, the occasional clicking of gears, and their own breaths as they pedaled across the sand.

"It's quiet," Tim remarked.

"Too quiet?" asked Nate. He thought of the silent machine in the walls of the Kavach building.

"Yeah, actually," Tim said. "You get used to operating with certain noise levels. There's nothing here."

"We're in the middle of a desert," said Veek.

"I've been in the desert before," said Tim. "Some nasty ones. You'd be amazed how many sounds there still are. Wind blowing, sand shifting. Plus you can hear for miles, so there's always something. But not here. Here there's nothing."

"I feel wind," said Roger.

"You feel the air on your face because we're moving. Not the same thing. Trust me, the only sounds out here are the ones we're making."

"Something else calling attention to us," said Nate.

"Oh, yeah," Tim said. "Not to mention the sand's just loose enough for us all to leave tracks." He shot a glance over his shoulder at the four trails tracing back to the building.

After a few more minutes Veek rolled her bike closer to Tim. "The tower's not moving much," she said. "I mean relative to us. That means it's close to the ridge, right?"

"I know what you mean," Tim said. "Parallax-wise, yeah. But remember what Xela was saying about how perspectives were tricky here? That might not mean anything."

Veek nodded on her bike. She looked ahead at Nate and gasped. "Shit."

Nate had leaped half a mile ahead. He straddled his bike and looked back at them, both feet on the ground. He waved to them.

"How'd he get so far ahead?" gaped Veek.

Tim shook his head. "Alien geometry, remember?"

She looked behind them. Roger's tire had almost been clipping hers. Now he was a good hundred yards behind them. She saw him mouth the words *what the fuck* before he leaned forward on his handlebars. Or maybe he hadn't mouthed it. The Kavach building was a speck on the horizon behind him.

"Look out!" yelled Tim. His voice sounded distant. She brought her head back around and caught a glimpse of him a few dozen feet away. Before she could get her eyes back to the front she crashed into Nate and knocked both of them over.

Nate grunted. His bike pinned one of his legs, and Veek pinned the bike. She tried to twist off him and he winced. "Easy," he said.

"Sorry."

Roger skidded to a stop inches from them. "Shit," he said. "Wham, here you are."

"Wham being the operative word," said Nate. He bit his lip as Veek shifted her weight. Roger helped her up and Nate untangled himself from the bikes.

Tim coasted up. "Sorry," he said. "I wanted to stop you but all of a sudden you were too far away. You okay?"

"A couple bruises, maybe," Nate said. "That's it. I got lucky and fell in some sand."

Veek snorted out a laugh and Roger grinned. Nate dusted himself off and they all smiled.

Tim tipped his head to Roger. "What did it look like to you? What happened?"

Roger shrugged. "Was weird," he said. "Wasn't like you guys sped up or anything. Just one second you were five feet in front of me, the next second you were five hundred. Like a movie skipping ahead because they edited stuff out."

Veek tilted her head. "What about when you almost hit us?"

"Same thing. You were way over there and then you were right in front of me again, down on the ground."

"So," Nate said, "we shouldn't get too separated."

"We *weren't* separated," said Roger. "Like Xela said, all the lines are messed up."

"Just before this," said Tim, "I was trying to tell Veek, I think the distances are off. We've been riding for twenty-five minutes, yes?"

Veek pulled out her phone, glanced at it, and sighed. "Sure, okay."

Tim pointed. "We should be close to the ridge by now. It was only two miles away, tops. But it doesn't look much closer than it did from the building."

Nate leaned over to Veek. "Phone's dead?"

"Fried," she said with a nod. "Just gibberish on the screen."

He glanced over her shoulder at the green squiggles. "Is that Arabic?"

"Don't think so." She shrugged. "Might be Thai and Arabic mixed together. Some default languages in the phone all spewing out at the same time."

"Looks kind of like the Matrix."

"So what do we do?" said Roger. "Think we're ever going to get there?"

Nate looked at the ridge. "Tough to say. For all we know, if we have another one of those...I don't know, ripples? Distortions? If there's another one of those we could be there in a few seconds. Or it might take us the rest of the day."

"Or the rest of the week," said Tim. He pulled his bag off his shoulder and rummaged around in it.

Roger looked over his shoulder. The building was a mile away now. They could still make out most of the big details on it. "What if the same thing happens going back? Could take us a couple days to get home."

"Or no time at all," said Veek. "Damned if we do, damned if we don't."

"Damn right," said Roger.

Tim pulled out a coil of cotton rope. He tied one end to the handlebars of his bicycle, pulled out a few lengths of rope, then did a quick hitch on Nate's handlebars. A few more quick lengths and he moved to Veek's bike.

"Okay," said Nate. "Here's what I'm thinking. We spend another hour heading for the ridge. If we don't make it, that's it. It's more important we get back to the building."

"Agreed," said Tim.

"And we're going off Tim's sense of time," Nate added, "because we don't have anything else that works. If he says it's been an hour, it's been an hour. We all agreed?"

Veek and Roger nodded. Tim tied the end of the rope to Roger's bicycle. "We've got ten feet between us," he said. "If it's just a perspective thing, nothing will happen. If we're actually moving somehow, we'll know through the rope. Make sense?"

"Let's try not to panic over any of it," said Nate. "Xela thought it might happen and it did. If we rush around, we're just going to get each other hurt." He rubbed his knee for emphasis.

Five minutes later they had another shift. Veek blinked and Tim vanished from the front of the line. Her eyes adjusted and saw him a mile down along the sand dune. Another blink and Nate joined him there.

Veek touched the rope connecting her bike to Nate's. It still had slack in it, just enough that she could hook her finger over it and feel it give when she tugged. The woven strands of cotton were still loose. She tried to follow the rope out to the other bicycle but it made her eyes hurt. She shook her head and the two men were in front of her again.

Nate glanced back at her. "You, too?"

She nodded.

"But we're all okay," he said. "It just looks weird. It doesn't hurt us."

"Not yet, anyway," muttered Tim.

SEVENTY TWO

Xela flipped through Veek's printouts and found a new schematic. Her eyes flitted from the picture to the bank of controls. She traced a line across the diagram with her finger, then followed it through the air with her eyes.

"I have no idea what I'm doing," she admitted to Clive.

He glanced at her. "Maybe you should've said that before everyone left."

"No one else knows anything, either," she said. "At least I've got a symbol key. There's just so much of this stuff, y'know? I get lost before I can figure out anything big."

"Maybe I can help," said Debbie. The side of her face was purple where Andrew had smacked her. She walked around the couch, where Mandy still sat in a near-fetal ball. "I know some basic electronics from undergrad courses."

"I don't think there's anything basic about this, hon," said Clive.

"It's better than nothing," Xela said. "I'm not even sure these are the diagrams of the control room. They might have something to do with the generators."

Debbie shook her head. "Too many switches," she said. "It's this room."

Xela spread a few diagrams across the arm of the couch. "Wow," Debbie said after a moment. "There really is a lot of it."

"Yup," said Xela. "But I'm sure an artist and a biochemist can figure it out."

The bicyclists went through another shift. This one made everyone seem claustrophobically close even though the ropes had no slack. Roger didn't deal well with it.

The next shift made them all seem miles away. It was like an extreme form of tunnel vision. Nate held his arm out in front of him and his fingernails vanished in the distance.

Their hour was almost up when they reached the ridge.

Veek looked back and saw the Kavach Building. It was a mile or so away. The ridge hadn't looked much higher than the roof, but she looked down on the building from here. She wondered if it was another trick of the world.

Nate looked at the crowned tower. From this position it was clear the tower was beyond the ridge, not on it. The skewed perspectives made it hard to be sure of size, especially since there was nothing around the tower to judge off.

"It's not glossy," said Nate. "It's kind of...hazy."

"Yeah," Roger said. "What's up with that?"

"Could be smoke," said Tim as he untied the bikes.

"Might just be the lighting," said Veek.

Nate shook his head. "If that's it, where's the light coming from?" He swung himself off the bicycle and set it on the ground.

Tim put a hand on Nate's shoulder and pushed down. "Stay low," he said. "If there's something over there, you don't want to be a silhouette against the sky."

They dropped to their hands and knees and shuffled up the last bit of the ridge. Nate felt a small drift of sand gather in his shirt against his stomach. He didn't picture it as sand, but as little squares of coarse glass, the remnants of a very tiny broken windshield. It felt too dry. He wondered if it would start to suck moisture from his skin. He tried not to think about it getting into his pants and reaching his crotch.

Their heads came up over the edge. They had a clear view of the tower.

"Fuck me," whispered Roger.

SEVENTY THREE

"I think we're doing this all wrong," Xela said. She looked at Andrew. He sat with his eyes closed and his chin tucked against his throat. His lips moved silently. "He doesn't know anything about electronics, either. He just came in here and attacked the controls."

attacked the canvas

She pictured herself starting a painting. Her brush reached out and touched the center of the canvas.

"Okay," said Xela. "Aesthetics and ergonomics. We all try to do things the easy way. It's how we're built."

Clive and Debbie exchanged a glance. Debbie shrugged. "Okay," she said.

Xela glanced down at the praying man again and balanced herself in front of the control panel on her good leg. "You said he was standing about here. Andrew and I are the same height. So if I was going to flip a random switch—"

She held out her hand. It came to rest just below shoulder height.

"—I'd probably go for something right in this area." Xela leaned in and studied the dusty switches. They were broad, steel pins with square tips. Some of them had crumbling rubber sleeves on them.

"All of them did something," said Debbie. "Andrew did most of it, but they all changed at least one."

Xela's head went up and down along the panel. She glanced at Debbie. "Do you guys have a flashlight handy?"

"I think so."

Clive nodded. "Check the tool chest. Should be a mini-mag in the top drawer, on the left side."

Debbie found the flashlight and tossed it to Xela. Xela played the beam across the panel. Then she pushed her head close to the controls and looked down the row of switches. A century of dust and grit was piled up on most of the switches.

A third of them gleamed in the flashlight beam.

"Okay," she said with another glance at Andrew. "He knew he didn't have a lot of time. Somebody could walk by, hear all the ruckus, maybe call the police. The quickest, easiest thing to do would be just to flip switches right? And it's not ergonomic to push them up. He'd push all of them down."

Debbie nodded. "Gotcha. Makes sense."

Xela pointed at the row of controls, careful not to touch them. "The squale blew off the dust bunnies, but a bunch of these switches have *all* the dust wiped off. You can see it when the light hits them. They're clean. There's even streaks on a few of them, like oil from someone's finger."

They glanced at Andrew. His head was down, but his lips had stopped moving. Clive raised the shotgun back up to Andrew's head.

"And this knob," Xela said, shining the light on it, "there's dust under it, but not on top. It's almost a full one-eighty from where it was before."

"Are you sure?" asked Clive.

"Pretty damned sure," said Xela. She took a cautious step away from the control panel. "It might take a little time, but I think I can figure out where everything was before dickless there turned the machine off. Do you have some paper? Even just a legal pad or something?"

"Sure," Debbie said. "I've got printer paper, too."

"Perfect. And a sharp pencil."

❖

The ground beyond the ridge dropped away. It was a massive crater, or maybe an excavation. It had to be at least half a mile deep. The far side blurred into the horizon.

At the center of it, reaching up to the sky, was the tower. It was hazy because it was so far away.

The tower was an obelisk of some sort, like a six-sided Washington Monument, and it was covered with engraved swirls and patterns. The top was a familiar arrangement of prongs and horizontal bars. Each of them had to be fifty or sixty feet thick to be visible from here, like the massive towers that held up freeways.

It took Nate a moment, then it struck him the whole thing looked like a gigantic jewelry setting for a ring.

He tried to guess how tall the tower was, but there was nothing near it to use for scale. Piled around its base were smaller obelisks and buildings and halls, like a sprawling castle or a small city. As far as Nate could see there were no windows. One archway near the edge of the complex looked small in comparison, but it could've been a hundred feet tall.

He brought his gaze closer and his eyes settled on something halfway down the slope. He almost gasped. Tim slapped a hand over his mouth before he could.

A few hundred yards below them hunched a line of men and women. Their skin was leathery, their hair matted into rough dreadlocks. Many of them were on their hands and knees, clawing at the sand. A few carried rocks.

"They're people," said Veek. Her voice dropped when she saw the others. "There's *people* here?"

"How?" said Tim. He opened his pack and pulled out two small sets of binoculars. One of them went to Nate. "There's nothing to eat. No water."

"Maybe it's all in the castle," said Roger. He jabbed a finger at the complex. "Could have *Star Trek* replicators and everything in there."

"They don't look too advanced," said Nate. He turned a wheel with his thumb and pressed his eyes to the lenses. "I think they're all naked."

"Seriously?" asked Roger. He peered down the slope.

"No," said Tim. He had his own set of binoculars to his eyes. "They're not naked. They all have collars on. Metal collars."

It took a moment for the implication to set in. "Let me see," said Veek. She took the binoculars from Nate and pushed her glasses up onto her forehead. Roger held out a hand for Tim's set, but the older man ignored him.

"I don't see a lock on any of them," said Tim, "but I do see what look like old scars. If I had to guess, I'd say they're riveted onto the people somehow. They don't come off."

"Do you see a...an overseer or something?" asked Nate. "A guard?"

Tim shook his head. "Not yet."

"Look at them," said Veek. "Their jawlines. It's like a gorilla. Even the women. Heavy brows, too."

"Eyebrows?" asked Roger.

"No, the actual brows. The bones of their skull." She shook her head. "They look like Neanderthals." She handed the binoculars back to Nate.

"What the fuck are cavemen doing here?" asked Roger.

"They look like them," said Tim. "It doesn't mean they are." He paused. "The guards aren't human."

"Where?"

Tim pointed without raising his hand or putting it out past the edge. "That group down there," he said. "The larger one. Look near the center. He blends in because his cloak's the same color as the sand."

Nate scanned back and forth. He passed the figure twice before his eyes caught its movement against the endless sand of the pit. It was almost invisible.

The guard was tall and lean. A good two or three feet taller than the cavemen, although it was hard to be sure with the slant of his crooked shoulders. A dust-colored cloak and hood covered most of his features, but Nate saw a sharp chin beneath the hood. Needle-like teeth jutted up out of the jaw. They looked too long for the mouth to close. Eyes gleamed inside the hood, but Nate couldn't see any details.

A spear leaned against the guard's body and its hands held the shaft in an easy grip, one above the other. The fingers and knuckles had the color and texture of wet clay, the same as the jaw.

The same as the old woman's skin.

The guard's other hand was twitching against his side. It was the motion of someone trying to keep a tally. Or maybe just a nervous tic of some kind.

Nate's mental gears jammed for a moment. He shifted the binoculars. Then he shifted them back. He did it again to be sure of what he was seeing.

The guard had two hands on the spear.

It also had one hand twitching at its side.

"No way," he said.

"There's another one," said Tim. His eyes pressed against the binoculars. "And another. Christ, there's a couple hundred of them. Maybe more."

"The arm?" asked Nate.

"They're all like that," Tim said. "And they're functional. It's not some freak mutation or something."

"What?" said Veek.

"The guards all have an extra arm," said Nate. "Like the roaches." He handed her the binoculars. She lifted them to her eyes.

"I'd guess there's around six thousand slaves down there," said Tim, "whatever they are. Maybe as many as five hundred guards."

Going off the lines of slaves and overseers, Nate guessed the tower was two miles away. He tried to calculate figures in his head and thought about times he'd climbed up Runyon Canyon to look down at Los Angeles. The view from up there helped give him a sense of scale. If he was right, the other buildings at the base of the tower were over a mile away. The tower itself had to be close to a quarter mile across at ground level. It stood five times taller than it was wide.

It wasn't just hazy because of the distance. It was reaching into the clouds.

"We'd never make it down there," Tim said. He lowered his binoculars and shook his head. "Count the crater wall and it's a couple of miles of open ground with a guard every hundred yards or so on the floor. I wouldn't try it with a machine gun and a case of grenades. Hell, it'd be tough with air support." He rolled onto his back and slid below the top of the ridge. "Even if we did make it, that's four or five Pentagons put together. We could spend years searching it for Oskar."

"Oh, hell," said Veek. Without lowering the binoculars, she fumbled for her phone.

"Got a call?" asked Roger.

"I wish," she said. She unlocked the phone to reveal the streaming gibberish. She glanced at the phone, then put her eyes back to the binoculars. "It's the same."

Nate looked at the phone. "What?"

"The squiggles on the phone," said Veek, "the stuff we couldn't figure out. It's all over the tower. It's on everything. It's all over the buildings and the..."

Veek choked. She held out the binoculars for anyone and slid a few feet down the slope. She tipped her head and let her glasses fall back into place.

Nate reached out and she grabbed his hand. "You okay?" he asked.

"I found Oskar," she said. Her eyes were wide.

Tim flipped back on his stomach and shuffled back up the slope. "Yeah?"

"Yeah," said Veek. "Most of him."

"Fuck," muttered Roger.

Tim scanned the crater with his binoculars. "Where?"

Veek pushed her glasses up and rubbed her eyes with her palms. "Left side of the tower, there's a big thing that looks like a barn with a silo. There's a dome just past it, and then a big plaza. He's there."

Nate took the binoculars from her hand and crawled after Tim. He found the barn and followed it to the dome. There was a huge covered walkway—more like a covered six-lane highway—that led to an enormous plaza of rough cobblestones. There were obelisks studding the end of it. A few dozen yards out from the arched entrance to the highway was a blob of ivory on the dark stones. He played with the dials until the blob solidified.

The bottom half of Oskar's body was gone. Nate tried to be clinical and noted it was a clean edge. Something had chopped

bitten

straight through him at the hips and taken his legs and crotch away. From the angle of the remains, it looked like most of his guts were gone. They'd left an empty torso supported by his rib cage. His skin was pale, and Nate wondered if Oskar's blood had all leaked out across the thirsty sand or if the squale had drained him like a gigantic vampire bat.

Roger took the binoculars from Nate and looked at the manager's body. "You think he was dead before it...bit him?"

"He probably just died of shock when it hauled him away," Tim said. His face didn't look as certain.

"Good," said Veek. "That's...good."

They all settled back down on their side of the ridge. "We should get out of here," said Nate. "Get back to Kavach and try to figure out the machine on our own."

A cloud passed in front of the sun, blocking the dim light for a moment. Another one hid it and they were in shadow. "Wind's picking up," said Roger. "Might be a rough ride back."

"Jesus," said Veek. "It's not wind."

The squales were back.

SEVENTY FOUR

The smaller ones swung in wide arcs, swooping around and approaching the crater from either direction. Their monstrous leader soared overhead, blotting out the sun. Its wings beat in wide arcs that covered hundreds of yards. The tentacles curled and stretched in the air, and its arms hung low, claws dragging behind it. Its thoughts hit them just before the wave of air roaring ahead of it.

Hungry So Hungry Food Prey Hunt My Prey All My Food

Wind and coarse sand tore at them. Nate felt it slice tiny cuts in his arms and cheeks and fingers and eyelids. He wrapped his arms around Veek and she grabbed back, pressing her face into his chest.

Sand piled up in the wrinkles of his clothes, enough that he could feel the weight of it. It slipped into his shirt and shoes and pants. The wind was burying them.

MY FOOD MY WORLD MY HUNGER MY CATTLE MINE MY FOOD

One stroke of the massive wings carried the alpha squale past them into the pit. Nate felt it go. The cavemen howled in fear. The guard-things howled in joy. The sounds didn't go well together.

He risked opening his eyes. Roger was curled up in a ball with his arms crossed over his face. The wind had dumped two or three buckets worth of sand on him. Tim had his hands pressed over his eyes and mouth. His legs were buried, and one of his knees poked up through the sand.

Veek's arms loosened around him and she raised her head. Her nose was bleeding again, and her ears. They all glanced at each other. There were lines of dark mud on Roger's cheeks and lips. Clots of sand and blood clumped under Tim's ears. Nate wiped the sticky mud from his own face.

They scrambled up to the top of the ridge.

The great squale reached the army of slaves and overseers. It soared over them like a bird passing over a pond stocked with fish. Tentacles snatched a baker's dozen of figures and they vanished up into the twisting mass of its face. Even this far off, Nate was pretty sure two of them were guards. The squale wasn't that discriminating.

One of the smaller squales pulled its wings close, went into a power dive, and grabbed three cavemen with its tentacles. Its wings spread for a moment to level it off. Without losing speed it shot past Oskar's remains and through the tall archway. They glimpsed it racing along the covered walkway and then it vanished inside the dome.

Another small one soared down toward the tall arch. As it flew by, it reached down a rope of muscle and snagged what was left of Oskar, almost as an afterthought. It disappeared into the dome.

The huge alpha reared up in the air, like a whale breaching the surface of the water, and then soared back down. The air thrummed against its wings like a huge sail. Its tentacles flexed before it.

Nate fumbled with the binoculars. The guards threw their arms open like happy children. Most of the Neanderthals cowered in terror. A few fled. The tentacles lashed out and grabbed even more of them. It looked to Nate like dozens of people were swept up by the curling limbs.

He noticed the squale grabbed the runners first. He wondered if it was a dinosaur thing, that it could only see them when they moved.

"It likes it," Veek whispered. "It likes it when they try to run."

The great squale beat at the air and the slaves and guards were scattered by the downwash. They tumbled and fell. Nate didn't have the binoculars up, but it looked like some of them were buried beneath tidal waves of sand thrown up by the hurricane winds.

The creature flew upward, circling the tower as it went. It reached the top, and its wings beat three or four times. The alpha beast hovered above the tower for a moment, and the air roiled through the pit as it did.

Its gnarled limbs unfolded and the talons spread wide. There were five of them, three at the front and two to the back. Each finger was forty feet, Nate guessed, without the claw at the tip.

The squale reached down with a set of talons and grabbed one of the bars of the jewelry setting. Then the second set took hold. It pounded the sky one more time with its wings and then settled its bulk between the prongs. Its tail reached down and wrapped around the tower twice.

"Jesus," muttered Tim.

Its wings settled against its body for a moment, then stretched up and out. Their shadows put half the crater floor in darkness. The tentacles opened up like a great green flower. Two amber eyes, each one the size of a swimming pool, gazed down at the milling crowds below.

The creature's thoughts hammered into their minds.

MY SERVANTS MY MORTALS WORSHIP BEG PLEAD PRAY PREY PRAY PREY TO ME FOOD MY FOOD MY SERVANTS MY CATTLE

The figures below scurried and scuttled. Some threw themselves to their knees. Others leaned back and opened their arms to the thing on the tower. Howls and cheers and cries rose up to the four people on the ridge and to the great squale.

MY WORLD MY HUNGER FOOD PRAY PREY FOR ME MY SERVANTS NEW WORLD NEW FOOD NEW PREY MINE MINE MY NEW WORLD

More cheers rose up from the crowd. Roger closed his eyes. "Shit," he said. He closed his eyes. Trails of blood were washing the sand from his face. "Can't take much more of that."

"It knows," said Tim. His nose gushed blood and his skin paled. "The damned thing knows about the machine being turned off. It knows it can get through. This is the last big farewell meeting before they cross over."

"How?" said Roger. "How's it know?"

"Because it's what these things live for," said Veek. "It's a predator, remember. It wants to move on and start hunting again."

"Not to argue," said Tim, "but it wants more than that." He threw a tight gesture at the mob below. "These things don't just want to eat, they want us praying and cheering to them. They want to be worshipped."

They all looked down at the crowd. The Neanderthals and the three-armed creatures were hollering and waving. "They want our souls," said Veek.

MY CATTLE

Nate glanced up from the binoculars and found himself staring into the amber pools. They were focused on him and he felt the awful weight of a trillion years. On one level he knew they were miles away, that the monster was perched on its tower like some monstrous, tentacled vulture. But he also knew how close it was, that for this creature seeing a place and being there were one and the same.

It saw into his mind. He slipped and fell past the tentacles into the Great Squale's eyes, tumbling down into their endless depths. Nate felt dream-hunger smothering him, the vague sensation that there may have once been a time before this, a time when there was no hunger, but it was impossible to remember. The hunger was all there ever had been, all there was, and all there ever would be. It just went on and on and on and on and on and on and on and on and

"Nate!" Veek slapped him hard across the jaw.

He was back on the ridge with the three of them. The sand was darker and had a red tint to it. He blinked and made a point of not looking up. He could feel the weight of the Great Squale's gaze on him from miles away.

"You guys just froze up," she said.

Tim had his hand over Roger's eyes and was dragging him down the slope. A shiny stain spread down one of Roger's thighs. Tim glanced back up at Nate. "Are you okay?"

"I think so," he said. His own crotch felt cold and clammy. "I think I wet my pants."

"You did," nodded Veek. Her face was redder, too, as if she'd been breathing hard. Her shirt had turned pink.

The images—ideas—of hunger still lurked in his mind, like the red spot after staring at a bright light. He shook his head to clear them away. "How long was I... "

"Five minutes, I think," she said. She squeezed his arm. "Thought I lost you there, Shaggy."

He shook his head again. "I think we need to get away from here."

"No thinking needed," said Roger. "Let's go." He sounded like he had a hangover. Both of his eyes were bloodshot, with large red blobs floating in them like extra irises.

Nate blinked and understood why everything he could see had a red tint now.

"Agreed," said Tim. "We need to get the machine running again." He helped Roger up and the two of them took a few steps toward the bikes.

Veek and Nate turned to slide down the ridge when the hammer hit their minds.

MY CATTLE MY NEW PREY THERE MY SERVANTS THERE

"Shit," said Roger. A fresh stream of blood raced from his nose. "It just say what I think it did?"

Nate and Veek looked down into the pit. As one, the crowd of Neanderthals and monstrous overseers turned and looked straight at them. A roar came from the crowd. It could've been anger or joy or even a cheer. Maybe they were welcoming them to the neighborhood. Welcoming them to the Family. But Nate knew it was something else.

It was a hungry roar.

SEVENTY FIVE

Clive glanced at the sheets of paper arranged on the couch. There were half a dozen of them so far. Xela had sketched the controls life-sized so there could be no confusion. Each lever and switch and pushbutton had been reproduced. It looked like concept art for an H. G. Wells movie.

He looked at Mandy. She still stared at the far wall with her mouth pressed flat. He gave her a smile, but she didn't respond.

Xela had another piece of paper pressed against the panels, the pencil tucked behind her ear as she studied another cluster of switches with the flashlight. After a moment she stretched three of her fingers away from the mini-Mag. Debbie reached in and held the flashlight without moving it. They had a system going at this point. Xela slid her hand free, pulled the pencil from behind her ear, and began sketching quick lines.

Clive turned his attention from the women back to Andrew. He'd been a model prisoner while the others were gone. A few minutes after Xela had started drawing he'd gone back to his silent prayers.

Something about his silence made Clive think of fish. He wasn't a huge documentary fan, but he'd seen a few undersea shows on the Discovery Channel back before he and Debbie realized how much money they were wasting on cable for the one or two nights a week they watched television. There were plenty of eerie things in the sea, but the part that always gnawed at him was how quiet everything was. It was natural and unnatural at the same time. Sharks hunted without a sound—-no growling or gnashing teeth or sniffing for scents. Fish swam in silent packs. When there was an attack, the victim would thrash and fight, but never made a peep. It was a whole world where everyone was mute.

Andrew was quiet that way. It looked okay on the surface, but his silence ran deep. Natural but unnatural.

Clive shifted his grip on the shotgun. It was heavy enough to be reassuring, but not to the point that it tired him to hold it.

"I think that's it," said Xela. She tucked the pencil behind her ear again and crouched by her assembled sketches. Her hand gestured at the controls. "I've got those three banks of switches, the upper and lower rows of knobs, the levers on both sides..."

"What about the dials?" asked Debbie.

The corner of Xela's mouth twitched. It almost looked like a grin. "We know where all the needles are supposed to be," she said. "No point in drawing those."

"Maybe just for reference," Debbie said. "Not having things written down is what's caused all this."

"Point taken." Xela pulled the pencil out and looked up at the panels again.

Clive leaned over her shoulder. "What's the shading mean?"

"Those are the ones that don't need to move," she said. "That way we can color them in as we flip them and know which ones are done. We don't want to be flipping the same switches back and forth."

"Maybe you should make another set of pictures," said Debbie. "Just in case something goes wrong."

"Also not a bad idea," said Clive. Something moved in his peripheral vision. His attention snapped back to the prisoner.

Andrew's head was up and his eyes open. He smiled and it stretched across his face. Clive thought it made him look like the Joker. Not the ragged-mouthed Heath Ledger one, but the curling, plastic Jack Nicholson one.

"The Lord is coming," said Andrew. He said it the way most people talked about grocery lists or the Netflix queue. His head drifted side to side, like a charmed snake. "He's coming to smash this awful place to dust."

Nate pumped the pedals of his bike. He could see Tim leaning over his handlebars and Veek churning her feet in circles. Roger grunted behind them.

They were ten minutes and a good quarter-mile away from the ridge when the first shift hit them. The Kavach Building jumped out to the horizon, a distant speck. They kept cranking the pedals.

Nothing had come out of the pit yet. At least, nothing they could see. There was noise, though. A low rumble. It was the sound of hundreds of feet in motion. An avalanche of footsteps. A stampede.

The four of them urged their bikes to go faster.

Tim glanced over his shoulder and frowned. "Why isn't it chasing us?" He sounded annoyed by the idea.

Nate looked back, too. The distance shifted again for a moment as he did, doubling or tripling behind them. He could see figures coming over the ridge, but the air was still empty. He thought about the Great Squale feeding in the pit and choosing its targets.

"We're running," said Nate with a glance at Veek. He looked forward again. "It likes it when we try to run."

"They're out of the pit!" shouted Roger.

"I saw," he called back.

Veek threw a glance over her shoulder. Her glasses shifted and she had to grab at them. The bike wobbled and she dropped back a few feet. "What are they riding?"

Roger turned his head back to the ridge. "Looks like they're riding big bugs or something."

"Bugs?" Nate checked where the other three bikes were and took a long look over his shoulder. He saw dozens of scuttling figures in the distance with their cloaks whipping behind them. Maybe hundreds. His mind fought the image for a minute, insisting it had to be another trick of the light.

The overseers had dropped to all fours. Two legs and two arms splayed out and grabbed at the ground. They looked like insects skittering up a wall, or crabs scuttling across the ocean floor. They clawed and pulled themselves across the sand after the bicyclists.

Their torsos folded back at an angle that would doom a human to life in a wheelchair. They looked like stunted centaurs, joined to their mount halfway up the ribs instead of the hips. Two legs and two arms on the ground meant they had one free to hold a spear up over their lopsided shoulders, ready to be thrown like a javelin.

Their hoods had fallen back. Nate was too far to see details of their faces. He was sure it wouldn't be pretty.

The overseers moved as fast as the bicycles, at least.

Roger let go of the handlebars with one hand and fumbled with his holster.

"Don't bother," Tim called over to him. "It'd be a tough shot if we were standing still. You're never going to hit anything."

"Might scare 'em," said Roger.

Veek shook her head. "They see that thing every day of their lives and you think a pistol's going to scare them?"

"Just keep going," yelled Nate. "The only place we're going to be safe is back in Kavach."

"And stop looking back," said Tim. "It just slows us down."

They pedaled hard for another ten minutes. Nate was sweating. It wasn't warm, but they'd been pushing themselves for almost half an hour now. His eyes flicked to either side. Veek was dripping and he could tell she was fighting to keep her breath even. Roger was panting but keeping up the pace.

Reality flickered again and the Kavach Building jumped a mile closer. It was a few hundred yards away. They could see the slabs of concrete between the windows, the faux columns, and the lintel over the door.

Nate risked a glance back. The overseer-bugs had fallen behind. Or maybe it was just the shifting perspective. One of them flicked its third arm, something rippled in the air near the shift, and a dark line raced past Nate's temple. A heartbeat later he felt a breeze shift his hair and heard something slice the air. A clatter came from the concrete slab of the building. He turned his head and saw Roger's wide eyes.

"Oh, shit."

Another spear whizzed by them like a bullet. Its tip cracked on the concrete ahead of them. A third one hit the ground and buried itself halfway in the sand.

"Jesus," said Tim. "How fast are they throwing those things?"

It was another three hundred feet to the building. Then two hundred. Veek wheezed hard but waved for them to keep going. Roger pulled ahead and took the lead of the little pack.

Tim coughed hard, and out of the corner of his eye Nate saw the other man pull something out of his shirt. He glanced over and remembered Tim was wearing a tee shirt. There was no way to pull something out of it. Or to hide anything under it.

Tim stopped pedaling. He was holding something up to his chest with one hand. It looked like a shorter version of the javelin the guards were throwing. This one was a foot long, and it glistened in the dim light as if covered with wet paint.

Tim plowed into the sand.

Nate skidded to an awkward halt. Veek swerved around him, saw what he was looking at, and stumbled to a stop. "Oh, hell."

Nate leaped off his bike and ran to him.

Tim's face stretched and twisted. He coughed and blood flecks sprayed across the sand. His shirt was red and slick where the spear had pushed between his ribs and his sternum. Five feet of it hung out his back and kept him lying on his side.

"Come on," Nate said. He squeezed Tim's hand. "Come on, we can make it. It's right over there."

Tim looked up at them and shook his head. He waved them away. "Go." Something wet filled his throat and made him gargle his words. The blood around the spear hissed and sucked at the air.

Nate looked up. The overseers were close. He tried to guess where the shift was and if they'd passed it already.

Veek grabbed Tim's arm. He shook her off and tried to roll away. The spear shifted in his chest and he screamed. He grabbed Nate's shirt with his bloody hand. "Go!" he yelled. "Get everyone safe."

"Everyone means you, too, old man."

He slapped Nate, but the strength was gone from his hand. "Told you I'd kick your ass," Tim wheezed. His head lolled back to look at the overseers and he pawed at his holster with weak fingers. "Get home. I'll buy you some time."

And then he died.

SEVENTY SIX

In the movies, Nate knew, he would stay by Tim's body and wail. Veek would break down and cry with him. Maybe he'd throw his friend over his shoulder and lumber back to the building where they'd save him with a last minute miracle. Or they'd make a quick booby trap of his body with some explosives they'd find in Tim's pack. At the least, they'd close his eyes, like people always did.

In reality, a pair of spears hit the sand a few feet from them moments after Tim's last words. Veek threw herself backwards on the sand. Nate yelped and fell on his ass. A third spear landed between his leg and his hand. His hip throbbed and blossomed red where it'd grazed him.

They scrambled to their feet, left Tim's body and the bikes, and ran the last hundred feet to the Kavach Building.

Roger was already up on the slab. A spear quivered on the concrete next to him. He reached down, grabbed Veek's arm, and hauled her up onto the landing. She rolled to her feet and dashed up the steps. "What about Tim?" he yelled down at Nate.

Nate shook his head and heaved himself halfway up onto the slab. Roger grabbed his belt and dragged him the rest of the way. Another javelin hit the sand below his feet, and one more cracked against the concrete to his right. The thought flickered through Nate's mind that it wasn't wood, but a long piece of bone.

They followed Veek up the steps. She sucked on her inhaler as she held the security door open for them. They yanked it closed behind them. Nate twisted the lock and a spear clanged against the metal mesh.

Roger was already on the second door, the big wooden door that was old-fashioned wide and always open. He slammed it shut and looked for a deadbolt or knob to twist. "Shit," he said. "This door doesn't lock?"

"No one ever closes it," said Veek.

Roger looked through the glass panes. "We got maybe two minutes," he said. "They're almost to Tim." He kicked his foot up against the base of the door, bracing his heel against the hardwood floor. The echo of another spear rang against the outside.

"Get Clive," Nate told Veek. "We need a hammer and nails and some boards."

She ran up the curving staircase.

Nate's hip throbbed as he ran to the mailboxes and looked for something to barricade the door. There were some dusty phone books and the trash can where people dumped junk mail. He thought about prying one of the brass plaques off the wall.

"They're past Tim," said Roger. "First one's here and climbing up."

Clive galloped down the stairs with his bright yellow screw gun. His other arm pinned some short boards against his side. He dumped the boards, caught one as it fell, and jammed it next to Roger's foot just as something large smashed into the security door. Nate glanced over Roger's shoulder and saw two bulging eyes glaring back at him.

No, he thought, *three eyes*.

The DeWalt *whirrrred* twice and the board stood on its own. Clive fired two more screws into it and then stood up a second jack. The security door rang like a cymbal set.

"They look pissed," said Roger. He still had his foot against the door and showed no sign of moving it.

"Yeah," Nate said.

"Tim dead?"

Clive stopped. He looked up at Nate with his mouth open.

Nate closed his eyes. He grabbed for memories of drinking beers on the roof and saw a glistening spearhead sticking out between ribs. He tried to remember Tim cheerfully deflecting questions about his past and saw the twisted head and blank eyes looking across the sand. "Yeah," he said. "He's dead."

Roger looked at the things outside the window. Three of them pounded the steel mesh and snarled. More climbed up behind them. "You sure?" he asked.

Nate looked out at the creatures and realized what Roger was really asking. "Yeah," he said again. "It was quick. He didn't...I don't think he suffered much."

Clive made a sound they couldn't decipher and bent back to work. He ran a third board flat on the floor alongside the door and fired a handful of screws into it. "Best I can do for now," he said. He pointed at the door and swept his arm back down the hall. "We can wrestle one of the big legs from the loft down here and I can run it right from the center of the door to...shit."

The word sounded clumsy, like he was speaking a language he wasn't fluent in. Nate realized he'd never heard Clive swear before.

He followed Clive's gaze down the hall.

The back door was open.

Debbie scooped up the shotgun when Clive ran downstairs. She didn't like guns. Not at all. But she'd come to realize she liked Andrew even less. The bruise on her jaw kept that fresh in her mind.

Andrew still hadn't moved. She hoped it was because he was intimidated by the shotgun. She kept her finger on the guard, not the trigger, just like Clive had been doing.

Xela showed Veek her diagrams and highlighted the dust with the flashlight. "I would've done most of them already," she explained, "but I didn't know if there was a tipping point. Maybe we'd get halfway through and hit the one that makes the building switch back. I didn't want to leave without you guys."

"I appreciate that," said Veek. She looked at the elaborate sketches. "How long is this going to take? To flip them all?"

Xela shrugged. "Five or six minutes, maybe. There's over fifty of them."

Veek glanced at the broken windows. The sound outside grew louder. She imagined it was the noise a swarm of angry lobsters would make.

"He only spent two or three shutting it off," Debbie said. She tipped her head at Andrew.

"Yeah, but he didn't care what he was doing," said Xela. "We want to make sure we get it right. Everyone's inside now, right?"

"Everyone..." *Except Tim*, Veek was about to say. Part of her wanted to believe the not-a-publisher was going to appear in the doorway. If there was a book on not dying from impalement and other traumatic chest wounds, his imaginary small press probably put it out. "Everyone's inside," she said with a nod.

Xela reached out to flip the first switch.

A sharp snap echoed in the apartment, the sound of plastic cords breaking. It was just loud enough to hear over the sounds outside. Debbie lifted the muzzle of the shotgun. She moved her finger to the trigger but she went too far and couldn't find the little lever. She was sliding her finger back and forth beneath the guard, not inside it.

Andrew stood right in front of her, baring his teeth in a smile. He swept the barrel away just as her finger found the trigger. The noise was like thunder in the apartment and the smell stung their noses.

Xela flinched and Mandy started screaming again. Veek threw up her hands and felt a hard kick. She'd gotten in a nasty fight once and been punched in the gut. It felt like that, but hard enough that she felt it straight through to her back. She wasn't sure who'd hit her this time.

Andrew snatched the shotgun away from Debbie. He swung it like a club and hit her across the face. The swing became a throw that hurled the weapon across the room at the windows. It hit one of the broken mullions and spun out over the desert.

Mandy howled and launched herself at Andrew. Her frustration, confusion, and anger all boiled over and she clawed and punched and kicked at him. He retreated for a moment and then the back of his hand sent her tumbling across the room. Fresh blood sprayed from her nose and mouth.

As Andrew marched out the door, Veek dropped to her knees and fell over.

Clive thundered down the hall with Nate a few steps behind him. His bleeding hip was getting numb, and he wasn't sure if that was good or bad. For now, it was good.

They dashed through the lower fire door and down the short flight of steps to the landing. The back door swung outward. He needed to reach outside and kick away the broken cinderblock everyone used to prop it open. Just opposite the door he could see a row of feet—the bodies of the Family.

Nate stepped outside. He felt exposed out on the broken slab of concrete. The wide expanse of sand stretched out behind the building. The blood-colored sky loomed over him.

The back door was much newer than the front one. It was wrapped in metal with a wire-reinforced window at the center. A hinged arm with a piston at the top made sure it wanted to stay shut. The knob was a ball of brushed steel. It had, much to his satisfaction, a small dial at the center to activate the lock.

Nate kicked at the cinderblock, missed, and his hip flared. He felt the block's rough edges grate on the bottom of his sneaker. He kicked again, lower, and it shifted a few inches. The door moved as much and they both came to rest again. He pulled back his foot to kick again and heard a noise behind him. It was a horror-movie sound. Clive made a strangled noise and he knew he was right.

It was a body shifting on concrete.

He looked over his shoulder while his foot felt around for the cinderblock. The old woman—Andrew had called her "Auntie"—had rolled up on her side, her back to them. For a moment Nate thought she was admiring the view, stretched out alongside the ten foot drop like a bloated poolside beauty. Her misshapen head hung limp and grazed the concrete.

Nate's toes found the cinderblock. This time he braced the ball of his foot on it and gave a steady push. It scraped free of the door and the hydraulic arm took the weight. He tried to pull it, but it hissed at him. The same damned arm that made it close automatically also made sure it closed at a slow, steady rate.

The old woman flopped back down onto her back and her arm bounced on the ground. Her sundress and one side of her cardigan were twisted into a ball on her chest. There was a distant sound, like someone grunting through a mouthful of water.

Clive dragged him back into the building and the door shut itself. There was a loud click as the latch struck the plate. Their hands smacked together reaching for the lock and both pulled back. They tried again and both hesitated. Nate's hand lunged in and locked the door.

There was a blur of movement and a dry rasp from outside.

A pair of hands sat at the edge of the concrete slab. They had spidery fingers and skin like an eel. Nate and Clive heard a low hiss and a third hand reached up. The top of a head appeared. It was bald with patches of hair. There were small spots that might have been melanomas, but Nate thought they were scales catching the light.

The head bobbed up for a moment, slipped down again, and reappeared as a forearm was heaved up onto the slab. The creature grunted with effort. Nate saw a jaw like a bear trap, bristling with narrow, glassy teeth. A swollen, pale eye the size of a silver dollar dominated one side of its head. The other side had two small eyes, the eyes of a rat or a spider. None of them had lids. It was the face of a deep sea monstrosity that should never see the sun. Not a sun in the prime of its life, anyway.

The overseer's hand shifted and landed on Auntie's arm. The limb shifted and her body slid toward the edge. The creature flailed for a better grip and sank its hand into the old woman's stomach. Her body rolled onto its side again, and this time it rolled all the way over and off the edge. The spidery hands vanished and they heard the distant sound of impact and chittering.

"If she hadn't been there," murmured Clive, "they would've gotten up."

"You think this door's going to hold?"

Clive looked at it. "Not much else we can do," he said. "Metal door, brick walls, concrete floor." He tapped his foot on the landing, then glanced back at the rear stairwell's institutional banister. "We could tie it off. Just tie the knob to the banister to hold it shut. I've got some sash cord upstairs."

Nate nodded. "Let's get it. And that big board for the front—"

The blast of the shotgun echoed down the stairwell.

They looked down the hall at Roger. He'd heard it, too. He locked eyes with Nate. "Go!" he yelled. "Get the damned machine turned back on!"

SEVENTY SEVEN

Veek curled up in a ball on the floor. "Jesus," she wailed. "Oh, *fuck* that hurts."

Xela dropped to the floor and winced as her leg flared. "Fuck, fuck, fuck!" She tried to pry Veek's hands away from her stomach. "Let me see it."

Veek howled again. Mandy moaned and pulled herself back into her ball of knees and arms.

"What happened?" yelled Clive as he ran in from the hall.

"She got shot," said Debbie. Her lip was split and blood trailed down her chin. "Andrew got loose and he hit the gun and—"

Nate limped in and ran to her. "How bad is it?"

"I don't know," said Xela. "She won't let me see."

He fell to his knees and leaned forward. Veek grabbed his arm. Something crunched under him. He glanced at the floor between them.

A lumpy circle of fabric sat just under his kneecap. He swiped at it and felt the pellets inside shift. It was still warm to the touch.

Xela followed his eyes. "What is it?"

"It's a little—it's a beanbag," said Nate. "He really loaded it with beanbags."

"I got *shot*," yelled Veek.

"With a beanbag," said Nate. He hugged her hard and planted a kiss on her head. "You're going to be okay."

"Well it hurts like all *hell!*"

He kissed her again and looked at Xela. "The machine?"

She nodded. "I think we can do it."

The chattering and grunting outside the window grew louder. Clive ran back downstairs with his rope, Debbie right behind him.

"Help me up, you bastards," growled Veek.

"God, you're such a wuss," said Xela. She hugged the shorter woman and then gathered up her scattered papers.

"What do we need to do?" asked Nate. He offered an arm to each of them and they stood up together.

"Okay," said Xela. "If I've got this all right, there's fifty-three controls that need to move. Almost all of them are the small switches and pushbuttons except for—" she double-checked her sketches, "—this dial, that one, that lever there, and that long one there." She gestured at each control as she named it.

Nate looked at the diagram and nodded. He set his hand on the last lever she'd pointed at. "So this goes up, right?"

"Right."

"Wait," said Veek. She kept one arm wrapped around her gut. "What if sequence matters? What if we crash the system or something because it boots in the wrong order?"

Xela's shoulders slumped. "Oh shit," she said. She looked at the wall of controls.

Nate shook his head. "Then we're all dead," he said. "It's this or nothing."

They looked at each other for a moment. Veek took a breath, crossed her fingers, and smiled at Nate. "Jinkies."

Xela snorted a laugh. Nate grinned and kissed Veek hard on the mouth. He set his hand on the lever. It was a brass bar with a knob the size of a golf ball at the end. It fit well in his hand. The lever slid up and settled against a contact. A faint *clunk* shivered up through the bar and it tingled with static electricity.

Roger still had his foot against the door. So far the security door outside had held against the monsters. He knew if they made it through, having his foot there wasn't going to make too much difference. But focusing on his foot kept him from putting the pistol to the window and emptying into the crowd of monsters.

He could smell his piss-soaked jeans and his own blood. Roger glanced toward the back door. Clive and Debbie were tying it off to the banister. From the front door, Roger saw the bruise puffing up one side of her face. He could see shadows moving, but the noise at his door drowned out whatever sounds the creatures made out back.

One of the overseers on the front stoop glared in at him between strikes to the door. The black mesh between them blurred its appearance, but he could see enough to know he didn't want a better look. As it was, there was no mistaking the rage in the thing's eyes. It wanted him dead. It wanted him and his friends dead in the most brutal way possible.

The creature gnashed its jaws, stepped back, and stabbed at the security door again with its spear. The overseers on either side added theirs and the weapons banged against the barrier.

One of the spears jammed deep into the security door. The mesh broke around it and made a rent an inch and a half long. The overseer at the other end of the spear twisted and levered its weapon and the rent tripled in size.

Without a pause or a word—at least, not a word he could understand—the growling horde switched from battering the door to prying at it. Spears jammed into the mesh and the creatures heaved side to side or up and down or twisted their spears in wide circles. There was a sound like popcorn cooking and Roger saw a handful of rivets shoot away into the mob. The mesh peeled away from the security door's frame.

"Guys!" he bellowed. *"They're getting in!"*

Xela held up the drawings one at a time while Nate and Veek reset controls. He checked the diagram again, counted along a row, and pushed up another switch. Xela marked it off with a scribble while he moved to the next one.

Veek had her hand on a knob. She peered at the sketch. "What does that say? Set it to...two-eighteen?"

"Two-sixteen," said Xela. "That's a six."

Roger's shout echoed up to them. Nate glanced at the open door of the apartment and then at the window. "How much more is there to go?"

"One more," said Xela. "There's only a couple things on the last page."

"Almost there!" Nate shouted at the doorway.

He flipped another switch and looked for the next one. Veek hit two side-by-side pushbuttons. Nate ran his hand down a line of switches and set his fingertip against one. He double-checked the picture and pushed the switch up with a solid *click*. "I think that's it for this sheet."

They compared the diagram to the control panel and all nodded in agreement. Xela let the sketch drop and held up the last one. Seven controls to adjust on the seventh page. "What if they come with us?" she asked. "What if we're bringing a hundred of these things back to Los Angeles with us?"

"They won't have a chance," said Veek. She shuffled over to the next section of the control panels. "They'll either get movie deals or beg for us to bring them back."

"Remember the cockroaches?" said Nate. He counted through a grid of buttons. "Debbie tried to take them away from the building and they died. If they come with us, I bet it'll be the same thing. Too much of our world kills them. They're not as strong as the squales. They have to stay near whatever little rifts are around the building."

Breaking glass and a pair of gunshots echoed up from downstairs. When the noise faded they heard another sound. It was a rural sound, but they all recognized it.

Wood was being chopped. Or hacked.

"Awesome," said Xela. "So they'll be trapped in the building with us."

A switch snapped into place. A button clicked. Another switch. A dial ticked off degrees as Veek turned it a third of the way around.

There was one lever left. It had a grip of crumbling rubber like an old bicycle handle. Nate set his hand on it and felt how stiff it was. He wrapped both hands around the black rubber. "We got everything, right?"

Veek took another look at the diagram. "Think so."

"Okay, then," he said. "Here we go." He pushed the lever up and felt it click into position.

Something shuddered inside the walls. They heard a faint hum of power. A few short sparks and an arc of electricity danced across the machinery.

And then faded.

The needles didn't move.

"Shit," said Xela.

Veek grabbed the sketches from the floor. "What did we miss? We must have missed something?"

"We didn't. I checked it all off as we went."

Nate looked around the apartment. It was still a shambles from the Great Squale's passing. Debbie had tried to straighten out some of it, but it was still a mess. The loft and its staircase were wrecked. Two of the kitchen chairs were smashed into kindling. The table—

"Oh, no," he said.

Veek followed his gaze. "What?"

Nate ran to the far wall across from the window, his hip throbbing with each step. The kitchen table still leaned up on its side. He grabbed the top edge and pulled. The table leaned forward and dropped back down onto its legs.

The bank of glass tubes was behind it. Ten high, six across. Nate's eyes skimmed over the rows. Most of them sparked and glowed with electrical current.

Five of them were broken.

SEVENTY EIGHT

"That's it, then," said Xela. She hobbled over to stare at the broken machinery. "Game over."

"No," said Nate. "There's got to be a way we can fix this or rig it for—"

"Storeroom!" shouted Veek.

Nate was a beat behind her. Xela was two. "Has to be," he said. "There have to be replacements."

Veek studied the bank of tubes. Her eyes went back and forth over them for a moment and then she nodded. "It's just like a fuse box. All the ones in this section are the same, all the ones down here—" her hand swiped at the bottom rows, "—are different. So we need five like this."

She pulled her shirt up and stretched it over her hand. Nate caught a glimpse of a huge bruise spreading across her stomach. She grabbed one of the tubes between her covered fingers. The tube shifted, wiggled, and popped out. It had brass caps on both ends. One of them had a trio of prongs like a grounded plug.

"Is it hot?" asked Xela.

Veek shook her head. "Tip from a hardware friend. Oil and sweat from your skin messes up glass components. Grab me a rag or something."

Nate found a banner of unrolled paper towels and tore off three of them. He met Veek at the door. "Let's go."

She wrapped the tube as they dashed down the hall to the back stairwell.

❖

Roger decided he could take his foot away from the door. The security door was gone and the overseer-things were gouging the door apart with their spears. A bone spear stabbed through the broken window and flailed in his direction.

He took a breath and fired another two shots. One of the overseers shrieked and leaped away from the window. Roger bit down and resisted the urge to keep pulling the trigger.

Clive and Debbie joined him in the lobby. They didn't have any weapons, but it was better than facing the monsters alone.

Roger raised the pistol again. He wasn't sure how many bullets it had left. Then he forced himself to take another breath.

There were less of them out there. He tried to focus harder, to make sure he wasn't imagining it, but it was true. Half of the overseers were gone. He could see the railing for the outside steps and one of the small trees from the front lawn.

While he watched, a few of the ones who were left stepped back away from the door. He straightened up and saw two of them down at the base of the stairs. They leaped off the cracked slab and back onto the sand.

He shot a glance to Clive. "Think I scared 'em off?"

The overseers had smashed the window of the back door, but it was too small for them to get though. Their pounding shook the door but it seemed to be holding. Bulging eyes focused on Nate and Veek, and there were more grunts and snarls. A spear reached through the door and jabbed at the air in front of them. A pair of arms—a pair of *right* arms—reached through the window and flailed in their direction.

"Come on," said Nate. He took a few more steps down the staircase, staying against the wall. Clive's rope stretched wire-tight across the landing. Going under forced them into a defenseless position. Over put them in an awkward, exposed position.

"I vote for under," said Veek, reading his mind.

"Good," he said.

He crouched low and duck-walked under the rope. Something swiped across his back in mid-waddle and he threw himself onto his knees, then over onto his ass. His hip burned, his fists came up, and he realized he'd grazed the rope.

Veek spent a moment figuring out what to do with the paper-wrapped tube, then shoved it down her shirt. She crawled on her hands and knees.

Halfway there one of the overseers crammed its head through the window and looked down. It howled and a wiry arm shot through and flailed for her. The claw-like nails passed through her hair and swung down to grab again. Nate reached out, hooked his hands in her armpits, and dragged her away. They slid-shuffle-crawled until they were off the landing. The overseers outside withdrew, as if they knew it was a waste of effort to go after the two humans now.

"You okay?"

"Just peachy," she said. Her arm wrapped around her gut again. She reached into her shirt and pulled out the tube. "Still in one piece."

They pushed themselves to their feet and skittered down the last few steps to the storeroom. The padlock hung on its hasp. The doorknob was locked.

Nate frisked himself, and hit something big near his throbbing hip. He glanced down and his eyes fell on the pistol Tim had given him. It was still clipped to Nate's waist.

"Stand back," Veek said.

She was one step ahead of him. She aimed her own pistol at the padlock, clutching it with both hands in a clumsy grip. Her first shot went off to the side and punched a hole in the door. It was deafening in the basement's concrete hallway. The second shot was high.

"Careful," he yelled. "You're shooting into a room full of fuses and light bulbs, remember?"

She squeezed the trigger again.

The padlock twisted. Her next shot shredded it apart.

Nate reached in and knocked the remains off the hasp. Veek lowered her aim and fired. There was a spark and the wood erupted next to the doorknob. She fired three more shots and the door around the knob turned into splinters. She glanced over at Nate and he nodded. He leaned back and kicked. The storeroom door twisted apart and swung open.

"Guys," Debbie called down the stairwell. "They're all leaving. The crab-bug-people are all going away."

They glanced at each other. "Why?" yelled Nate.

"We don't know."

"That can't be good," Veek muttered.

"Agreed," Nate said. "Let's find the fuses and get out of here."

She shoved the pistol back into its holster and led them into the storeroom.

They each pulled a box down and yanked it open. Nate had plastic pipe fittings. Veek's was a dusty collection of old videotapes. They both shoved them aside, glanced at labels, and grabbed again. This time Nate had a case of spiral light bulbs, still in packaging that declared them energy-efficient. Veek shoved her carton aside and reached for the next one. Nate dropped to one knee and slid a box from one of the bottom shelves.

A minute later Veek cried, "Here!"

Nate had seen the box she was looking in and ignored it because it was new. The cardboard was flat and smooth. The corners weren't blunted and the tape was still clear. Veek hadn't been so dismissive.

The inside of the box was divided into twenty tall slots. Each one held a package wrapped in a thin sheet of foam. Veek slid one out, broke the paper seal around it, and unrolled the bundle.

It was one of the glass tubes. She held out the one she'd pulled from the machine. Unlike hers, this one was clear and spotless. The brass gleamed and the filaments and tiny circuits inside shined like new.

Too new, thought Nate for a moment. But only a moment. He saw something coming at him from the door. A foot wearing a faux-leather shoe lashed out and smashed into the box of tubes. It skidded across the floor and Veek scrambled after it.

Andrew took another step and slammed an awkward punch down at Nate. He got his head out of the way but the fist cracked against his shoulder and a wave of pain washed down his arm. Another punch caught him in the elbow and he felt something crack.

"You filthy, degenerate heathens," spat Andrew. His eyes were wide and angry. His voice was thick and wet, as if he was drowning in his own rage. "How dare you interfere with my Lord's plan? How dare you ruin *my wonderful day?*"

His foot came back and he drove a kick into Nate's stomach. Nate *woofed* out some air but managed to grab hold of the leg. Andrew lunged back and dragged him across the floor. He shifted his weight and his free foot swung in and caught Nate in the hip. He roared and the adrenaline let him wrestle Andrew down to the floor.

Nate threw himself on top of the other man and landed a couple of punches, but Andrew didn't even notice them. He brought his hand around and slapped Nate hard in the side of the head again and again. Nate slammed his head down. His forehead cracked against Andrew's nose and drove the man's skull back to *clunk* against the concrete floor.

Andrew's eyes glazed over for a moment, blood gushed from his nostrils, and Nate pushed himself away.

Nate reached down for the bucket of tools near the door, grabbed a solid looking handle, and swung his arm around. Andrew was already up and lunging forward. The hammer caught the edge of his hand, just under the little finger, and Nate saw the palm crumple.

Andrew howled and brought his other arm around. It wasn't a punch, just a wild, angry flail, but the blow hit Nate like a baseball bat. He staggered back and the room spun. *One too many in the head*, he thought. His legs felt weak and then the floor slammed up against his knees.

"You will not pollute my Lord's divine form with your filth," growled Andrew. His face was a mask of blood below his crooked nose and one of his wide eyes was puffy. "You will not ruin this glorious day with your heresies."

There was a blast of noise and Andrew twisted back. He straightened up and Nate saw the dark spot below his shoulder. While he watched, it spread and soaked out through the sweater vest. The stain caught the light and showed the same red as his face.

Veek clutched her blocky pistol in both hands. A tiny wisp of smoke slipped out of the barrel, thinned, and vanished. The smell of powder wafted around her.

Andrew snarled at her. For a moment his twisted face looked more like one of the overseers than a man. He took another step toward Nate. She fired again. The sweater vest unraveled across the top of his other shoulder and they heard the sharp chime of the bullet ricocheting off the concrete walls. He stopped.

"I'm sorry," said Veck. Her eyes were wide. "I didn't want to."

He glared at her, then at Nate. He reached up and swept his hair back into its helmet-like perfection. Then he turned and staggered to the door. He glared back at her.

"I would've made it quick for both of you," Andrew said. "Now you can die in the rubble of this place."

He vanished into the basement hallway. His shoes scraped on the concrete stairs for a moment and the sound faded away.

"The tubes," said Nate. He tried to shake the dizziness out of his head and realized that was not the way to go. "Are they okay?"

"Yeah, they're packed really well," she said. "He only broke three of them. I didn't want to shoot him. I really didn't."

"I know," he said. "It's okay."

She helped him to his feet and tucked the box under her arm. There was no sign of Andrew in the hallway. They went up the stairs cautiously. Clive's rope lay on the landing in a tangle. The back door was open, but pulling itself closed.

Veek shook her head. "He went out?"

Nate shrugged. "Maybe this is his idea of heaven. If he wants to stay, let him."

"Guys!" This time it was Roger yelling down the stairwell. They looked between the railings and saw him up above. "Move it! *The Squale's coming!*"

SEVENTY NINE

When they reached the second floor they could look straight down the hall to the front window. They couldn't see the Great Squale itself, but they saw the landscape going dark in the distance. They ran to the control room.

The others had cleaned out the remains of the broken tubes. Veek set the box down on the floor in front of the array. She pulled the new tubes from their slots one by one and handed them out. "Try not to touch the glass," she told everyone. "Use the packing like a wrapper and take it off once they're in place."

Clive spun his two different ways until he figured out how to slot it between the other tubes. Roger got his in position but couldn't get it to lock. Xela's snapped into place and sparked on the ends. She peeled off the foam wrapping and the tube was filled with a soft glow. "Get the prongs in first," she said, "then twist the flat end into the bracket."

Roger's tube sparked and he beamed at her. Clive got his and then stepped aside so Debbie could put one in under it. Veek handed the last one to Xela. The tube snapped into place and a few threads of electricity raced out across the array.

They felt the hum begin in the floor. Sparks flashed behind some of the other controls. Clive and Debbie held each other. Roger hugged Xela. Nate and Veek squeezed their hands together.

Nothing happened.

"No," said Debbie. "No, no, no, no."

The machine remained quiet.

Veek shook her head. "We missed something. We must've missed something."

Nate looked around. "Where are the sketches? The diagrams."

"They're on the couch," said Xela. She broke free of Roger and limped for them. Debbie tailed her. Mandy flinched away from them. They each picked up a handful of pictures and then staggered under the weight of the Great Squale's thoughts.

My People My Prey My Food My Way The Way The Open Way

Veek wiped her eyes. The hand came away streaked with red. "Maybe it's the order," she said. "Maybe we needed to do it in a certain order."

Nate grabbed one of the diagrams. He wasn't sure which one, and something in his mind—something buried under the growing presence of the Great Squale—told him it didn't matter. "Explain it again," he said. "How'd you figure out which ones to reset?"

"The dust," Xela said. She gestured at the diagrams with her free hand and tried to ignore the drops of blood falling from her nose. "All the buttons and switches Andrew and his people touched had the dust wiped off them. With the buttons the dusty ones went in and the ones that popped out had been in the wall, so they were clean. And the dials all had dust on the top, so we turned them back so it was all on top again."

THE OPEN WAY MY WAY TO PREY MY PREY MY CATTLE

Nate looked at the wall of controls. They'd forgotten something and it had been on the edge of his mind before the Great Squale hammered it back down.

It got dark outside. The beast was close. It would destroy the building this time. They could all sense that under the dark imagery of its thoughts. Debbie wrapped her arms around Clive and they closed their eyes. Mandy sobbed behind her arms.

Nate looked at the gaping holes in the wall that had been windows back when the control room had just been Clive and Debbie's apartment. The same windows he'd first seen the Great Squale from. And he knew it was the same one. None of the others were big enough to make themselves known like that, to press up against another world the way it had that first time.

The first time they—

Nate looked at the control panels. At all the shiny levers and knobs and switches they'd adjusted and readjusted and—

"Roger!" he shouted. "Which switch did you touch?"

He blinked and tears of blood ran from his eyes. "I didn't touch any—"

"Two weeks ago when you hit one of the switches," said Nate. He had to raise his voice over the noise of the Squale's wings and the wind that came with them. "When we caused the earthquake. *You wiped the dust off it then.*"

Veek stared at the controls. Xela's mouth dropped open.

"Your switch was already clean!" Nate yelled. "We turned it *back off!*"

DESTROY SMASH OPEN THE WAY THE WAY TO PREY MY CATTLE MY PREY

"Which one was it?" Clive shouted at Roger.

Roger stared at the wall of controls. He looked down at the floor, then around for furniture that had been tossed away from its usual place. "I don't know."

"Think!" shouted Nate. The wind was picking up. "You can do it!"

"Just look at the controls," said Debbie. "Where were you standing compared to the controls?"

Sand whipped in through the window and stung their skin. The diagram flapped in Nate's hand and he let it slip from his fingers. It flew into the air, made a quick circle around the room, and plastered itself on a panel above the bank of glass tubes.

"I don't know!" shouted Roger.

"How high was your arm?" yelled Xela. "Try to remember."

The walls trembled. Outside was black as night. They could hear the overseers chanting under the wind's roar.

"Come on, you ignorant jackass!" shouted Veek. "Use your brain for once in your life."

Roger glared at her and then he looked at the controls. A trail of blood raced out of his nose and across his lip. He grinned. "Fuck you, bitch!" he yelled back at her.

He stabbed out and flicked his switch down.

The Kavach Building roared to life.

A buzz of power filled the air as the machinery engaged. Electricity raced around the panels. The hum in the floorboards cancelled out the shaking walls.

On the control panel, the needles rose to attention. They centered on zero.

Xela threw her arms around Roger and kissed him savagely on the mouth.

For a moment it was bright outside, as if unseen lightning had lit up the sky. A new tremor ran through the Kavach Building. There was a sensation of lifting—of casting off, as if an enormous mass had been tossed aside—and a wave of nausea and shifting gravity knocked the residents to the ground.

NO MY PREY MINE MINE MY PREY MY NEW WORLD NO NO NO

The thoughts of the Great Squale faded as if it were falling away. Energy clotted the air around them. A ripple ran through the walls, the aftershock of a quake that never happened.

The Kavach Building took them home.

Andrew stood with the overseers. His voice joined theirs in song. The Lord of All Things filled the sky above them. It *was* the sky, and it filled their minds as surely as air filled their lungs. The winds flaying their skins were a sign of its greatness.

The Kavach Building flickered before them. A ripple of brilliant color raced around the building like a New Year's Eve light show, and it was gone. The dead air shook with its sudden absence.

The Lord of All Things roared its anger. The heretical machine, the machine that kept nature from taking its course, had vanished. The way was sealed.

The faithful had failed.

Andrew felt a wave of nervousness wash over him as his god's wrath became known. Still, he knew he was favored. He was blessed for all he had done, and the proof was that he stood in the presence of the Great One itself.

He closed his good eye and angled his face to the sky. He raised his arms and smiled as he felt his god's love wrap around him and lift him up.

It was the most wonderful day ever.

ADDITION

EIGHTY

"Did we make it?"

Nate heard Debbie's question, but didn't know how to answer it. His arms were wrapped around Veek and hers around him. He could smell her hair and the masculine shampoo she used because it was cheaper.

He opened his eyes and they were sticky with blood. Veek shifted in his arms and he got one of his hands up to wipe his eyelids as best he could.

Xela yelped. "We're not dead," she announced. "My leg still hurts like all hell."

"You and me both," muttered Veek, putting her hand on her stomach.

Nate sat up. The seven of them were sprawled on the floor of Clive and Debbie's apartment. Blood streaked their faces. Around them, the brainchild of Aleksander Koturovic and Nikola Tesla hummed as it had for over a century.

"Dark out," said Roger.

"No," said Debbie. She was smiling. "There's a building in the way."

They got up and staggered to the shattered window like a pack of grinning drunks. A wall of rust-colored bricks faced them, even darker in the twilight hours. They looked up and saw a little girl staring back at them. She waved at the strange looking grown-ups and they all waved back.

"Hang on," said Veek. Her phone was powering up, and Nate saw a spinning icon as it tried to sync itself with the network it had been separated from. She let out a little laugh. "It's Tuesday night," she said. "We've been gone for four days."

"Fuck," said Roger. "So gonna get fired."

They hugged each other and laughed. And after a few minutes, some of the laughter became tears.

Roger got fired, but found a new job by the end of the week. Veek had been fired, too, but didn't care. By a stroke of luck, Clive didn't have any work scheduled for the days they'd been somewhere else. Debbie and Xela both had classes to catch up on.

There was no other sign anyone had noticed their absence. No news crews. No police activity. No concerned notes. Somehow the Kavach Building had kept its presence in the real world even as it carried them somewhere else. The other tenants who hadn't crossed over were more concerned with the sudden wave of vandalism—half the windows broken, the front door wrecked, and the steps cracked in three places.

The bodies vanished from the slab of concrete in the back. Aside from the blood in the hallway, there was no sign of them. Once Nate and Veek mopped the halls, even that was gone.

They found sheets of plywood out back by the now-restored fence. Clive put them over the broken windows.

Debbie went to Health Services on her campus and learned Andrew had cracked two of her teeth. She couldn't afford crowns so they were both pulled. The gap was far enough down her jawline it didn't show, but she talked with a lisp for a few days.

Xela also went to Health Services and said she'd been injured while moving an oversized picture frame. The doctor told her she was lucky the glass had missed arteries, berated her for taking so long to get it checked, and explained it was too late for stitches. She was going to end up with a scar. Her leg was wrapped and taped. He said to keep it clean and gave her a pair of aluminum crutches along with a bottle of Vicodin.

Nate's hip got better and the bloodshot eyes he and Roger shared healed up in a week. For most of that time Veek had a grapefruit-sized bruise just under her ribs and winced whenever she laughed or breathed too hard.

Mandy was past her shock and well into denial. She'd sat silently in Debbie and Clive's apartment for almost a day after they got back. Then she got up and walked back to her apartment. Two days later Nate saw her on the stairs and she acted confused when he asked how she was doing. "I fell down and hit my head," she told him. "That's all. Nothing else happened."

He decided not to push it.

They went up one night to watch the sunset, but the roof was a different place without the wooden deck. It didn't feel the same for a number of reasons. One of the big ones being the lack of a retired publisher-who-wasn't-a-publisher.

Nate and Veek stayed together every night. They worked in his room and slept in hers. Her room was once again at a constant sixty-nine degrees. Sometimes, late at night, they talked about the machinery in the walls and the things on the other side.

One night they talked about Andrew and the Family of the Red Death.

Two weeks passed. And when they couldn't avoid the issue any longer, they all met in the lounge.

"Rent's due the day after tomorrow," said Nate. "Someone's going to notice Oskar's missing, if they haven't already."

"What if we all just put our checks under his door?" offered Xela.

"Don't think that'll cut it," said Roger. "Anyone's gonna know something's up."

Nate nodded. "I'm just thinking..." He paused and wondered if there was a better way to phrase his suggestion. Veek knew what was coming and squeezed his hand. "I'm thinking maybe no one wants to be here this weekend."

Debbie raised an eyebrow. "Why?"

"Because I think there are going to be a lot of questions," said Nate, "and I don't think we're going to be able to answer them."

"You think we should all move?" asked Clive.

"I just think you should all be somewhere else," Nate said. "Go stay with friends out of town for a night or two."

Roger shook his head. "Just come looking for us, won't they?"

"Yeah," said Xela. "I mean, this is all super-secret government stuff, right?"

"They won't," said Nate. "Because they're going to find me."

"No," said Clive.

Debbie shook her head. "Nope," she said.

"It'll be okay," said Nate.

"Why you, bro?"

"Because I'm the guy in charge," Nate said. "Remember?"

"Captain goes down with his ship," snorted Clive. "That's messed up."

Nate shrugged. "I owe it to Tim," he said. "And Oskar and Mrs. Knight. They're all dead because...because of what we started. They deserve a little bit of...I don't know. Justice? Peace?" He shrugged again. "You can stay if you want. But you don't have to, and I won't blame you if you don't."

Veek squeezed his hand. Xela reached out and grabbed the other one. The surviving tenants of the Kavach Building's trip to the other side took each other's hands and said nothing for a few minutes.

"You know what I want?" said Nate, breaking the spell. "I want to be around people. Lots of people."

"Yes," said Debbie. "Somewhere that smells good."

"Thai food," said Roger. He patted his backside and his hand came back with a wallet. "On me."

"I want to change my shirt real quick," said Xela.

"It's just the Thai place," said Clive.

"I've got paint on me," said the blue-haired woman. "And I stink."

"I should change, too," said Debbie.

"Yeah," said Nate. "I could grab a different shirt."

"Fine," said Roger. "Five minutes, in the lobby. If you're all not there, I'm going without you and eating eggrolls alone."

"You'll wait," said Xela. She kissed his cheek.

"Not for eggrolls," said Roger.

Nate squeezed Veek's hand and climbed up the back staircase. He looked at his door, 28, then turned to look at Mandy's. He turned his head down the hall to 26. He half-expected to see Tim there, giving him a casual wave. His eyes drifted down, staring through the floor to impossible apartment 14. He opened the door and tried to remember if his favorite striped shirt—his deep space shirt—was clean. Then he froze.

There was a man in a dark suit waiting inside his apartment.

EIGHTY ONE

The man was standing next to the entertainment center. Nate realized he was examining the DVD collection. His hand was out and he was inching a case out as a place marker.

He had black hair, cut conservative-short, with a bit of gray streaked through it, but not enough to look old. His nose was a little large, his eyes a little small, but neither enough to stand out. He was the same height as Nate, just under six feet tall, and had a body that showed enough time in the gym to keep off the pounds. The kind of guy who would blend effortlessly into any crowd if not for his sharp suit.

"Hello, Nate," said the man. "I figured it was time we had a talk. Rent's almost due, after all."

"Who are you?"

The man gestured at the entertainment center. "You're old enough to remember before DVDs, right? Back when you'd visit someone and learn about them by what was on their bookshelves. Don't get me wrong, I love my movies, but it's harder to get a good grasp of somebody with them. Movie tastes always seem a bit random." His mouth formed a tight, professional smile. "You've got seventeen of the same ones I do."

"I asked who you are," Nate said. He tried to sound confident.

"We're on the same side," said the man. "That's probably the most important thing right now, isn't it? After all you've gone through, I bet you're not too keen on trusting strangers right now, are you?"

"Not particularly."

"If it helps, the FBI has arrested all the top members of the Family, and most of the congregation's been detained for questioning. The ones that aren't being locked up forever are heading for years of federally-funded therapy."

"Really?"

The man nodded.

"So who are you?"

He put up a hand and shook his head. "Let's not complicate things with names. Speaking of which, is it okay if I call you Nate? Overt familiarity's a curse of the job. Would you be more comfortable with Nathan? Mr. Tucker, maybe?"

"Nate's fine."

"Great." He took a long look at Nate. "You know, I've got to be honest. Part of me has been dreading this."

"Dreading what?"

"You," said the man. "I've been dreading the day I had to meet you. I've been waiting years for it, but now that it's here..." He shook his head and then gave a shrug.

"You've been waiting...for me?"

"Well, not you specifically. If you'll pardon the melodrama, I knew this day was going to come, and I knew I'd be having this conversation with someone. I'm glad it's you, Nate."

A moment stretched out between them.

"You're Locke Management," said Nate. "You're who puts out the ads and hires the actresses and all that."

"Guilty as charged."

"You decide who lives here."

He gave another calm nod.

"So, you're...what? Some government agency that protects the building?"

The man in the suit shook his head. "I never said I was with the government."

"You're not?"

"For the record, I haven't said that, either. Really, I could just be another actor hired to play a role." His mouth formed a pleasant smile that felt sincere, but also a bit too practiced for Nate's liking. "Besides, it's not like the building needs much protecting, is it? Not with folks like you living here."

"People *died* here," snapped Nate. A wave of frustration washed over him. "Fuck, people have been dying here since this place was built. *Because* of this place."

"Yes," said the man, "they have. A lot more than you probably know about."

"Why haven't you studied it? If you had some kind of...back-up building or something, or if people *knew* about it, none of this ever would've happened."

"We've tried to study it," said the man, "and we've managed to copy some elements. That's why you've got a room full of replacement parts downstairs. There are light bulbs, too, if you want to swap out the ones in the tunnels."

"But that's nothing," said Nate. "It's minor stuff. That's like trying to copy an airplane and coming away with how to make tires."

The man put up his hands. "It's the best we can do. You can't examine an airplane in mid-flight, especially the engine."

"The right people could."

"They probably could," the man agreed. "There are some electronic and mechanical geniuses out there. The problem is recruiting them. I'm sure you'll agree, we have good reason to keep this building as secret as possible."

Nate bit his lip and looked over at the wall where Aleksander Koturovic had spent some of the last minutes of his life making sure the world stayed safe.

"I know it doesn't mean much," the man said, "but I'm sorry for your losses. I understand you and Tim Farr had become friends."

"We were. What's going to happen to him? Officially?"

"There'll be a funeral. Closed casket, full military honors. You can attend, if you like. He doesn't have any next of kin."

"I'll take care of his stuff."

"It's already taken care of," said the man. He hooked his thumbs on his pockets. "Nate, let's stop beating around the bush. You're not in handcuffs. We're talking alone, like civilized gentlemen. You know what this meeting's about."

Nate found Veek waiting for him in the lobby. "Hey," she said. "I was just about to come looking for you."

"Sorry."

"Roger was serious. They all headed over a couple of minutes ago. Debbie said they'd save us some egg rolls. I told her to order chicken pad thai for us if we missed the waiter."

He nodded. "Good."

She tilted her head at him. "You okay, Shaggy?"

Nate reached out and took her hand. "I just got a job."

Veek blinked. "Just now?"

"Yeah."

"Did someone call you or something?"

He shook his head.

The man in the suit came down the staircase, speaking quietly into a cell phone. He paused to nod at Nate, and before she knew he was doing it he shook Veek's hand. "Miss Vishwanath," he said. "Pleasure to meet you in person. For the record, my money was on you from the start, but I'm glad we'll still have you on the team."

He was out the door before she could respond. "What was that all about?" she asked Nate.

"I'm the new building manager."

Her jaw dropped. "What?"

He led her back up the curving stairs. "The only catch is they want me to be more active than Oskar was. They're hoping I can learn more about the building and maybe fill in some of the holes in their records."

"They have records?" asked Veek.

"Yup. They're giving me copies of all of their files so my staff and I can be up to date."

"Your staff?"

He squeezed her hand and guided her down the hall to apartment 12. There was a gleaming brass sign next to the door. It fit the Kavach Building's classic style.

NATHAN TUCKER MANAGER

She smiled. "So I'm on your staff, is that what you're saying?"

"If you want to be."

"Are there rules about office relationships?"

"We could make some up. And then break them."

"Cool." She kissed him. "I think I could be up for this. How many files are we talking about?"

"Well," he said, "let's check it out."

He turned the knob and opened the door of his new apartment.

AFTERWORD

It would be easy to say that ***14*** has been kicking around in my brain for about four or five years.

The truth is, though, that this story started many years back when I was a little kid watching the most terrifying television show at the time—*Land of the Lost.* I wasn't just scared because this show was obviously a documentary shot with live dinosaurs. I was unnerved by the fact that no one else seemed to know about it. They'd teach us about dinosaurs in elementary school, but why was there no mention of lost cities or pylons? Why was no one teaching us about Sleestaks? Were they covering it up for some reason or did they honestly *not know*? How could there be this whole section of history so many adults seemed willfully ignorant of?

That thought has stuck with me for ages—that there's more to the world than we'll ever know or understand—and I've tried to work little threads of it into several short stories and books. The specific ideas that eventually became ***14*** were kicking around in my mind for about five years, but the truth is I've wanted to tell a story like this since eight-year-old me first realized that Enik wasn't the descendant of the feral Sleestaks in the Land of the Lost... he was their ancestor.

How's that for a geek reference?

Naturally, for a story that long in the making, it took more than a few people to help me pull it out and shape it. As such, some thanks and recognition are in order.

First, many thanks to Jacob Kier at Permuted Press, who let me take some time away from zombies and superheroes to tell a very different kind of apocalyptic story. After the last time I tried it, he had every right to say no.

Thom Brannon, author of *Lords of Night* and co-author of *Pavlov's Dogs*, offered me a pile of Tesla research he'd built up from one of his own projects, which I gladly accepted. Bob Spencer at the Los Angeles County Public Works Department spent an afternoon on the phone talking about what happens to old building plans. Any deviations from the facts in either case were my own choice for dramatic reasons, not from any misinformation on their parts.

Chitra helped with Marathi names, pronunciations, and translations after I fumbled around on the internet trying to find certain words.

Tim is named after a friend of mine who's also lent his name to a silver dragon. He's always willing to help me with technical and computer issues in books, like designing Veek's computer.

The usual suspects helped by reading early drafts and convincing me this book wasn't *too* crazy and sprawling. Larry, John, Patrick, and David offered fantastic suggestions, encouragement, and also caught many things that slipped past me. Double that thanks for Felicia, my editor at Permuted Press.

And many, many thanks to my lovely lady Colleen, who continues to offer advice, critiques, harsh truths, kind words, and the still sometimes-needed reminders that I can actually do this.

—PC

Los Angeles, November 5th, 2011

MORE TITLES FROM PERMUTED PRESS

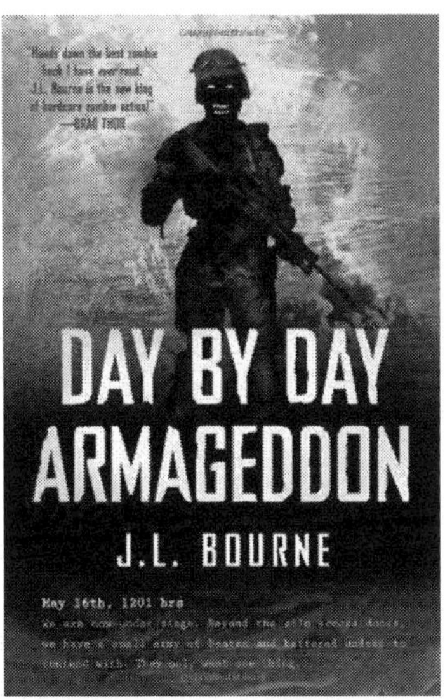

MORE DETAILS, EXCERPTS, AND PURCHASE INFORMATION AT

www.permutedpress.com

MORE TITLES FROM PERMUTED PRESS

MORE TITLES FROM PERMUTED PRESS

MORE DETAILS, EXCERPTS, AND PURCHASE INFORMATION AT

www.permutedpress.com

MORE TITLES FROM PERMUTED PRESS

More details, excerpts, and purchase information at

www.permutedpress.com

MORE TITLES FROM PERMUTED PRESS

MORE DETAILS, EXCERPTS, AND PURCHASE INFORMATION AT

www.permutedpress.com

Made in the USA
Lexington, KY
11 May 2014